Bernard Shaw and His (

Series Editors
Nelson O'Ceallaigh Ritschel
Pocasset, MA, USA

Peter Gahan
Los Angeles, CA, USA

The series *Bernard Shaw and His Contemporaries* presents the best and most up-to-date research on Shaw and his contemporaries in a diverse range of cultural contexts. Volumes in the series will further the academic understanding of Bernard Shaw and those who worked with him, or in reaction against him, during his long career from the 1880s to 1950 as a leading writer in Britain and Ireland, and with a wide European and American following.

Shaw defined the modern literary theatre in the wake of Ibsen as a vehicle for social change, while authoring a dramatic canon to rival Shakespeare's. His careers as critic, essayist, playwright, journalist, lecturer, socialist, feminist, and pamphleteer, both helped to shape the modern world as well as pointed the way towards modernism. No one engaged with his contemporaries more than Shaw, whether as controversialist, or in his support of other, often younger writers. In many respects, therefore, the series as it develops will offer a survey of the rise of the modern at the beginning of the twentieth century and the subsequent varied cultural movements covered by the term modernism that arose in the wake of World War 1.

More information about this series at
http://www.springer.com/series/14785

Robert A. Gaines
Editor

Bernard Shaw's Marriages and Misalliances

Editor
Robert A. Gaines
Auburn University at Montgomery
Montgomery, AL, USA

Bernard Shaw and His Contemporaries
ISBN 978-1-349-95749-1   ISBN 978-1-349-95170-3   (Ebook)
DOI 10.1057/978-1-349-95170-3

Cover credit: © Everett Collection Historical/Alamy Stock Photo

Printed on acid-free paper

This Palgrave Macmillan imprint is published by Springer Nature
The registered company is Nature America Inc.
The registered company address is: 1 New York Plaza, New York, NY 10004, U.S.A.

*In memoriam
Blair Riepma Gaines,
Beloved Wife and Mother
1945–2014*

"These diverse, illuminating essays show Shaw, from first to last, consistently subverting and challenging convention as he redefines marriage and its permutations—legal, sham, wished-for, spiritual—for his own ends. A most welcome addition to Shaw studies!"
—Sally Peters, *is the author of the Choice award-winning biography* Bernard Shaw: The Ascent of the Superman

"Gaines has enlisted a lively and distinguished array of commentators on the vagaries of marriage, and its shadow, misalliance, in Shaw's works and life experience, all deftly organized and contextualized. I especially liked Jennifer Buckley's forceful, cogent, and subtle essay on the Pleasant Plays; L. W. Conolly's on their Unpleasant predecessors; R.F. Diedrich on Shaw's early writings; Peter Gahan on the symbolism of clothing and the structural patterns in the Discussion Plays, Fanny's First Play, and Barker's Madras House; D.A. Hadfield's lucid and cogent take on Shaw's evolving positions on marital relations between the wars, with unexpected sidelights from the pædeutics of Maria C. Stopes, Matthew Yde on Shaw's later-play versions of companionate marriages (with distracting interludes) like his own, along with his critique of democratic populism. These, and as much more, offer a variety of perspectives, and form a comprehensive overview, on a subject at the heart of Shaw's lifelong critical anatomy of modern life, its idols of the tribe and the marketplace, and what became his evolutionary politics."
—Martin Meisel, *is the author of* Shaw and the Nineteenth-Century Theater *and* Chaos Imagined: Literature, Art, Science

"Bernard Shaw's controversial views on marriage as a societal institution, expressed in Man and Superman, so offended public sensibilities that the head of the New York Public Library circulation department in 1905 had the book pulled from open shelves and placed on restricted shelves inaccessible to minors. In contrast, Robert Gaines's Bernard Shaw's Marriage and Misalliances, a cleverly commissioned and edited collection of essays by a team of international scholars, should be placed on unrestricted shelves everywhere for all to discover its comprehensive and incisive discussions from a political perspective of how Shaw represented marriage in his plays. The varied perspectives on marriage ideals, marriage laws, and marriage realities in Shaw's plays and other writings provide much provocative analysis. The volume fills a real gap in Shaw studies."
—John A. Bertolini, *Ellis Professor of English and the Liberal Arts*
Middlebury College, VT USA

"Bernard Shaw's Marriage and Misalliances is a topic which has not yet (as Robert Gaines divulges in his Preamble) been focused on by scholars, so this book is very original, at the same time demonstrating that its topic is central to Shaw's plays, while Gaines' choice of authors offers a really appropriate take on this gender-focused topic, with half the writers – 6 out of 12 – being women. Similarly this list includes at least three younger academics, as well as three emeritus professors giving a wide range of attitudes, although the vantage point is typically American since only one of the authors is from outside North America: Audrey McNamara a vital young scholar from Ireland. In addition, there are historical and factual appendixes backing up the chapters, with one giving an insightful collection of legal and church documents, demonstrating how attitudes were changing during the nineteenth century. Offering a focused interpretation of all Shaw's plays, this is an excellent and insightful addition to Shaw studies, which should be extremely useful to all: Gaines has done an excellent job."
—Christopher Innes, *is the author of 16 books on modern drama. He has*
featured Shaw in Modern British Drama *and edited a study of Shaw*

ACKNOWLEDGEMENTS

Few create a book all alone and so I take great pleasure in acknowledging with grateful appreciation the contributions of some of the many others who have made this work possible. First to Richard F. Dietrich, who founded the International Shaw Society, and served two terms as its first president. Dick is the intellectual and spiritual godfather of all North American Shavians. He suggested the title for this volume and has gently but firmly pushed me ever forward. To L.W. Conolly, the ISS's second president, who suggested to me the need for this volume and has constantly provided information, support, and guidance throughout this endeavor. He also contributed the Chronology and Appendix B. To Stanley Weintraub, who always knew the right book and where to find it. To A.M. Gibbs and Jesse Hellman, who contributed much-needed materials.

To Nelson Ritschel, the Bernard Shaw and His Contemporaries Series Editor for Palgrave Macmillan, who not only provided good cheer but held the steady editorial reins that keep us all in harness and on track. To Peter Gahan, who graciously stepped aside from his shared editorial duties with Ritschel for this series, and who contributed a chapter for this book when altered circumstances prompted me to press him into service. To Palgrave Macmillan's Film, Cultural, and Media Studies Editor, Shaun Vigil, for good communication that began early in the process and keeping me constantly updated as to where the book was in the publisher's internal processes. To Palgrave Editor Jenny McCall and her assistant April James, who cheerfully answered every question and helped keep the book on track. Finally, to Palgrave Editor Tomas Rene, who brought us home.

Auburn University Montgomery, where I was a member of the faculty for 30 years, also provided invaluable assistance. Chancellor Guin Nance, Vice-Chancellor for Academic Affairs Roger Ritvo, and Dean of Liberal Arts Marion C. Michael provided badly needed time and assistance from the very top of the academic ladder. Honors Program Director Donald Nobles and Librarian Ricky Best ran down obscure journal articles and inter-library loan requests. International Shaw Society bibliographer Charles Carpenter reviewed the proposal to ensure there was no duplication with an existing book. John McInerney and Toni Burke provided invaluable proofreading services. Elizabeth Gaines served as the Manuscript Supervisor. Zach Burke provided vital computer assistance on Appendix A. Dorothy Hadfield went above and beyond by graciously volunteering to do the index. Finally, Michel Pharand reviewed, edited, and re-edited the proposal, and served as my "Father Confessor" throughout this project, dispensing sage advice and much-needed absolution in equal measures. My sincerest thanks to them all. While each contributed much, all errors are my own.

CONTENTS

EDITOR AND CONTRIBUTORS

About the Editor

Robert A. Gaines Professor Emeritus at Auburn University Montgomery, Alabama, USA, and a Ph.D. from Indiana University, spent 35 years in university positions (i.e., professor/administrator/director of theatre). His research interests are in classical theatre production, as are his publications, including a book on the Stratford Shakespeare Festival as well as various articles. He has been a member of the International Shaw Society since its inception in 1994.

Contributors

Jennifer Buckley University of Iowa, Iowa City, USA

L.W. Conolly Trent University, Peterborough, Canada

Richard Farr Dietrich University Press of Florida-Shaw Series, Gainesville, USA; University of South Florida, Tampa, USA

Ellen Ecker Dolgin Dominican College of Blauvelt, Orangeburg, New York, USA

Peter Gahan Los Angeles, USA

D.A. Hadfield Department of English Language and Literature, University of Waterloo, Waterloo, Canada

Audrey McNamara University College Dublin (UCD), Dublin, Ireland

Michel W. Pharand Kingston, Canada

Jean Reynolds Polk State College, Winter Haven, FL, USA

Lawrence Switzky University of Toronto, Toronto, Canada

Rodelle Weintraub Philadelphia, USA

Matthew Yde University of New Mexico, Albuquerque, USA

NOTES ON COLLECTION ABBREVIATIONS

CL   Bernard Shaw. Bernard Shaw Collected Letters 1874–1950. Under the editorial supervision of Dan H. Lawrence. 4 vols. Vols. 1–2 London: Max Reinhardt, 1965 and 1972   Vols. 3–4 New York: Viking, 1985 and 1988

CP   Bernard Shaw, *The Complete Prefaces*. Under the editorial supervision of Dan H. Laurence and Daniel J. Leary. 3 vols. London: Allen Lane, Penguin Press Group, 1993–1997

CPP   Bernard Shaw, *Collected Plays with their Prefaces*. Under the editorial supervision of Dan H. Laurence. 7 vols. London: Max Reinhardt: The Bodley Head, 1970–1974

Holroyd   *Bernard Shaw*. Michael Holroyd. 5 vols. London: Chatto & Windus, 1988–1992

Shaw   *Shaw, An Autobiography*. Selected from his writings by Stanley Weintraub. 2 Vols, New York: Weybright and Tally, 1969–1970

BERNARD SHAW: A BRIEF CHRONOLOGY
BY L.W. CONOLLY

For a comprehensive and detailed chronology of Shaw's life, see A.M. Gibbs, *A Bernard Shaw Chronology* (Basingstoke: Palgrave, 2001). Dates of British and foreign productions of Shaw's plays are given in Raymond Mander and Joe Mitchenson, *Theatrical Companion to Shaw* (New York: Pitman, 1955).

1856   Born in Dublin, 26 July, to George Carr Shaw and Lucinda Elizabeth Shaw.
1871   Leaves school and takes an office job with a Dublin property agency.
1876   Moves from Dublin to London.
1879   Completes his first novel, *Immaturity* (published 1930).
1880   Completes his second novel, *The Irrational Knot* (published in serial form 1885–1887, book form 1905).
1881   Completes his third novel, *Love Among the Artists* (published in serial form 1887–1888, book form 1900).
1882   Completes his fourth novel, *Cashel Byron's Profession* (published in serial form 1885–1886, book form 1886).
1883   Completes his fifth (and last) novel, *An Unsocial Socialist* (published in serial form 1884, book form 1887).
1884   Joins the Fabian Society.
1885   Publishes first music and drama criticism in the *Dramatic Review*.
1891   Publishes *The Quintessence of Ibsenism*.
1892   His first play, *Widowers' Houses*, performed by the Independent Theatre Society, London.
1893   Completes *The Philanderer* and *Mrs Warren's Profession*.
1894   *Arms and the Man* performed at the Avenue Theatre, London, and the Herald Square Theatre, New York; completes *Candida*.

1895   Begins writing theatre criticism for the *Saturday Review*.
1896   Meets Charlotte Payne-Townshend, his future wife. Completes *You Never Can Tell* and *The Devil's Disciple*.
1897   *Candida* performed by the Independent Theatre Company, Aberdeen. *The Man of Destiny* performed at the Grand Theatre, Croydon. American actor Richard Mansfield produces *The Devil's Disciple* in Albany and New York.
1898   Copyright performance of *The Philanderer* at the Bijou Theatre, London (30 March). Marries Charlotte Payne-Townshend. Publishes *Plays Pleasant* [*Arms and the Man, Candida, The Man of Destiny, You Never Can Tell*] and *Unpleasant* [*Widowers' Houses, The Philanderer, Mrs Warren's Profession*]. Completes *Caesar and Cleopatra*.
1899   *You Never Can Tell* performed by the Stage Society.
1901   Publishes *Three Plays for Puritans* [*The Devil's Disciple, Caesar and Cleopatra, Captain Brassbound's Conversion*].
1902   *Mrs Warren's Profession* performed by the Stage Society. Completes *Man and Superman*.
1903   Publishes *Man and Superman*.
1904   Begins his partnership with Harley Granville Barker and J.E. Vedrenne at the Court Theatre (until 1907). *John Bull's Other Island* performed there.
1905   Première of *The Philanderer* by the New Stage Club, Cripplegate Institute, London (20 February). *Mrs Warren's Profession* performed (then banned) in New Haven and New York. *Man and Superman* and *Major Barbara* performed at the Court Theatre, London.
1906   *The Doctor's Dilemma* performed at the Court Theatre; *Caesar and Cleopatra* performed (in German) in Berlin.
1907   *The Philanderer* performed at the Court Theatre, London (5 February).
1909   *The Shewing-up of Blanco Posnet* banned in England, but performed in Dublin. *Press Cuttings* banned in England. Completes *Misalliance*.
1911   *Fanny's First Play* performed at the Little Theatre, London. Runs for 622 performances (a record for a Shaw première).
1912   Completes *Pygmalion*.
1913   American première of *The Philanderer* at the Little Theatre, New York (27 December). *Pygmalion* performed at His Majesty's Theatre, London.
1914   Outbreak of World War I. Publishes *Common Sense about the War*.
1917   Visits front-line sites in France. Completes *Heartbreak House*.
1918   End of World War I.
1920   *Heartbreak House* performed by the Theatre Guild, New York. Completes *Back to Methuselah*.

1922   *Back to Methuselah* performed by the Theatre Guild, New York. Meets T.E. Lawrence (Lawrence of Arabia).

1923   Completes *Saint Joan*. It is performed in New York by the Theatre Guild.

1924   First British production of *Saint Joan*, New Theatre, London, with Sybil Thorndike as Joan.

1926   Awarded the 1925 Nobel Prize for Literature.

1928   Publishes *The Intelligent Woman's Guide to Socialism and Capitalism*.

1929   *The Apple Cart* performed (in Polish) in Warsaw.

1931   Visits Russia; meets Gorky and Stalin.

1932   Travels on a world cruise.

1936   *The Millionairess* performed (in German) in Vienna.

1938   *Pygmalion* is filmed, starring Leslie Howard and Wendy Hiller.

1939   Outbreak of World War II. Wins an Oscar for the screenplay of *Pygmalion*.

1940   *Major Barbara* is filmed, starring Rex Harrison and Wendy Hiller.

1943   Charlotte Shaw dies.

1944   Publishes *Everybody's Political What's What?*

1945   *Caesar and Cleopatra* is filmed, starring Claude Rains and Vivien Leigh. End of World War II.

1950   Dies, 2 November, aged 94, from complications after a fall while pruning a shrub in his garden.

BERNARD SHAW'S MARRIAGES AND MISALLIANCES

There is no subject on which more dangerous nonsense is talked and thought than marriage.
CPP III:452

However much we may suffer through marriage, most of us think so little about it that we regard it as a fixed part of the order of nature like gravitation. Except for this error which may be regarded as constant, we use the word with reckless looseness, meaning a dozen different things by it, and yet always assuming that to a respectable man it can have only one meaning.
CPP III:454–455

...the respectable British champion of marriage ... sometimes ... does not mean marriage at all. He means monogamy, chastity, temperance, respectability, morality, Christianity, anti-socialism, and a dozen other things that have no necessary connection with marriage. He often means something that he dare not avow; ownership of the person of another human being, for instance.
CPP III:455

PREAMBLE

The idea for this book was born when I reached for it on the library shelf, and it was not there. More specifically, I was preparing a paper on *Major Barbara* for an academic conference and wanted to see what others had to say about Bernard Shaw's use of marriage in his novels and plays, only to discover that no such book existed. To be sure, there was the occasional article as well as some less helpful but more widely scattered dibs and dabs—mostly just mentions of the word "marriage." But no single volume existed devoted to exploring the themes and issues Shaw portrayed in the marriages throughout his major works.

In the final act of *Major Barbara*, Adolphus and Barbara argue about several issues pivotal to whether they will choose to marry. At times, they are almost bartering their strengths/moralities like commodities on the open market. Looking up the word "commodity" in several dictionaries, I found the expected answer: it is something for sale. But in checking a reprint of the *1811 Dictionary of the Vulgar Tongue*, I found that the only definition given for "commodity" was "the private parts of a modest woman and the public parts of a prostitute."[1] The seedling idea for this book suddenly grew roots in fecund soil.

I admit the *1811 Dictionary* is one of slang and also was nearly 75 years old when Shaw began writing. Still, classifying women as either modestly pure or as prostitutes, depending on who was privy to their privates, was an idea that seemed welded to the soul of the nineteenth and twentieth centuries. Indeed, some might argue that this pernicious notion thrives in the present day.

The story of how Shaw uses marriage in his works is inexorably bound up with the cause of women's equality, a cause he championed. Even as late as 1937, when Shaw was entering his early 80s, a new Irish Constitution declared: "In particular, the state recognizes that by her life within the home, a woman gives to the state a support without which the common good cannot be achieved."[2] Against such notions, Shaw, all of his adult life, made speeches, wrote pamphlets, and gave voice to his better angels in his novels and plays. But it was a battle not easily won. "Women ... have all the vices of men but their follies are never quite so foolish as masculine follies," said Shaw when interviewed by the London *Sunday Express*.[3] He shared his secret for being able to write such women: "I have always assumed that a woman was a person exactly like myself, and that is how the trick is done."[4] Marriage and women's equality are so melded in Shaw's mind that the story of one often becomes the story of both.

To explore these topics, I asked twelve Shavians each to write a chapter addressing the marital void in Shaw criticism: six are women and six are men. They represent Canada, Ireland, and the United States. I gave ten of these scholars a specific series of plays to examine in whichever manner they wished. I asked another one to do the same with Shaw's novels. The remaining scholar was asked to look at Shaw's sexual conduct. In addition to all of Shaw's full-length plays and his novels, we collaboratively decided to include certain of his short stories and one-act plays. The book is organized chronologically through his *oeuvre*, except where thematic concerns overrode a strict adherence to dates. Doubtless, some readers will notice the absence of a favorite short story, one-act, or essay; but all should sympathize with the limits of a single volume.

Richard Dietrich begins the discussion with an evaluation of Shaw's earliest works, the at-first-unpublished *My Dear Dorothea* (1877) and the unfinished dramatic piece called *Passion Play* (1878), followed by his five completed novels (1879–1883) and some short stories typical of his early writing, in all of which Dietrich finds the playwright establishing a dialectical approach to theme, story, and characterization that led easily to the play form Shaw would adopt. Shaw began by writing fiction like a playwright, as he later would write plays like a novelist. Dietrich explains how in such early works Shaw fictionalized the attraction and repulsion to domesticity he himself felt as a young Londoner, between his desire for marriage with a soul mate and his passion for "world betterment" which he feared would be thwarted if he ever succumbed to the domesticating influence of marriage, no matter how "advanced" the woman might be, and even if she tried to follow his own fictional prescriptions for the New Woman. Misalliance had been Shaw's experience within his own family, and so the fear of it is mirrored in this early writing.

In Chaps. 2 and 3, Jennifer Buckley and L.W. Conolly tackle Shaw's earliest plays. Buckley, writing about *Plays Pleasant*, contends that the dividing line between these is not always as sharp as might be thought. She contends that Shaw's turn toward the commercial theatre was for purposes of cultural permeation, arguing that, after setting up some definite obstacles to marriage, Shaw skirts the central issue by allowing the Life Force to propel the couple down the aisle. Conolly, covering *Plays Unpleasant*, after a brief discussion of the history and the state of the marriage laws in England, dissects Shaw's purposes in each play. Years and customs had provided for the intertwining of these grossly unfair marriage laws with religious doctrine. Shaw sought to uncouple this alliance and bring both into the light of day for rational discussion.

In *Three Plays for Puritans*, written between 1897 and 1900, Shaw began to conceive of marriage not only as a legal procedure or a religious rite, but also as a social contract that might be most meaningful when decoupled from self-interest or erotic attraction. In Chap. 4, Lawrence Switzky describes several impersonal, "decoy marriages" in these plays— feigned marriages without legal sanction—as tests of disinterested interpersonal obligations. Through these decoy marriages, Shaw rehearsed his conflicting beliefs about human plasticity and altruism.

Chapter 5 does not look at Shaw's works but rather at his own self-confessed sexual conduct in light of his celibate marriage. Rodelle Weintraub discusses Shaw's sexual exploits as she tackles the question of whether he was a philanderer. As the story of his marriage to Charlotte has been covered in some detail elsewhere, there is no chapter devoted to their marriage here. Nevertheless, Shaw was a sexual being and exercised his heterosexual nature before and most probably after his marriage to Charlotte.

In Chap. 6, Michel Pharand, while examining *Man and Superman*, *John Bull's Other Island*, and *Major Barbara*, concludes that whatever else marriage is, it is a compromise both with one's self and with one's partner. Often the Life Force pushing two people together demands compromise—but it does not dictate its nature. Pharand suggests that, as none of these plays includes a marriage, at least on stage, much less a happy life for the couples after marriage, there is no guarantee that they have indeed achieved workable compromises for the survival of their union.

Peter Gahan, in Chap. 7, works from the sartorial context prominent in comedies written between 1908 and 1911 that highlight marriage as a social institution. Civic roles and social responsibilities are ostentatiously signified by costume in *Getting Married* and in *Fanny's First Play*'s framing play. With *Misalliance*'s underwear manufacturer as well as the underwear retailers in *Fanny's* inner play, Shaw throws his comic spotlight on clothing that is more usually concealed, while Granville Barker's contemporaneous *Madras House* features social ramifications in marriages across the classes of the clothes manufacturing process and fashion industry. All four plays suggest that with marriage, human beings become something more than autonomous individuals, assuming positions within a more complex system of social signification—society.

In Chap. 8, Ellen Dolgin deals with four plays from the last decade before World War I: *The Doctor's Dilemma, Androcles and the Lion, Pygmalion*, and *Overruled*. In the first three plays, she finds that Shaw warns his audiences and readers of the danger of misalliances that result from the pressure of obligatory matches when marriage was often the only career choice a woman had for economic survival. Shaw proposed instead a life of hard work and self-fulfillment, which were much the same choices faced by men. In so doing, he was turning his back on the accepted notions of a woman's place in marriage. Even in *Overruled*, a one-act play set in a conventional drawing room, Shaw features wives reflecting the empowerment of the New Woman.

In Chaps. 9 and 10, Audrey McNamara and D.A. Hadfield tackle the interwar years, when women were being turned out of the factories where they had worked during the war, so that men could resume their work there. While surveying *Heartbreak House, Back to Methuselah*, and *Annajanska the Bolshevik Empress*, McNamara believes that after World War I, Shaw realized the impossibility of going back to a pre-war society. He also knew that without marriage, society had no way of healing itself from the scars war had inflicted, but that marriage in its pre-war form was equally intolerable. Shaw thus used his twin concepts of the Life Force and Creative Evolution to help people see beyond the present and to fashion a change that would make marriage—and the nation—stronger and more independent.

D.A. Hadfield's treatment of *Saint Joan, Too True to Be Good, The Millionairess*, and *The Six of Calais* suggests that Shaw's views of marriage often show him ahead of his literary and social contemporaries when he advocates for women's autonomy and empowerment, and sometimes even for their independence from marriage. The latter was a particularly difficult proposition during a period when women's postwar experiences of financial and physical independence conflicted with an economic need to eliminate them from the workforce. Hadfield concludes that even so, Shaw's plays support an institution that is reformed to accommodate independent women empowered by their experiences, and their need for something more from married love.

In Chap. 11, Jean Reynolds, looking at *Village Wooing, On the Rocks*, and *The Simpleton of the Unexpected Isles*, finds that the three couples at the heart of these three plays define marriage very differently. In one instance, a woman simply wants to be married and has selected her mate; in another, the husband of a long-married couple is quite content, while his wife is bored and frustrated; and in the last case, group marriage is tried unsuccessfully, suggesting that, in the end, a marriage is what each couple makes of it.

Matthew Yde, in the concluding chapter, considers *In Good King Charles's Golden Days, The Apple Cart*, and *Geneva*. While acknowledging that Shaw's opinions on marriage are various and often contradictory, Yde suggests that the best place to look for Shaw's overriding view of the topic is in his own childless yet seemingly happy marriage to Charlotte, as reflected in *The Apple Cart* and *In Good King Charles*.

Appendix A charts year by year the slow but steady increase in the number of divorces or marital separations over time. The efforts of Shaw and others to change the marriage laws were in reality campaigns to make divorce easier and more equable for women. Appendix B, by L.W. Conolly, lays out in Part I the Anglican Marriage Ceremony and in Part II some of the changes in the laws governing divorce.

Part of what makes a novel or play timeless is its ability to be read in many different ways. Part of what makes this collection of essays interesting is its variety of authors' opinions and perspectives. No attempt was made to bring all into alignment. Instead, the editor hopes that inconsistencies between various writers will generate fresh ideas and further discussion on this long-neglected topic.

While some authors referenced particular staged productions of Shaw's plays and/or the personalities that brought them to life, this book aims to offer insights on the texts themselves, as Shaw wrote and rewrote them. All contributors used the authoritative Constable editions of the novels and the Bodley Head edition of the plays.

Major Barbara in particular had piqued my curiosity. Did Shaw's characters always barter their strengths/moralities as a prelude to marriage? As with the best philosophical questions, the answer is both yes and no. Yes, because the element of marriage as commodity remains a constant, although frequently not the primary or even secondary, focus of a particular work. No, in the sense that his views on marriage over his entire body of work reflect his evolution as a maturing writer and thinker, ever expanding with insight, nuance, and definition. Shaw does not change his views on marriage from one work to the next so much as he expands on views previously expressed, and follows them to their natural conclusions. As a result, no play, preface, or essay can sum up his views on marriage. Each work is a snapshot, showing us, in still frame, the specific moments that cumulatively outline his arc of ever-expanding marital perspectives.

Thus no matter how fully formed Shaw's ideas appear in the prefaces to some plays, especially *Getting Married* or *Misalliance*, for example, or in essays such as *The Quintessence of Ibsenism* or *The Intelligent Woman's Guide to Socialism and Capitalism*, Shaw always supplements and changes the focus of those ideas, returning to them later. Sometimes he speaks through a housewife (*Candida*) and sometimes through a reigning monarch *(King Charles)*; but none of his characters has the complete picture. Therefore, the only way to get a summation of his marital views is to go through his works novel by novel and play by play charting their development, which is the purpose of this book.

Several issues need further exploration before beginning; thus, this essay is a preamble as much as it is an introduction. Those issues include Shaw's views of his parents' marriage. Perhaps their union taught him that "marriage" and "misalliance" are not mutually exclusive. They can exist within the same domestic scene. Placing Shaw among his nineteenth-century contemporaries will help explicate his stature in his own day and perhaps in ours as well. One of those contemporaries, Henrik Ibsen, influenced Shaw greatly. For this reason alone, Ibsen deserves a short mention.

SHAW AND HIS PARENTS

The marriage of Shaw's parents, Lucinda Gurley, hereafter called Bessie, and George Carr Shaw, was a misalliance. Shaw's impressions of that marriage, subconsciously or not, helped shape all the marriages and misalliances of the characters that flowed from his pen. Bessie's mother died when Bessie was 9 years old and the child was raised by her maiden aunt, Ellen Whitcroft, who educated her in the social graces and prepared her to take her place in Dublin society. George Carr Shaw was a sometimes corn merchant with a weakness for alcohol, which Bessie's family had warned her about before the wedding. But when she asked him about it, he assured her that he was a teetotaler. Shaw believed one missed an essential part of his father's character if one failed to realize how sincerely George Carr despised alcohol (*CL* III:365). Then 38-year-old George wed 22-year-old Bessie on June 17, 1852. Soon, because of George's drunken behavior, the newly married Shaws were excluded from the very society Bessie had been trained to enter.[5] There were three children born to the couple in rapid succession: two daughters, Lucinda Frances (1853–1920) and Elinor Agnes (1855–1876), and the last and the only son, George Bernard (1856–1950), born on July 26.

Bessie was gifted with a beautiful singing voice and came under the tutelage of George John Vandeleur Lee, a singing instructor with original methods of voice training. Although the exact date Lee and Bessie first met is not known, the Amateur Musical Society began in 1852, the same year Bessie and George Carr Shaw were married. Bessie became indispensable to Lee in arranging his concerts and other business of the Musical Society, and she even completed his four-year voice training program.

Perhaps due to George's lack of income, the entire Shaw family moved in with Lee. Although the date is difficult to ascertain, biographer B.C. Rosset, tracing the date through real estate records, believes that "There seems little doubt that the Shaw-Lee *household* was first constituted in 1866 and ... existed for one year in Torca Cottage (on Dalkey Hill) prior to its more permanent establishment in Hatch Street."[6] This unconventional arrangement lasted until Lee moved to London in 1873. Bessie and her daughter Lucy followed Lee shortly thereafter, presumably so Lucy could continue her voice lessons. Nevertheless, once arrived in London, Bessie and Lucy did not share a house with Lee, perhaps since Bessie was disappointed in him because he had abandoned his voice training methods and because he had turned "sentimental" in his attentions to Lucy.[7]

The Hatch Street living arrangements inevitably led to speculation about George Bernard Shaw's real father. Although the Shaws did not move into Hatch Street with Lee until Shaw was 9 or 10 years old, Holroyd acknowledges that Lee and Bessie moved in the same musical circles and could have met anytime in the 1850s (*Holroyd* I:24). One proponent of the idea that Shaw was fathered by Lee was Beatrice Webb, who, with her husband Sidney, was a fellow member of the Fabian Society. (Sidney, along with Shaw, was the co-founder of the London School of Economics.) Beatrice wrote in her diary: "About G.B.S.'s parentage. The photograph published in the Henderson Biography makes it quite clear to me that he was the child of G.J.V. Lee—that vain, witty, and, distinguished musical genius who lived with them. The expression on Lee's face is amazingly like G.B.S. when I first knew him."[8] Shaw always stoutly defended his mother's honor: "My mother was one of those women who could act as a matron of a cavalry barracks from 18 to 40 men and emerge without a stain on her honor" (*CL* III:356).

One would-be biographer, Thomas Demetrius O'Bolger, while acknowledging George as Shaw's father, suggested that Bessie and Lee did have an affair. Shaw countered: "My mother wasn't that sort of woman: there you have the whole difficulty in seven words" *(CL* III:770). Nevertheless, Holroyd observes that "themes of consanguinity and illegitimacy reoccur obsessively in [Shaw's] plays" *(Holroyd* I:24).

In his biography, Rosset, after extensive research, concludes that Shaw was haunted by the uncertainty of his paternity, particularly as a young man, but also all of his life.[9] Yet if he was so haunted, why the denials? Rosset answers: "He was absolutely convinced that disaster would follow exposure and that the contumely of a mocking world, would silence his voice, cancel his works, nullify his selection by the Life Force as a link in the apostolic succession from Shakespeare and thus destroy forever his claim to immortality."[10] If Rosset is correct, those doubts color all of the fictional marriages and misalliances that Shaw would produce.

SHAW'S PLACE IN HIS TIME

The nineteenth century was when melodrama took the stage by storm. Shaw was not immune from its impact. Many helpless but virtuously modest pre-Shavian heroines—with nothing but their modesty to recommend them, and certainly not brains enough to help themselves—awaited a man to come and rescue them from danger. *The Perils of Pauline* is a title that evokes that modest kind of woman.[11] On the other side of the ledger, Alexandre Dumas *fils*'s (1824–1895) *La Dame aux Camélias* (1848) told the story of the prostitute with the heart of gold whom he tried to raise to an acceptable social position, but his audiences would not have it so.[12] Melodrama, with its stereotypical characters and implausible plots, did the cause of marriage, with its accompanying question of women's equality, little good.

Then onto that stage steps Shaw. In his first play, *Widowers' Houses*, he gives us his heroine, Blanch Sartorius, who rages against her perceived injustices, beats her maid, and shows "flashes" of an exotic passion. Yet what the critiques complained about, says Shaw scholar Martin Meisel, "was the sheer indecorum of Shaw placing a woman of this type … in the plot position normally reserved for the fair, innocent and sweet tempered heroine."[13] In short, Shaw sometimes, but by no means always, uses some melodramatic devices. Although when he does, he stands the genre on its head by developing psychologically complex characters and turning them loose in the drama in place of those conventional two-dimensional ones so loved by straight melodramatic authors.

Shaw enthusiast Michael Billington, drama critic of London's *The Guardian*, commented on a more recent feminist playwright Caryl Churchill's (b. 1938) play *Top Girls* (1982): "What Churchill was saying, with her usual formal audacity, was that feminism will never seriously advance until we restructure society."[14] What Shaw does, with his usual formal audacity, is to offer society just such a restructuring by giving his women characters the same brains and ingenuity as his males. Frequently they have more resolve and ingenuity. Admittedly, there is a huge gap between restructuring society in a play and restructuring it in reality. But Shaw never let the world as it was interfere with that more equitable world he saw in his head.

Being the first dramatist in England to speak so eloquently on marriage and equality while writing comedies in a realistic style was no easy feat.[15] It certainly escaped the talents of such popular English dramatists as Henry Arthur Jones (1851–1929) and Arthur Wing Pinero

(1855–1934). Perhaps Jones's greatest hit was *The Silver King* (1892), which never rose above conventional thoroughgoing melodrama. Pinero's later efforts to produce more serious drama did not achieve the same success as Shaw's work. Likewise, Pinero specialized in social drama with intriguing titles like *The Second Mrs Tanqueray* (1893) and *The Notorious Mrs Ebbsmith* (1895), suggesting he was poised to make serious statements on the social conventions of the day. Yet in the end, Pinero was not able to follow through with the piercing social critique that became the keystone of Shaw's style.

Shaw's fellow Irish playwright Oscar Wilde (1854–1900) was similarly unprepared to help Shaw restructure the world. In his most popular play, *The Importance of Being Earnest* (1894), Wilde was content merely to satirize both the realistic style as well as its content, while at the same time taking a good-natured swipe at stereotypical melodrama. Gwendolyn and Cecil—although properly modest—are not helpless heroines in need of rescue. They are perfectly capable of taking matters into their own hands, with exemplary results. Modern satirist Carl Hiaasen (b. 1953) says, "Good satire comes from anger."[16] Both Wilde and Shaw, seeing the inequalities of their day, would have agreed satire was an indispensable tool in their war chests. But only Shaw drew a complex world from a palette rich in shades of gray as a backdrop for his satire, adding in a level of sophistication and nuance that was out of Wilde's grasp.

A word should be offered to distinguish the works of Shaw from those of Henrik Ibsen (1828–1906), the Norwegian playwright whose influence over Shaw was monumental. Ibsen married Suzannah Thoresen (1836–1914), 8 years his junior, in 1858; not much has been written about their married life, but it is worth noting that his wife did not attend his funeral.[17] Both Ibsen and Shaw wrote of women and marriage. Both wrote with great sympathy for their women characters. But while Ibsen wrote problem plays, Shaw opted for using some melodramatic conventions at times, although he never fully adopted that medium. Comedy was his forte. Ibsen gave little or no background to the marriages, since his women were married when his plays opened. As a result, he wrote of women who come to crisis after marriage in plays like *A Doll's House* (1879), *Ghosts* (1881), *The Lady from the Sea* (1888), and *Hedda Gabler* (1890). In contrast, Shaw generally chose women who considered their options prior to marriage and seldom showed what happened once a marriage did or did not take place. Yet from Shaw's pre-marital considerations, a more hopeful future might be anticipated by the characters and their audiences or readers.

Robert A. Gaines

NOTES

1. Grose, Capitan. Original Compiler. Considerably altered and enlarged with The Modern Changes and Improvements by a Member of the Whip Cub assisted by Hell-Fire Dick, James Gordon, and William Soames. *The 1811 Dictionary of Buckish Slang, University Wit and Pickpocket Eloquence.* (London: Studio Edition Ltd, rpt. 1994). This volume has no page numbers, but the entries are listed alphabetically. The back cover proclaims, "As a living social history it brings the reader in touch with the past as lively, bright, and chaotic as the present."
2. The Constitution of Ireland, Article 41, Section 2.1, Enacted by the People July 1, 1937.
3. Church, Hayden. *George Bernard Shaw: Eight Interviews* (Peacham, VT: The Perpetua Press, 2002), 9. The interview appeared originally in The Sunday Express of December 28, 1924.
4. Weintraub, Rodelle, Ed. Fabian Feminist: Bernard Shaw and Woman (University Park: Penn State Press, 1977), 114.
5. A.M. Gibbs asserts an alternative theory. He says George Carr had abandoned drinking by 1869 and previously had a period—16 months—of complete abstinence before that—A.M. Gibbs. *Bernard Shaw: A Life.* (Gainesville: University Press of Florida, 2005), 24.
6. Rosset, B.C. *Shaw of Dublin: The Formative Years* (University Park: The Pennsylvania State University Press), 1964, 120.
7. O'Donovan, John. *Shaw and the Great Charlatan Genius.* (Dublin: Dolmen Press, 1965), 90.
8. Webb, Beatrice. Typescript Diary May 12, 1911. Online at http://digital.library.lse.ac.uk/objects/lse:six767gol.
9. Rosset. xiii.
10. Rosset. 348.
11. *The Perils of Pauline* was actually a 1914 movie serial with 20 episodes which were shown in theatres weekly. Pauline displayed a lot of ingenuity and solved many of her own problems, but that scenario is not the one conjured up in our minds by that title. *The Perils of Pauline.* Imdb.com. Web.

12. To return to the good graces of his social world Dumas *fils* had to write another play, *Le Demi Monde* (1855), in which his compromised heroine's attempts to rise to an acceptable social position are rudely rebuffed.
13. Meisel, Martin. *Shaw and the Nineteenth Century Theatre*. (Princeton, NJ: Princeton University Press, 1963), 29–30.
14. Billington, Michael, *State of the Nation: British Theatre since 1945*. (London: Faber and Faber, 2007), 307.
15. In Shaw's time, the term realism was used by its critiques to condemn a work for dealing with surface issues and not with substantive content. Professor Richard Dietrich argues that Shaw wrote the *Quintessence of Ibsenism* to refute that charge. Indeed, according to Dietrich, Shaw and Ibsen use the word "to denote the sort of vision that sees behind appearances to the deepest truths, as available to intuitions but scientifically unverifiable." Dietrich, Richard Farr. *Bernard Shaw's Novels*. (Gainesville: University Press of Florida, 1996), 20. Dietrich further discusses the word realism in another article. Dietrich, Richard Farr "*Shaw and Yeats: Two Irishman Divided by a Common Language.*" SHAW: *The Annual of Bernard Shaw Studies* 15 (1995): 65–84. This essay uses the term realism in the same way to convey psychologically complex and complete characters acting in accordance with their natures.
16. Hiaasen, Carl. brainyquote.com. Satire.
17. Saether, Astrid. Interview (27 February 2008) with Saether about her biography of Suzannah Thoresen Ibsen. Online at ibsen.nb.no/id/11163880.0.

LIST OF FIGURES

CHAPTER 1

Shaw's Early Writings: A Prologue to the Playwright

Richard Farr Dietrich

The past is prologue for all, of course, but we are especially fascinated by the lessons to be learned from applying it to people of fame and fortune, a category into which it was very unlikely that young Bernard Shaw, when he escaped from provincial Dublin in 1876 at the age of 19 to join his mother and sister in London, would ever fall into, as eventually he did. What caused this improbable future? Many things, no doubt, but his very successful and sustained portrayal of "marital misalliance" is considered in this book, chronologically through his work. His parents provided that theme, and he did not thank them at the time, but maybe he should have, because making the marital skeletons in the family closet dance to entertain us and provide grist for his comic mill had much to do with his eventual success.

Shaw wrote about other kinds of misalliances, which were all connected, but the focus of this study is on the primary misalliance for

R.F. Dietrich (✉)
University Press of Florida-Shaw Series, Gainesville, USA
e-mail: dietrich@usf.edu; dietrich@shawsociety.org

R.F. Dietrich
University of South Florida, Tampa, USA

© The Author(s) 2017
R.A. Gaines (ed.), *Bernard Shaw's Marriages and Misalliances*,
Bernard Shaw and His Contemporaries,
DOI 10.1057/978-1-349-95170-3_1

1

everyone who experiences it, especially if a child, the sort that happens in the home in which one lives, often destroying a family, as illustrated by his mother's abandonment of his father and a move to London about three years before Shaw too abandoned his father. The marital misalliance between his parents was a scarring experience that had life-long consequences for him, not the least of which was his understandable fear of marriage, however comically he typically handled it. He brought with him to London and finished there a poem entitled "Calypso"[1] in which he bade farewell to his own, dangerously captivating "dark lady" back in Dublin, essentially as a farewell to marriage, at least of the conventional sort.

Yet it was not just that. Another reason for leaving Dublin was his despised work for a land agent, which introduced him to "landlordism" and the misalliance between rich and poor, capital and labor. By 1876, Shaw was succeeding all too well as a capitalist-in-the-making, the boss offering him a raise and a way up the ladder of success, with the boss's daughter a distinct marriage prospect. That Shaw instinctively ran from this likely future of financial and social success presages the socialist to come, socialism as he conceived it providing a marriage of wealth and labor in the family of man.

The parental split and his breach with capitalism may have been enough to send him off to London, but he did not actually make the move until after his older sister Agnes's death from tuberculosis on the Isle of Wight, where her mother had taken her from London to be in a milder climate. There is nothing like a death in the family to provide a compelling reason to get on with one's life. It was only four days after Agnes died, a day that coincided with his final day at the land agent's, that Shaw took the ferry to England.

His experience of an indifferently cruel universe that so mercilessly cut down his sister must have contributed to his growing sense of a misalliance between man and the universe as well. This in turn contributed to his eventual invention of a means of addressing it that he called "Creative Evolution," in which man (or whatever else evolves) slowly improves the universe, in the billions of years to come ("I believe in the Life Everlasting," said Shaw[2]), by making it more godly, more caring of life, fairer to all. As a world betterer he would marry a Becoming God to the universe. The God of desperate fantasy was dead, all right, as Nietzsche had proclaimed, but Shaw imagined we were all experiments in creating His replacement by trial and error, this one not a fantasy. The purpose of life is to create purpose in the universe.

Shaw came to London with all these misalliances already becoming templates in his mind for future use, between husband and wife, between rich and poor, between man and the universe. London's being, in fact, at the center of this puzzling universe, as well as of a questionable empire, did not at first help this "divorced child" to resolve any of them; but it did challenge the "moral passion" he had brought with him to take action. Of great help was the anomaly of the Reading Room of the British Museum, which not only became his "university" but also, in providing him with a free education and an office for writing, served as a model for how an essentially socialist institution such as a free library could civilize a capitalist society. Might London and the world and the universe just need more of that sort of thing, on all levels of existence? Maybe Shaw could contribute to its becoming by writing. As writing was creative, Creative Evolution could be served by writing.

An omnivorous reader, Shaw became self-taught in many phases of intellectual and artistic life, but perhaps most importantly awoke to the power of writing to change the world. He read widely in all genres, but as prose fiction was the choice of most Victorians, he, in hopes of earning his bread as a writer, began with that, in the form of novels, after a couple of "false starts" in other genres. Since publishers would not touch the novels at first, it was not a very promising start, and the wonder is that he persevered.

Since nothing in his early prose fiction was considered major work, regardless of what good reading it was, how prophetic it was, and how innovative, this "apprentice work" has been considered a prologue to the major literary works that eventually followed from 1892 on, mostly in the dramatic mode that gained Shaw fame and fortune. Yet there was a consistency in this: just as he later wrote plays like a novelist, with elaborate stage directions serving as a substitute narrative voice, so too did he write novels like a playwright, with large patches of dialogue that could be lifted to make a play (and, in fact, several of the novels have been converted into plays). However slow to emerge as dominant, the dramatist was there from the beginning.[3] Why was that?

A credible explanation for Shaw's dramatic inclinations can be found in a quotation from Henri Bergson: "what is called wit is a certain 'dramatic' way of thinking. Instead of treating his ideas as mere symbols, the witty man sees them, hears them, and above all makes them converse with one another like persons. He puts them on the stage, and himself, to some extent, in the bargain."[4] And since, as Shaw said, in drama "conflict is indispensable: no conflict, no drama" (*CPP* I:373), it thus was inevitable that dialectics, as we call conflicts between ideas, should materialize in the witty Shaw's fictional conversations and debates among characters from the outset, with theses conflicting with antitheses in many guises, jawing away at one another on page after page, in scene after scene. There was no shortage of misalliances to dramatize, in families, in society, in the universe.

Primary, then, in the early days and certainly present from the beginning, was the dialectic of "marriage and misalliance," played in these early works as a major introductory chord to be developed symphonically later, in the full orchestral scoring of it that is to follow in his plays, with its ingenious variations and antiphonies of harmony and discord, as his male and female characters frequently come girded for the battle of the sexes, mated or misallied or studying for one of those operatic roles.

But why that particular dialectic? Probably because, given his sense that "world betterment" was the only thing that he was suited for (*The World Betterer* was the working title for his late play *Buoyant Billions*, in acknowledgment of his lifelong identity), the young Shaw, prior to becoming famous as a playwright, found himself caught between ordinary human desires for a marital soul mate and extraordinary ambition justified by the sort of singular mind and talent that often thrive best in a dedicated single life. By projecting that inner conflict into fictional characters, with much ambivalence stirred in, he was able to study that most crucial problem from all those perspectives and see its universality. Though his case was more extreme than most, he was not alone in being trapped in this conflict so central to all the young, to ally or not to ally, given how often alliance turns into misalliance. All the testimony to this that Shaw needed was that his father lived in Dublin and his mother lived in London, seldom communicating.

This dialectic was first embodied in the two aforementioned "false starts," worth examining for their startling revelations about the proto-Shaw. First came an odd little book, about the last thing you would expect Shaw to start with, *My Dear Dorothea: A Practical System of Moral Education for Females Embodied in a Letter to a Young Person of That Sex* (written early in 1878 and published posthumously in 1956),[5] which becomes less odd when you think through its implications and its place in Shaw's development.

Later in 1878 came the even stranger work, a fragment of a play in blank verse originally called "Household of Joseph" and later called

"Passion Play" (*CPP* VII:481–527), which focuses on the relationship between Jesus and Judas. This was odd not for its interest in the sort of historical phenomenon in which a self-appointed world betterer like Shaw would be interested, but for the attempt at Shakespearian embodiment. This made the contrast between the styles of these two works extreme, but both the comic didacticism in the relatively modern prose of *My Dear Dorothea* and the general dramatic form of "Passion Play," if not its archaic blank verse, would later combine very successfully in Shaw's playwriting. And among the many themes they have in common, the principal one that "this world in which we live is a very badly arranged one"[6] is Shaw's grand theme throughout his life, accounting for both his ambivalence toward marriage arrangements (all too often "badly arranged") and his reformist/revolutionary mentality.

More specifically, in his earliest work, the epistolary *My Dear Dorothea*, we see the witty provocateur at work, counseling 5-year-old Dorothea to "let your rule of conduct always be to do whatever is best for yourself. Be as selfish as you can."[7] And then he continues to provide the sort of "bad advice" to a young girl that if followed might very well result in her becoming the sort of "New Woman" to whom a world-bettering Shaw might be attracted. In effect, he was ordering his bride! On the lay-away plan? Well, you have to start them young may have been his thinking. At any rate, the irreverent, iconoclastic, and seemingly avuncular but ultimately seductive *My Dear Dorothea* could be understood as a manual for creating women who might actually prefer a limited marriage that had room for world betterment—even on the part of both sexes in the relationship. It would not be long, in fact, before more than one of the actual "New Women" Shaw encountered considered such a limited marriage with him and he with them. If Shaw, more playfully than not, could later claim that he had invented the "New Woman," it is because, with *Dorothea* as his start in 1878, he henceforth devoted much time and effort to the educating of young females to be the flag bearers for the march into a better future, educating partly by exemplifying them in his works. But of course his teaching style, often of the personal tutorial sort, also just happened to keep such aspiring "New Women" always around him and, ahem, interested in him, "the philanderer," as some called him who did not understand the Irish gallantry in his style and the options in the new fellowship (Fig. 1.1).

He ultimately married a woman who did understand, but not until other candidates for a Mrs. Shaw had been passed by him or passed

Fig. 1.1 An older
Shaw gazes up at a pastel
of a young Charlotte
Payne-Townshend, the
New Woman he actually
married

him by and he was well launched as a playwright. Until then he put the majority of his time and effort into being a world betterer on his own, not excepting the company of his fellow Fabian reformers, because that still left him bereft of a soul mate. Michael Holroyd entitled the first volume of his biography of Shaw *The Search for Love*, because he saw in Shaw's *Candida* the shy young poet Eugene Marchbanks's "I go in search of love" (*CPP* I:549) as speaking for the whole Shaw. This takes that identification way too far when you consider that Marchbanks himself ultimately declared that search unworthy for the likes of him, but there is no doubt that Shaw understood how his extraordinary ambition and talent made him achingly lonely at times (as revealed most explicitly, perhaps, in his diaries[8]).

Taking it to the highest level, it seems Shaw often felt as lonely as the Jesus or Caesar of his own characterizations of them, the martyrdom of a savior portrayed as one kind of loneliness (so searing that this may be one reason why he could not take his dramatization of Jesus to its biblical conclusion),[9] the loneliness of the world-bettering conqueror shown as another kind. But while in his fiction he tried them both on for size, he found neither extreme suitable in practice. For one thing, neither Jesus nor Caesar was known for his sense of humor, which was a prime requirement for the devilishly smiling Irishman who once used the pseudonym of "GBS Larking."[10]

The savior option first appears in the dramatic fragment now known as "Passion Play,"[11] which shows the enticement of Jesus by Judas away from the bickering misalliance of his parents' household and illustrates the sort of flight from domesticity a calling as savior inspires him to, even if loneliness was to be his fate. Even though Shaw knew he was writing a closet play because its biblical subject would not have been allowed on the stage, that this play was left a fragment suggests not just that Shaw realized that blank verse was neither appropriate to the day nor his own writer's inclinations, but also that martyrdom was not, after all, his personal style (as suggested in the quip he gave to Burgoyne in *The Devil's Disciple*: "Martyrdom ... is the only way ... a man can become famous without ability" (*CPP* II:115).

Thus Shaw's first two works, although neither was published in his lifetime, nevertheless set the pattern for a lifetime of fictionalizing (in both prose and play) the attraction and repulsion to domesticity he felt, between a longing for companionable marriage and the fear implied in "Passion Play" that his desire to be the savior of mankind would be thwarted if he ever succumbed to the domesticating impulse, no matter how "New" the woman might be. His first two works thus amounted to a Point Counter Point, a dialectic which continued throughout his life.

The five novels that followed, one a year from 1879 to 1883, fictionalize and dramatize this same dialectic, between that longing for a fellowship of hearth and home that marriage ideally brings and his fear that marriage would be followed by a homeless misalliance after the breakup, of the painful sort his own childhood had been witness to in Dublin, of course, but multiplied many times over by his adult singularity that led him to fear in marriage the thwarting of his passion for world betterment, "the only thing I am suited for."[12] We should not ignore that some of the potential marriages nipped in the bud in those early days were so ostensibly because of his poverty, a very real consideration, but remember that he *was* poor largely because of his uncompromising dedication to his world-bettering career as a radical writer. He turned down or quit some decent-paying jobs.

Shaw's first novel, *Immaturity* (1879), was well named for its extensive coverage of that theme as it pervades all cultures, but "immaturity" also applies to its would-be hero. It introduces us to the ur-Shaw in the character of an aspiring young poet rather anonymously named Robert Smith (Shaw was mysteriously called "Bob" when very young), who at 18 (his author was 23) is intellectually ambitious and morally passionate in his inveterate criticism of society, but is very shy and lacking a positive identity. "Smith" as a name is ambiguous in suggesting both nonentity and, as in "smithy," the creator of identity, which sums up his often contradictory behavior, that of a nobody striving to become somebody. Seemingly parentless (and thus, figuratively, self-created or seeking to be), Smith is living in a London boarding house[13] and working as a clerk for a wholesaler in a job he despises, an echo of the anti-capitalist template established in Dublin.

Smith flirts a little with an attractive but more practical-minded fellow lodger named Harriet Russell, who might have been Shaw's first attempt at a "New Woman" (if you do not count the prepubescent Dorothea). They go back and forth over her favorite subject, what it takes to get on in the world; but they also discuss male–female relationships and his sense of being stalemated, she taking the position that he has only himself to blame for the turnoff to women of purposelessness in a man who does not want to "get on" in the usual ways. Passing him by, and rather disgusted by his romantic fantasies inspired by an exotic dancer at the Alhambra Theatre, Harriet eventually marries the artist Cyril Scott (sense married to sensibility) in a commonsensical marriage that is typical of how most accommodate themselves to the world and, with luck, maybe avoid misalliance. Such compromises are not for Smith, however.

Later Smith is aggressively pursued by another woman, the very attractive Belle Woodward, the daughter of an Irish MP for whom Smith works as a super-efficient secretary after angrily quitting his unfulfilling clerk's job (goodbye to capitalism!) and stumbling into the new role. Belle is a coquette who, when inspired by her mistaken estimates of the seemingly superhuman Smith, turns on him all the sexual charm of which the Life Force has made her capable. However, Smith's shyness, decorousness, and monstrous sense of propriety (although he did snatch a few kisses in moments of mad impulsiveness) discourage her from pursuit, and he breathes a huge sigh of relief when he learns she has married an older man. As for marriage for himself, he tells Harriet, with whom he is still good friends, it seems to have nothing to do with him: "if it did not exist I should never dream of inventing it."[14]

That is partly because he is otherwise occupied with what might be called an anthropological expedition in which he conducts the sort of research among the natives necessary to any prospective world betterer. Through encounters with a broad sampling of London life, Smith ends his probing discovery of the moral immaturities that surround him in Victorian times with a dawning realization of an immaturity of purpose in himself to match. The human world desperately needs bettering (in the sense of "maturing" as a species), and he wishes to do great things in a world so desperately needing that rather than piddle his life away in domesticity, but he ends with little clue as to how to accomplish that, and there are always young women about to distract him with the allure of domestic bliss, so what to do?

Near the end of the novel, there is a clue about a certain direction in which he might be headed when, after quitting his role as secretary to the Irish MP, he takes a job as a civil servant. This last of an ominous progression of jobs suggests he is a natural permeator of government, however apolitical he strangely seems to be, but the playing of a small part in government *that* portends is still way less than adequate to the needs of a world betterer. The novel ends with Smith feeling rather lost and uncertain of his future. He has learned from contrasting himself with others what he is not, but he does not yet know who he is. Most significantly, as a man of great dignity and propriety he intensely dislikes being made a fool of, a dislike that his creator will eventually overcome as he finds the role of court jester the perfect role for a world betterer of his sort, the sort who does not want to be either a dictator imposing his will or a martyr to the imposition of somebody else's will. And someone who cannot resist a good joke.

One of the best features of *Immaturity* is that it is about a real person who was well known to Shaw—his younger, immature self—whose placement under a narrative microscope made it clear that there was no future for him. Having come to that realization, Shaw wrote four more novels in which he experimentally fashioned various theoretical selves that might allow him to proceed as the world betterer he wanted to be, which accounts for the sense of work-in-progress about the constructed heroes of each of the remaining novels. The first two novels (of the last four) contain in their heroes rather an overstatement of a part of the author that gets a chance, in his narrative, to dominate the whole, but, failing to convince, is replaced in the next novel by its antithesis. In the last two novels Shaw attempts to find a synthesis for this dialectic, coming close but leaving himself to finish the work of personal transformation in person when he moves into the practical world-bettering of the Fabian Society and journalistic criticism. Through all four novels, the familiar dialectic of marriage and misalliance is there to try the souls of all four of their heroes.

Shaw focuses in his second novel, *The Irrational Knot* (1880), on what it means to have an unusual mind, conceived of here as an unusually *rational* mind, and the problems that creates for him in relating to others, especially women. The novel could also be read as an attempt to replace Smith's negativity with a more positive attitude, while his author struggles to do the same, but it is one that overshoots the mark by taking positivity to extremes.

While today we would read Smith as an "anti-hero," this second novel has an actual, traditional "hero" in it, one Ned Conolly, a mature, suave, organized, inventive, cultured man, admirable in so many ways but super-rationalistic to the point of annoyance to those lacking such command. He is a successful American electrical engineer working in London who is bent on improving the world with technology. Did Shaw have intimations of the future that led him to guess that being a high-tech guy might be a way of fulfilling the ambition to be a world betterer? Shaw might have gotten such intimations from meeting in 1879 that human calculating machine and future Fabian luminary Sidney Webb!

Conolly probably owes most of his fictional existence to Shaw's recent work in London, temporarily, for the Edison Telephone Company, charged with persuading people to allow telephone lines and poles on their property, and his encountering of a very different attitude toward life on the part of the Americans with whom he worked. Their contemptuousness of English class consciousness did wonders, it seems, for changing his own attitude. And, to the point of this book, Shaw allows Conolly, social climbing into the aristocracy, actually to attempt marriage with the beautiful Marian Lind (thus tying "the irrational knot"), a marriage on her part largely in defiance of her relatives' disapproval of the workman Conolly (who insists he is an inventor, not a workman). Though minor characters illustrate variations on the themes of the novel, the bulk of the work from then on is devoted to a struggle for compatibility between a very rational husband and a wife who craves conventional emotionalism in her marriage. She wishes for romance and he gives her reason.

Eventually, an exasperated Marian decides for incompatibility and runs off with a romantic rogue named Sholto Douglas, who satisfies her need for emotionalism (by faking it), but leaves her stranded and pregnant in poor lodgings in New York. Conolly gallantly tries to rescue her, but when she thinks her "respectability" lies in not accepting a return to London with an illegitimate child, the novel ends with a misalliance acknowledged as final, the first in a long series to come, which might sound to us now something like Beethoven's opening of the Fifth Symphony were it not for the suggestion of comedy it contains.

Speaking of Beethoven, the third novel has a tell-tale title, *Love Among the Artists* (1881), featuring a Welsh composer and musical genius, Owen Jack (a pun on his poverty), a somewhat brutish, Beethoven-like whirlwind of passion and truth telling, who takes Shaw's experimentation with the hero to the opposite extreme, replacing Conolly's extreme rationalism with its antithesis, extreme passion. Shaw had plenty of both and soon enough understood the need for synthesis, but that is reserved for experimentation in the last two novels.

In this one, Jack "among the artists" gets caught up in a general mating dance, a metaphor reminding us that the original title of *Immaturity* was *Quadrille*, which puts the emphasis upon the dance of life among prospective partners in which the unmarried often find themselves, *Quadrille* perhaps being a good title for the entire quintet of Shaw's novels. In this work's dance, Jack is attracted to a spirited, rebellious girl named Madge who wants to go into acting, against her father's wishes, and much time is spent between them in Jack's Pygmalion-like attempts to teach her elocution and other tricks of the trade. But when she becomes successful on the stage, she rebuffs his marriage proposal, which forces upon Jack the discovery that genius and marriage do not mix (his magnum opus is "Prometheus Unbound," so no irrational knot for him), a motif that will brilliantly and tunefully reoccur many times in Shaw's subsequent work, but nowhere better than in *Candida*, which reminds us that the poet Marchbanks's escape from a domestic romance is one way to avoid the inevitable misalliance. Out into the lonely night goes the solitary poet, or, in this case, musician, to punish the keyboard with his frustrations.

Cashel Byron's Profession (1882), Shaw's fourth novel, surprises us with a reversal, ending with a seemingly successful marriage between the professional boxer Cashel Byron and Lydia Carew, an aristocratic lady of considerable means and even more brains. That Shaw took boxing lessons around this time and sparred a bit reminds us of his development in the 1880s into a public fighter for the causes he thought would lead to world betterment, with verbal feints and jabs replacing actual fisticuffs.[15] Byron exemplifies not only the fighting spirit but also the "executive force" that Shaw sought to add to his debating weaponry, and all the more effective is Byron in retirement from boxing when, after discovering a hidden ancestry in the aristocracy (as indeed Shaw's "downstart" family in Dublin had relatives in that club), he becomes an MP and enjoys a public career made especially successful by his marrying wealth,

Fig. 1.2   Shaw in his
all-wool Jaeger suit in
1885

social grace, and brains. It seems it was possible after all to have a marriage without a misalliance—at least in this fantasy of a plot, where opposites attract and synthesis triumphs for once in the dialectical struggle.
But the wishful thinking in this fantasy came true in a way with Shaw's
eventual marriage to millionairess Charlotte Payne-Townshend, with
eventual lodgings for them in the plush Whitehall Court on the Thames
within spitting distance of Parliament, which Shaw as a Fabian as well as
a creative artist spent much effort trying to permeate (Fig. 1.2).

Yet that was in the future. Meanwhile, Shaw's fifth novel, the wacki-
est, *An Unsocial Socialist* (1883), seemingly returns to the more usual
routine of marriage followed by misalliance, albeit with a surprising
U-turn near the end. One of the wacky things about it is how suddenly
a misalliance is declared when the wealthy hero, Sidney Trefusis, discovers a few weeks after his marriage to wealthy heiress Henrietta Jansenius
that he has made a mistake and runs away to his country retreat,[16]
Sallust's House, which just happens to be close to an exclusive school
for wealthy girls. Trefusis makes his escape by preposterously disguising
himself as his proletarian opposite, a handyman he names "Jeff Smilash"
and who gets employed at the girls' school. Afterwards Trefusis has a
sort of Superman/Clark Kent relationship with Smilash, with sometimes
Smilash darting into a building and Trefusis coming out or vice versa.
High comedy! Conveniently for the development of this split-personality
plot, when Henrietta pursues Trefusis to his country retreat to reclaim
their marriage, she contracts pneumonia that goes undiagnosed and soon

kills her, leaving Trefusis to his higher calling and shortcomings with women. That he does not attend Henrietta's funeral is one of the reasons for the original title of the novel being *The Heartless Man*, but it is more because of his sacrificing everything to world bettering, except some innocent "philandering" now and then.

However, Trefusis ran away not because he disliked his wife, but because he was too powerfully attracted to her, her attractiveness making it impossible for him to do the great work he wants to do. He, a millionaire by inheritance who has made the mistake of reading Karl Marx and thus is plagued with a guilty conscience due to his unearned income, escapes his marriage in favor of conducting a comic Marxist showdown with the plutocratic society of his peers (Trefusis precedes Jack Tanner as an M.I.R.C., Member of the Idle Rich Class, and may be capable of writing a "Revolutionist's Handbook" of his own one day). That he effects his escape by donning the proletarian disguise of Smilash, who speaks humbly but ironically and sarcastically of conformity to the status quo out of one side of his mouth while implying revolution out of the other side, is the principal thing that makes for a very bizarre plot, as Shaw experiments with a clowning Smilash in his playing the fool to the madness of King Capitalism, a role Shaw will later expertly embody in his own person.

This ironic Marxist revolution, however, is undercut and complicated by Trefusis/Smilash's addiction to sweet-talking every pretty girl who comes his way, the girls' school Smilash works at giving him plenty of opportunity. Significantly, Shaw later inserted the following lines for Trefusis to say: "With my egotism, my charlatanry, my tongue, and my habit of having my own way, I am fit for no calling but that of saviour of mankind."[17] But with equal significance, no sooner is this spoken than the "saviour of mankind" enquires of the headmistress about a blonde schoolgirl named Agatha "who is like a golden idol."[18] Though the Marxist Trefusis argues that the more satisfying domesticity is that of being part of a socially responsible society, he, after disappointing a few other girls, eventually plans for marriage to the "golden idol," she being a young radical of his own sort, who sometimes behaves as though she has read *My Dear Dorothea*, for she likes to do whatever is forbidden. This endears her to Trefusis, who thinks marriage to another world betterer might work, especially when he is hit with the sudden realization, *à la* Jack Tanner in his "Don Juan in Hell" dream, that he "was meant to carry a house on his shoulders."[19] In this novel we are reminded that a second marriage can follow a misalliance.

Yet with this idea of a community-minded society itself being the best home for the world betterer, it is likely that Trefusis will soon be looking for something like the Fabian Society to begin the task of constructing that larger home. It was in a Fellowship of the New Life (an actual group Shaw later joined which partially transmuted into the Fabian Society) that Shaw hoped to find his more perfect union, his "marriage." And the reason there were "Christian Socialists" in the world like the Reverend Morell in *Candida* is precisely because Shaw knew that it was the idea of a loving Christian community that, in the West, gave impetus to socialism in the modern world. Sidney Trefusis's philandering is an expression of that communal feeling that so overpowered Shaw and that led some Victorian radicals to entertain notions of "free love" as crucial to the utopian community so planned. But not, ultimately, Shaw; he thought "holidays" and "Sunday husbands" would suffice to break the routine of marriage.

This dialectic between marriage and misalliance is at the center of all the novels (and the unfinished one as well in 1887–1888, with a *ménage à trois* added to the fun), and many examples of this among the minor characters have not even been mentioned, so there is no gainsaying its importance. Yet the novels are about other things as well, and you can make a case for any of the many themes being the most important. Perhaps all the themes are connected, or best connected, by the realization that all plot actions serve the larger purpose of helping Shaw to develop a public personality (which turned out to be GBS) fit and apt for dealing with a difficult, discouraging, unloving world, as with each novel he tries on a different mask of personality, accepting features that seem to work for him and dismissing features that do not, with the trying out of more features always a possibility in the next work.[20]

Some of that experimentation occurred in a few short stories Shaw wrote prior to the playwright years, but as the dialectic of marriage and misalliance typically takes some room to develop, short fiction was not as conducive to it. Nevertheless, of the short stories written in this period, two of the longest, "The Miraculous Revenge" (1885) and "Don Giovanni Explains" (1887), employ the battle of the sexes to develop plots that may reveal some self-questioning by Shaw of his world-bettering proclivities and how easily distracted they were by pretty women.

In "The Miraculous Revenge,"[21] a cardinal archbishop in Dublin, rudely visited in the middle of the night by his cultured, witty, but energetically self-centered and atheist nephew, Zeno Legge, decides to get this young man out of his house by asking him to investigate a miracle down in Wicklow, counting on the young man's skepticism to lend credence to the miracle if found genuine. The miracle is that when a heretic, Wolfe Tone Fitzgerald (called "Brimstone Billy"), is buried in the town graveyard on one side of a river, the next morning all the Catholics buried there are found to have moved to graves across the river, leaving the original graveyard to the heretic. In this miracle of prejudice, Shaw amusingly turns a figurative expression—"wouldn't be caught dead with that person"—into a literal action.

Although Zeno writes to his uncle that he finds the miracle genuine, he complicates matters by falling in love with a pious Irish lass, Kate Hickey, niece of the local priest, Father Hickey, who originally reported the miracle to the cardinal. Unfortunately, Kate takes an immediate dislike to Zeno, hating him for his rude, sarcastic, skeptical, and superior manner, and is immediately supported in this dislike by everyone else. Much of the remaining story is devoted to Zeno's revenge on the people who have insulted and hurt him. At night he transplants Brimstone Billy, for whom he has compassion as another outcast, from his lonely spot in the original cemetery to the new graveyard with all the others, as payback to the religious snobs. However, Zeno is amazed when, as soon as he buries Billy in the new cemetery, all the graves there disappear and reappear in the original cemetery across the river, a far more miraculous revenge than he had planned, which has the added benefit of getting the original miracle debunked in all the newspapers and Father Hickey removed from office. It is as if Shaw were practicing his skill with ironic reversals for the sake of the joke. Yet what is left with Zeno is a bitter residue of questioning why everyone so dislikes him. And one wonders if Shaw, in keeping with the experimentation found in the novels, is here questioning aspects of personality that were counterproductive to either a world betterer or a man seeking love.

"Don Giovanni Explains" is narrated by a self-described "very pretty woman" who is bored by men's company and is independent enough to take a train by herself to an opera, *Don Giovanni*, to which she had been invited by friends in the city. She is disappointed by a poor performance and heads back home by train, in a first-class compartment by herself. She passes the time musing about how much better she might have got on with the real Don Giovanni if they had met because she realizes how "wheedled or persecuted into love affairs"[22] he might have been, as indeed she has been. Kindred spirits, it seems.

And then, as if invoked, suddenly Don Giovanni appears in appropriate stage garb, admitting himself a ghost through which, after her first fright, she can reach. In answer to her questions about his afterlife, he responds with most of the themes of "Don Juan in Hell" from *Man and Superman*, except his time in Hell is narrated rather than shown. This Don Giovanni is one of the few among the dead who occasionally visit the earth in ghost form, and the story he tells is the one from "Don Juan in Hell" about how he has been misrepresented as a seducer of women, when in fact he had found women as tiresome in their pursuit of him as the beautiful narrator had found men in pursuing her. Finding Hell unsatisfactory as well, he had bid the Devil adieu as he heads for Heaven, which is not portrayed as it will be in Shaw's play as a congenial place for the likes of him, partly because he is not identified yet as a philosopher who will enjoy contemplation. Taking her sense of kinship with the Don seriously, the beautiful narrator ends her story by declaring her love for him and insisting that she will *make* him love her, an action seemingly contrary to her character but, perhaps, not to Shaw's experience of such women. Applied to the author, the joke seems to be that a marriage between a flesh-and-blood woman and the ghostly Shaw could not help but be a misalliance, although women who felt themselves kindred were ready to try anyway.

So what was behind all the mating and misalliance in these early works, other than personal aspirations and apprehensions? The Life Force, of course, the centerpiece of that new religion of Creative Evolution, first fully proposed in *Man and Superman*, that resolves all the apprehensions and fulfills the aspirations in the artist-philosopher's understanding that there is a great power at work in the world, deemed the Life Force, that requires sexual mating to achieve its evolutionary ends, realized as divine when the end of endings is the becoming of God. This becoming God learns, as it grows in consciousness and wisdom, by making mistakes and correcting them. On the human level where this cosmic drama is mostly played out on this planet, complications arise in this divine plan with such realizations as that good breeders do not always make good house mates or even good parents, and so that is cause for more dialectical play of a frequently comic nature in Shaw's plays, as the mating dance goes on no matter what and institutions that fail to accommodate its realities are questioned and ridiculed. Yet this was all to come, and so it is all to come in this book.

NOTES

1. Gibbs, *Bernard Shaw: A Life*, 48.
2. Gibbs, *Interviews and Recollections*, 520.
3. For a detailed account of how Shaw's early work was often echoed in the later playwriting or subsequently mined for ideas, see Stanley Weintraub's *Bernard Shaw Before His First Play: The Embryo Playwright* (ELT Press, 2015), 213 pp (Weintraub 2015).
4. It is significant that this quotation can be found in the frontispiece of Eric Bentley's seminal 1947 book (amended in 1957), *Bernard Shaw 1856–1950* (New Directions Paperback), which more radically changed the critical reaction to Shaw than any other work. The quotation from Bergson goes on to say, "But if wit consists, for the most part, in seeing things 'sub specie theatric' it is evidently capable of being specifically directed to one variety of dramatic art, namely, comedy" (Bentley 1947).
5. Bernard Shaw, *My Dear Dorothea: a Practical System of Moral Education for Females Embodied in a Letter to a Young Person of That Sex*, Illustrated by Clare Winsten with a note by Stephen Winsten (New York: The Vanguard Press, 1956), 55 pp (Shaw 1956).
6. *My Dear Dorothea*, 28.
7. Ibid., 25.
8. See Weintraub's *Bernard Shaw Before His First Play: The Embryo Playwright*, 42–53.
9. See Richard F. Dietrich's "Shaw and the Uncrucyifying of Christ," *The Annual of Bernard Shaw Studies*, vol VIII (1988), 13–38 (Dietrich 1988).
10. Found in a letter entitled "Who Is the Thief" in *Justice* (the Journal of the Social Democratic Federation, 15 March 1884) and referred to in Dan H. Laurence's *Soho Bibliography* (Vol. I, p. 182 and vol. II, pp. 524–525) and in A.M. Gibb's *A Bernard Shaw Chronology* (p. 47).
11. For a detailed treatment of this work, see Weintraub's *Bernard Shaw Before His First Play: The Embryo Playwright*, 5–18.
12. Bernard Shaw, *An Unsocial Socialist*. London: Constable & Co 1932, 104 (Shaw 1932).
13. Shaw did not actually live in a boarding house, except for the fact that while living with his mother he often had to put up with the boarders she sometimes took in.

14. Bernard Shaw, *Immaturity*, 423–424.
15. For a treatment of Shaw's interest in boxing throughout his life, see Weintraub's *Bernard Shaw Before His First Play: The Embryo Playwright*, 30–41. See also Jay Tunney's *The Prizefighter and the Playwright, Gene Tunney and Bernard Shaw* (New York: Firefly Books, 2010), 287 pp (Tunney 2010).
16. Trefusis's country house is called Sallust's House, Sallust being a Roman philosopher who had much in common with Shaw, including the coining of moral aphorisms, all of which is explained in Weintraub's *Bernard Shaw Before His First Play: The Embryo Playwright*, 85–90.
17. *An Unsocial Socialist*, 104.
18. Ibid., 104.
19. Ibid., 225.
20. The many other themes that can be found in Shaw's novels are treated in Richard Farr Dietrich's *Bernard Shaw's Novels: Portraits of the Artist as Man and Superman*, University Press of Florida, 1996 (Dietrich 1996).
21. Both "The Miraculous Revenge" and "Don Giovanni Explains" are to be found in a collection called *Short Stories, Scraps & Shavings*, to be found in both The Constable Edition, vol 6, 1932, and a Dodd, Mead edition of 1934, 1935.
22. "Don Giovanni Explains," Constable & Co. LTD, 1932, 98.

REFERENCES

Bentley, Eric. 1947. *Bernard Shaw 1856–1950*, Amended Edition. New York: New Directions Paperback.

Dietrich, Richard Farr. 1988. Shaw and the Uncrucifying of Christ. *SHAW: The Annual of Bernard Shaw Studies* 8: 13–38.

Dietrich, Richard Farr. 1996. *Bernard Shaw's Novels: Portraits of the Artist as Man and Superman*. Gainesville: University Press of Florida.

Shaw, Bernard. 1932. *An Unsocial Socialist*. London: Constable.

Shaw, Bernard. 1956. *My Dear Dorothea: A Practical System of Moral Education for Females Embodied in a Letter to a Young Person of that Sex*. New York: Vanguard Press.

Tunney, Jay. 2010. *The Prizefighter and the Playwright: Gene Tunney and Bernard Shaw*. New York: Firefly Books.

Weintraub, Stanley. 2015. *Bernard Shaw Before His First Play: The Embryo Playwright*. Greensboro, NC: ELT Press.

AUTHOR BIOGRAPHY

Richard Farr Dietrich Professor Emeritus at the University of South Florida, USA, was the Founding President of the International Shaw Society, is a member of the Editorial Board of *SHAW: The Journal of Bernard Shaw Studies*, and was the Series Editor for the University Press of Florida's Bernard Shaw Series. He is the author of *Bernard Shaw's Novels: Portrait of the Author as Man and Superman* as well as *British Drama 1890–1950: A Critical History*.

CHAPTER 2

The "Mystical Union" De-Mystified: Marriage in *Plays Unpleasant*

L.W. Conolly

As weddings go, it was a bit of a shambles. Held on a cool and showery first day of June in 1898 in a registry office on Henrietta Street,[1] just a few steps away from the smells and cacophonies of London's Covent Garden fruit and vegetable market (where Eliza Doolittle was subsequently to display her wares), the brief civil ceremony in which Charlotte Payne-Townshend and Bernard Shaw were married was short on glamour, but long on farce—at least according to Shaw. Surgery to his left foot had left him ungainly, tottering on crutches, and such was his indifference to sartorial niceties that the registrar assumed that one of his better-dressed witnesses was the groom and Shaw just "the inevitable beggar who completes all wedding processions" (*CL* II:46).

Shaw made light of the occasion, but the institution of marriage itself was no laughing matter as far as he was concerned. His parents' own marriage had broken down irretrievably when his mother moved from the family home in Dublin to London in 1873 leaving Shaw, aged 16, with his father. And between the time that Shaw followed his mother to London (in 1876) and his marriage to Charlotte 22 years later, he

L.W. Conolly (✉)
Trent University, Peterborough, Canada
e-mail: lwconolly@gmail.com

© The Author(s) 2017
R.A. Gaines (ed.), *Bernard Shaw's Marriages and Misalliances*,
Bernard Shaw and His Contemporaries,
DOI 10.1057/978-1-349-95170-3_2

21

witnessed plenty of marital misalliances among a wide circle of friends and colleagues. Some of his own numerous dalliances before he married Charlotte (and some afterwards as well) were, unwisely, with married women. His relationship with May Morris, for example, albeit platonic, seems to have been at least partly responsible for her divorcing her husband in the hope that Shaw would marry her.[2] Shaw was also close to fellow socialist Annie Besant, legally separated (but not divorced) from her clergyman husband and the father of her two children. In 1877 she drew up a common-law marriage contract for the two of them, but Shaw declined the offer.[3]

That Shaw married at all is testament both to his respect and affection for Charlotte and to the power of marriage as a Victorian social convention (*CL* 111:778). That marriage became such a prominent theme in his plays is testament to its power to disrupt and blight lives across all levels of society—from Kitty Warren's half-sister in *Mrs Warren's Profession*, struggling to raise three children in a London slum on the paltry money that her drunken husband spares her (*CPP* I:311), to the real-life aristocratic friend of Shaw, Lady Colin Campbell, whose divorce case against her adulterous and syphilitic husband was shamefully rejected by the courts in 1886.[4]

By the time Shaw married Charlotte, he had become one of London's most prominent and disputatious critics (art, music, theatre) and a high-profile writer and lecturer for the Fabian Society. Moreover, his prominence as a playwright was growing on both sides of the Atlantic, with commercial successes for *Arms and the Man* in London in 1894 and *The Devil's Disciple* in New York in 1897. Shaw welcomed those successes—the money was useful—but his all-important political convictions were better reflected in the first three plays that he had written before he married Charlotte: *Widowers' Houses, The Philanderer* and *Mrs Warren's Profession*, published together as volume one, *Plays Unpleasant*, in *Plays: Pleasant and Unpleasant* in April 1898. All three plays make the case for fundamental social reform. A myriad of entrenched political, economic, and social policies, Shaw believed, were in dire need of change. Among them was the cherished Victorian institution of marriage.

There were several pieces of marriage and divorce legislation in place in Great Britain (excluding Scotland, which had its own, more liberal marriage laws) when Shaw got married. They represent the legal context for Shaw's career-long interest in the issue.

The basic legislation was the 1753 Marriage Act, which replaced canon law of the Church of England, often flouted or contravened, thereby creating uncertainty about the legal status of thousands of marriages.[5] The 1753 Act stipulated that marriages had to be performed in an Anglican church, by an ordained minister of the Church of England, following the publication of banns (i.e., public announcements in the parish where the marriage was to take place) and the acquisition of a marriage license. (Jews and Quakers were exempted from the Act; Catholics were not.) The Church of England marriage service (see Appendix B1), "The Solemnization of Matrimony," among many other charges required the groom to affirm that he will "love ... comfort ... honour, and keep" his wife "in sickness and in health," while "forsaking all other" and keeping "only to her, so long as ye both shall live." The same commitment was asked of the bride, with the important addition that she must also promise to "obey" and "serve" her husband.[6]

It is very hard to imagine that either Shaw or Charlotte would have agreed to participate in such a service, the preamble to which states that matrimony is "an honourable estate, instituted of God in the time of man's innocency, signifying unto us the mystical union that is betwixt Christ and his Church." Shaw had many views on marriage, but they emphatically did not include the opinion that it signified "the mystical union that is betwixt Christ and his Church."

If the law on marriage had not been relaxed, it is unlikely that Shaw and Charlotte would ever have married. The 1753 Act remained unaltered until 1836, when a new Marriage Act, for the first time in English history,[7] allowed for civil marriages, thereby creating, Lawrence Stone notes, "a two-track system for marriage in England": "One was conducted by a minister in holy orders in a church or chapel, and regarded as a sacred religious ceremony. The other was conducted by a state official in an office, and regarded as a purely secular contract. It was swift and cheap, and was intended to lure the poor back into matrimony."[8]

The brevity of a civil ceremony was doubtless more important to the Shaws than the cost, but what really mattered was that they could marry without having to endure the Church of England marriage liturgy.[9] The only requirements of the civil ceremony were that both parties declare that they know of no legal impediment to their marriage, that they make a formal commitment to each other ("I take thee to be my lawful wedded wife/husband"), and that there be two witnesses. And that is exactly what Shaw and Charlotte did in the Henrietta Street registry office on that rainy day on June 1, 1898.

It certainly helped as well that as a result of the Married Women's Property Act of 1882, Charlotte—a woman of considerable wealth—was not deprived of her rights to own property and conduct her financial affairs independently of her husband, as she would have been prior to 1882. Under the Act, a married woman retained the rights of a single woman, as opposed to becoming what in the legalese of British common law was called a "feme covert" (i.e., in modern French, a "femme couverte," a "covered woman," a woman whose very identity is assimilated by her husband).

Getting married was one thing; getting divorced was another—not that the Shaws ever contemplated it, but, inevitably, many British couples did. The problem was that the law did not make divorce easy, as Shaw frequently pointed out in his prefaces and plays. In fact, given that all divorce cases had to go through a full trial process in court, the law made divorce inaccessible to all but the wealthiest in society. And women, whatever their wealth, faced more barriers than men.

The legislation relating to divorce in Great Britain that was in effect for most of Shaw's life was the 1857 Divorce and Matrimonial Causes Act (see Appendix B2). While taking divorce out of the control of the Church and placing it under civil law, the 1857 Act, like the Church of England marriage liturgy, blatantly discriminated against women. To gain a divorce, a man was required simply to prove that his wife had committed adultery. Period. A woman, on the other hand, was required to prove not only that her husband had committed adultery, but that he had committed adultery *in conjunction with* at least one of a lengthy list of additional acts: incest, bigamy, rape sodomy, bestiality, desertion, cruelty.[10] Not until the 1937 Divorce and Matrimonial Causes Act were women treated equally with men in divorce law.[11]

In the circumstances, it is not surprising that divorce rates remained very low in Victorian and Edwardian England. Statistics for 1901, just 3 years after Shaw's marriage, show that only 477 divorces were granted that year, which amounted to a mere 0.08 divorces per 1000 married couples.[12] The virtual impossibility of gaining divorce was akin, Shaw argued, to enslavement. "To impose marriage on two unmarried people who do not desire to marry one another would be admittedly an act of enslavement," he wrote in the preface to *Getting Married*. "But it is no worse than to impose a continuation of marriage on people who have ceased to desire to be married" (*CPP* III:519). The solution? "Make divorce as easy, as cheap, and as private as marriage," and "Grant divorce at the request of either party, whether the other consents or not; and admit no other ground than the request, which should be made without stating any reasons" (*CPP* III:542). But that kind of visionary thinking did not fit at all comfortably with the prevailing religious and political ideologies of marriage and divorce.

This, then, was the legal context for Shaw's first explorations of marriage in his plays. That Shaw was knowledgeable about the legalities of marriage and divorce laws in Great Britain, the United States, and other countries is clearly evident from his original final act of *The Philanderer* (see below), as well as from later plays such as *Getting Married*. His interest in marriage goes far beyond legalities, however, encompassing a wide range of the moral, emotional, and economic complexities involved in the lives of those of his characters who are contemplating marriage, or are married but wish they were not, or have decided not to get married, or multiple permutations of those situations. While the principal subject matter of the first and third of his *Plays Unpleasant—Widowers' Houses* and *Mrs Warren's Profession*—ostensibly has little to do with marriage, both plays, through characters such as Blanche Sartorius and Vivie Warren, raise deeply unsettling questions about marriage. Just as Victorian hypocrisies about housing the poor (*Widowers' Houses*) and about prostitution (*Mrs Warren's Profession*) are exposed in these plays, so is the piousness about "the mystical union that is betwixt Christ and his Church" shown to be a sham.

At the instigation of and in collaboration with critic William Archer, Shaw began writing *Widowers' Houses* in 1884. After various lengthy delays, the exit of Archer from the collaboration, and numerous revisions, *Widowers' Houses* was accepted for production by Jacob Grein at his recently formed Independent Theatre Society (at the Royalty Theatre on Dean Street in Soho). It opened there on December 9, 1892, with a second (and last) performance on December 13.[13] It was first published in 1893 in London, and subsequently, with further revisions, simultaneously in London and New York in volume one of *Plays: Pleasant and Unpleasant* in 1898.[14]

In explaining the textual development of *Widowers' Houses*, Jerald Bringle identifies "dual themes of matrimonial and commercial contamination" in the play.[15] They remain dual themes in the published texts, but not equal themes, at least in terms of the attention Shaw gives them.

What early critics by and large detected in the play was Shaw's "scorn and hatred [of] the morality, or rather the immorality, of those who batten on rents torn from the miserable occupants of slum-dwellings."[16] So did the conservative boo-boys in the gallery at the Royalty Theatre quick to show their distaste for "a succession of Socialistic tirades and rhetorical speeches."[17] Nonetheless, as Sandra Joy Russell has more recently pointed out, "*Widowers' Houses* works within [the] binary of spatial and social, placing the housing crisis alongside shifting notions of gender and marriage."[18]

There are only five characters in *Widowers' Houses*. One (Sartorius) is a widower, though his wife is never mentioned; two (Lickcheese and Cokane) are married, but their wives are neither seen nor heard; two (Harry Trench and Blanche Sartorius) are single. We do not, then, witness a marriage in action, as it were, in *Widowers' Houses* (or, for that matter, in *Mrs Warren's Profession* and the published version of *The Philanderer*), but the relationship between Blanche and Trench, closely intertwined with Sartorius's business and social ambitions, ensures that marriage is an issue integral to the play.

Sartorius has become a wealthy man on the backs of the poor who rent rooms, or portions of rooms, in his dilapidated London tenement buildings. What he wants now is social status, which can be achieved by marrying off his daughter, Blanche, to Harry Trench, a young doctor with upper-crust relatives. In that sense, marriage, from Sartorius's point of view, falls into the category of what Shaw calls "a political necessity" in the preface to *Plays Unpleasant* (*CPP* I:33).

Shaw describes Blanche as "*a well-dressed, well-fed, goodlooking, strong-minded young woman*" (*CPP* I:49). According to her father, her education like Vivie Warren's, "has been of the most expensive and complete kind obtainable" (*CPP* I:68), though what, exactly, it has consisted of (in addition to extensive European travel) he does not say. In any event, it has given Blanche enough self-confidence and guile to take the initiative to strike up a conversation with Trench when she first encounters him on holiday in Germany, and to manipulate him into a proposal of marriage shortly afterwards. When wedding plans collapse after Trench discovers the source of the Sartorius fortune and, on principle, refuses to countenance accepting any of it as part of the marriage settlement, Blanche calculatingly exploits her sexuality—"*undisguised animal excitement*," says Shaw (*CPP* I:119)—to overcome Trench's scruples. That "animal excitement" is reflected as well in her brutal treatment of the maid (*CPP* I:97–98) and her frequent outbursts of anger. Clearly, her education has not taught her much about self-control, nor has it done a very good job of inculcating a social conscience. In this regard she is, as Shaw says (*CPP* I:49), her father's daughter. Like Vivie, Blanche has been kept in the dark about the source of her parents' income. When she discovers that Sartorius is well known as "the worst slum landlord in London" (*CPP* I:109), she momentarily challenges him to explain and justify what he does (again, not unlike Vivie's challenge to her mother about *her* occupation). Sartorius, however, easily swats aside her half-hearted objection, leaving her merely to express a concern that the family name might be tainted by being involved with "those dirty, drunken, disreputable people who live like pigs" (*CPP* I:110).

Blanche is Sartorius's bargaining chip for entry into polite society. "There shall be no difficulty about money," he tells Trench. "But I must have a guarantee on my side that she will be received on equal terms by your family" (*CPP* I:62). He trades his daughter for social status. Blanche, despite her concerns about marrying "a fool" (*CPP* I:99), is a willing partner in what is essentially a commercial and political transaction. And so, ultimately, is Trench. His qualms about Sartorius's business operations are more deep seated than Blanche's. He accuses Sartorius of making his fortune "out of a parcel of unfortunate creatures that have hardly enough to keep body and soul together—made by screwing, and bullying, and threatening, and all sorts of pettifogging tyranny" (*CPP* I:91). When, however, Trench learns that his own income in fact derives from the interest on a mortgage he holds on one of Sartorius's properties—"Do you mean to say that I am just as bad as you are?" (*CPP* I:94)—he is reduced to feebly apologizing for "making such a fuss" (*CPP* I:95). Subsequently, on learning that Sartorius is about to enter into a shady property deal that will significantly diminish his income unless he joins the scheme, Trench again allows self-interest to overcome principle and he agrees to participate. At that point Lickcheese, the former rent collector turned property shark, encourages Trench and Blanche to make things up: "Why not have a bit of romance in business when it costs nothing?" (*CPP* I:117), he says. Indeed, why not? And so *Widowers' Houses* reaches its entirely plausible and wholly depressing conclusion as the five business partners (Trench's friend Cokane is also one of them) head off to celebrate both the forthcoming marriage and their new scam planned around Sartorius's dining table.

In *Widowers' Houses*, Shaw said, "I have shewn middle-class respect-ability and younger son gentility fattening on the poverty of the slums as flies fatten on filth" (*CPP* I:33). In the first Tract he wrote for the Fabian Society (no. 2, 1884), he had declared that "wealth cannot be enjoyed without dishonour." In the case of *Widowers' Houses* the dishonor is shown emphatically to encompass marriage as well as the more spectacu-larly odious capitalist enterprises.

Shaw's second play, *The Philanderer*, was written shortly after the première of *Widowers' Houses*, but in many ways Shaw's third play, *Mrs Warren's Profession*, has more in common with *Widowers' Houses*. Both deal with a recognized social problem (slum housing and prostitution, respectively) while at the same time successfully integrating the subject of marriage into the fabric of the play.

Shaw began writing *Mrs Warren's Profession* in August 1893, and had completed the first draft by early November. Between then and the play's first publication in *Plays Unpleasant* in 1898 he made several revi-sions, but his final version was denied a performance license by the Lord Chamberlain. Over the coming years there were several private perfor-mances, but the first public performance of *Mrs Warren's Profession* in England did not take place until 1925. The first performances in the United States in 1905 (in New Haven and New York, one performance in each city) were highly controversial, the New York performance lead-ing to the arrest of the whole cast on the charge (subsequently dropped) of an offense against public decency.[19]

Widowers' Houses has five characters; *Mrs Warren's Profession* has six, only one of whom, the Reverend Samuel Gardner, is married. There are references to Mrs. Gardner, but, like the wives in *Widowers' Houses*, she is kept out of sight. Mrs. Warren herself is unmarried (the "Mrs" pro-vides a faux respectability), though as a prostitute she has, of course, had numerous sexual partners, one of whom is the father of her daughter, Vivie (Mrs. Warren never reveals the identity of Vivie's father, and may not know it). Vivie is unmarried, though the possibility of her marry-ing Frank (Gardner's son) or Sir George Crofts (Mrs. Warren's business partner)—ugly misalliances in both cases—forms an important thematic and narrative element in the play. Praed, an architect and one of Mrs. Warren's more cultured confidants (though not sexually involved with her), is also single.

As with *Widowers' Houses*, Shaw explained very clearly why he had written *Mrs Warren's Profession*. He wrote it, he said in the preface to the

1930 edition of *Plays Unpleasant*, "to draw attention to the truth that prostitution is caused, not by female depravity and male licentiousness, but simply by underpaying, undervaluing, and overworking women so shamefully that the poorest of them are forced to resort to prostitution to keep body and soul together" (*CPP* I:231). And, as with slum housing in *Widowers' Houses*, capitalism has found ways of creating profit out of poverty and destitution. Prostitution, Shaw noted, is not only "carried on without organization by individual enterprise in the lodgings of solitary women," but also "organized and exploited as a big international commerce for the profit of capitalists like any other commerce" (*CPP* I:231). That is the kind of business carried on by Mrs. Warren and Crofts in their chain of European brothels. Although we never learn the details of Mrs. Warren's wealth, Crofts tells Vivie that he makes 35% ("in the worst years") on his investment of £40,000 (*CPP* I:328).

When Vivie asks her mother why she continues to run her brothel business, Mrs. Warren responds with a rhetorical question—"do you know how rich I am?"—and goes on to explain how much in love with Mammon she is and what it means to her: "it means a new dress every day; it means theatres and balls every night; it means having the pick of all the gentlemen of Europe at your feet; it means a lovely house and plenty of servants; it means the choicest of eating and drinking; it means everything you like, everything you want, everything you can think of" (*CPP* I:350). Like Sartorius, then, Mrs. Warren has become an unapologetic capitalist, the great seductress herself seduced by Mammon and all his trappings. She treats the tenants of her brothels more compassionately than Sartorius treats the occupants of his tenements, but her values, like his, permeate and contaminate her relationship with her daughter and her daughter's future, which will, Mrs. Warren has no doubt, include marriage.

Mrs. Warren has firm views on marriage. Growing up in poverty, watching her mother struggle to raise four daughters by herself, seeing her half-sister die from workplace lead poisoning, being exploited herself in demeaning jobs—all this has led her to understand that one of the few ways for a young woman to escape poverty is "to catch some rich man's fancy and get the benefit of his money by marrying him ... as if a marriage ceremony could make any difference in the right or wrong of the thing!" (*CPP* I:313). Mrs. Warren has taken a different route from this: rather than prostituting herself in marriage, she has gone several steps further and joined her sister (now retired) in building and managing a successful European brothel operation. Unbeknownst to Vivie, the profits from the business have paid for her Cambridge education, but even though Mrs. Warren assures Vivie that she will continue to benefit from her mother's largesse, Mrs. Warren's view of marriage as a commercial transaction remains firm. Seemingly unaware that Vivie and Frank Warren may be half-siblings (Samuel Gardner is a former client of Mrs. Warren's), Mrs. Warren's main concern is about Frank's financial suitability as a husband for her daughter. When it becomes clear that Frank has no money—on the contrary, he is keen to marry Vivie for *her* money—she flatly tells him "that settles it: you cant have Vivie" (*CPP* I:297).

Mrs. Warren also rejects Crofts as a suitor for Vivie. Since Crofts has been a sexual partner, and could even be Vivie's father (though Mrs. Warren denies it), having the near-50-year-old as her son-in-law is out of the question; she is, say the stage directions, "*revolted*" by Crofts's proposition and looks at him with "*contemptuous disgust*" (*CPP* I:302). But Crofts knows the kind of proposition that accords with Mrs. Warren's values. He offers Vivie social position (he is a baronet), money, property, and for Mrs. Warren herself there will "a cheque … on the wedding day … any figure you like—in reason" (*CPP* I:302–303). Just as Sartorius wants to buy a husband for his daughter, so Crofts wants to buy himself a wife. Later in the play Crofts makes the offer directly to Vivie. When she rejects him, he spitefully reveals to her the extent to which dubious capitalist business ventures, including her mother's, have infiltrated and benefited the upper echelons of British society—church, politics, education—and damns her for refusing to cooperate, especially since, as Crofts points out, she has been a beneficiary herself.

Vivie, then, faces the same dilemma as Harry Trench in *Widowers' Houses*. Like Trench, Vivie moves from a state of economic innocence to an awareness of her complicity in a business she finds abhorrent. Both Trench and Vivie are offered marriage as the means of accepting and affirming their complicity. Marriage is the portal, not to a "mystical union" as the Church would have it, but to an unscrupulous capitalist ethos.

In the preface to the 1898 edition of *Plays Unpleasant*, Shaw wrote that marriage was viewed by some as "that worst of blundering abominations, an institution which society has outgrown but not modified, and which 'advanced' individuals are therefore forced to evade" (*CPP* I:33). By agreeing to marry Blanche in *Widowers' Houses*, Harry Trench excludes himself from this "advanced" group; by rejecting Crofts (and, later in that same scene, Frank), Vivie allies herself with it. Vivie's reasons for rejecting Frank and Crofts are specific to those particular men and their circumstances. Frank is off limits, among other reasons, because he may be her half-brother; Crofts is simply morally repugnant. If that were all, one might imagine Vivie finding a more like-minded partner at a later stage in her life. Vivie is adamant, however, that not only is she rejecting marriage suitors, she is rejecting marriage itself. Marriage is simply not compatible with her goals as an independent, professional woman, a New Woman. "I must be treated as a woman of business, permanently single ... and permanently unromantic," she tells Frank and Praed in her actuarial office toward the end of the play (*CPP* I:342). A few minutes later, as she dismisses her mother from her life, she also dismisses marriage: "I do not want a mother; and I dont want a husband" (*CPP* I:354).

At the end of *Widowers' Houses* there is a business and family cohesion around Sartorius that depends on his daughter's marriage to Trench. No such cohesion exists in *Mrs Warren's Profession*. Vivie is the spoiler, setting off on her own career, a career that remains, to be sure, in the capitalist economic orbit, but one free of the exploitative blight of slum housing and prostitution—and simultaneously free of marriage as well.

Although still classified by Shaw as an "unpleasant" play, *The Philanderer* differs in striking ways from *Widowers' Houses* and *Mrs Warren's Profession*. There is again a relatively small cast (eight characters, one of whom, the Page in Act II, makes only a brief appearance). Among the seven main characters there is one married man (Cuthbertson), but he is legally separated from his wife (who does not appear); a widower (Craven); a widow (Grace Tranfield); and four singles (Paramore, Julia Craven, Sylvia Craven, and Leonard Charteris—the philanderer). But none of them can lay claim to being a capitalist of the kind we encounter in *Widowers' Houses* and *Mrs Warren's Profession*: the protagonist (Charteris) is a philosopher, Paramore is a doctor, Cuthbertson a theatre critic, and Craven a retired soldier. Grace Tranfield appears to receive income from her late husband's estate, and the Craven sisters (Julia and Sylvia) live with and off their father. Moreover, there is no discussion in *The Philanderer* of issues that most Victorians would have acknowledged as problematic. Few would have conceded (openly, at least) that the issue that *is* discussed in *The Philanderer*—marriage—was a problem at all, let alone of the magnitude of slum housing and prostitution. Shaw begged to differ. In *The Philanderer* marriage takes center stage.

When Shaw wrote in the 1898 preface to *Plays Unpleasant* that the three plays included in the volume are intended "to force the spectator to face unpleasant facts" (*CPP* I:32), no one who went on to read the plays would have been left in any doubt about the unpleasantness of *Widowers' Houses* and *Mrs Warren's Profession*. Slum housing and prostitution are, indisputably, unpleasant subjects. But to argue that marriage, that "mystical union that is betwixt Christ and his Church," is unpleasant would have puzzled and, no doubt, offended many readers.

Nonetheless, Shaw insists in the 1898 preface that *The Philanderer* exposes "the grotesque sexual compacts made between men and women under [British] marriage laws," and that the events and atmosphere in the play, from beginning to end, are "unpleasant" (*CPP* I:33).

The action of *The Philanderer*, which has a much higher comic element than seen in either of the other two "unpleasant" plays, is built around the (successful) efforts of Leonard Charteris to avoid entering a sure-fire misalliance by marrying Julia Craven, a discarded but still persistent lover. An early verbal skirmish between the philanderer and his current lover, Grace Tranfield, reveals Shaw's agenda. In response to Charteris's confession that his marriage proposal to Grace is merely a strategy to escape from Julia, Grace replies that she declines "to be made use of for any such purpose," and that she "will not steal [Charteris] from another woman." Charteris quickly pounces on Grace's response to ask her if Julia belongs to him: "Am I her owner—her master?" "Certainly not," says Grace. "No woman is the property of a man. A woman belongs to herself and to nobody else" (*CPP* I:142). On this they are agreed, which, Charteris declares, allies them with the ideas of his champion, Henrik Ibsen ("Ibsen for ever!"). He might also have pointed out that this Ibsenite point of view is totally at odds with the Church of England marriage liturgy, in which the bride is asked "Who giveth this Woman to be married to this Man?" (traditionally her father), as if the bride is indeed someone's property. A few moments later Julia herself bursts into the room, and promptly reverses the Church's (and Ibsen's) position by telling Charteris that "You belong to me" (*CPP* I:144), a claim that, once Grace has beaten a hasty retreat to another room from Julia's onslaught, leads to an unevenly matched but revealing conversation between Charteris and Julia about marriage.

According to Charteris, his relationship with Julia has been between two people with "advanced views": "As a woman of advanced views, you were determined to be free. You regarded marriage as a degrading bargain, by which a woman sells herself to a man for the social status of a wife and the right to be supported and pensioned in old age out of his income. That's the advanced view: our view" (*CPP* I:147). And then, uniquely among *Plays Unpleasant*, Charteris brings up the matter of divorce. With a direct allusion to the prevailing legislation governing divorce (the 1857 Divorce and Matrimonial Causes Act), he reminds Julia that if she married Charteris (or anyone else, of course) and he turned out to be "a drunkard, a criminal, an imbecile, a horror to you ... you could not have released yourself." That is, such kinds of behavior were not sufficient grounds for a woman to divorce a man (even if coupled with adultery). In those circumstances, Charteris concludes, marriage is just "too big a risk. ... That's the rational view: our view" (*CPP* I:147).

It becomes increasingly clear to Charteris, however, that while it may be his view, it is not her view, so she must endure another admonition from him. "Advanced people," he tells her, "form charming friendships: conventional people marry. Marriage suits a good many people: and its first duty is fidelity. Friendship suits some people; and its first duty is unhesitating, uncomplaining acceptance of a notice of change of feeling from either side. You chose friendship instead of marriage. Now do your duty, and accept your notice" (*CPP* I:150).

Julia's unwillingness to behave as an "advanced" woman drives the action of Act II of *The Philanderer*, which is set in the fictional Ibsen Club, in which membership is limited to "unmanly men" and "unwomanly women." Determined to marry Julia off to someone else, Charteris targets a doctor, Percival Paramore, who apart from being a potential spouse for Julia also provides Shaw with an opportunity for a hearty dose of medical satire (a trial run for his later play, *The Doctor's Dilemma*). The result of Charteris's conniving is that by the end of the act, Julia is all but engaged to the hapless Paramore, and the match—another surefire misalliance—is finally sealed in Paramore's rooms at the beginning of Act III.

At that point, Shaw changes the mood of the play. The satire and frolics of the second act (at one point Julia frantically pursues Charteris around the library of the Ibsen Club) take a more serious turn. Claiming that she is "alone in the world," and that Paramore, unlike Charteris, at least shows some respect for her, she is on the point of accepting his proposal of marriage when, anticipating an embrace, he "*approaches her eagerly.*" This provokes "*a violent revulsion*" from Julia, and she *"rises with her hand up as if to beat him off."* When Paramore asks "Is it Charteris?" Julia is jolted back into the recognition of Charteris's treatment of her and she—still hesitatingly—agrees to marry Paramore (*CPP* 1:213).

It is here that Shaw's prefatory remark on the "grotesque sexual compacts" of marriage comes to mind, but in an unexpected way. Julia's acceptance of Paramore has a major proviso. "If I say yes," she asks him, "will you promise not to touch me? Will you give me time to accustom myself to our new relations?" (*CPP* 1:213). That is, there is to be no sex at least in the early stages of the marriage, perhaps longer. This is the opposite of what Shaw took to be the norm in the relationship between marriage and sex with sex holding such power that "when two people are under the influence of the most violent, most insane, most delusive, and most transient of passions, they are required to swear [in the marriage liturgy] that they will remain in that excited, abnormal, and exhausting condition continuously until death do them part" (preface to *Getting Married, CPP* III:474–475). Shaw's own attitude toward sex and marriage was entirely the opposite. As he expressed it in a letter to Frank Harris, sex was "hopeless as a basis for permanent relations," and he "never dreamt of marriage in connection with it" (*CL* IV:192).[20] But Julia is not quite so cerebral about sex Every indication is that her affair with Charteris has been passionate, and that she would expect passion, including sexual passion, to be an important aspect of her marriage. Thus the "grotesque" element of her marriage arrangement with Paramore is the exclusion of sex. It is not surprising, then, that at the end of the play, the marriage with Paramore now inexorably confirmed, Shaw's stage direction tells us that everyone except Charteris (who is "*amused and untouched*") looks at Julia "*with concern, and even a little awe, feeling for the first time the presence of a keen sorrow*" (*CPP* 1:227). The sorrow is twofold: Charteris is lost to her, Paramore is substituted. The past is bitter; the future is bleak.

In the published text of *The Philanderer*, readers and audiences are left to imagine the future of the Paramore–Julia marriage, based on what they have learned about the two of them during the play. Only the most naively optimistic could imagine anything but disaster from this misalliance and that is precisely what Shaw himself envisioned. In *Pygmalion* Shaw gives us a sequel to describe what happens to Eliza after she leaves the home and laboratory of Henry Higgins (*CPP* IV:782–798). There is no published equivalent for *The Philanderer* But Shaw's original intention was to show in the final act of the play that, 4 years later, the marriage had failed. Paramore has begun a relationship with Grace Tranfield (Charteris's lover at the beginning of the play) and seeks a divorce from Julia. At first resistant, Julia eventually agrees, but what Paramore calls England's "pigheaded" divorce law prevents a civilized, dignified, and mutually beneficial settlement.[21] The solution to the problem involves a lengthy trip to the United States, specifically South Dakota, where more liberal divorce laws give Paramore his freedom to marry Grace, and Julia hers to continue her pursuit of Charteris—or anyone else, for that matter.[22]

Shaw begins his preface to *Getting Married* (first performed in 1908) with a section headed "The Revolt against Marriage," in which he declares that "There is no subject on which more dangerous nonsense is talked and thought than marriage." English marriage law, he adds, "is inhuman and unreasonable to the point of downright abomination" (*CPP* III:452–453). He spends the rest of one of his longest prefaces developing these observations, and then explores them in dramatic form in *Getting Married: A Disquisitory Play.* None of the *Plays Unpleasant* achieves the focus on marriage that Shaw realized in *Getting Married*, though *The Philanderer* comes close, particularly when the discarded final act is taken into account. But that marriage has such a consistent and provocative presence in *Plays Unpleasant* speaks to Shaw's ongoing sense of how important it was to wrest the subject from religious doctrine and bring it into the cold light of rational discourse.

NOTES

1. The offices of Grant Richards, who published Shaw's *Plays: Pleasant and Unpleasant* on April 19, 1898, just a few weeks before Shaw married Charlotte, were also on Henrietta Street. According to Shaw, it was Charlotte who found the registry office there (*CL* II:45) (Shaw 1898).
2. A.M. Gibbs, *A Bernard Shaw Chronology* (Basingstoke: Palgrave, 2001), 371 (Gibbs 2001).
3. Ibid., 344.
4. Bernard Shaw, *The Philanderer* ed. L.W. Conolly (Peterborough, ON: Broadview Press, 2015), 14–15 (Shaw 2015).
5. Lawrence Stone, *Road to Divorce. England 1530–1987* (Oxford: Oxford University Press, 1990), 128–137 (Stone 1990).
6. The full text of the marriage service as it was when Shaw married is in Appendix B1 (p. 211–216). The service has changed since then, notably

omitting the requirement that the bride agree to obey and serve her husband.

7. Except, Stone notes (133), for "a brief period in the 1650s."
8. Ibid., 133.
9. At the time that Shaw and Charlotte married, roughly 18% of marriage ceremonies were conducted in a registry office (Stone, 133).
10. The key clauses of the 1857 Act are given in Appendix B2 (p. 211–216).
11. The 1937 Act also added desertion, cruelty, and a spouse's mental condition ("incurably of unsound mind") as grounds for divorce. See Stephen Cretney, *Family Law in the Twentieth Century. A History* (Oxford: Oxford University Press, 2003), 250–273 (Cretney 2003).
12. Stone, 435.
13. There is a detailed discussion of the genesis and development of the text of *Widowers' Houses* in Bernard Shaw, *Widowers' Houses. Facsimiles of the Shorthand and Holograph Manuscripts of the 1893 Published Text,* ed. Jerald E. Bringle (New York: Garland, 1981), and, with a more focused time frame, in Stanley Weintraub, "Shaw Decides to Become a Playwright: July–December 1892," *SHAW: The Annual of Bernard Shaw Studies* 14 (1994): 9–23 (Shaw 1981; Weintraub 1994).
14. See Charles H. Shattuck, "Bernard Shaw's 'Bad Quarto,'" *Journal of English and Germanic Philology*, 54 (October 1955): 651–663 for a discussion of the differences between the 1893 and 1898 texts. Shaw made minor revisions for the version of *Widowers' Houses* in the Collected Edition (1930); the text used for the play in volume I of *Collected Plays* published by the Bodley Head in 1970. The history of the published texts of the play is given by Dan H. Laurence in *Bernard Shaw: A Bibliography* (Oxford: Clarendon Press, 1983) particularly items A20 (1893), A30 (1898), A198*a* (1930), and A296 (1970) (Shattuck 1955; Laurence 1983).
15. Shaw, *Widowers' Houses*, ed. Bringle, xx.
16. T.F. Evans, ed., *Shaw: The Critical Heritage* (London: Routledge & Kegan Paul, 1976), 42 (Evans 1976).
17. Ibid., 45
18. Sandra Joy Russell, "The Devil Inside: London's Slums and the Crisis of Gender in Shaw's *Widowers' Houses*," *SHAW: The Annual of Bernard Shaw Studies* 32 (2012): 87 (Russell 2012).
19. See L.W. Conolly, "*Mrs Warren's Profession* and the Lord Chamberlain," *SHAW: The Annual of Bernard Shaw Studies* 24 (2004): 46–95, and editions of *Mrs Warren's Profession* by Conolly (Peterborough, ON: Broadview Press, 2015), Kent (London: Methuen, 2012), and Peters (New York: Garland, 1981) for extensive discussion of the textual and

performance history of the play (Conolly 2004; Shaw 1981, 2012, 2015).

20. In that same letter to Harris, Shaw says that by the time he married Charlotte he was "too experienced to make the frightful mistake of simply setting up a permanent whore," and Charlotte likewise avoided "making the complementary mistake." Shaw also told Harris that "as man and wife" he and Charlotte "found a new relation in which sex had no part" (Bernard Shaw, *Sixteen Self Sketches* [London: Constable 1949], 115) (Shaw 1949).

21. The "pigheaded" law is the Divorce and Matrimonial Causes Act of 1857. See earlier discussion.

22. Soon after Shaw had finished writing *The Philanderer* (in June 1893), he read it to friend and journalist colleague Lady Colin Campbell, who bluntly told him that the last act "ought to be put into the fire." He did not do that, but he did write an entirely new act, the one published in *Plays Unpleasant* in 1898. The original final act is held in the British Library (Add MS 50596A–50596G), and is reproduced in facsimile in *The Philanderer. A Facsimile of the Holograph Manuscript*, ed. Julius Novick (New York: Garland 1981). A transcribed and annotated version is included in the Conolly edition of *The Philanderer*, 139–163. See the same edition, 29–35, for discussion of various productions of the play that have used the original final act. Details of Lady Colin Campbell's involvement can be found in the introductions of both the Conolly and Novick editions of *The Philanderer* (Shaw 1981).

REFERENCES

Conolly, L.W. 2004. *Mrs. Warren's Profession* and the Lord Chamberlain. *SHAW: The Annual of Bernard Shaw Studies* 24: 46–95.

Cretney, Stephen. 2003. *Family Law in the Twentieth Century. A History*. Oxford: Oxford University Press.

Evans, T.F. (ed.). 1976. *Shaw: The Critical Heritage*. London: Routledge & Kegan Paul.

Gibbs, A.M. 2001. *A Bernard Shaw Chronology*. Basingstoke, UK: Palgrave.

Laurence, Dan H. 1983. *Bernard Shaw: A Bibliography*. The Soho Bibliographies, 2 vols. Oxford: Clarendon Press.

Russell, Sandra Joy. 2012. The Devil Inside: London's Slums and the Crisis of Gender in Shaw's *Widowers' Houses*. *SHAW: The Annual of Bernard Shaw Studies* 32: 86–101.

Shattuck, Charles H. 1955. Bernard Shaw's 'Bad Quarto.' *Journal of English and Germanic Philosophy* 54: 651–653.

Shaw, Bernard. 1898. *Plays Pleasant and Unpleasant*, vol. II. London: Grant Richards.

Shaw, Bernard. 1949. *Sixteen Self Sketches*. London: Constable.

Shaw, Bernard. 1981. *Widowers' Houses. Facsimiles of the Shorthand and Holograph Manuscripts of the 1893 Published Text*. Intro. Jerald E. Bringle. New York: Garland.

Shaw, Bernard. 2012. *Mrs. Warren's Profession*, ed. Brad Kent. London: Methuen.

Shaw, Bernard. 2015. *The Philanderer*, ed. L.W. Conolly. Peterborough, ON: Broadview Press.

Stone, Lawrence. 1990. *Road to Divorce. England 1530–1987*. Oxford: Oxford University Press.

Weintraub, Stanley. 1994. Shaw Decides to Become a Playwright: July–December 1892. *SHAW: The Annual of Bernard Shaw Studies* 14: 9–23.

Author Biography

Leonard W. Conolly is Emeritus Professor of English at Trent University, Peterborough, Ontario, Canada, an Honorary Fellow of Robinson College, Cambridge, a Senior Fellow of Massey College, Toronto, and a Fellow of the Royal Society of Canada. A former President of the International Shaw Society, he has published extensively on Shaw, including critical editions of *Mrs Warren's Profession* (2005), *Pygmalion* (2008), and *The Philanderer* (2015).

CHAPTER 3

The Pragmatic Partnerships of *Plays Pleasant*

Jennifer Buckley

At the midpoint of Bernard Shaw's *You Never Can Tell* (1896), Gloria Clandon declares, "I do not think the conditions of marriage at present are such as any self-respecting woman can accept" (*CPP* I:735). Deeply if narrowly well read and self-consciously modern, Gloria knows that if she married her suitor Valentine, he would legally own her body. Given that she considers John Stuart Mill's *The Subjection of Women* suitable beach reading (*CPP* I:725),[1] she is unlikely to have been satisfied by the Married Women's Property Act of 1882, which established wives as legal persons—without the vote.[2] If the marriage were to fail for any reason, they could divorce if Valentine provided the courts with evidence of her infidelity; Gloria, however, would have to prove that he had committed adultery and at least one of several other acts, among them abuse, incest, and bestiality. Yet she need not have studied the law in depth to understand its disastrous consequences: the Clandon family has lived them. Just before delivering this condemnation, Gloria had argued with her estranged father, a bad-tempered alcoholic from whom her mother had

J. Buckley (✉)
University of Iowa, Iowa City, USA
e-mail: jennifer-buckley@uiowa.edu

© The Author(s) 2017
R.A. Gaines (ed.), *Bernard Shaw's Marriages and Misalliances*,
Bernard Shaw and His Contemporaries,
DOI 10.1057/978-1-349-95170-3_3

"rescued" herself and her young children by securing a separation and leaving the country (*CPP* I:761).

Had Shaw written *You Never Can Tell* along the lines of the earlier plays he classified upon their publication as "unpleasant," Gloria might have gone on to explain her objections at length and to remain unmarried. This play, however, is one of the four Shaw consigned to the other volume of *Plays: Pleasant and Unpleasant* (1898), so Gloria provides no further detail. By the end of the act, Valentine has kissed her and made his own declaration—"we're in love with one another"—to which Gloria responds with distressingly mixed feelings (*CPP* I:740). By the end of the play, she has literally dropped her copy of Mill, rejected her wage-earning mother's tutelage, forcefully kissed Valentine, demanded that he announce their engagement to her family, and obtained a commitment from her wealthy father to provide her fortune-hunting but now frankly terrified husband-to-be with a financial settlement. Though Gloria has reasserted a certain degree of control over her emotions and a certain form of mastery over Valentine and thus her future, Shaw sweeps them both away with what he would later call the "Life Force—the power, at once physiological and mystical, to which John Tanner will succumb at (much) greater length in *Man and Superman* (1903).

Audiences who see the curtain fall on this state of affairs—an "unwise" marriage newly contracted (*CPP* I:793) and an unhappy one permanently suspended—are more likely than not to be swept away with them. *You Never Can Tell* has its grim moments, but concludes with the characters being drawn into a seaside party featuring dancing so exuberant that even the imposing QC Bohun waltzes off with Gloria. However, readers of this play and those with which it shares a volume may well question Shaw's categorization, as did his contemporary G.K. Chesterton.[3] Of course comedy, as a genre, has always been able to accommodate far nastier situations than those in the Pleasant plays. (Consider the more problematic comedies of Shakespeare, whose oft-noted influence upon *You Never Can Tell* is so obvious that the Clandon twins Dolly and Philip quote his plays, and call the hotel waiter "William" because they see a resemblance to the Stratford memorial bust.) But "pleasant" is not a conventional genre designation; it is an adjective Shaw applied to a group of plays that do not, in any straightforward way, forward the more trenchant critiques of contemporary marriage and gender roles and relations evident in earlier and later dramatic works. Nor do they clearly promote the positions Shaw had articulated in non-dramatic writings including *The Quintessence of Ibsenism* (1891). There he famously declared that "Woman" must "repudiate duty altogether. In that repudiation lies her freedom."[4] What, then, is ultimately "pleasant" about *You Never Can Tell*, in which the "Woman of the Twentieth Century" proclaims her "duty" to "obey nothing but my sense of what is right" and "respect nothing that is not noble" (*CPP* I:730–731), but then contracts herself, in a legal arrangement she knows not to be right, to a man who is in no sense noble, as her miserably married parents look on? However fizzy the farce, surely this is more disquieting content than Shaw's account of the Pleasant plays as concerned with "romantic follies, and with the struggles of individuals against those follies" can bear (*CPP* I:34)?

It is, and to an extent that made its author intermittently uneasy. Like its Pleasant companions, *You Never Can Tell* constitutes an early attempt by Shaw to incorporate his politics and philosophy into plays that adhered closely enough to conventional comedic forms—here, farce—to appeal to commercial producers and "commonplace" audiences (*CPP* I:377). With his first three plays Shaw had taken a comparatively aggressive approach, writing "propagandist" (*CPP* I:373) dramas for experimental theatres where select audiences would be "force[d] … to face unpleasant facts" (*CPP* I:32). Yet only *Widowers' Houses* (1892) had been performed; *The Philanderer* (1893) was rejected by managers, and *Mrs Warren's Profession* (1894) by the Lord Chamberlain's Examiner of Plays. Not content to remain a propagandizing prophet relegated to the theatrical wilderness, Shaw made his first, partially successful attempts to enact what we might call a Fabian strategy, pursued both dramaturgically and institutionally.

Shaw's crucial role in the development of the Fabian Society is among the best-known aspects of his career. A socialist organization of middle-class reformers, the Fabians promoted gradual change via "permeation" of the extant political structure. Discussing a slightly later period, J. Ellen Gainor details how Fabians and "fellow-travelers" also pursued a strategy of "cultural permeation," contributing to subscription-supported experimental theatres like the Stage Society, to provincial theatres, to efforts to establish "financially and culturally superior … national, municipal, and endowed theatres," and in some cases to commercial theatres. Shaw's plays would find their first hospitable English homes at theatres managed by Fabians, most famously the Court under Harley Granville Barker.[5] In 1895, however, Shaw was focusing his cultural permeation efforts on the commercial West End. Infiltration of the corrupt capitalist theatre was unlikely to be achieved by writing the equivalent of Mrs. Warren's ferocious attack on bourgeois marriage as a legal form of prostitution. To maximize his chances of success, Shaw adopted an incrementalist dramaturgy which would "bring the manager what his customers want and understand, or even enough of it to induce them to swallow at the same time a great deal that they neither want nor understand." Critique could be spoken—briefly, as in *You Never Can Tell*, or at somewhat greater length, as in *Candida*—and then structurally superseded in plays that skirted the political and generic "commercial limits" (*CPP* I:378).

With *You Never Can Tell*, however, Shaw feared that he had pulled back too far from those boundaries. As Kerry Powell notes, Shaw both deplored and deployed the "'tricks'" of fashionable farcical comedy, and he worried that this last Pleasant play remained a "prisoner of its genre."[6] Powell's argument that Shaw ultimately succeeded in his attempt to "'humanize'" that genre rests on the psychological depth of his characterizations: the splenetic father grieves his lost family, while the lust-driven dentist tries to reason away his passion. From a dramaturgical point of view, if such realistic shading constitutes an advance (an argument Powell does not fully endorse), then *You Never Can Tell* improves upon its "mechanical" genre. From a sociopolitical point of view, Gloria and Valentine's marriage can be seen as an incremental advance upon her parents', which began in mutual ignorance and ended (in all but law) in mutual acrimony. The pair may be ill matched in every respect other than sexual attraction; at the (very) least their efforts to demystify that attraction, and the legal union that will sanction it, suggest that theirs will be a marriage devoid of what Shaw calls, in the *Quintessence* and elsewhere, "ideals"—romantically inflated notions that enable traditionalists to justify "graft[ing] pleasure on necessity by desperately pretending that the institution forced upon them is a congenial one."[7] It is a thoroughly Shavian partnership of pragmatists who warily enter, rather than overthrow, institutions they know to be corrupt.

However pleasant the plays, Shaw's permeation of the commercial theatre progressed slowly enough to frustrate the most committed gradualist. With the publication of *Plays: Pleasant and Unpleasant*, he hoped to make in print the "breaches in the English survival of the harem" he had not achieved with productions (*CPP* I:25). The military metaphors Shaw employs in the Unpleasant volume's preface to describe his verbal assault on "home life" seem warranted by the relative force and precision of those plays' attack. What critique did he hope the Pleasant plays would charm readers—and, eventually, mainstream theatre audiences—into "swallowing"? Testing but rarely exceeding the boundaries of popular genres, these plays conclude with either the contraction or the consolidation of pragmatic marriages devoid of "ideals," though not necessarily of desire or affection.

Although the chief pragmatist of *Arms and the Man* (1894), the Swiss mercenary Captain Bluntschli, aims squarely at Raina Petkoff's idealization of war, he also manages to make collateral damage of her fantasies of romantic love. In a scene worthy of the military melodramas that Shaw's first act parodies, Bluntschli seeks refuge in the Bulgarian woman's bedroom after fleeing a battle against the army in which her father and fiancé serve. She begins the play absurdly venerating the victorious fiancé's portrait and ends up agreeing to marry the beaten bourgeois anti-hero Bluntschli. Theirs is one of three potential, and potentially troubled, marriages in the play; less frequently noted is the happy marriage of Raina's parents. Undistinguished and unsophisticated, Major Paul and Catherine Petkoff would seem to be perfect targets for Shavian satire, yet the play submits the couple to only the gentlest mockery. Catherine bosses the loving but hapless Paul, who loves being bossed. Upon his return from battle, she embraces him, then immediately condemns the peace treaty he secured—whereupon the two settle in for a bout of the affectionate mutual henpecking permissible only in a long, satisfying partnership. His characteristic response to her exposure of his social and professional deficiencies is "quite right, my love: quite right" (*CPP* I:440).

Such agreeably deflationary self-awareness is lacking in Raina's fiancé Sergius Saranoff. As bombastic in his chaste wooing of her as he is in hot-blooded pursuit of her maid Louka, Sergius is so poorly matched to his betrothed in every aspect except class that even Raina says so when provoked (*CPP* I:431). Inclined to theatrical stagings of her person and her officially acknowledged passions, the novel-reading, opera-loving Raina overacts the role of unworthy subject to her "hero" and "king," while Sergius exalts her as his "lady" and "saint" (*CPP* I:424–425). Shaw makes it immediately clear that this is a doomed courtship; the play's first scene has already revealed Raina to be just enough of a skeptic to be vulnerable to Bluntschli's disenchantment campaign, against which Sergius could mount no serious defense. Exhausted by the extravagant performance of self-abasement demanded of the asexual "higher love," he seeks "relief" by verbally and physically harassing the servant Louka (*CPP* I:425–426). Shaw exposes Sergius's hollow idealization of the well-to-do Raina by staging its flipside: his aggressively sexualized displays of the class and gender privilege he wields over her maid. But Louka is also a realist when it serves her social ambitions; she deflates Sergius's heroic postures and punctures all of his claims except the last: "You belong to me" (*CPP* I:467).[8] Faced with three possible futures, all of which require some form of submission—one as a maid temperamentally unsuited for service; one as the spouse of another servant who threatens to be "master in my own house" (*CPP* I:451); and one as the wife of a wealthy fool who woos her with phrases like "provoking little witch" (*CPP* I:427)—Louka cannily chooses the option that will elevate her economic status while legally sanctioning what she calls "my love" (*CPP* I:462).

Shaw may have subtitled the play an "anti-romantic comedy," but he also wrote it to fill the seats of London's Avenue Theatre for his actress-manager friend Florence Farr. *Arms and the Man* debunks military heroism, yet allows both matches to stand unchallenged. Louka's "love" enables audience members to laugh away the personal problems likely to bedevil the marriage, while Bluntschli's briefly stated approval of the pairing on "good Republican" principles glosses over cross-class complications (*CPP* I:467). The threat that his own marriage to Raina will traverse class boundaries is dismissed in a humorously extended enumeration of property inherited upon the death of his hotelier father. Raina protests that she is "not here to be sold to the highest bidder," but relents, within five lines, at the slightest sign of affection from the almost inhumanly rational Bluntschli (*CPP* I:470–471). And so *Arms* concludes comically with the prospect of thoroughly practical partnerships subjected to capitalist logic but softened, to some extent, by something approximating affection (Fig. 3.1).

The bourgeois domesticity inhabited or aspired to by the couples of *Arms* comes under greater scrutiny in Shaw's next Pleasant play, *Candida* (1894). Though he affords the title character a speech in which she pragmatically assesses the affective and physical labor expected of middle-class wives, Shaw tended to insist in feminist-unfriendly terms that it was Candida herself whom the play's real protagonist must and does escape. Wife of a popular Christian Socialist minister, daughter of a vulgar factory owner, love object of a slumming aristocratic aesthete, Candida could be seen as a

Fig. 3.1   Actress Florence Farr

beautiful, interestingly "immoral" (Shaw's term), but ultimately dismissible excuse for the expression, evaluation, and evolution of men's ideas about marriage, morality, economics, and art. Satisfied in her conventional marriage without adhering to conventional morals, Candida absorbs young Eugene Marchbanks's adulation and her husband James Morell's admiration until the poet's declaration of love makes it impossible to sustain what had been a tacit *ménage à trois*, and they demand she choose between them. It is not only the men's affections Candida adroitly administers; she also admits to knowing that Morell's typist Proserpine Garnett performs household labor because she is in love with him (*CPP* I:563). Humorously uptight in Act I, hilariously tipsy in Act III, and pining throughout, Miss Garnett serves the structural function of "ineffectual comic foil" to her employer's wife, as Powell notes.[9] Whatever the quantity of good Candida does by divesting her smug husband of his ideals of wifely purity, by showing him how much of his success he owes to her support, or (more dubiously) by sending Marchbanks down the high road to asexual artistic glory, the benefits are confined to at most three people—two of whom conclude the play by reaffirming their partnership with enough warmth that early audiences appeared to miss or ignore Shaw's critique of his title character and the marriage she manages.[10]

Indeed, the domestic comedy's politics are only marginally more evident than those of *You Never Can Tell*. J. Ellen Gainor writes of *Candida* that "the social issues of women in society" discussed by the characters "ultimately serve only as backdrops."[11] While Morell espouses socialist values, Tracy C. Davis contends that "the play's focus on a woman's choice of male companion is totally devoid of economic critique and is separate from" those values.[12] Such appraisals remain compelling, and not only because Shaw's statements support them. Writing to William Archer, he depoliticized Candida completely, describing her as "a mother first, a wife twenty seventh, and nothing else" (*CL* II:137).[13] Moreover, what Shaw designated in a later letter as a "counterblast" to *A Doll's House* can be seen as something like a counterpunch to the pioneering actresses who risked their careers and personal finances to bring Ibsen's plays to English stages.[14] When Archer proposed in 1900 that the title role go to Elizabeth Robins, the first London Hedda Gabler and Hilda Wangel, Shaw had the gall to reply that she had misunderstood Ibsen's plays as well as his own. Robins, he assumed, had failed to notice that *Candida* dispenses with "the happy home ideal" by liberating the male poet from the domestic "cage" (*CL* II:137). The fact that Shaw had written the play to showcase the talents of Janet Achurch— who had so powerfully performed Nora Helmer's desire to become "before all else … a human being"—makes his verbal confinement of Candida to the "cage" troubling.[15] If, like Margot Peters, we consider the Marchbanks-like role Shaw was playing in Achurch's marriage while writing *Candida*, his scripting of the male poet's escape from what Peters describes as the "suffocating commonplaces" of female-dominated "domesticity" into the "sublime and lonely renunciation of the artist" looks both politically suspect and blatantly self-serving.[16]

Candida is neither a straightforwardly feminist nor socialist play. But it is a play more concerned with women's work—with the physical and affective labor wives perform to support themselves, their partners, and their households—than is acknowledged by either Shaw or many critics. Before the audience hears a word from Morell or Marchbanks, they hear and see a woman at work: Miss Garnett operating her "*clattering*" typewriter at a table next to her employer's desk (*CPP* I:518). Heidi

J. Holder points out that in Shaw's play, unlike other fidelity-themed society dramas of the period, "the drawing room we see is actually a workplace" in which the labor of wives and female employees is both performed and discussed.[17] Whether or not Proserpine approves of the radical political groups whose meetings overfill the schedule she keeps for her employer, it is she who defends the general dignity of labor here. When the Oxonian curate "Lexy" Mill arrives late, it is Proserpine who upbraids him: "It will do you good to earn your supper before you eat it, for once in a way, as I do" (*CPP* I:521).

The unseen working women of Morell's parish so exploited they cannot earn their supper are the subject of a more heated discussion. Candida's father Burgess, a sweatshop boss, has returned uninvited to the house years after a battle with Morell over what the reverend calls the "worse than starvation wages" Burgess paid the women in his factory. In an accusation that echoes Mrs. Warren's, Morell contends: "Your wages would have driven them to the streets to keep body and soul together" (*CPP* I:527).[18] Burgess insists that he has changed his ways, becoming a "moddle hemployer": he has "sacked" the women, replacing them with machines operated by better-paid men (*CPP* I:528). While Morell is disappointed that Burgess made these moves only to secure public contracts, he seems unconcerned that the women have been driven back into the brutal labor market rather than trained for positions that might enable them to support their families. But then, Morell has a sizable blind spot when it comes to the labor conditions faced by the women working in his own home. Despite his self-satisfied admission to Marchbanks that he does household chores, Morell is so clueless about the size and intensity of Candida's workload as a minister's wife and mother of their children that he blithely piles on more duties, offering her up as a nurse for Lexy should he catch the measles from a parishioner (*CPP* I:521). He is no less blithe about the housework he inflicts upon his harried assistant. Money is tight, he explains, and the family's servant Maria "isn't a slave," so "everyone has to lend a hand. ... Prossy and I can talk business after breakfast while we're washing up" (*CPP* I:556).

Marchbanks has no problem with the demands made upon Miss Garnett, whom he judges "coarse-grained" enough for such work (*CPP* I:556). But he is horrified at the prospect of Candida laboring in any capacity whatsoever. The copy of Titian's *Assumption of the Virgin* hanging over the fireplace (his gift) depicts Mary suspended between heaven and earth, but Marchbanks envisions the woman he exalts as a Virgin

Mother safely transported to paradise. He becomes frantic upon hearing that Candida fills oil lamps and polishes boots, and he nearly falls into a fit when confronted with the apron-clad figure of his goddess complaining about a misused scrubbing brush (*CPP* I:557). She, too, works in this drawing room–office, and seeing her do so fills Marchbanks with "horror!"—not because she is working for Morell, but because she is working at all (*CPP* I:558). He professes his desire to liberate Candida from "slavery" to her husband's "ideas" (*CPP* I:545), but Marchbanks seems more concerned about the paraffin oil besmirching her "beautiful fingers" than he does about anyone's philosophy (*CPP* I:557). When he rhapsodizes about the labor-less faraway dream world to which he wants to whisk Candida via "tiny shallop," she appreciates the beauty of his expression but knows that it is the vision of a pampered child, whom she soothes by "*petting*" (*CPP* I:558) as if he actually were the "great baby" she calls him in jest (*CPP* I:537). To Marchbanks's proclamation that she should not "talk about boots! Your feet should be beautiful on the mountains," Candida replies prosaically, "My feet would not be beautiful on the Hackney Road without boots," before hauling him off to help in the kitchen (*CPP* I:559).

All of this, of course, leads up to Candida's choice of partner. It is true that, as Davis suggests, her choice has nothing to do with the men's stances on gender, labor, or gendered labor. Candida does not remain with Morell because he voices a (schematic) critique of the "idle, selfish, and useless" segment of the aristocracy to which Marchbanks belongs, and she does not reject Marchbanks because he wishes to transform her into one of the decorative women of that class (*CPP* I:558). She does not so much rebuff Marchbanks as pre-emptively emancipate him from domestic entanglements that might impede his progress toward the aesthetic heights she believes him capable of reaching. Whether or not this constitutes criticism of those entanglements has been a subject of critical debate; if so, it is softened enough by a domestic comedy conclusion that the fans Shaw called "Candidamaniacs"—the conventional "New York Hausfraus" who flocked to the play during its 1904 run there—could have interpreted the play as a vindication of bourgeois marriage and its gendered division of labor. Either way, Shaw himself rarely described this play in *Quintessence*-era Ibsenist terms. Writing to James Huneker about that New York production, Shaw grants Candida "brains and strength of mind," "freedom from emotional slop," and the "immoral[ity]" and "unscrupulous[ness]" of Wagner's Siegfried, though none of his courage, and no politics to speak of (*CL* II:415).[19]

Notably for a playwright who had written *Mrs Warren* and would go on to pen the *Getting Married* preface in which marriage and prostitution are compared to "Trade Unionism and unorganized casual labor" (*CPP* III:501), Shaw rarely emphasized that Candida herself frames all of the labor she performs—including loving Morell—in economic terms. "Ask me what it costs," she says in her long third-act speech, to "build a castle of comfort and indulgence and love for [James], and stand sentinel always to keep little vulgar cares out" (*CPP* III:592–593). In doing so, she aligns herself with the other women whose work has enabled him to become the man and the minister he is. They include not only the mother and sisters who "save James the trouble of doing anything but be strong and clever and happy," but also the employees who keep the "troublesome" house functioning both as an emotionally sustaining home and an efficient workplace (*CPP* III:592). This is very far from a developed sociological account of how women's domestic work is conjoined with affective labor. Yet Candida does take and share credit for both kinds of work, insisting that they *are* work, which does not pay wages but which does exact a cost.

Torvald Helmer, whose last-scene discussion with his wife served as a formal inspiration for this one, continues to insist that it is Nora whose "education"—by him—will repair their marriage.[20] He only realizes belatedly that Nora is giving him the lesson of his life, but Morell accepts Candida's instruction without hesitation, though without fully recognizing the degree to which her "loving care" *is* labor (*CPP* III:593). Nora becomes increasingly grim as she educates her husband, but Candida smiles indulgently as she enlightens the two "boys" who, at different points, occupy the children's chair. While this tutelage can be seen as yet another traditionally feminine task she is compelled to discharge within a private sphere separated from the public one influenced by Morell, Burgess, and Marchbanks, the home appears less hermetically sealed if we note that she tutors another "pupil" during the play—a woman working outside the home, in the very oppressive labor conditions Morell deplores. In Act II, while Marchbanks bothers Proserpine, Burgess tells him that Candida is "hupstairs heducating of a young stitcher gurl she's interested in" (*CPP* III:552). Given that Burgess's once-compliant "Candy" has become a woman who criticizes her husband for failing to appreciate the intellectual independence he had himself encouraged, audiences are invited to wonder about the content of the lessons she is teaching the "stitcher gurl" (*CPP* III:566).

Marchbanks ignores Burgess's comment, because to him all labor—other than the household tasks Candida performs—is invisible. Neither does he recognize the heavy emotional lifting Candida does to set him on his feet and down the path toward poetic glory. The play concludes with his flight "*out into the night,*" as Candida and Morell embrace. Between his completion of the manuscript and the publication of *Plays Pleasant*, Shaw added a line to the stage directions, giving Eugene the last (written) word: "*But they do not know the secret in the poet's heart*" (*CPP* III:594).[21] Readers could be told that the real beneficiary of this happy ending is Marchbanks. Audiences, however, could and can assume that it is the man forced to recognize what it costs the women who lovingly ensure that the Reverend James Morell show plays to packed houses of worship and political meetings.

No dishwashing, boot-blacking, typing, or stitching is done in *How He Lied to Her Husband*, which Shaw wrote in 1904 partly to poke fun at the "Candidamaniacs" more interested in the Morells' marriage than in Marchbanks's secret. (Although not included in *Plays Pleasant*, *How He Lied* is so closely associated with *Candida* that I address it here.[22]) Shaw himself dismissed the one-act play as "trifling," a "knockabout farce" dashed off to provide the American actor-manager Arnold Daly with a curtain raiser for *The Man of Destiny*, to which Daly had turned in desperation after running afoul of the Comstock Laws with his 1904 New York production of *Mrs Warren's Profession* (*CPP* II:1031). This is not to say the play presents no challenge to the ticket buyers with whose money Shaw bolstered Daly's finances. The absurdly named Aurora Bompas is a purely ornamental woman, muse to poet Henry Apjohn and trophy wife to city man Teddy Bompas. Even as she spends Bompas's cash, Aurora accrues social capital for him with every carefully staged public display of her beauty, attracting the eyes and admiration of what he boasts are "the smartest" and "most experienced" men among "the best people" (*CPP* II:1048). She is just the kind of "silly" woman Vivie Warren refuses to become, one who does little but "advertise [her] dressmaker" and jeweler (*CPP* II:352). Aurora's appeal is an effect of consumer items: she is "*a very ordinary*" woman whose costume, more than the body it adorns (and much less any brains it might contain), is what attracts men. Apjohn bestows more passion upon her fan, gloves, and hair ornaments than he does upon her person once she appears (*CPP* II:1032–1033). This is funny, especially for audiences who had seen Daly or Barker (the first London Apjohn) as Marchbanks, but it is also farcically fetishistic. The husband learns of his wife's entanglement with the poet, but he takes it rather better than does Morell: Bompas values the social capital she brings him more than her fidelity. Having been given Apjohn's poems, he is offended when the poet tries to lie his way out of the situation, and finally determines to resolve the love triangle by going public. Bompas suggests investing his own money in a "first class" edition of the poems that will testify to his wife's socially advantageous desirability (*CPP* II:1051). She, of course, is delighted, and apparently so were the audiences for whom Daly played the farce at upscale vaudeville houses—a rather different sort of commercial theatre than Shaw intended the Pleasant plays to permeate.[23]

The play with which Daly followed that curtain raiser features another woman who charms powerful men in public and private to amass cultural and political capital for herself and her husband. The political stakes of such liaisons, however, are significantly higher in *The Man of Destiny* (1895) than they are in any other Pleasant play. While the wife never appears on stage, the audience can identify her as Marie-Josèphe Rose de Beauharnais, *née* Tascher de la Pagerie, better known by the title later bestowed by her second husband: Joséphine, Empress of the French. The woman they do see also remains anonymous. During one of their testier exchanges, the young General Napoleon Bonaparte calls her "Dalila," but she is "the Strange Lady" in Shaw's stage directions (*CPP* I:634). It takes Napoleon some time to realize that the Lady is not out to sabotage his efforts to defeat the Austrians. She has stolen a packet of letters, but she is uninterested in the battle-related correspondence that would be the target of a proper spy. The Lady wants a letter Joséphine wrote to her lover Barras, a director of the executive council ruling France. The socially graceless Corsican soldier had used his attachment to the glamorous widow Beauharnais as a toehold in Paris's upper echelon, while Joséphine had banked on his military prowess to stabilize her hard-won post-revolutionary position. By stealing the compromising letter, the Lady hopes to protect her adulterous former school mate.

She lies, steals, and dons military drag to prevent Joséphine's ruin, but the Lady also spends much of the play persuading Napoleon that disregarding the letter serves his interests. By ignoring its contents, Napoleon can remain half of what could become European history's most formidable power couple. The Lady accomplishes this not by appealing to the sanctity of marriage or to his love for Joséphine, but rather to the "strong simplicity" of his own character (*CPP* I:656), the only possible temperament for a man she predicts—only partially as a ploy—will be "Emperor of France; then of Europe; perhaps of the world." Articulating a condensed version of the Shavian superman's creed, the Lady urges Napoleon to embrace "your own destiny," a destiny accessible only to those who ruthlessly exercise their own will (*CPP* I:633). (Though unconventional, no such destiny awaits her: she "had the misfortune to be born good" [*CPP* I:632].[24]) *Candida* suggests that only mediocre men need marriage to achieve whatever victories they manage, while great men can and must go it alone. In *Destiny*, however, a great man is urged by a spousal proxy to preserve his marriage purely for its strategic value. Candida expends great emotional effort teaching Marchbanks that "happiness" is inimical to greatness, but the Lady easily enables Napoleon to affirm what he already knows to be true: that he could not "be what I am if I cared for happiness" (*CPP* I:636). Napoleon needs no Candida to educate him beyond ideals, yet the Lady does perform crucial affective labor on his behalf. Playfully but strenuously steering him through an overtly theatrical battle of wits and wills, she acts as a kind of histrionic helpmeet, finally getting him to affirm that "Caesar's wife is above suspicion"—and thus to claim the title of Caesar for himself (*CPP* I:661).[25]

In his preface, Shaw describes a theatricalized culture in which "the modern Emperor is 'the leading man' on the stage of his country."[26] The Lady rehearses Napoleon for this stage, prompting him to take up and abandon role after role, from discipline-dispensing general to jealous husband to platitudinous politician. Finally, however, he drops the well-worn roles drawn from a grab bag of well-made plays, melodramas, and tragedies, as the stagy pose of "*Talma ... gives way*" to an entirely new part, fit for the unbuilt stage of the First French Empire (*CPP* I:657). Likewise, the conventional drama scripted by the Lady—so replete with stray handkerchiefs (perfumed, of course), stolen letters, and disguises that Bernard F. Dukore called it a "spoof," and Shaw himself a "harlequinade" (*CL* I:546)—momentarily gives way to an utterly serious monologue in which Napoleon declares that he will "go over all the mobs and all the courts of Europe as a plough goes over a field" (*CPP* I:657).[27] Having burned the distracting letter with the surrogate spouse who aptly draws the strongest sexual charge when, dressed in an officer's uniform, she presents him with a near-mirror image, Napoleon becomes the man of the play's title, directed onto his destined path by a proxy for the wife he will later discard in pursuit of his indomitable will.[28] Like most of the marriages in *Plays Pleasant*, Napoleon and Joséphine's is thoroughly demystified over the course of the play. Stripped of every last illusion, their partnership can now function openly as the mutually beneficial strategic arrangement it always has been. Threatening but ultimately preserving the marriage, Shaw attempts to deliver the mainstream audience the structurally comedic conclusion they "want and understand," while inducing them to "swallow" an early, concentrated form of his Life Force doctrine.

Cleverer and more ruthless than any of their Pleasant counterparts, Napoleon and his spousal surrogate spar until the play's last moments. The marriage-related conflicts in which the plays' other couples engage conclude on terms devised to be soft enough to appease West End playgoers and "New York Haufraus" alike. Even Valentine, who had made such extravagant use of military metaphors to explain the "duel of sex" to Mrs. Clandon, finds himself totally disarmed at the conclusion of *You Never Can Tell*, cheered into his impending marriage by the Waiter, who assures him, and the audience, that he may be "very happy indeed" (*CPP* I:794). However happily Shaw concluded the Pleasant plays, none would immediately advance his cultural permeation program by garnering the high-profile productions he sought. They did, however, inaugurate his own pragmatic partnership with the commercial theatre which he would go on to manage with as little sentimentality as he affords his anti-romantic heroes and heroines.

NOTES

1. In the play's first edition, Gloria is reading Schopenhauer, presumably the Haldane–Kemp translation of *The World as Will and Idea*, and not *On Women*. Bernard Shaw, *Plays: Pleasant and Unpleasant*, vol. 2 (London: G. Richards, 1898), 259 (Shaw 1898).
2. See Mary Lyndon Shanley, *Feminism, Marriage, and the Law in Victorian England* (Princeton: Princeton University Press, 1989), 103–130 (Shanley 1989).
3. G.K. Chesterton, *George Bernard Shaw* (London: The Bodley Head, 1909), 115–116 (Chesterton 1909).
4. Bernard Shaw, *The Quintessence of Ibsenism* (London: Constable & Company, 1926), 40 (Shaw 1926).
5. J. Ellen Gainor, "Fabian Drama," in *George Bernard Shaw in Context*, Ed. Brad Kent (Cambridge: Cambridge University Press, 2015), 78. On the Court venture as Fabian cultural permeation, Ian Britain, *Fabianism and Culture: A Study in British Socialism and the Arts, c. 1884–1918* (Cambridge: Cambridge University Press, 1982), 176 (Gainor 2015; Britain 1982).

6. Kerry Powell, "Farcical Comedy," in *George Bernard Shaw in Context*, 93. Powell takes up and then departs from the account of farcical comedy given by Martin Meisel, *Shaw and the Nineteenth Century Theater* (Princeton: Princeton University Press, 1963), 242–68. On Shaw's ambivalence about the play, see also Margot Peters, *Bernard Shaw and the Actresses* (New York: Doubleday, 1980), 174 (Meisel 1963; Peters 1980).

7. Shaw, *Quintessence*, 26.

8. On Louka as a social climber, see Peters, *Bernard Shaw and the Actresses*, 76.

9. Kerry Powell, "New Women, New Plays, and Shaw in the 1890s," in *The Cambridge Companion to George Bernard Shaw*, ed. Christopher Innes (Cambridge: Cambridge University Press, 1998), 78. See also J. Ellen Gainor, *Shaw's Daughters: Dramatic and Narrative Constructions of Gender* (Ann Arbor: University of Michigan Press, 1991), 30 (Powell 1998; Gainor 1991).

10. Gainor contends that neither the "womanly" or "New" woman "has an impact outside the Morrell household, despite the specter of the Woman Question in their midst. … Shaw safeguards the larger, extant patriarchal order" (*Shaw's Daughters*, 30).

11. Ibid., 29.

12. Tracy C. Davis, *George Bernard Shaw and the Socialist Theatre* (Westport, CT: Greenwood Press, 1994), 51 (Davis 1994).

13. Quoted in Gail Finney, *Women in Modern Drama: Freud, Feminism, and European Theater at the Turn of the Century* (Ithaca: Cornell University Press 1991), 187 (Finney 1991).

14. Bernard Shaw, "Candida Was Not Ellen Terry," *The Evening Standard*, November 30, 1944. Quoted in Stephen S. Stanton, *A Casebook on Candida* (New York: Thomas Y. Crowell Company, 1962), 158 (Shaw 1962).

15. Henrik Ibsen, *A Doll's House*, in *Ibsen's Prose Dramas*, trans. William Archer (London: Walter Scott, 1890), 384 (Ibsen 1890).

16. Peters, *Bernard Shaw and the Actresses*, 139–140. Contemplating a 1900 production of the play starring Achurch, Shaw wrote to her husband Charles Charrington, "If Eugene plays Morell & Candida off the stage, he will exactly fulfill my intention" (*CL* II, 170).

17. Heidi J. Holder, "Shaw, Class, and the Melodramas of London Life," *SHAW: The Annual of Bernard Shaw Studies* 32 (University Park: Penn State University Press, 2012), 74 (Holder 2012).

18. Meisel emphasizes that in this and other ways, "both the Pleasant Play and the Unpleasant Play are joined at the root," though in the Pleasant Plays, "the possible serious consequences of the subject matter are avoided" (*Shaw and the Nineteenth Century Theater*, 135).

19. On Wagnerian resonances in *Candida*, see Peter Gahan, *Shaw Shadows: Rereading the Texts of Bernard Shaw* (Gainesville: University Press of Florida, 2004), 199–203 (Gahan 2004).
20. Ibsen, *A Doll's House*, 382.
21. Cf. Bernard Shaw, *Candida & How He Lied to Her Husband: Facsimiles of the Holograph Manuscripts*, ed. Dan H. Laurence, intro. J. Percy Smith (New York: Garland Publishers, 1981), 181 (Shaw 1981).
22. Shaw cut explicit references to *Candida* in later editions. See J. Percy Smith, introduction to *Candida & How He Lied to Her Husband: Facsimiles of the Holograph Manuscripts*, XXII.
23. Leigh Woods, "'The Wooden Heads of the People': Arnold Daly and Bernard Shaw," *New Theatre Quarterly* 22, no. 1 (2006): 54–69 (Woods 2006).
24. Davis contends that the Lady is one of Shaw's "new types" whose behavior defies conventional gender roles (*George Bernard Shaw and the Socialist Theatre*, 50).
25. On the play's overt theatricality, see Charles A. Berst, "*The Man of Destiny*: Shaw, Napoleon, and the Theater of Life," *SHAW: The Annual of Bernard Shaw Studies* 7 (University Park: Penn State University Press, 1997): 85–118 (Berst 1997).
26. Bernard Shaw, *Plays: Pleasant and Unpleasant*, vol. 2 (London: G. Richards, 1898), xi. Cf. *CPP1*, 378, in which "Emperor" has been altered to read "Kaiser, Dictator, President or Prime Minister" (Shaw 1898).
27. Here, J.L. Wisenthal writes, Shaw's Napoleon "rises above" the conventional hero of Victorien Sardou's *Madame Sans Gêne*. Introduction to *The Man of Destiny & Caesar and Cleopatra: Facsimiles of the Holograph Manuscripts*, ed. Dan H. Laurence (New York: Garland Publishing, 1981), XIV. For GBS's scathing review of the 1897 Lyceum production of Sardou's play, see Bernard Shaw, *Our Theatres in the Nineties*, vol. 3 (London: Constable, 1932), 110 (Wisenthal 1981; Shaw 1932).
28. See Gainor on the "symbolic narcissism of the closing tableau" (*Shaw's Daughters*, 118).

REFERENCES

Berst, Charles A. 1997. *The Man of Destiny*: Shaw, Napoleon, and the Theater of Life. *SHAW: The Annual of Bernard Shaw Studies* 7: 85–118.
Britain, Ian. 1982. *Fabianism and Culture: A Study in British Socialism and the Arts, c. 1884–1918*. Cambridge: Cambridge University Press.
Chesterton, G.K. 1909. *George Bernard Shaw*. London: The Bodley Head.
Davis, Tracy C. 1994. *George Bernard Shaw and the Socialist Theatre*. Westport, CT: Greenwood Press.

Finney, Gail. 1991. *Women in Modern Drama: Freud, Feminism, and European Theater at the Turn of the Century*. Ithaca: Cornell University Press.

Gahan, Peter. 2004. *Shaw Shadows: Rereading the Texts of Bernard Shaw*. Gainesville: University Press of Florida.

Gainor, J. Ellen. 1991. *Shaw's Daughters: Dramatic and Narrative Constructions of Gender*. Ann Arbor: University of Michigan Press.

Gainor, J. Ellen. 2015. Fabian Drama. In *George Bernard Shaw in Context*, ed. Brad Kent, 76–84. Cambridge: Cambridge University Press.

Holder, Heidi J. 2012. Shaw, Class, and the Melodramas of London Life. *SHAW: The Annual of Bernard Shaw Studies* 32: 58–84.

Ibsen, Henrik. 1890. *A Doll's House. Ibsen's Prose Dramas,* trans. William Archer. London: Walter Scott.

Meisel, Martin. 1963. *Shaw and the Nineteenth-Century Theater*. Princeton: Princeton University Press.

Peters, Margot. 1980. *Bernard Shaw and the Actresses*. New York: Doubleday.

Powell, Kerry. 1998. New Women, New Plays, and Shaw in the 1890s. In *The Cambridge Companion to George Bernard Shaw*, ed. Christopher Innes, 76–100. Cambridge: Cambridge University Press.

Shanley, Mary Lyndon. 1989. *Feminism, Marriage, and the Law in Victorian England*. Princeton: Princeton University Press.

Shaw, Bernard. 1898. *Plays Pleasant and Unpleasant*, vol. II. London: Grant Richards.

Shaw, Bernard. 1926. *The Quintessence of Ibsenism*. London: Constable.

Shaw, Bernard. 1932. *Immaturity*. London: Constable.

Shaw, Bernard. 1981. *Candida & How He Lied to Her Husband. Facsimiles of the Holograph Manuscripts*, intro. J. Percy Smith. New York: Garland.

Stanton, Stephen S. (ed.). 1962. *A Casebook on Candida*. New York: Thomas Y. Crowell.

Wisenthal, J.L. 1981. Introduction. *The Man of Destiny & Caesar and Cleopatra. Facsimiles of the Holograph Manuscripts*. New York: Garland.

Woods, Leigh. 2006. 'The Wooden Heads of the People': Arnold Daly and Bernard Shaw. *New Theatre Quarterly* 22 (1): 54–69.

AUTHOR BIOGRAPHY

Jennifer Buckley is Assistant Professor of English at the University of Iowa, USA, where she teaches courses in modern and contemporary drama, performance studies, and print cultures. Her essays have appeared in *Modernism/modernity, Theatre Survey, Comparative Drama, SHAW: The Annual of Bernard Shaw Studies*, and *Theater*. She is currently completing her first book, *Beyond Text: Theater and Performance in Print*.

CHAPTER 4

Three Plays for Puritans: Decoy Marriages and Social Contracts

Lawrence Switzky

Bernard Shaw often claimed that he experienced sexual attraction as a kind of metaphysical terror. When she was traveling in Rome in March of 1898, he wrote to his future wife, Charlotte Payne-Townshend, that though he missed her beautiful green eyes,

> then [I] think of the terrible Charlotte, the lier-in-wait, the soul hypochondriac, always watching and dragging me into bondage, always planning nice, comfortable, selfish destruction for me, wincing at every accent of freedom in my voice, so that at last I get the trick of hiding myself from her, hating & longing for me with the absorbing passion of the spider for the fly.[1]

Despite his misgivings, Shaw married his soul hypochondriac that June. They agreed to a chaste marriage and, initially, to separate residences. When he later explained to fellow Fabian Beatrice Webb why he had surrendered to marriage, Shaw said that it no longer seemed like pursuit and entrapment, but instead like a tool for managing unwieldy passions: "I found that my objection to my own marriage had ceased

L. Switzky (✉)
University of Toronto, Toronto, Canada
e-mail: lawrenceswitzky@gmail.com

© The Author(s) 2017
R.A. Gaines (ed.), *Bernard Shaw's Marriages and Misalliances*,
Bernard Shaw and His Contemporaries,
DOI 10.1057/978-1-349-95170-3_4

with my objection to my own death."[2] Charlotte had overcome her "corrupt personal interest in me" and the profits from *The Devil's Disciple*, Shaw's first sustained commercial stage success, "relieved me of the appearance of a pecuniary interest (more than was reasonable) in her. The thing being cleared thus of all such illusions as love interest, happiness interest, and all the rest of the vulgarities of marriage, I changed right about face on the subject and hopped down to the Registrar ...."[3]

Shaw's hyperbole at once masks and expresses an oddly de-personalized approach to marriage: not the gaining of a wife, in-laws, and a dowry, but a tabulation of losses, a trimming of "interests" and "illusions." It is not surprising, then, that before, during, and after his own marriage, Shaw scripted similarly impersonal marriages in *The Devil's Disciple* (1897), *Caesar and Cleopatra* (1898), and *Captain Brassbound's Conversion* (1899), which he grouped together in the volume *Three Plays for Puritans* (1901) as fictional adjuncts to the social arrangements he was practicing in life. By Puritanism, Shaw meant a rejection of the gratification of the "sex instinct" then prevalent on English stages, as opposed to the seminars on sex in the plays of Ibsen and Strindberg. But he also intended to interrupt the merely personal interests of his audiences, as though they too were in training for Shavian marriages:

> the theatre is a place which people can endure only when they forget themselves: that is, when their attention is entirely captured, their interest thoroughly aroused, their sympathies raised to the eagerest readiness, and their selfishness utterly annihilated. (*CCP* II:20)

For Shaw, self-forgetfulness is as important a precondition for marriage as it is for attentive spectatorship. But a marriage, like a theatre, that encourages the abandonment of "interests" has further resonances in *Three Plays for Puritans*. The preface and the plays continually take up the question of goodness decoupled from personal motivations, including love. Why, asks Shaw, does anyone do anything virtuous on behalf of anybody else, particularly when it requires personal risk? The usual answer, Shaw claims, is "the romantic metaphysic": "Why should a blackguard save another man's life, and that man no friend of his, at the risk of his own? Clearly, said the critics, because he is redeemed by love" (*CCP* II:34). Shaw asks us instead to reimagine virtue as impersonal and multiply motivated—he dismisses those "penny-in-the-slot heroes, who only work when you drop a motive into them" (*CCP* II:35)—and acts of bravery as disinterested, philosophical, and not (wholly) libidinal.

The *Three Plays for Puritans* are often read as transitional plays, positioned between the amatory optimism of *You Never Can Tell* (1896), in which love is capable of uniting an estranged family and resistant lovers, and *Man and Superman* (1901), in which love is figured as a numinous evolutionary force. We might think of the prose and plays of 1897–1901 as a nursery for nearly all of Shaw's later pronouncements on marriage. As he completed *Captain Brassbound's Conversion*, for instance, Shaw wrote a letter of support to a socialist debater that auditions many of his arguments in the preface to *Getting Married* (1908), including the argument that marriage is so variously defined that it is nearly incoherent (and therefore available for reinvention): "your opponent defines marriage. What does he mean by marriage? Is it legal marriage? If so, according to what law and what canon?"[4]

Marriage in these plays becomes protean, negotiable, an institution that is at once embedded in social conventions and yet murky in its contours and potential. Each of the *Three Plays for Puritans* stages at least one decoy marriage and sometimes a series of them. These simulated marriages are primarily heuristic: they allow otherwise aloof, self-interested, or excessively passionate characters to establish personal obligations, while also assuring that any virtuous actions they perform on each other's behalf are not based in the "interests" of love, legal contracts, or sexual desire. Decoy marriages are rehearsals for the social contract in miniature. In each play, a decoy marriage collapses in the face of an actual marriage proposal or an open profession of desire, as though the heuristic value of the decoy marriage would be compromised if it too closely approximated conventional love matches.

THE DEVIL'S DISCIPLE: THE THEATRICAL DECOY MARRIAGE

In 1896, the year Shaw began drafting *The Devil's Disciple*, he also wrote *Fabian Tract 70*, which proclaimed the Fabians' "singleness of aim" as the creation of a more democratic political constitution in England and the socialization of industry. Other issues might dilute this focus, so the Fabian Society professed "no distinctive opinions on the Marriage Question" in addition to "Religion, Art, abstract economics, historic Evolution, Currency, or any other subject ...."[5] Shaw could hardly have established a sharper wedge between his official Fabian persona and his personal concerns as a thinker and a playwright. According to Gareth Griffith, the Fabians avoided discussing marriage because they did not want to become embroiled in debates about free love that might brand them as sexual radicals.[6] Shaw, on the other hand, believed that marriage could not help but be shaped by economic and democratic change, though his public views tended toward reform (the creation of rational divorce laws, for example) rather than demolition.

At the outset of *The Devil's Disciple*, marriage hardly seems capable of redemption. The marriage between Annie and the now deceased Timothy Dudgeon that dominates the first act is a stalemate of recrimination and neglect. Annie is Shaw's type of the "dead Puritan," a proud and bitter woman who conceives of goodness as self-denial which is *"easily extended to others-denial"* (*CCP* II:53). The Dudgeon marriage is rooted in a pattern of refusals that Annie has attempted to construe as virtues. Shaw most directly demonstrates the cool enmity of a marriage predicated on denial (and self-denial) at the climax of the first act, when the reading of Timothy's will spectacularly denies Annie both her house and the right to dispose of her inherited fortune. The most troubling symptom of this unhappy marriage emerges when Timothy's will requests that his children care for their mother, even though he has "stood between them and her as far as I could to the best of my ability" (*CCP* II:75). A bad marriage is envisioned as standing between or against, canceling or impeding action and feeling rather than enabling them to find expression. Anderson will later describe how common this kind of marriage is in Act II: "Think of how some of our married friends worry one another, tax one another, are jealous of one another, cant bear to let one another out of sight for a day, are more like jailers and slave-owners than lovers" (*CCP* II:88).

As often happens in Shaw's drama, the reorganization of a family is an occasion to think about the arrangement of social and kinship structures more broadly. *The Devil's Disciple* encourages us to compare the central Dudgeon marriage to at least two other marriages as social arrangements: the future marriage of Christy, the lumpish Dudgeon son, to Sarah Wilkins, which is unapologetically an accrual of money and property; and the comparatively "holy" marriage of Anderson and Judith. Despite their apparent happiness, the Judith–Anderson marriage is nearly a misalliance Judith is 20 years younger than Anderson, but she is sentimental and vain and therefore less "vital" than he is: *"One feels, on the whole, that Anderson might have chosen worse, and that she, needing protection, could not have chosen better"* (*CCP* II:65). The Anderson marriage is based on Anderson's indulgence of Judith rather than his denial of their passions, though Judith's melodramatic emotions often translate into self-absorption while Anderson's protectiveness is frequently a form of inattention.

The most successful marriage in the play is not a marriage, legally speaking, at all. When a sergeant from the British army comes to arrest and hang Anderson, who has stepped out to attend to the dying Annie Dudgeon, he mistakes her son, Dick Dudgeon, for the absent minister. The sergeant makes his judgment based on a superficial survey of the scene: Dick is standing in Anderson's house in close proximity to Judith; he puts on Anderson's black coat; and he coerces Judith into a performance of wifely devotion: "And now, my dear, I am afraid the sergeant will not believe that you love me like a wife unless you give me one kiss before I go" (*CCPII*, 97). Shaw teases us, through the sergeant's misrecognition and its continuation in the third-act trial, with the possibility that marriage is simply a kind of performance: to be married Shaw reminds us, you only need to stand where a groom usually stands, to wear his costume, and to get someone else to say "That's my husband!" In this sense, Shaw seems to anticipate speech-act theorist J.L. Austin, who named "I do (sc. take this woman to be my lawful wedded wife)" as a pivotal example of performative speech: a verbal statement that produces a change in situation.[7] But marriage is only one of several sudden conversions that occur in the play. When Anderson learns that the soldiers came for him, not for Dick, "*the man of peace vanishes, transfigured into a choleric and formidable man of war*" (*CCP* II:105). Likewise, Dick, the disciple who swore his allegiance to the devil when he saw the wickedness that was done in God's name in his family home, is transformed into "the Reverend Richard Dudgeon, and [will] wag his pow in [Anderson's] own pulpit" (*CCP* II:139) at the end of the play.

Is Shaw telling us that marriage is nothing more than a performance? Not entirely: Judith and Richard have feelings for each other that pre-exist their decoy marriage and that inform their feigned nuptials. Anderson notices, for example, that Judith's amplified disgust for Richard is a kind of fascination: "After all, my dear, if you watch people carefully, you'll be surprised to find how like hate is to love ... you really are fonder of Richard than you are of me" (*CCP* II:88). Dick, meanwhile, waives his customary contempt for Judith, and even attacks British Major Swindon when he tries to remove Judith from his courtroom: "Why do you raise the devil in me by bullying the woman like that? You oatmeal faced dog, I'd twist your cursed head off with the greatest satisfaction" (*CCP* II:128). At the same time, Dick and Judith are almost always conscious that their roles are play-acted. Dick takes pleasure in the idea of impersonating a minister—"*he looks down at the sleeve on his arm, and then smiles slyly at Judith*" (*CCP* II:96)—while Judith tactically reserves the knowledge that Dick is her husband until she can deploy it most devastatingly in the courtroom.

As in the preface to *Three Plays for Puritans*, marriage in *The Devil's Disciple* is likened to serious theatre: one that requires attentiveness and a sacrifice of personal interests to better perform a role. Dick and Judith are predisposed to be good audiences for each other, partly as a result of a shared libidinal itch. In an earlier essay, "Acting, by One Who Does Not Believe in It" (1889), Shaw had similarly aligned Puritanism (as a kind of skepticism towards received wisdom) with marriage and role playing. Shaw's argument in the essay is that true acting is not pretense or deception, but an opportunity to show more aspects of the self than the constraints of social decorum usually allow. Great acting is "not acting: it is the final escape from acting, the ineffable release from the conventional mask ...."[8] Shaw goes on to insist that marriage is a similar structure in that it likewise requires "striving to get cast for the part which most fully realizes us" (*CPP* II:98): a wife who is straitened by poverty might "find a social career in which she can be fully herself" (*CPP* II:98) when her husband becomes wealthy, whereas a wife who is frugal would be "uncomfortable, regretful, exacting, and out of place on the higher scale of expenditure" (*CPP* II:98). A fruitful marriage requires not simply finding the right partner, but also the right circumstances to give the self the most latitude for an expressive performance.

A decoy marriage predicated on a non-binding negotiation of roles, is a ramification of this theatrical model. In pretending that he might be virtuous in the same way as Anderson, Dick discovers that he is already "naturally" inclined to goodness. Pretending to be good, like pretending to be Judith's husband, reveals mysterious and neglected aspects of Dick's character—to Dick most of all:

> I had no motive and no interest: all I can tell you is that when it came to the point whether I would take my neck out of the noose and put another man's into it, I could not do it. I don't know why not: I see myself as a fool for my pains; but I could not and I cannot. I have been brought up standing by the law of my own nature; and I may not go against it, gallows or no gallows. (*CCP* II:113)

Judith likewise discovers concern for Dick that exceeds her parochial vanity and morality. Her melodramatic hand-wringing over loyalties in the second act also signals self-expansion, surprise, and even horror that she could feel as much affection for her husband as she could for a man she thought she had despised: "He must be saved—no: you must be saved: you, you, you" (*CCP* II:100).

As the characters of Dick and Judith stretch and deform, the setting also shifts to accommodate their widening perspectives. While the unhappy Dudgeon house is the backdrop to an unhappy marriage and the Anderson house the setting for a partially happy marriage, the decoy marriage that dominates the third act takes place in a courtroom: a public place in which a marriage that is not legally binding becomes, ironically, a means of confusing, evading, and questioning British law. "We are bound to make an example of somebody" (*CCP* II:124), Burgoyne explains as a glib apology for hanging Dick. Judith and Dick, on the other hand, are *unbound* by their feigned contract, loosened from their habitual roles of sardonic malcontent and conceited housewife by their collaborative play-acting.

Shaw does not fully reject love as a factor in legal or decoy marriages in *The Devil's Disciple*. If anything, love is a more important factor in these heuristic marriages than it is in legal marriages. Instead, he resituates love as one ingredient in an intricate concoction of motives. "Was it for my sake?" (*CCP* II:110), Judith asks Dick, presuming that his sacrifice was a sublimated gesture of love. "It must have been a little for your sake" (*CCP* II:110), Dick admits. The point is not that love cannot be a spur to virtuous actions or happy marriages, but rather that we should avoid taking love as an exhaustive rather than a partial factor in any account of a complex action.

Even as Shaw demotes legal marriages as incapable of accommodating human flexibility, he assigns philosophical importance to marriage as a performative goad. Shaw's plays anticipate the ideas of philosopher Stanley Cavell, who likewise locates a philosophical "comedy of remarriage" in film comedies of the 1930s. (Shaw's plays were first filmed at the same time as Cavell's sample comedies). According to Cavell, the comedy of remarriage requires divorce, bigamy, or some other interruption of marriage. Because marriage is not taken for granted as an outcome of a tryst and may even seem unlikely, it becomes a topic of debate. Love, in Cavellian (as in Shavian) terms, is a "metaphysical" rather than an individual problem, and comedies of remarriage "trace the progress from narcissism and incestuous privacy to acknowledgement of otherness as the path and goal of human happiness," where the "achieving of one's private self and the creation of the social" are mutually reinforcing projects.[9]

Cavell takes Shaw's *Pygmalion* (1912) as an ur-text of the comedy of remarriage that deliberately thwarts the romance between Higgins and Eliza, while nevertheless containing features of the genre. In his later study of moral perfectionism, *Cities of Words*, Cavell considers *Pygmalion* at greater length. As an account of moral striving, Cavell contends that Shaw's comedy is concerned with the collateral benefits of self-creation—"it is the woman who seeks creation and the man is shown to suffer education (hence further creation) through her"—even as *Pygmalion* demonstrates Shaw's "limited" ability to imagine other minds.[10] I would argue, though, that Shaw's plays of the 1890s are a better match with Cavell's thesis, since they more insistently demonstrate the invention of social and personal roles through virtual marriages. *Caesar and Cleopatra* is the Play for Puritans that is most concerned with education and moral perfection, and Cavell's notion of collateral creation applies most clearly to it.

Caesar and Cleopatra: The Tutelary Decoy Marriage

Shaw establishes Caesar and Cleopatra as unsuitable marriage partners, but excellent conversational partners, at their first meeting. Although both have vigorous sexual appetites, Cleopatra immediately rejects Caesar because of his physiognomy: "I like men, especially young men with round strong arms; but I am afraid of them. You are old and rather thin and stringy; but you have a nice voice; and I like to have somebody to talk to, though I think you are a little mad" (*CCP* II:185). Since she is already fixated on Mark Antony as a husband who matches her physical expectations their decoy marriage will primarily be a conversational rhapsody, often, as in *The Devil's Disciple*, on the theme of play-acting. (When Cleopatra first hears the sound of a bucina, a Roman war trumpet, Caesar describes it ironically as "Caesar's voice" (*CCP* II:188), as though to demonstrate what he is not—a man who can only command, but cannot discuss.)[11]

Caesar and Cleopatra form a pseudo-marriage in order to learn how to govern Egypt and themselves. Shaw structures the first two acts of the play to set two models of rule, relationship, and instruction in apposition: the improvisatory and humane regime of Caesar against the hierarchical, codified approach of Pothinus and Ptolemy. In their meeting by the Sphinx in Act I, Caesar playfully instructs Cleopatra in how to perform queenliness—to issue orders firmly, to keep her voice from quavering. In exchange, Cleopatra promises to make him part of her royal harem: "you shall always be my king: my nice, wise, good old king" (*CCP* II:191). This game of collaborative performance absorbs and strengthens the erotic tension of the relationship while imagining its future in a chaste marriage punctuated by libidinal excitement. This stands in contrast to the following scene that opens Act II of Ptolemy's instruction by Pothinus, an older eunuch, in which Ptolemy simply repeats a speech by rote. "Which is the King? the man or the boy?" (*CCP* II:198), Caesar asks, which is a kind of performance critique. Caesar detects that either the tutor wishes to usurp the place of the king rather than to collaborate with him or that the boy has not been taught to perform kingship persuasively, through flirtation rather than fiat. In either case, he does not buy the performance: it does not throb with the pleasure engendered by an educative pseudo-marriage.

The continuum of flirtation, instruction, and leadership provides a thematic scaffolding that organizes the otherwise episodic struc- ture of *Caesar and Cleopatra*. Lessons in governance become intimate as they mark both displays of expertise and tokens of concern between the decoy partners. "You must learn to look on battles" (*CCP* II:223), Caesar admonishes Cleopatra before he departs to capture the Pharos of Alexandria. When she threatens her servant Ftatateeta with death if she does not obey and makes Caesar squeamish, Cleopatra's response is at once affectionate and didactic: "You are very sentimental, Caesar; but you are clever; and if you do as I tell you, you will soon learn to govern" (*CCP* II:212).

Their difference in experience and moral development makes the decoy marriage between Caesar and Cleopatra less balanced than that in *The Devil's Disciple*. As the beneficiary of Caesar's tutelage in clemency, Cleopatra begins to mirror him in Act IV: "Now that Caesar has made me wise, it is no use my liking or disliking: I do what must be done, and have no time to attend to myself. ... If Caesar were gone, I think I could govern the Egyptians; for what Caesar is to me, I am to the fools around me" (*CCP* II:256). Her court assumes that she can only be motivated by infatuation or love. But Cleopatra describes her transformation as the discovery of a capacity for impersonal virtue, and her own kindness as an attempted impersonation of Caesar's kindness: "His kindness is not for anything in me: it is in his own nature" (*CCP* II:257). The combination of care and indifference is characteristic of the decoy marriage, and Cleopatra has learned it more than her fellow Egyptians by being in a relationship that is at once attentive and disinterested, bound by mutual fascination and unbound by law—"neither mother, father, nor nurse have ever taken so much care for me, or thrown open their thoughts to me so freely" (*CCP* II:257).

One form that Caesar's disinterested virtue takes is his disgust at and dismissal of the cult of vengeance in Alexandria and Rome. Cleopatra betrays Caesar most when she tries to save him from Pothinus by ordering his murder—countering one act of revenge with another. But it could also be argued that their decoy marriage performatively honors and instantiates Caesar's creed. The structure of marriage itself is also a rejection of vengeance, as Marc Shell demonstrates, drawing on Claude Levi-Strauss's studies of kinship: "Marriage appears to solve the fundamental issue of taliation [the injurious return of like for like] by creating or hypothesizing a condition of identity in difference where 'both are two but each is one,' and it appears to solve the fundamental issue of sexual exchange by hypothesizing an essentially chaste relationship."[12] Through their decoy marriage, in other words, Caesar and Cleopatra embody an alternative to the rule of vengeance, a fruitful confusion of identities where self and other are mixed rather than opposed.

By this account, nearly all the tutelary value of the decoy marriage benefits Cleopatra. What does Caesar get out of it? One possibility is that the lonely proto-Superman Caesar strengthens his bond with the people he must govern by internalizing a durable relationship with one of them. At the beginning of the play, Caesar, addressing the Sphinx as a fellow hybrid—"part brute, part woman, part god"—feels alienated from human relations and concerns:

> I have wandered in many lands, seeking the lost regions from which my birth into this world exiled me, and the company of creatures such as I myself. I have found flocks and pastures, men and cities, but no other Caesar, no air native to me, no man kindred to me, none who can do my day's deed, and think my night's thought. (*CCP* II:182)

Cleopatra, who also insists on her tripartite heritage (she is a woman, she is descended from the Nile, she claims kinship with sacred cats), is a partial doppelganger for Caesar, if not a partner than a fellow trave-ler.[13] She is not as evolutionarily advanced, but she pierces his autonomy and stifles what might become contempt for the more primitive subjects he superintends. (Cleopatra's partial mirroring of Caesar manifests itself in her impatience with her servants: "Caesar has spoiled me for talk-ing to weak things like you" [*CCP* II, 258–259].) Dennis J. Leary has described Shaw's Caesar as embroiled in a quest to reconcile his dialecti-cal tensions: "a general who is a saint must live a tense life of compro-mise between matter and spirit."[14] Cleopatra is a collateral beneficiary of Caesar's self-creation, but she is also an intrinsic part of it, a representa-tive of fleshly desire and martial inclinations who becomes his extension and double as she is folded into his project of dialectical self-fashioning.

While a decoy marriage between Caesar and Cleopatra cannot resolve their constitutive antitheses, Shaw positions it as an indispensable step in the endlessly pursued and endlessly deferred project of human perfec-tion. In *Captain Brassbound's Conversion*, Shaw's final Play for Puritans, a decoy marriage again softens the desire for vengeance and encourages self-expansive improvisation. But Shaw also stretches the pseudo-mar-riage conceit to fantastic extremes, at once testing and parodying the elasticity of marriage as a structure that can accommodate human trans-formative potential.

Captain Brassbound's Conversion: The Limits of Universal Indifference

Slavoj Žižek is not often acknowledged as a disciple of Shaw, though his distinction between intimate–erotic love (*eros*) and political love (*agape*) could be conceived as a descendant of Shaw's attempt to transmog-rify romantic love into social awareness quickened by an erotic charge. Žižek argues that *eros* flexes between contractive and expansive forms, "between erotic self-immersion and the slow work of marking a space defined by the couple's love (children, common projects etc.)."[15] *Agape*, on the other hand, is not a contraction from a collective into a couple, but "an emphatic *yes* to the beloved collective and ultimately to all of humanity" whereby "love emerges out of a universal indifference," while hatred, for Žižek, is only possible where love is an exclusive or unique condition.[16]

Cleopatra is confused when Pothinus asks if Caesar loves her, because she can only understand love as *eros*. To call Caesar's indifference love seems to her like a confusion of categories:

> Caesar loves no one. Who are those we love. Only those whom we do not hate: all people are strangers and enemies to us except those we love. But it is not so with Caesar. He has no hatred in him: he makes friends with everyone as he does with dogs and children. (*CCP* II:257)

Caesar seeks to convert law, which is organized vengeance, into *agape*, which is impersonal affirmation, both through the decoy marriage with Cleopatra and via an attempted political rapprochement (another counterintuitive "marriage") between Egypt and Rome. The generally optimistic "idealist-imperialist" vision of the play, according to M. Sean Saunders, emerges from Caesar's fitness to govern in the interests of the whole species.[17] If Caesar is not quite patriarchal, he is certainly parentarchal: he views his subjects like children in his care, generally but not specifically loveable (though Cleopatra seems to be, for a time, his favorite).

In *Captain Brassbound's Conversion*, by contrast, Lady Cicely Waynflete is a blander version of Caesar, a woman who reduces *agape* to etiquette, and the ethical injunction to preserve life to the reminder to be "nice." "Why do people get killed by savages?" Cicely asks. "Because instead of being polite to them, and saying How dye do? like me, people aim pistols at them. Ive been among savages—cannibals and all sorts. Everybody said theyd kill me. But when I met them, I said Howdyedo? and they were quite nice. The kings always wanted to marry me" (*CCP* II:339). As the recipient of 17 proposals of marriage before the start of the play, Cicely's benign tolerance straddles, and elides, the line between *eros* and *agape*. She has made the flexibility and impersonality of the decoy marriage a way of life, and the play she inhabits is a catalogue of the diversity of her pseudo-roles, as well, finally, as a limit case of the effectiveness of marriage as a heuristic.

While earlier decoy marriages pressed characters to discover untapped virtual selves, in *Captain Brassbound's Conversion* nearly every character is already "multiple" by virtue of their tangled biological and social heritage. Shaw's final Play for Puritans is set on the periphery of the British Empire, in a fantastic version of Morocco occupied by mongrels of class, race, gender, and parentage. The cockney Felix Drinkwater, for instance, is of "*inscrutable*" age (he might be younger than 17 or older than 40), speaks in a dialect that combines a "*base nasal delivery*" with the tone of "*smart London society*," is dressed in "*somebody else's very second best*" (*CCP* II:322), and, like so many other characters in the play, has at least one other name, in this case "Brandyfaced Jack" (*CCP* II:345). Captain Brassbound, also known as "Black Paquito" (his mother's nickname) or "Mr Hallam," is the son of a West Indian mother and an aristocratic English father, while English judge Sir Howard Hallam is the unacknowledged uncle of Brassbound. Lady Cicely is perhaps the most fraught case of crossed and multiple selves in the play, since she is at once Sir Howard's sister-in-law, therefore also Brassbound's aunt and love interest, as well as a traveler, nurse, seamstress, and litigator, to name only a few of her many roles.

In contrast to these fluvial and motley figures, Shaw associates both English law, incarnated in paternalistic Sir Howard, and the counter-law of vengeance, incarnated in Brassbound's mother and the denial of the title to her West Indies property by Hallam, with a fixation on autonomy and rigidity. Sir Howard defines the law as a force that transcends kinship: "Cicely: an English judge has no nephews, no sons even, when he has to carry out the law" (*CCP* II:390). Brassbound likewise presents his will to revenge as a force that denies other familial and social attachments. When Cicely reminds him that his monomania yokes him to his uncle Howard despite their differences in class and heredity, Brassbound furiously denies the resemblance: "If I thought my veins contained a drop of his black blood, I would drain them empty with my knife. I have no relations. I had a mother: that was all" (*CCP* II:370). As a whirlwind of relationality, Cicely sets to work establishing points of commonality between antagonists, first by arguing Brassbound out of his mother's claim, and then by reminding him of the "brave things" he did while serving under General Gordon in the Sudan. Ironically, despite his disgust with British power and its destructive effects on his family, Brassbound owes his military discipline and greatest display of heroism to his past role in a watershed of British imperialism.

A decoy marriage might be a way of freeing Brassbound from the grip of his real and symbolic parents and of broadening his capacity for impersonal goodness. But even a rudimentary love match with Cicely fizzles. At their first quasi-romantic encounter in Act II, Cicely "*puts her hand kindly on his shoulder*" (*CCP* II:374). Brassbound interprets this as an invitation to further physical contact: "*He looks up at her for a moment;*

then kisses her hand. She presses his and turns away with her eyes so wet that she sees Drinkwater, coming in through the arch just then, with a prismatic halo around his head" (*CCP* II:374). This sedate flirtation is echoed by a more explicit demand for erotic involvement at the end of the play. Brassbound's final seduction of Cicely reverses the logic whereby *eros* is more personal than *agape* by trying to persuade her that marrying a man she does not love is the final triumph of "universal indifference":

Lady Cicely [shaking her head]:	I have never been in love with any real person; and I never shall. How could I manage people if I had that mad little bit of self left in me? Thats my secret.
Brassbound:	Then throw away the last bit of self. Marry me.
Lady Cicely [vainly struggling to recall her wandering will]:	Must I?
Brassbound:	There is no must. You c a n. I ask you to. My fate depends on it.
Lady Cicely:	It's frightful; for I dont mean to — dont wish to.
Brassbound:	But you will. (*CCP* II:416)

If the benign management of people is the highest achievement of *agape*, *eros* is figured here as a hallucinatory failure of self-management that recalls the ecstatic self-erasure in Wagner's *Tristan and Isolde*—an opera that Shaw would also appropriate and mock in his next major play, *Man and Superman* (Fig. 4.1).

In one sense, the conclusion to *Captain Brassbound's Conversion* features Shaw's most daring decoy marriage. It lasts only an instant and is interrupted by the distant gunfire from an American ship, and yet that intense encounter is enough to show Brassbound how erotic seduction can be instrumentalized for the impersonal good of leadership. "I have blundered somehow on the secret of command at last" (*CCP* II:417), he tells Cicely, kneeling and kissing her hand. Although his "secret" remains enigmatic, it is plausible that Brassbound has—like Dick and Judith, like Caesar and Cleopatra—discovered how marriage, enacted by virtual rather than legal means, can reciprocally broaden one's awareness of another person's claims even as it bolsters individual development. So much of the play is taken up by the question of how to wield authority over others, with Cicely's benign, coyly manipulative strategies counterpoised

Fig. 4.1   Ellen Terry as Lady Cicely Waynflete at the Court Theatre in 1906 in Shaw's *Captain Brassbound's Conversion*. Reproduced by the kind permission of the Society of Authors on behalf of the Bernard Shaw Estate, the National Trust and the London School of Economics

to Brassbound's severe, grimacing style of command. Perhaps when Brassbound *"turns and flies"* from Cicely it is to take on a series of enlightened command posts, each of which will be like a little decoy marriage, informed by passion but tempered by playful disinterestedness.

While Cicely's saint-like manner allows her to establish non-binding kinship with anybody, it also keeps her at a placid—and sometimes patronizing—remove, and refuses all experience that cannot be contained in the bounds of what is "nice." In Act II, Drinkwater compares Cicely as a leader to a Sunday school teacher, treating men like a "bloomin lawt o cherrity kids" (*CPP* II:382), like Caesar stripped of his libido and his existential anxiety. Shaw's last Play for Puritans may finally be both an attempt to imagine a way past the decoy marriage and its emotional exposures and confusions as well as a parody of an emotionless, flexible, gently amused *agape*. Shaw continues to goad us by refusing to endorse (or deny) either Brassbound or Cicely, and likewise by refusing to jettison or fully celebrate marriage. Is there such a thing as love or politics without "interests"? Certainly there is not much drama without them. Ellen Terry, for whom Shaw wrote the part of Lady Cicely, turned down the role, preferring the more emotionally textured (and glamorous) part of Cleopatra. When Gertrude Kingston took on the part of Cicely in 1912, she tried to replace the play's final line—"How glorious! And what an escape!"— with, "How glorious! And what a disappointment!"[18] However atavistic, entrapping, or terrifying Shaw and his characters might find marriage to be, they also find life stale without the idea of marriage and the erotics of courtship and flirtation.

Throughout the rest of Shaw's dramatic career, "real" marriages do occur off stage or are planned after the end of a play. But although decoy marriages are most prevalent in his plays of the late 1890s, they persist well into the plays of the 1920s: in the "marriage" of Shotover and Ellie Dunn in *Heartbreak House* (1916), for instance, or the spiritual consultations of King Magnus and Orinthia in *The Apple Cart* (1928). Shaw's skepticism about marriage, like his dismissals of love and sexual desire as experiences necessary for human flourishing, have generated lasting controversy and even disgust among his critics.[19] The challenge for Shaw, and for us, is how to think of marriage as a transitive verb in search of new objects and new occasions for performances rather than as a complacent and static condition—to approach marriage as a rehearsal for and sustenance during a passional life of social work rather than an end in itself.

NOTES

1. Bernard Shaw, *Collected Letters*, Vol. 2, ed. Dan H. Laurence (New York: Dodd, Mead & Company, 1972), 24 (Laurence 1972).
2. Ibid., 51.
3. Ibid., 51. Shaw hopped because he was still recovering from an operation to correct two slipped toe joints.
4. Shaw, *Collected Letters*, 81.
5. Bernard Shaw, *Political Tract 70: Report on Fabian Policies and Resolutions* (London: The Fabian Society, 1896), 3 (Shaw 1896).
6. Gareth Griffith, *Socialism and Superior Brains: The Political Thought of Bernard Shaw* (London and New York: Routledge, 1993), 170 (Griffith 1993).

7. J.L. Austin, *How to Do Things with Words* (Cambridge: Harvard University Press, 1975), 5 (Austin 1975).
8. Bernard Shaw, "Acting, by One Who Does Not Believe in It" in *The Drama Observed*, vol. 1, ed. Bernard Dukore (University Park: Penn State UP), 97 (Shaw 1993).
9. Stanley Cavell, *Pursuits of Happiness: The Hollywood Comedy of Remarriage* (Cambridge and London: Harvard UP, 1981), 102 (Cavell 1981).
10. Stanley Cavell, *Cities of Words: Pedagogical Letters on a Register of the Moral Life* (Cambridge: Belknap Press of the Harvard University Press, 2004), 409 (Cavell 2004).
11. Marjorie Morgan argues that Shaw was abetted in his vision of an amorous but asexual relationship between Caesar and Cleopatra by Theodore Mommsen's *History of Rome* (1854–1856), one of Shaw's main sources for the play. Mommsen misrepresents Cleopatra's age as 16 instead of 20 and neglects to mention their child, Caesarion. See *The Shavian Playground* (London: Methuen, 1972), 242 (Morgan 1972).
12. Marc Shell, *The End of Kinship: Measure for Measure, Incest, and the Ideal of Universal Siblinghood* (Baltimore: Johns Hopkins UP, 1995), 169 (Shell 1995).
13. M. Sean Saunders suggests that Cleopatra is a deliberately abject copy of Caesar whose "incapability perpetuates the 'need' for rulers from the colonizing nation," in "From Metropolis to 'Impossible Edges': Shaw's Imperial Abjects," *SHAW*, vol. 22, 105. Their pseudo-marriage contains elements of a fantasy of colonial reconciliation (and subjugation) that Shaw variously reproduces and critiques. He would develop the fuller implications of marriage as a questionable model for national reconciliation in *John Bull's Other Island* (1904).
14. Daniel J. Leary, "The Moral Dialectic in *Caesar and Cleopatra*" in *The Shaw Review*, Vol. 5, No. 2 (May, 1962), 52 (Leary 1962).
15. Slavoj Žižek, *Living in the End Times* (London, New York: Verson, 2011), 98 (Žižek 2011).
16. Ibid., 98, 100.
17. Saunders, 102.
18. Holroyd, Michael, *Bernard Shaw* (New York: Random House, 1988), 278 (Holroyd 1988).
19. See Matthew Yde, *Bernard Shaw and Totalitarianism: Longing for Utopia* (New York: Palgrave Macmillan, 2013) and Arnold Silver, *Bernard Shaw: The Darker Side* (Stanford: Stanford UP, 1982), for two of the most incisive accounts of how the dismissal of love was ethically catastrophic for Shaw (Yde 2013; Silver 1982).

REFERENCES

Austin, J.L. 1975. *How to Do Things with Words*. Cambridge, MA: Harvard University Press.
Cavell, Stanley. 1981. *Pursuits of Happiness: The Hollywood Comedy of Remarriage*. Cambridge and London: Harvard University Press.
Cavell, Stanley. 2004. *Cities of the Words: Pedagogical Letters on a Register of the Moral Life*. Cambridge, MA: Belknap Press of the Harvard University Press.
Griffith, Gareth. 1993. *Socialism and Superior Brains: The Political Thought of Bernard Shaw*, 170. London and New York: Routledge.
Holroyd, Michael. 1988. *Bernard Shaw*. New York: Random House.
Laurence, Dan H. 1972. *Bernard Shaw. Collected Letters, vol. 2, 1898–1910*. New York: Dodd, Mead.
Leary, Dennis J. 1962. The Moral Dialectic in *Caesar and Cleopatra. The Shaw Review* 5 (2 May): 43–54.
Morgan, Margery. 1972. *The Shavian Playground: An Exploration of the Art of George Bernard Shaw*. London: Methuen.
Shaw, Bernard. 1896. *Political Tract 70: Report on Fabian Policies and Resolutions*. London: The Fabian Society.
Shaw, Bernard. 1993. Acting by One Who Does Not Believe in It. In *The Drama Observed*, vol. I, ed. Bernard F. Dukore, 92–104. University Park: The Pennsylvania State University Press.
Shell, Marc. 1995. *The End of Kinship: Measure for Measure, Incest, and the Ideal of Universal Siblinghood*. Baltimore, MD: Johns Hopkins University Press.
Silver, Arnold. 1982. *Bernard Shaw: The Darker Side*. Stanford, CA: Stanford UP.
Yde, Matthew. 2013. *Bernard Shaw and Totalitarianism: Longing for Utopia*. New York: Palgrave Macmillan.
Žižek, Slavoj. 2011. *Living in the End Times*. London and New York: Verso.

AUTHOR BIOGRAPHY

Lawrence Switzky an Assistant Professor of English and Drama at the University of Toronto, Ontario, Canada, specializes in modern and contemporary drama, media theory, and modernism across the arts. He is currently completing a manuscript, *The Rise of the Theatre Director: Negotiations with the Material World, 1880–1956* (forthcoming from Northwestern University Press), which demonstrates how the evolution of an artistic executive responsible for the interpretation and sensuous materialization of theatrical texts shaped fundamental ethical and aesthetic debates on the modern stage. He is guest editor of *SHAW* 35.1, "Shaw and Modernity."

CHAPTER 5

Not Really a Philanderer

Rodelle Weintraub

Philanderer: One who engages in love affairs frivolously or casually
American Heritage Dictionary of the English Language[1]

A man who readily or frequently enters into casual sexual relationships with women
Oxford Dictionary of English[2]

Shaw's play *The Philanderer* (1893) has a scene in which two women fight over Leonard Charteris, the philanderer of the title (*CPP* I:166–167). Based on an incident in which Jenny Patterson and Florence Farr, both mistresses of George Bernard Shaw, got into a hair-pulling tussle over him, the play ends with Charteris as a failure at philandering.[3] Was Shaw suggesting that he himself was or was not a philanderer?

In April 1876, the almost 20-year-old Shaw emigrated from Ireland to London, joining his mother and sister Lucy who had preceded him. The unsophisticated young man, tall, red-haired with a wispy beard, embarked upon a self-education of singing lessons from his mother; improving his piano skills; going to the theatre; studying for a Civil Service Examination, which he abandoned; learning French; becoming

R. Weintraub (✉)
Philadelphia, USA
e-mail: rodellew@yahoo.com

© The Author(s) 2017
R.A. Gaines (ed.), *Bernard Shaw's Marriages and Misalliances*,
Bernard Shaw and His Contemporaries,
DOI 10.1057/978-1-349-95170-3_5

a regular visitor to the circular reading room of the British Library, his "university"; listening to speakers in Hyde Park and other venues; and joining radical organizations. After working for the telephone company for less than a year, Shaw was unemployed, except for doing occasional music reviews for fringe London newspapers, until 1885.[4] Not until 1878 did he begin his first novel, *Immaturity,* the title well describing both the young writer and his work. Unemployed, the impoverished young man could not afford liaisons with the many young women he met through his and their involvement with radical groups, nor with his mother's pupils (he often played the piano accompaniment for their lessons); nor could he afford the services of prostitutes, had he wanted them.

His first London romance came in 1876 with "la Carbonaja" (possibly a pun on coal), one of the Collier sisters. The Colliers lived in the Brompton Square area, near the Roman Catholic Brompton Oratory. Mabel, who tried to convert Shaw to Roman Catholicism, gave him a medal of the Virgin Mary.[5] At her request, he visited with Father Addis at the Oratory. Rather than the priest being able to convert Shaw, the iconoclastic GBS arguing about first causes almost destroyed the priest's faith.[6] The relationship ended in 1879, but Shaw kept the medal for the rest of his life.

In 1882, the 26-year-old Shaw fell in love with Alice Lockett, a nursing student who was taking singing lessons from Bessie Shaw. This provided him the opportunity to see her at least once a week. Shaw played the piano and they sang duets. The cautious affair lasted until 1885 and influenced the writing of the "proper" characters of Alice in *Cashel Byron's Profession* (1883) and Gertrude in *An Unsocial Socialist* (1883), the last two of his five completed novels.

In the middle 1880s, many of the young women in the new Fabian Society such as Grace Gilchrist and Grace Black found Shaw sexually attractive and were disappointed when he did not reciprocate. To Bertha Newcombe, who painted a notable portrait of him at this time, "G.B.S. Platform Spellbinder," (1896),[7] he wrote, "Heavens! I had forgotten you—totally forgotten you … You may play me as a trump card for all I am worth; but I cannot play myself … Twas ever thus, Bertha. Your sex likes me as children like wedding cake, for the sake of the sugar on the top" (*CL* I:619–621). To Janet Achurch he wrote, in 1895, "everybody seems bent on recommending me to marry Bertha."[8] The society and its women members, Shaw's "New Women," appear in Act II of *The Philanderer,* where the society becomes the Ibsen Club. Other

New Women in his plays are the Polish acrobat Lina Szcepanowska and Hypatia Tarleton (*Misalliance*, 1909), Vivie Warren (*Mrs Warren's Profession*, 1893), and Epifania Ognisani di Parega Fitzfassenden (*The Milllionairess*, 1934). Epifana loses her husband not to a womanly woman but to a conventional woman, "the angel in the house" (*CPP* VI:899). In *The Philanderer*, Charteris tells the womanly woman Julia that despite her membership in the Ibsen Club, "all your advanced views were merely a fashion picked up and followed like any other fashion." In the end, Julia gets her man—though not the philandering Charteris, settling instead for the medical scientist Dr. Paramore.[9]

Young women physically pursuing the men they want turn up in *Man and Superman* (1902), where Ann Whitefield chases John Tanner through France and Spain until she finds him and wears him out.[10] As he succumbs to the inevitability of marriage with Ann, Tanner laments: "I never asked her. It is a trap for me" (*CPP* II:730). Erica Cotterill, a Young Fabian infatuated with Shaw, who in 1908 pursued him even to his home, where Charlotte barred her entry, would provide the model for Hypatia in *Misalliance*. Hypatia chases Joey Percival into the woods until, as she runs faster and faster, he "runs slower and slower"—and she catches him (*CPP* IV:240).

Shaw met Mrs. Annie Besant in 1884 when she joined the socialist movement. As their friendship deepened, she became infatuated with him. By 1887 "it nearly became an intrigue." She even drew up a "marriage contract" about their living together. Considering this a result of his carelessness in which he had behaved inconsiderately, he nevertheless rejected any romantic entanglement with Annie. She returned his letters, but remained friends with him. The idea of a marriage contract appears in *Getting Married* (1908), in which the young couple to be married object to the conditions imposed by the Marriage Act, such as the man being responsible for the woman's debts and legally liable for her actions. When the characters' subsequent attempt to draw up a reasonable marriage contract flounders as none of the characters can agree on the terms, the young couple elopes.

Not until July 26, 1885, his 29th birthday, could Shaw record in his diary what he described as "a new experience" (*Shaw* I:99). In anticipation, he had purchased "French Letters" (condoms) shortly before, on July 18 (*Shaw* I:97). The considerably older Mrs. Jenny Patterson was a friend and singing pupil of his mother Bessie. Shaw often played the piano during these lessons and had become a frequent visitor to the

Irish-Scottish, socialist mother figure, sometimes accompanied by his mother and sister. In a later letter to his classicist friend Gilbert Murray about the Greek incest play *Oedipus*, Shaw wrote: "I very seldom dream of my mother; but when I do she is my wife as well as my mother" (*CL* III:17). With Jenny, Shaw in effect put his dream into practice. In some ways she acted in a motherly fashion, giving him supplies of cocoa, fruit, and slippers, and, having collected his *World* articles, helped him get his papers in order. The affair gradually became a burden to him as Jenny became more and more possessive, even rifling through his letters from other women. Shaw, as did other Victorians such as Sir Arthur Sullivan, put a code in his diaries indicating sexual intimacy. Why Shaw stopped entering the numerals (0, 1, 2) at the end of November 1887 we do not know, but his diminishing sexual encounters with Jenny continued.[11]

In October 1891, Shaw and actress Florence Farr Emery had begun seeing each other frequently. She performed the role of Blanche Sartorious, Shaw's first stage heroine, in *Widowers' Houses* (1892). Her husband, the actor Edward Emery, left her after 4 years of marriage and went to America in 1888. Younger than Shaw by 4 years, Florence met him when visiting May Morris in Hammersmith. He had already seen her perform at Bedford Park in John Todhunter's *A Sicilian Idyll* (1890). By the end of 1891 Shaw had fallen in love, and he and Florence became lovers. Jenny, jealous and feeling betrayed, burst in on the couple in February 1893. An argument ensued and only by force did Shaw prevent the hefty Jenny from physically assaulting Florence. The brawl became the opening scene in *The Philanderer* (1893), which Shaw began writing that November as a romantic role for *FE*, as he referred to her in his diary. Still, the Shaw–Patterson–Farr triangle lasted another two and a half years. Shaw worked with Florence, becoming her tutor in elocution, his Henry Higgins to her Eliza Doolittle as in his much later *Pygmalion* (1912). She was a New Woman who could have been the model for Madge Brailsford in the third of his novels, *Love Among the Artists* (1881).[12] Madge rejected her middle-class upbringing to become an actress whom Owen Jack coaches. Blanche in *Widowers' Houses* reflects the feistiness, the cool self-possession and sexuality of Florence, who performed in that role. In 1894 she played Louka in *Arms and the Man*, Shaw's fifth play and first commercial success, which she produced at the Avenue Theatre. Florence, who wanted to play Raina, the lead, stole the show as the sexy, conniving Louka.

Florence's season at the Avenue Theatre was anonymously financed by Annie Horniman, and both were members, along with W.B. Yeats, in the Order of the Golden Dawn hermetic society. Florence became more and more interested in mysticism, writing, much to Shaw's distress, *Egyptian Magic* in 1886. In W.B. Yeats she found someone compatible with her growing interest in mysticism. Her affair with Shaw ended in 1894 when Yeats briefly replaced Shaw as her lover. Shaw and Florence remained friends until her death. She had left England in 1912 to teach in Ceylon, where she died in 1917. Shortly before her death she let Shaw know that she was dying. Aware that she had limited funds, he immediately cabled her asking that she cable him collect. The cable arrived too late.

In June 1886, fellow Fabian and writer Edith Nesbit, the wife of Hubert Bland, fell in love with Shaw. He often visited the Blands at their home and by the summer of 1886 she was pursuing him, visiting him almost daily at the British Museum. He realized that Edith Nesbit Bland, a married woman with children, had "become passionately attached" to him (*Shaw* II:34). The Bland *ménage à trois* included Hubert's mistress, Alice Hoatson. Edith took care of their child along with her own. Rather than take advantage of the situation, Shaw spurned her attentions, claiming she had to "live down her fancy." Shaw, who did not wish to cuckold his friend Bland, was satisfied to remain a "Sunday husband." In Shakespeare's *Much Ado about Nothing* when Prince Pedro asks Beatrice "Will you have me?" he is told "No, my Lord, unless I might have another for working days: your grace is too costly to wear every day," thereby relegating him to what Shaw would describe as a "Sunday husband," attributing the term to Shakespeare. Edith appears as the unhappy Mrs. Maddick in Shaw's *An Unfinished Novel* (1887–1888). Mrs. Maddick convinces Dr. Kincaid to accompany her on a shopping trip and walk in the country: "Kincaid, a good listener, allows. Maddick to be 'happy in the full play of her egotism' as they walked. But abruptly … she stops, and begins to draw aside the transparent pretenses between them." There the manuscript breaks off.[13] Although Edith was bitter that Shaw did not wish to consummate their affair, they remained good friends.

Another marriage in which he performed the role of a Sunday husband was that of Henry and Kate Salt. Kate worked for Shaw as an unpaid secretary. Her marriage to Salt was unconsummated, but there was little chance of Shaw and Kate being intimate. She was a lesbian. Kate, Shaw later wrote, "loved me as far as she could love any male creature. Once, towards her end, when I had been absent for years and turned up unexpectedly .... she flung her arms round me. She was a queer hybrid."[14] It is debatable as to whether Lesbia, who rejects marriage in *Getting Married* (1907–1908), and Vivie Warren (*Mrs Warren's Profession*) are lesbians.

Shaw and May Morris, daughter of William Morris, were, Shaw thought, merely good friends in a "Mystic Betrothal." The socialist Morris was a father figure for Shaw; May, in effect, his "sister." For May, however, it was an unrequited love affair. Even after her marriage to Henry Sparling (1890), she and Shaw continued to meet regularly at Sunday-evening gatherings at Morris's Kelmscott House. They acted in several plays together in Socialist League productions, sang duets, played chess, and went on outings, such as rowing and sailing on the Thames. With and without Sparling they took long walks together, skated, and danced. In November 1892, exhausted from overwork and with the Shaw family residence in Fitzroy Square being renovated, Shaw moved into the Sparling home, becoming her Sunday husband. He remained until January, but continued occasionally to stay with the Sparlings after they moved to Hammersmith. On one occasion he remained with May while Henry was away in France. Despite the opportunities, their relationship remained unconsummated. The frustrated May knew about his ongoing affairs with Jenny Patterson and Florence Farr. In *Getting Married*, Leo enjoys the attention of Sinjon, her Sunday husband. Unlike in the play, in which Leo and Reginald call off their divorce, once Shaw moved out of the Sparling household the marriage ended. In her later years, May finally found domestic contentment with a woman.[15] In *Candida* (1894), the young poet, Eugene, does not move into the Morell household, but seriously interferes in their marriage. Candida loves her husband and rejects Eugene, choosing Morell over the smitten, immature poet.[16]

In June 1889, Shaw commenced upon the most unusual of his liaisons. He met the actress Janet Achurch at a dinner celebrating the English première of Ibsen's *A Doll's House*. Janet was playing Nora; Florence Farr was her understudy. Married to the actor Charles Charrington, who played Helmer in *A Doll's House*, Janet was much the better actor of the two. She smoked, drank, and eventually took drugs. She was a buxom bottle blonde. She was not a vegetarian. She was everything that Shaw abhorred; yet he was utterly smitten. Shaw avidly pursued her and within a few days of meeting her, their affair had begun.[17]

Only three weeks later when she and Charrington left for their prearranged theatrical tour of Australia, she was pregnant with Nora, her only child. Might Shaw have been the father? Might he have thought he was? Given morphine because of a difficult childbirth, she became addicted, with Charrington her willing supplier.[18] After their return to England, the affair with Shaw continued. In what was a most ironic twist even for the iconoclastic Shaw, he wrote *Candida* for Janet and insisted that she be cast as the seductive model of purity—Candida (Fig. 5.1).

Shaw enjoyed the children of his friends and even paid for the schooling of some.[19] His relationship with Nora, however, was especially close. He baby-sat for her; Janet brought the young girl to visit him in his lodgings, and also to see him at Battersea Park.[20] Even into her

Fig. 5.1 Nora Charrington taken at the time of the first Fabian Summer School in 1907 held at Llanbedr Gwynedd (Wales). The photo was probably taken by Shaw himself. Reproduced by the kind permission of the Society of Authors on behalf of the Bernard Shaw Estate, the National Trust and the London School of Economics

adulthood, Shaw often met Nora in this park. It is where she informed him that she was engaged to be married. He included her in a group of young women who were children of his friends at a première performance in a box at a theatre. Married, she died in 1914, possibly in childbirth or of influenza.[21] When Janet died in 1916, Shaw wrote to Charrington: "I don't feel sorrow; death doesn't catch me in that way, ... I feel much worse about Nora, whose death was a sort of murder on the part of Nature ... Remember how much I may change and deny it, that I really did love her [Janet] once ...."[22] GBS paid for Janet's funeral expenses and sent death notices to *The Nation* and *New Statesman*, and then financially supported Charrington until his death.

On June 1, 1898, Shaw and Charlotte Payne-Townshend, his Irish "green-eyed millionairess," were married.[23] Both over 40, the marriage, at her insistence, was not consummated. Nevertheless, it put an end to Shaw's affairs with other women, at least until 1912. Not that young women ceased to pursue him. As with young Fabian (and cousin to Rupert Brook) Erica Cotterill in 1908, Charlotte sometimes had to bar the door to protect him and prevent them from entering the house.

Shaw long admired the actress Stella (Mrs. Patrick) Campbell, complimenting her in print and writing to her. In 1897 he had visited her, wooing her to act in *The Philanderer* and *Mrs Warren's Profession*. He had spent 2 years prior to the London opening of *Pygmalion* (1914) trying to persuade her to play Eliza. Although the 48-year-old actress was far too old to portray the teenaged heroine, she pulled off what has been described as the greatest vanishing act in London. Shaw was horrified at the production, in which actor-manager Herbert Beerbohm Tree as Henry Higgins suggests an ultimate love affair between the young woman and the middle-aged bully.

Things changed from Shaw's wooing Stella professionally to doing so romantically, when he fell "violently and exquisitely in love" with "Stellatissima" (*CL* III:95). Their affair, which although physical may not have been consummated, shows up in the passionate love talk in his one-act play *Overruled* (1912), written the year after his feelings for Stella changed. She nicknamed him "Joey" (circus clown) as he had named the young man whom Hypatia chases in *Misalliance*, Joey Perceval. Charlotte, aware of his fascination with Stella, could do nothing to prevent him from visiting Stella as often as every day when she was bedridden and confined to her room. He even photographed her in bed (*CL* III:95). Coquettish, cruelly manipulative, and teasing, Shaw admitted to Stella that she was the model for the black-haired manipulative siren Hesione in *Heartbreak House* (1916–1917). The stress of the triangle of Stella, Charlotte, and Shaw later played out in the interlude scene of *The Apple Cart* (1928). Based on an episode which occurred in Stella's Kensington home when a servant interrupted the two in a similar situation, the scene ends with King Magnus's mistress Orinthia and the King tumbling across the floor as she tries to prevent him from leaving and a courtier enters the chamber. Earlier in that scene, Orinthia, who wants to be Queen, demands that Magnus leave the dowdy Jemima, crying, "Heaven is offering you a rose; and you cling to a cabbage." Magnus responds, "But what wise man, if you force him to choose between doing without roses and doing without cabbages, would not secure the cabbages" (*CP* VI:338–339). Shaw, however, not following his later character's advice, made plans to elope with Stella in April 1914, after Charlotte had sailed for America. Such an action would have seriously hurt his reputation and would have destroyed her career. He followed Stella to a hotel at a seaside resort in Sandwich, but when he refused to leave, she did. Instead of eloping with Shaw, she married the much younger George Cornwallis-West only hours after his divorce from Jenny Churchill. Shaw was deeply hurt, writing to her "Very well, go: … It is not the end of the world. The sun shines: it is pleasant to swim: it is good to work: my soul can stand alone. But I am deeply, deeply, deeply wounded … Farewell, wretch that I loved" (*CL* III:191–195). He resumed domestic life with his comfortable "cabbage" on Charlotte's return to England.

There would be only one more affair about which we know. In 1921, when Shaw was in his 70s, 23-year-old American Molly Tompkins, along with her husband and son Peter, arrived in London hoping to establish her career as an actress. Shaw befriended the couple and took Molly under his wing. On his advice she enrolled in the Royal Academy of Dramatic Art and took elocution lessons. During the summers of 1926 and 1927, the Shaws and Tompkinses vacationed together in Italy. In 1927 they even shared a villa on Isola San Giovanni. It became the Tompkinses' permanent home, until the financial crash of 1929 forced them to give it up in 1931. Shaw's affair with Molly began at Lake Maggiore. Following a stormy beginning, in the words of Anthony Gibbs, "the first period of happiness between the two occurred."[24] The affair came to an abrupt end when the pregnant Molly got an abortion. Shaw, who according to her son was the father, begged her to keep the child. She did not, and the affair ended. Still, he helped her through the "troubled time of the 1930s," and assisted with Peter's education. She influenced the feisty character of Sweetie in *Too True to Be Good* (1931). After Charlotte's death in 1943, when Molly offered (October 1945) to come to Ayot St. Lawrence to live with him, Shaw responded: "I have had enough of marriage … No woman shall ever live with me again. Put it out of your very inconsiderate head at once and forever … I should be justified in shooting you if there no other way of preventing you from crashing my gates."[25] In 1948, he wrote: "Do you realize that I am 92, and that I can no longer be of any use or interest to you."[26] And as late as 1949, he urged Molly to remarry her husband, whom she had divorced although they were not estranged.

Shaw's philanderer Charteris says: "I shall have to go on philandering now all my life. No domesticity, no fireside, … Nobody will marry me."[27] But was Shaw a philanderer?

One who engages in love affairs casually or frivolously? With Jenny Patterson it had been a carefully prepared-for learning experience, although one with which he quickly became disenchanted and found some difficulty in ending. Shaw fell madly in love with Florence Farr, Janet Achurch, Stella Campbell, and possibly Molly Tompkins, yet he enjoyed the domestic comforts of marriage living with Charlotte for over 40 years.

One who readily or frequently enters into casual sexual relationships with women? One cannot say that having four affairs in 50 years was especially frequent, and they were hardly casual. He even went so far as risking the end of his marriage to Charlotte in his failed attempt to elope with Stella Campbell. Molly Tompkins, taking advantage of a 70-year-old man's sexual reawakening, flattered him and stoked his ego to advance her faltering career. Despite the painful end to the affair, they remained friends for the rest of his life. He never, so far as we know, engaged in one-night stands or paid for sex with prostitutes, nor did he take advantage of the many young women who pursued him before and during his celibate marriage. While his character might be a philanderer, Shaw never was.

NOTES

1. *The American Heritage Dictionary of the English Language* (Boston, MA: Houghton Mifflin Co.: 1976), 984.
2. *The Oxford Dictionary of English*, Oxford University Press (ebook 2010), Loc. 296738.

3. Josephine Johnson, *Florence Farr: Bernard Shaw's 'New Woman,'* (Totowa, NJ: Rowman and Littlefield, 1975), 55 (Johnson 1975).

4. He later did reviews under the pseudonym Corno Di Bassetto.

5. Biographical information unless otherwise noted is from A.M. Gibbs, *Bernard Shaw: A Life*, (Gainesville, FL: University Press of Florida, 2005) and Michael Holroyd, *Bernard Shaw*, (New York: Random House, 1988), and interviews with Stanley Weintraub, who with 60+ years of Shaw research and scholarship might be considered a virtual GBS encyclopedia (Gibbs 2005; Holroyd 1988).

6. *Shaw: An Autobiography 1856–1898*, Stanley Weintraub, ed., (London, Sydney, Toronto: Max Reinhardt, 1969), 80 (Weintraub 1969).

7. Reproduced in Shaw's *Sixteen Self Sketches*, (London: Constable, 1949). And on dust jacket of Stanley Weintraub's *Bernard Shaw Before His First Play: The Embryo Playwright.* (Greensboro, NC: ELT Press, 2015) (Shaw 1949; Weintraub 2015).

8. Qtd. in Gibbs, 201.

9. Op.cit., 148.

10. Tanner, in the *Don Juan in the Hell* scene and as the socialist author of "The Revolutionist's Handbook," bears a remarkable similarity to the playwright. Tanner's ineffectiveness as a socialist missionary was also seen in Sidney Trefusis in Shaw's last novel, *An Unsocial Socialist.*

11. Holroyd speculates that Jenny Patterson may have had an abortion of Shaw's child (*Holroyd I*, 251). This seems most unlikely, as Shaw had purchased and most likely used condoms and Jenny, at age 45, may have already been in menopause, had never conceived a child before, so far as we know, and saw a medical friend of Shaw's, Kingston Barton. In 1886 a woman seeking an illegal abortion would not have seen an established physician to obtain one. It is likely that she had what was commonly referred to as "women's trouble," which would have necessitated a D&C.

12. Published 1900.

13. *An Unfinished Novel by Bernard Shaw*, Stanley Weintraub, ed. (London: Constable, 1958), 25–26 (Weintraub 1958).

14. *Shaw: An Autobiography 1856—1898 vol. 1*, Selected from his writings by Stanley Weintraub (London: Reinhardt, 1970), 123 (Weintraub 1970).

15. After the rest of her family died, May Morris lived happily at Kelmscott Manor with Mary Lobb, who came to work there as a farm girl during World War 1. See Jan Marsh, *Jane and May Morris: A Biographical Story 1839–1938*, (London: Pandora Press, 1986) (Marsh 1986).

16. In a letter of November 28, 1944, to the *Evening Standard*, in denying the assertion of its critic Beverley Baxter that "the boy [the poet Marchbanks] has no beard, but he was Shaw," Shaw wrote, "I certainly never thought of myself as a model." Qtd. in CP1, 602–603.

17. Gibbs in his biography speculates that the affair may never have been consummated (Gibbs, 157). But their correspondence leaves open the possibility, as does Shaw's unusually supportive relationship with Janet's daughter Nora, for whom he might have been, or thought he might have been, her father. Unable to get permission to publish the letters between Shaw and Janet Achurch, Tullah Innes Hanley converted them into dialogue in the novel *Strange Triangle of G.B.S.* (Boston: Bruce Humphries, Inc., 1956), about "the true, secret love which lasted from his thirty-second to his sixtieth year." The Harry Ransom Humanities Research Centre at the University of Texas, Austin, holds 93 items of correspondence from Shaw to Janet Achurch, and 161 to Charles Charrington. See Dan H. Laurence *Shaw: an Exhibit* (Austin: University of Texas, 1978), item 127 (Laurence 1978).

18. Margot Peters claims that Janet became addicted after being given large doses of morphine during Nora's birth. Margot Peters, "As Lonely as God." In italics. Michael Holroyd Ed. (New York: Holt Rinehart and Winston, 1979), 192 (Peter 1979).

19. For Shaw's interest in the children of his friends, see "Shaw's Children" by Dan H. Laurence in *SHAW: The Annual of Bernard Shaw Studies* Vol. 25 (University Park: The Penn State University Press, 2005), 22–26 (Laurence 2005).

20. "I learn that you and Miss Charrington honored me with a call on Saturday" (*CL* I:493).

21. Hanley says Nora died of influenza (Hanley, 322).

22. Qtd. in G.C.L. DuCann, *The Loves of Bernard Shaw* (New York: Funk & Wagnails, 1963), 184 (DuCann 1963).

23. See Rodelle Weintraub's "The Irish Lady in Shaw's Plays," in *The Shaw Review*, May 1980, and "Shaw's Celibate Marriage: Its Impact on His Plays, "*Cahiers Victoriens & Edouardiens*," No 9/10, October 1979, 37–61, for the influence on Shaw's plays of Charlotte and his marriage to her (Weintraub 1979).

24. Gibbs, 387.

25. *To a Young Actress: The Letters of Bernard Shaw to Molly Tompkins*, Peter Tompkins, ed., (New York: Clarkson N. Potter, 1960), 180 & 184 (Tompkins 1960).

26. Ibid., 186.

27. Act III in the published edition of *The Philanderer* (*CP* I:225).

REFERENCES

DuCann, G.C.L. 1963. *The Loves of Bernard Shaw*. New York: Funk & Wagnails.
Gibbs, A.M. 2005. *Bernard Shaw: A Life*. Gainesville: University Press of Florida.

Holroyd, Michael. 1988. *Bernard Shaw*. New York: Random House.
Johnson, Josephine. 1975. *Florence Farr: Bernard Shaw's New Woman*. Totowa, NJ: Rowman and Littlefield.
Laurence, Dan H. 1978. *Shaw: An Exhibit*. Austin: University of Texas.
Laurence, Dan H. 2005. Shaw's Children. In *SHAW: The Annual of Bernard Shaw Studies*, vol. 25, 22–26. University Park: The Penn State University Press.
Marsh, Jan. 1986. *Jane and May Morris: A Biographical Story 1839–1938*. London: Pandora Press.
Peters, Margot. 1979. As Lonely as God. In *The Genius of Shaw. A Symposium*, ed. Michael Holroyd, 185–199. New York: Holt, Rinehart and Winston.
Shaw, Bernard. 1949. *Sixteen Self Sketches*. London: Constable.
Tompkins, Peter (ed.). 1960. To a Young Actress: The Letters of Bernard Shaw to Molly Tompkins, 180, 184. New York: Clarkson N. Potter.
Weintraub, Rodelle (ed.). 1979. Shaw's Celibate Marriage: Its Impact on His Plays. *Cahiers Victoriens et Edouardiens* 9/10: 37–62.
Weintraub, Stanley. 1970. *Shaw: An Autobiography 1856—1898*, vol. 1, 123. London: Reinhardt.
Weintraub, Stanley. 2015. *Bernard Shaw Before His First Play: The Embryo Playwright*. Greensboro, NC: ELT Press.
Weintraub, Stanley (ed.). 1958. *An Unfinished Novel by Bernard Shaw*, 25–26. London: Constable.
Weintraub, Stanley (ed.). 1969. *Shaw: An Autobiography 1856–1898*. New York: Weybright and Talley.

Author Biography

Rodelle Weintraub has been involved in Shaw studies for more than half a century. She was assistant editor of the *Shaw Bulletin* and *Shaw Review* (now the *SHAW Journal*). The Shaw plays she has edited for publication include *Captain Brassbound's Conversion*, *Arms and the Man* and *John Bull's Other Island*. She is also editor of *Fabian Feminist: Bernard Shaw and Woman*, and has written numerous articles. She is married to Stanley Weintraub and has assisted him in his research and as an editor.

.

CHAPTER 6

Shaw's Salvation Trilogy: *Man and Superman, John Bull's Other Island, Major Barbara*

Michel W. Pharand

In a press release published in *The Sun* (New York) on December 26, 1915, Shaw described *Man and Superman, John Bull's Other Island*, and *Major Barbara*, with characteristic immodesty, as "a group of plays of exceptional weight and magnitude on which the reputation of the author as a serious dramatist was first established" (*CPP* II:193). Written within a few years of one another—1901–1902, 1904, and 1905, respectively— the plays may owe some of their "weight and magnitude" to the controversial themes that, by the turn of the century, had become typical Shavian fare: politics and power, religion and nationalism, the Life Force and Creative Evolution, the importance of money, the nature of love and of the sex instinct, and the role of marriage.

To believe Jack Tanner (in *Man and Superman*), "Marriage is a mantrap baited with simulated accomplishments and delusive idealizations." Ironic as always, Shaw rounds out his trilogy with marriage—specifically, marriages yet to come, some of them destined to be, perhaps, misalliances.

M.W. Pharand (✉)
Kingston, Canada
e-mail: michelpharand@yahoo.com

© The Author(s) 2017
R.A. Gaines (ed.), *Bernard Shaw's Marriages and Misalliances*,
Bernard Shaw and His Contemporaries,
DOI 10.1057/978-1-349-95170-3_6

89

(Not so Shaw's own marriage to Charlotte Payne-Townshend, who he had married in 1898, only a few years prior to beginning *Man and Superman*: their union lasted over four decades, until Charlotte's death in 1943.)

As we shall see, Shaw in these three plays treats marriage as a commodity, as a means to an end, one that might be termed "salvation" in the word's secular meaning: the preservation or deliverance from harm, ruin, or loss. In *Man and Superman*, that end is "a father for the Superman!" via the triumph of the Life Force, with the marriage-vilifying Tanner finally succumbing to Ann Whitefield. (Conversely, Violet Robinson's secret marriage to Hector Malone, Jr., is a love match that disregards marriage-as-commodity, that is, Hector's father's will disinherit him if he does not marry into the aristocracy.) In *John Bull*, Nora Reilly will marry future Member of Parliament Tom Broadbent and in due course bolster his career. And in *Major Barbara*, Adolphus Cusins and Barbara Undershaft will join forces to ensure the ongoing success of Barbara's father's armaments factory, Cusins at the helm and Barbara attempting to save the souls of its workers.

In all three plays, then, marriage and its attendant domesticity (and possible progeny) are portrayed by Shaw as world-bettering processes that will eventually bring about "salvation": of the human race, of political success, and of private enterprise. Lofty goals—especially for a "mantrap"!

MAN AND SUPERMAN: MARRIAGE AND THE LIFE FORCE

In his 1903 Epistle Dedicatory, Shaw explains to drama critic A.B. Walkley that he accepted the latter's challenge of writing a "Don Juan play" because "we have no modern English plays in which the natural attraction of the sexes for one another is made the mainspring of the action" (*CPP* II:495). This natural attraction—which Don Juan himself will call "a perfectly simple impulse of my manhood towards her womanhood"—is the crux of *Man and Superman*, and it is closely allied with marriage and with what Jack Tanner calls, in his appended Revolutionist's Handbook, "conjugation."

What Shaw illustrates in this play, then, is the conflicted relationship between personal freedom, sexual attraction, and married domesticity, as well as the role of moral propriety and financial security. His Epistle informs the reader that in "a trumpery story of modern London life … the ordinary man's business is to get means to keep up the position and habits of a gentleman, and the ordinary woman's business is to get married." And she "must marry because the race must perish without her travail" (*CPP* II:504–508). In this play, what one might term the procreative imperative is embodied in Ann Whitefield, herself standing for all females: "Ann is Everywoman," Shaw reminds us (*CPP* II:519).

The play opens with Roebuck Ramsden informing young Octavius Robinson that his dear friend, the recently deceased Whitefield, had hoped young Tavy would one day marry his daughter Ann. Although it is soon apparent that they are as mismatched as are Candida and Marchbanks in *Candida* (1894)—Tavy and Marchbanks are romantic sentimentalists—neither is Ann temperamentally suited to Tanner, described in Shaw's stage directions as an independent, "*restless, excitable ... megalomaniac.*" Ramsden dismisses her as a mere "young and inexperienced woman," and even Ann herself admits to Tanner that "I do not think any young unmarried woman should be left quite to her own guidance" (*CPP* II:541, 546, 551). Hence Tanner's panic at the revelation that he, a self-proclaimed revolutionary, has been appointed Ann's co-guardian (with Ramsden): "I cant control her; and she can compromise me as much as she likes. I might as well be her husband." He enjoins Tavy: "you must marry her after all and take her off my hands" (*CPP* II:543–545).

Shaw's concept of the Life Force is perhaps nowhere more prominently illustrated than in this play—whose subtitle is, after all, "A Comedy and a Philosophy"—and Ann Whitefield is its earthly incarnation. A woman's purpose, Tanner warns Tavy, "is neither her happiness nor yours, but Nature's. ... her highest purpose and greatest function—to increase, multiply, and replenish the earth" (*CPP* II:556, 560). Shaw expounds at length on this idea in the "Don Juan in Hell" scene, with Tanner's alter ego explaining to Doña Ana (Ann's avatar) that "Sexually, Woman is Nature's contrivance for perpetuating its highest achievement. Sexually, Man is Woman's contrivance for fulfilling Nature's behest in the most economical way" (*CPP* II:659). According to Don Juan, one of Nature's highest achievements is "the philosophic man: he who seeks in contemplation to discover the inner will of the world, in invention to discover the means of fulfilling that will, and in action to do that will by the so-discovered means" (*CPP* II:664). Don Juan speaks for Shaw in this much-quoted passage: "I tell you that as long as I can conceive something better than myself I cannot rest easy unless I am striving to bring it into existence or clearing the way for it. That is the law of my life. That is the working within me of Life's incessant aspiration to higher organization, wider, deeper, intenser self-consciousness, and clearer self-understanding" (*CPP* II:680–681). The culmination and embodiment of that process will be a Superman, and when told by The Devil that this being has yet to be created, Doña Ana exclaims, "Then my work is not yet done. I believe in the Life to Come. A father! a father for the Superman!" (*CPP* II:689) (More about this "Hell scene" later.)

Those, then, are the intellectual and theoretical underpinnings of the workings of the Life Force through nature via woman. The moral and social ones are marriage and money, which Shaw critiques by introducing the sub-plot of a marriage that, albeit a *fait accompli*, is being kept a secret. When it is disclosed that Tavy's unmarried younger sister Violet is pregnant, consternation abounds, her brother calling the unknown impregnator "a heartless scoundrel" and Ramsden echoing with "a damned scoundrel"—in other words, a sexually unscrupulous cad. And yet they insist that the culprit make reparation by marrying Violet. "So we are to marry your sister to a damn scoundrel by way of reforming her character!" Tanner exclaims. "On my soul, I think you are all mad" (*CPP* II:562).

In this instance, marriage becomes the hypocritical barometer of respectability, which must be upheld no matter what the consequences to the parties involved. Tanner later dismisses the righteous indignation displayed by Tavy and Ramsden as "their silly superstitions about morality and propriety" (*CPP* II:581). Perhaps. Yet readers and audiences would have known that the stakes were serious, not silly. The "Victorian" era may have ended with the Queen's death a mere six months before Shaw, on July 2, 1901, began mapping out the scenario for *Man and Superman*, but the unwed Violet faced a lifetime of ignominy for having borne a "bastard."[1]

When she finally discloses that she is in fact married (but has kept things dark for her husband's sake), Tanner tells Ramsden that he "must cower before the wedding ring like the rest of us" (*CPP* II:584). Violet's integrity and virtue have been intact all along.

This secret union affords Shaw some fine opportunities to have his characters expound on the nature of marriage. When Tanner informs Hector Malone (Violet's husband, unbeknownst to Tanner) that Violet is married, Malone replies, "Surely marriage should ennoble a man." To which Tanner counters: "Get married and try. You may find it delightful for a while: you certainly wont find it ennobling" (*CPP* II:605–606). In fact nobility, or social rank, is at the heart of the father–son conflict, as Malone *père* insists that his son marry a woman with a social pedigree:

"Here's my silly old dad ... who would shew me the door for marrying the most perfect lady in England merely because she has no handle to her name. Of course it's just absurd" (*CPP* II:607).

Malone Senior explains his rationale to Violet, whose marriage to his son he ignores: "Let [Hector] pick out the most historic house, castle, or abbey that England contains. The very day he tells me he wants it for a wife worthy of its traditions, I buy it for him, and give him the means of keeping it up." He readily admits that his own grandmother came from common stock: she was "a barefooted Irish girl. ... Let him raise himself socially with my money or raise somebody else: so long as there is a social profit somewhere, I'll regard my expenditure as justified. But there must be a profit for someone. A marriage with you would leave things just where they are" (*CPP* II:703). We soon learn that Malone's "prejudice" (as Violet calls it) in obtaining a titled bride for his son has its origin in deep-seated, if wrongheaded, political motives: "Me father was starved dead; and I was starved out to America in my mother's arms. English rule drove me and mine out of Ireland. Well, you can keep Ireland. Me and me like are coming back to buy England; and we'll buy the best of it. I want no middle class properties and no middle class women for Hector" (*CPP* II:704).

Before Malone learns the truth, however, we come to Act III, the "Don Juan in Hell" interlude, where sex and marriage are discussed at some length, as they have been by Shaw's *raisonneur* Jack Tanner, who has already debated the nature and aftermath of marriage, and the conflict between the mystical and the mundane aspects of being in love. "It is a woman's business to get married as soon as possible," he had told Tavy, "and a man's to keep unmarried as long as he can." Shaw himself followed Jack's precept, as he married at the rather late age of 42.

To Tavy's reply that he "cannot write without inspiration. And nobody can give me that except Ann," Tanner reminded him that Petrarch and Dante saw very little of Laura and Beatrice: "They never exposed their idolatry to the test of domestic familiarity; and it lasted them to their graves. Marry Ann; and at the end of the week youll find no more inspiration in her than in a plate of muffins." Ann will tell Tavy (in the last act) that she will "have to live up always to your idea of my divinity; and I dont think I could do that if we were married" (*CPP* II:592–593, 714).

These views are echoed by Tanner's avatar Don Juan, who is as garrulous with Doña Ana as his earthly counterpart is with Ann, and as fiercely against marriage: "The Life Force respects marriage only because marriage is a contrivance of its own to secure the greatest number of children and the closest care of them. ... And a woman seeking a husband is the most unscrupulous of all bears of prey." (Tanner has compared Ann to a boa constrictor and a lioness.) "The confusion of marriage with morality has done more to destroy the conscience of the human race than any other single error. ... marriage is a mantrap baited with simulated accomplishments and delusive idealizations" (*CPP* II:670). To believe the Don, all marriages are misalliances.

When Ana insists that "most marriages are perfectly comfortable," Juan compares the conjugal arrangement to that of galley slaves: "Many such companionships, they tell me, are touchingly affectionate; ... But that does not make a chain a desirable ornament nor the galleys an abode of bliss. Those who talk most about the blessings of marriage and the constancy of its vows are the very people who declare that if the chain were broken and the prisoners left free to choose, the whole social fabric would fly asunder." Virtuous women have done their best "to bend Man's mind wholly towards honorable love as the highest good, and to understand by honorable love romance and beauty and happiness in the possession of beautiful, refined, delicate, affectionate women. You have taught women to value their own youth, health, shapeliness, and refinement above all things. Well, what place have squalling babies and household cares in this exquisite paradise of the senses and emotions?" (*CPP* II:671–672).

He later grumbles that the purpose of "breeding the race ... to heights now deemed superhuman ... is now hidden in a mephitic cloud of love and romance and prudery and fastidiousness." This, however, may one day not be the case: "The plain spoken marriage services of the vernacular Churches will no longer be abbreviated and half suppressed as indelicate. The sober decency, earnestness, and authority of their declaration of the real purpose of marriage will be honored and accepted, whilst their romantic vowings and pledgings and until-death-do-us-partings and the like will be expunged as unbearable frivolities" (*CPP* II:674).

Juan explains to Ana that while on earth he was told by prospective inamoratas that they would countenance his advances "provided they were honorable." This, he learned, meant "that I desired her continual companionship, counsel, and conversation to the end of my days, and would take a most solemn oath to be always enraptured by them above all, that I would turn my back on all other women for ever for her sake." He was prostrated, he says, by their "extraordinary irrelevance," replying "that unless the lady's character and intellect were equal or superior to my own, her conversation must degrade and her counsel mislead me; that her constant companionship might, for all I knew, become intolerably tedious to me; that I could not answer for my feelings for a week in advance, much less to the end of my life; ... that, finally, my proposals to her were wholly unconnected with any of these matters, and were the outcome of a perfectly simple impulse of my manhood towards her womanhood" (*CPP* II:676–677).[2]

This unearthly interlude—in which Juan (speaking for Shaw) has debunked the romantic idealism of marriage—ushers in the final confrontation between Tanner and Ann in the last act. But first comes Hector's revelation of his secret marriage to Violet, which leads Malone to disinherit his son: "She's married a beggar." And to show he is in earnest about finding employment and will not need an inheritance, Hector hands over his father's latest remittance (a thousand dollars). Yet when Tavy and Tanner offer to help Hector financially, Malone does an about-face: "Who wants your duty money? Who should he draw on but his own father? ... I take it all back. She's just the wife you want: there!" (*CPP* II:709–710). Violet then asks him for the remittance, which Malone duly hands over; from now on, she will control the finances: "Y'understand that this is only a bachelor allowance" (*CPP* II:711).

The debate between Ann and Tanner resumes with increased fervor and builds in vehemence during the closing minutes of the play, with Jack struggling in vain against the grip of the Life Force. "It seems to me that I shall presently be married to Ann whether I like it myself or not," he tells her mother, only to counter moments later that "[*emphatically*] I havnt the slightest intention of marrying her" (*CPP* II:720). He tells her that Ann is a "coquette" ("a woman who rouses passions she has no intention of gratifying"), a "bully," a "liar," and, because "she habitually and unscrupulously uses her personal fascination to make men give her what she wants," she is "almost something for which I know no polite name." Then, alone with Ann, he is adamant: "[*explosively*]: Ann: I will not marry you. Do you hear? I wont, wont, wont, wont, WONT marry you." And yet, wavering again: "everybody treats the thing as settled. It's in the air." In fact, "I have a frightful feeling that I shall let myself be married because it is the world's will that you should have a husband" (*CPP* II:725).

But before surrendering, Tanner fires a final volley: "Marriage is to me apostasy, profanation of the sanctuary of my soul, violation of my

manhood, sale of my birthright, shameful surrender, ignominious capitulation, acceptance of defeat." Yet he knows he is weakening: "The Life
Force. I am in the grip of the Life Force" (*CPP* II:726). In fact, he has
apparently had no choice from the outset. Ann reveals that her father,
prior to drawing up his will, had asked her whom she would have as a
guardian. "I chose you!" she tells Tanner, who now realizes "The trap
was laid from the beginning." Ann agrees: "[*concentrating all her magic*]
From the beginning—from our childhood—for both of us—by the Life
Force" (*CPP* II:728).

Tanner finally succumbs: "I love you. The Life Force enchants me:
I have the whole world in my arms when I clasp you. But I am fighting for my freedom, for my honor, for my self, one and indivisible"
(*CPP* II:729). From this point the dialogue increases in frantic intensity, and Shaw's stage directions provide not-so-subtle clues as to its
powerful sexual subtext, with Ann in Tanner's arms, Tanner "*groan-
ing*" and Ann "*panting*" and, she tells him, on the verge of fainting—
which she does moments after all the other characters arrive: "I have
promised to marry Jack," she says, and then "*swoons*" and faints, caus-
ing a general panic on stage.

Tanner later takes Tavy aside and tells him: "I never asked her. It is
a trap for me." The play closes with Jack's peroration to the assembled
crowd, including a revived Ann: "What we have both done this afternoon is to renounce happiness, renounce freedom, renounce tranquillity,
above all, renounce the romantic possibilities of an unknown future for
the cares of a household and a family." He enjoins the gathering that
any wedding gifts "will be instantly sold," including "copies of Patmore's
Angel In The House in extra morocco," with proceeds going to circulat-
ing free copies of his "Revolutionist's Handbook" (*CPP* II:732).

That Shaw makes a point of naming Coventry Patmore's popular narrative poem *The Angel in the House* (1854, expanded often until 1862) is
interesting, as its topic is the nature of ideal womanhood. The expression
"angel in the house" soon became widespread shorthand for a woman
who embodied that ideal: a mother selflessly devoted to her children and
a wife dutifully submissive to her husband. Ann, we are meant to understand—Shaw's audience (and readers) would have known Patmore's
book—will be no such wife.[3]

Although the stage play ends here, "The Revolutionist's Handbook,"
Tanner's credo—and, in part, Shaw's—has a section on "Property and
Marriage" that concludes with a prediction, one that seems to run

counter to his own capitulation to conjugal life: "the progressive modification of the marriage contract will be continued until it is no more onerous nor irrevocable than any ordinary commercial deed of partnership." Moreover, "one of the changes in public opinion demanded by the need for the Superman ... is nothing less than the dissolution of the present necessary association of marriage with conjugation, which most unmarried people regard as the very diagnostic of marriage." In truth, it "is essential to nothing but the propagation of the race; and the moment that paramount need is provided for otherwise than by marriage conjugation, from Nature's creative point of view, [it] ceases to be essential in marriage."

The section concludes with a summary of marriage's "two functions of regulating conjugation and supplying a form of domesticity," and "domesticity is the only one of the two which is essential to the existence of marriage, because conjugation without domesticity is not marriage at all, whereas domesticity without conjugation is still marriage; in fact it is necessarily the actual condition of all fertile marriages during a great part of their duration, and of some marriages during the whole of it" (*CPP* II:746–748). These views are reflected in Shaw's own marriage, a domestic partnership that was—at least according to Shaw—celibate by mutual agreement.

Interestingly, the Handbook's "Maxims for Revolutionists" has a section devoted to "Marriage," an institution whose "essential function," we read, "is the continuance of the race, as stated in the Book of Common Prayer. The accidental function of marriage is the gratification of the amoristic sentiment of mankind. The artificial sterilization of marriage makes it possible for marriage to fulfill its accidental function whilst neglecting its essential one. The most revolutionary invention of the XIX century was the artificial sterilization of marriage" (*CPP* II:784–785).[4] (We know from his early diaries that Shaw purchased—and presumably used—condoms.)

That Jack Tanner and Ann Whitefield will avail themselves of that invention seems unlikely, however, as only "conjugation" would ensure the possible emergence of a Superman. As one critic has phrased it, "All of Act IV (as indeed the whole play) has prepared for Tanner's anagnorisis, the recognition of his love for Ann, his husbandness, above all his fatherness."[5] Thus, despite Jack's inveighing against marriage as surrender, capitulation, and defeat—a true "battle of the sexes"—the Life Force, in this instance at least, has triumphed.

JOHN BULL'S OTHER ISLAND: MARRIAGE AND POLITICS

Although the treatment of marriage in *John Bull's Other Island* and *Major Barbara* is far from as ideologically thorough or as thematically pervasive as it is in *Man and Superman*, the plays nonetheless offer further insights into Shaw's views on the topic. In the case of *John Bull's Other Island*, the scrutiny is on marriage as it relates to one's career: in this case, politics.

Civil engineer Tom Broadbent proposes to go to Ireland to develop a large estate, complete with hotel and golf club, for the Land Development Syndicate. His business partner in this grandiose venture is the restless Irishman Larry Doyle, who, after an absence of 18 years, will revisit his native land, where his childhood sweetheart, the rather frail and insecure Nora Reilly, has been waiting for him. Yet according to Larry, Nora "has a fortune": £40 per annum. "A girl with a dowry of *five* pounds calls it a fortune in Rosscullen. Whats more, £40 a year is a fortune there; and Nora Reilly enjoys a good deal of social consideration as an heiress on the strength of it" (*CPP* II:917).[6]

Despite their history—Larry and Nora were 17 when her father died and she moved in with Larry's family—"Nora would wait until she died of old age sooner than ask my intentions or condescend to hint at the possibility of my having any," Larry tells Broadbent. "You dont know what Irish pride is" (*CPP* II:919). Nora, who is described as *"slight"* and *"weak,"* possesses a *"comparative delicacy of manner"* and *"caressing plaintive Irish melody of her speech,"* giving her a charm that makes her, for Broadbent at least, *"an attractive woman, whom he would even call ethereal."* Doyle, on the other hand, finds her *"helpless, useless, almost sexless, ... an incarnation of everything in Ireland that drove him out of it"* (*CPP* II:927). This Broadbent–Nora–Larry triangle mirrors, to a degree, the Tanner–Ann–Tavy relationship of *Man and Superman*, in that the women possess an ineluctable attraction (Nora's is more unconscious than Ann's) for the men, with two of them falling under their spell.

In Nora's case, it is Broadbent who, upon first meeting her, is instantly enraptured. It is love at first sound: he has been bewitched, he tells her, by "the charm of your Irish voice." Nora (like Tanner in dealing with Tavy's infatuation) is more realistic: "Youre breaking your heart about me already, I daresay, after seeing me for two minutes in the dark," she tells him. "Is it making love to me you are?" To which Broadbent replies, "all the harps of Ireland are in your voice." And although he reassures her that she should "accept the fact that I'm an Englishman as a guarantee that I am not a man to act hastily or romantically," only moments later he asks, "Will you be my wife." "Deed I wont. The idea! ... I think youre not accustomed to potcheen punch," of which Broadbent had had a mere two tumblers. He is now aghast at his own lack of self-control: "I must be drunk; frightfully drunk; for your voice drove me out of my senses," and he apologizes for his "disgusting state." He is so tipsy that Nora has to help him walk home (*CPP* II:941–945).

The following day, he tells Larry that "potcheen goes to the heart, not to the head" (*CPP* II:954) and reiterates his declaration to Nora: "I was in earnest last night. ... and I am prepared to wait as long as you like, provided you will give me some small assurance that the answer will not be unfavorable." Following further admissions of love—"you have inspired in me a very strong attachment"—Nora breaks down: "Oh, go away from me: I wont get married at all: what is it but heartbreak and disappointment?" Broadbent goes on, tenacious: "I love you. I want you for my wife. [*In despair*] I cant help your refusing. I'm helpless: I can do nothing." Like Tanner, Broadbent has been seized by the Life Force. Nora gives in to the "*hurt and petulant*" Broadbent: "I think you might understand that though I might choose to be an old maid, I could never marry anybody but you now," she confesses; to which he gives "*a crow of immense relief and triumph.*" Why does Nora give in? When they first met, she now tells him, "I let you be kind to me, and cried in your arms, because I was too wretched to think of anything but the comfort of it. And how could I let any other man touch me after that?" (*CPP* II:1001–1003) Nora, it seems, is driven by a strong personal morality, and in marrying Broadbent she will secure for herself a safe haven for the preservation of her female integrity.

Broadbent's own motives are more mundane—if not opportunistic: "We're not going to have any rows: we're going to have a solid four-square home: man and wife: comfort and common sense. And plenty of affection, eh?" Broadbent (and indeed Shaw) considers marriage an arrangement necessary to both parties' psychological and physiological well-being: "its an absolute necessity of my nature that I should have somebody to hug occasionally. Besides, its good for you: itll plump out your muscles and make em elastic and set up your figure."

Later in the evening, as they walk through the garden, he begins to plan his political campaign: "Youll be a great success as a canvasser, Nora: they call you the heiress; and they'll be flattered no end by your calling, ... I get engaged to the most delightful woman in Ireland; and it turns out that I couldnt have done a smarter stroke of electioneering" (*CPP* II:1004–1007). Broadbent may be in love, but his emotional drive has now been eclipsed by his political ambition, with his own Life Force propelling him to form an alliance that will further his career. Whether his stage-managing of Nora's future role as helpmate will result in a misalliance or whether the union will succumb under what Jack Tanner called "the cares of a household and a family," no one can know.

Larry, too, sees advantages in Nora marrying Broadbent: "Nora Reilly was a person of very little consequence to me or anyone else outside this miserable little hole. But Mrs. Tom Broadbent will be a person of very considerable consequence indeed. Play your new part well," he advises her, "and there will be no more neglect, no more loneliness, ... but real life and real work and real cares and real joys among real people: solid English life in London, the very centre of the world. You will find your work cut out for you keeping Tom's house and entertaining Tom's friends and getting Tom into parliament; but it will be worth the effort" (*CPP* II:1009). Marriage, apparently, will widen Nora's horizons to an unimaginable degree.

And although her future now appears to be in London, she will also, presumably, support and assist her husband in turning her small town into a prosperous and vibrant community: "I shall raise wages," boasts Broadbent. "I shall found public institutions"—among them a library, polytechnic, gymnasium, and cricket club—"perhaps an art school. I shall make a Garden city of Rosscullen: the round tower shall be thoroughly repaired and restored" (*CPP* II:1015). This is not the advent of a Superman but the birth of a Supertown—almost on the order of Andrew Undershaft's Perivale St. Andrews in *Major Barbara*.

If marriage in *Man and Superman* was the inevitable result of the workings of the Life Force on a recalcitrant Jack Tanner, in *John Bull's Other Island* it is the natural outcome of Tom Broadbent's determination to succeed professionally. Whereas one is led to believe that Ann Whitefield will be no angel in the house, one cannot be so sure about Nora Broadbent.

MAJOR BARBARA: MARRIAGE AND BUSINESS

As it is in *John Bull*, marriage in *Major Barbara* is related to social prosperity, financial success, and, in this instance, success in business. The play opens with Lady Britomart Undershaft predicting to her only son Stephen that Charles Lomax, her daughter Sarah's fiancé, 10 years hence "will be a millionaire at 35." For the moment, however, he has a mere £800 a year, and "Sarah will have to find at least another £800 a year for the next ten years; and even then they will be as poor as church mice." (Everything being relative, of course: recall Nora Reilly's £40 a year!) Meanwhile, Lady Britomart's other daughter Barbara, having joined the Salvation Army,[7] "lives on a pound a week," her mother claiming that she "will need at least £2000 a year." Her fiancé, Adolphus Cusins, although impecunious, has impeccable intellectual credentials as a professor of Greek. According to Lady Britomart, "nobody can say a word against Greek: it stamps a man at once as an educated gentleman" (*CPP* III:70–71).

As with *Man and Superman, Major Barbara* is full of secrets and revelations. Lady Britomart informs Stephen that his father, munitions magnate Andrew Undershaft, "broke the law when he was born: his parents were not married" (*CPP* III:73). She enlightens her son on his dubious family pedigree, which can be traced to the reign of James I, when a foundling was adopted as an armorer and gun maker. Ever since, the cannon business has been left to an adopted foundling, who married and always adopted and trained a foundling to succeed him in business.

Summoned by his rather imperious wife (her daughters now need dowries), the absentee industrialist returns home after many years—so many that he fails to recognize his own progeny! The awkward reunion is soon followed by intense discussion of his profession. Undershaft has no qualms about proclaiming himself "a profiteer in mutilation and murder" in charge of a "death and devastation factory"—one that Cusins, upon completing a tour of the Perivale St. Andrews munitions plant and housing facilities, declares "horribly, frightfully, immorally, unanswerably perfect" (*CPP* III:89, 153, 158). This garden city of prosperous homes and happy employees is a far cry from the impoverished West Ham shelter where Barbara toils amidst the indigent.

If Undershaft has succeeded in business, he has failed in marriage: the magnanimous employer is an estranged husband and father. His courtliness—"Time has stood still with you," he tells Lady Britomart—soon gives way to bewilderment: his children are now strangers to him. Why, one could ask, did the Undershafts remain married? Although wealthy enough to have ended his marriage through the courts, the social cost of divorce—in a word, scandal—would have been too high even for Undershaft.[8]

But the more pressing question in the play is: who will take over the family business? The only candidate appears to be Adolphus Cusins, whose eligibility, we learn, rests on a legal technicality: as his parents' marriage, although legal in Australia, is not so in England, "in this island I am consequently a foundling" (*CPP* III:165). This revelation immediately leads to a bidding war: Undershaft offers him £1000 a year; Cusins asks for £2500 a year for 2 years, but wants another £5000 if he succeeds in business. Undershaft offers him half, then three-fifths. It is agreed: Cusins will assume control of the armament factory, but with one proviso: "I shall sell cannons to whom I please and refuse them to whom I please." Undershaft, who has always lived by his motto, "Unashamed," dismisses that idea as "morality mongering" (*CPP* III:169). Still, Cusins may yet summon the Life Force within him and become a world betterer, provided he curtail the indiscriminate distribution of deadly weapons.

However, the issue of marriage is by no means settled. Sounding as conflicted about wedlock as Tanner, Cusins tells Undershaft: "I don't like marriage: I feel intensely afraid of it; and I dont know what I shall do with Barbara or what she will do with me. But I feel that I and nobody else must marry her" (*CPP* III:118). As tempting as Undershaft's entreaties may be, Cusins remains insecure about what Barbara will think of his taking over the family munitions business: "But perhaps Barbara will not marry me if I make the wrong choice," he tells Undershaft, who replies rather unhelpfully, "Perhaps not" (*CPP* III:178). Yet even Barbara, who has lived a very comfortable life thanks to her father's financial support, needs money to save souls. Although she had refused the small fortune he had offered her to help keep the West Ham shelter from closing down—she considered the money tainted—Barbara nonetheless tells Cusins that, had he refused her father's offer, "I should have given you up and married the man who accepted it" (*CPP* III:183). For Barbara, the end apparently does justify the means.

Like Broadbent and Nora in *John Bull*, Barbara and Cusins are poised to form a successful professional partnership. Although having accepted to live on the profits of armament sales, Barbara will nonetheless remain true to her strong Christian morality: her future husband will presumably make judicious (moral) choices in selecting his business partners, while Barbara Cusins, in turn, will have every opportunity to evangelize his employees. The couple can now begin their new life together "unashamed."

Marriage as Compromise

Shaw inaugurated the new century with three plays that close with the promise of future marital unions. Whether they will be happy and successful ones is another matter. Although as the curtains fall the unions cannot be deemed "misalliances" in the sense of being "unhappy or unworkable" (as the word is usually defined), the question of long-term compatibility remains. Our three couples will have to make compromises: Jack Tanner must give up his view of marriage as "apostasy" and "profanation" and pass "the test of domestic familiarity"; Nora Broadbent must encourage and support her husband's social and political aspirations; and Adolphus Cusins must adhere to his ethical (pacifist) principles in running his munitions business.

If all this happens, then all three marriages have a strong potential for world betterment: nothing less than the birth of better (Super)humans, social improvements through political reform, and the perpetuation of world peace through maintaining the balance of power among nations. No wonder Shaw called *Man and Superman, John Bull's Other Island,* and *Major Barbara* "plays of exceptional weight and magnitude."

Notes

1. *Post factum* legitimization of an illegitimate child would occur only with the passage of the Legitimacy Act 1926, which allowed that child to inherit on the intestacy of his parents; a child had to be legitimized by the subsequent marriage of his or her parents, provided neither parent had been married to a third party (hence an adulterous relationship) at the time of the child's birth.
2. In one of his many grandiloquent speeches, Tanner had told Ann that he believed "the first duty of manhood and womanhood is a Declaration of Independence" (*CPP* II: 599).
3. Neither was Charlotte Shaw, but she was a perennial, crucial helpmate to Shaw's career (as Nora Reilly will be to Tom Broadbent's in *John Bull's Other Island*).
4. E. Lambert and Sons (founded 1877) became the leading early manufacturer of condoms in Britain. Joan Lane, *A Social History of Medicine* (Abingdon, UK: Routledge, 2001), 38. For Shaw's relationship with birth control advocate Marie Stopes, see Chap. 10 (Lane 2001).
5. John A. Bertolini, *The Playwrighting Self of Bernard Shaw* (Carbondale and Edwardsville: Southern Illinois University Press, 1991), 50 (Bertolini 1991).

6. Shaw, like Doyle an Irish expatriate, married his own Irish heiress.
7. The Salvation Army (founded 1865) was a mere 40 years old when *Major Barbara* was written.
8. Obtaining a divorce at this time was expensive and difficult, and its aftermath often humiliating. A man could "petition the court" for a divorce on the basis of his wife's adultery, which had to be proved (along with the absence of collusion), while a woman was required to prove an additional aggravating factor (such as rape or incest). Moreover, as one could obtain a divorce only in London's High Court, where proceedings were public, scandalous personal details became common knowledge. For more on this topic, see Chap. 2 and Appendix B2.

REFERENCES

Bertolini, John A. 1991. *The Playwrighting Self of Bernard Shaw*. Carbondale and Edwardsville: Southern Illinois University Press.
Lane, Joan. 2001. *A Social History of Medicine*. Abingdon, UK: Routledge.

AUTHOR BIOGRAPHY

Michel W. Pharand, formerly Adjunct Associate Research Professor of Arts and Science at Queen's University in Kingston, Ontario, Canada, is general editor of *Benjamin Disraeli Letters IX: 1865–1867* (2013) and *X: 1868* (2014), and advisory editor for Broadview Press, for *ELT: English Literature in Transition, 1880–1920*, and for Palgrave Macmillan's Bernard Shaw and His Contemporaries series. He is the author of *Bernard Shaw and the French* (2000) and editor of Robert Graves's *The Greek Myths* (2001), *Bernard Shaw and His Publishers* (2009), and of *Bernard Shaw on Religion* (2016).

CHAPTER 7

Marriage and Mating in the Plays of Bernard Shaw and Granville Barker, 1908–1911

Peter Gahan

> LORD SUMMERHAYS: *The great question: which particular young man some*
> *young woman will mate with.*
> PERCIVAL: *As if it mattered!*
> Bernard Shaw, *Misalliance* (1910: 238)

INTRODUCTION: MARRIAGE AND FAMILY LIFE

Critics have generally failed to appreciate the scale of what Bernard Shaw achieved with the group of full-length marriage or courtship plays, *Getting Married* (1908), *Misalliance* (1910), and *Fanny's First Play* (1911).[1] Written in spite of reviewers' resistance to his practically *sui generis* new type of theatre, they provide an excellent opportunity for understanding Shaw's distinctive dramaturgy.[2] Shaw confronts head-on criticisms that his drama was all talk, or that in contravening long-established rules of playwriting, especially concerning plot making, they should not be considered legitimate plays. He reflexively integrates talk,

P. Gahan (✉)
Los Angeles, USA
e-mail: pgahan@me.com

© The Author(s) 2017
R.A. Gaines (ed.), *Bernard Shaw's Marriages and Misalliances*,
Bernard Shaw and His Contemporaries,
DOI 10.1057/978-1-349-95170-3_7

105

language, reading, and writing, as well as the origins of western drama in Ancient Greece, into these plays' highly intricate thematic and formal structures, before finally launching a full-scale satire on London theatre critics in *Fanny's First Play*'s frame play.

In adding Harley Granville Barker's *The Madras House* (1910), written in tandem with *Misalliance*, the group becomes an informal tetralogy showcasing the non-commercial New Drama. All four plays are based on sartorial metaphoric foundations, belonging in a literary tradition that includes such diverse works as Swift's *Tale of a Tub*, Carlyle's *Sartor Resartus*, and H.G. Wells's *The Misery of Boots*. In the theatre, where costume is so important, such metaphoric use of clothes goes right back to the Athenian playwrights. Aristophanes in his comedy *Acharnians*, for example, satirized Euripides as the hoarder of old costumes because the latter often chose to clothe the gods in rags; Shaw draws on both Athenian dramatists.

Set on a wedding day, everyone in *Getting Married* is dressed up—with the exception (Shaw's irony to the fore) of the bride. Rather than the expected wedding dress with veil and orange blossoms, Edith wears a *"dressing-jacket and petticoat"* (*CPP* III:589) that acts as a sartorial question mark placed over the dramatic action. Specially costumed are those who perform specific civic roles, like the Bishop, the Sexton, the General, an Alderman, the Lady Mayoress, and her uniformed Beadle (a public official), one of the few Shavian characters to serve a purely symbolic function as bearer of the emphatically phallic mace designating her official civic capacity. In a play that boasts of its return to Greek forms in a prefatory note, this acknowledges the thyrsus (phallic staff) bearers of Dionysus, the Greek God of theatre, like Xanthius in Aristophanes's *Archaians*.[3]

With the exception of the frame play, the Induction and Epilogue to *Fanny's First Play*, where the Count, his footman, and the leading critic wear formal eighteenth-century dress, the sartorial discourse of the other three plays is handled differently. All involve families working in the clothes manufacturing and/or retailing business, underwear in the case of the mischievous playwright's *Misalliance* and *Fanny's First Play*. Underwear points to what is essential but hidden. The metaphoric significance of such in-between or liminal clothing can be understood better once it is realized how Shaw constructs these plays on structural patterns of binary oppositions. In *Misalliance*, one of the most basic is whether something is inside or outside, visible or hidden, or in between. That the main character, John Tarleton, is named after tarlatan, a cotton textile of open-mesh weave that when stiffened can be used as an under layer providing support, for example, to a ballerina's costume, is no coincidence. As a special type of underwear that is neither transparent nor opaque, tarlatan has a liminal status both physically and visually.[4]

Fanny's First Play's basic reflexive conceit, a play within a play, implies doubling and mirroring. Granville Barker's looser, if also unorthodoxly structured *The Madras House* shows the rag trade's treatment of women in relation to marriage under several aspects.

As courtship/marriage plays written at the height of the Suffragette campaign, all four portray sexuality, marriage, children's rights, and divorce within the modern English family. Although the heyday of British imperialism, this same period also saw a surge in support for Fabian socialism, with Shaw and his friend H.G. Wells the avatars of social change. Encouraged to shake off their parents' Victorian shackles and dismantle Britain's notoriously rigid class structure, Young Fabians, many of them women, provided a significant proportion of the new audience for the New Drama.

EQUALITY AND THE WOMAN QUESTION

As socialists, both Shaw, a long-time leader with Sidney Webb of the Fabian Society, and Granville Barker, an Executive Committee member, campaigned for that prerequisite of democracy, social equality, and what—beyond the mere right to vote—it might mean in social and political terms, especially for women in marriage.[5] Abolishing the social barriers to any two people *getting married* would allow, for example, the son of an earl to wed the daughter of a chambermaid. Rather than such a marriage being frowned upon as a *misalliance*, intermarriageability between people from all types of background would be facilitated, rendering the notion of misalliance redundant. Responding to Lillah McCarthy (May 13, 1908), who hoped to play the lead role of the common coal merchant's wife Mrs. George in *Getting Married*, Shaw pointed out that "though the play is so largely a discussion on Marriage, [it] is really a sermon on Equality. There could have been no rebuke whatever to the snobbery of Hotchkiss if Mrs. George had been what you call an uncommon woman."[6]

The status of women in society is inextricably interwoven with equality: women as autonomous sexual and economic beings whether within or outside marriage, or as workers, or as part of the franchise. Each play highlights young, single adult women seeking independence both from their parents and in any prospective marriage by playing an economic role in society. Middle-class Edith and Hypatia in *Getting Married* and *Misalliance*, respectively, along with upper-class Fanny O'Dowda in the frame play and lower-middle-class Margaret Knox in the main play of *Fanny's First Play*, are all daughters in a state of incipient revolt both within and outside the family, wanting more than simply knowing who to mate with, while in *The Madras House* the unmarried factory worker, made pregnant by the owner, remains unashamed.

A surprisingly ignored feature of Shaw's general discourse in the critical literature can be noted: his concern for the soul, like that of the wicked cowboy in his one-act Western melodrama from this same period, *The Shewing-up of Blanco Posnet* (1909).[7] This concern for his characters' souls and their salvation, and, by extension, those of his audience, is part of his fundamentally religious insistence on human equality, distinguishing Shaw to some degree from his modernist literary contemporaries.

In a prefatory note to *Fanny's First Play*, Shaw declares that "the young had better have their *souls* awakened by disgrace, capture by the police, and a month's hard labor, than drift along from their cradles to their graves doing what other people do for no other reason than that other people do it" (*CPP* IV:345). Mrs. George in *Getting Married*, speaking for all women speaking to all men, declaims: "We spent eternity together; and you ask me for a little lifetime more … I gave you your own *soul*: you ask for my body as a plaything. Was it not enough?" (*CPP* III:645). She adds to the Bishop, referring to his sermon on human equality: "You spoke to my *soul*, … you opened the doors of my salvation to me, and now they stand open for ever" (*CPP* III:646). And *Misalliance*'s manufacturer of Tarleton's Underwear imagines, with some sartorial irony, how a painter might paint him: "Tarleton meditating on his destiny. Not in a toga. Not in the trappings of the tragedian or the philosopher. In plain coat and trousers: a man like any other man. And beneath that coat and trousers a human *soul*. Tarleton's Underwear!" (*CPP* IV:173). Granville Barker also in *The Madras House* is concerned with the soul in these Shavian terms when Philip Madras explains to his wife why he wants to forsake his role of running the prosperous Fashion House to go into politics: "To save my *soul* alive"[8] (all italics added).

All the characters in these epochal plays seek their souls' salvation, whether through money ("the one hopeful fact in our civilization," according to Shaw the paradoxical socialist), through marriage, or through a fiercely independent, even reckless pursuit of life's challenges.[9] In opening out for his audience such possibilities and hopes, Shaw became the representative literary artist of the pre–World War I period.

Getting Married

Getting Married, a wedding play as well as a marriage play, commands most attention here. Shaw originally intended to write a double-wedding play, as Margery Morgan explains: "The cast list Shaw wrote in his notebook, when first he started work on this play in Llanbedr in August 1907, includes two engaged couples and so provides for a double wedding."[10] The play as finished early the following year, however, contains only one wedding, and even that does not take place as planned, for the young couple sneak out to get married *offstage*, unbeknownst to both the other *onstage* characters in the play (with the significant exception of the phallic mace-bearing Beadle as witness) and the *offstage* audience of wedding guests, who have by then deserted the cathedral church, as well as that other *offstage* audience in the theatre. Still, as we shall see, more than one wedding might be said to take place.

Fully justifying the label dramatic poet, Shaw often devises a formal or structural technique for a particular play. The delayed impromptu wedding highlights the abstract difference or binary opposition between *on*- and *offstage* symptomatic of the structuring devised for *Getting Married*: one or more significant events happens offstage while the audience attends to onstage proceedings. Learning of the *off-stage* events later enables retrospective understanding, which makes the displacement of simultaneous events temporal as well as spatial, while setting up a thematic relation between *on*- and *offstage* action.

The single set and the stage entrance, in both of which this abstract onstage/offstage distinction is crucial, can be seen as key elements in Shaw's structural design. Like the institution of marriage, the imposing Norman kitchen of the Bishop's Palace is a massive structure "built to last forever"[11] (*CPP* III:547). The stage characters' entrance into the kitchen lies in one corner: "a *vaulted circular chamber* with a *winding stair* leading up through a *tower* to the upper floors of the palace" (*CPP* III:548; italics added). In a play about marriage that makes much of phallic symbols, this requires little explanation. Apart from the Beadle's mace, Mrs. George brandishes a poker in an exchange with Hotchkiss, while much is made of the Bishop's ring, worn on a symbolically phallic finger, with which the sexually wise Mrs. George is summoned. Shaw uses abstract circular and straight shapes as analogues for (the congress of) male and female in marriage, most obviously this circular vault with its tower, and, combining both, the winding stair that the characters wind around as they descend and ascend to make their entrances and exits.

The essence of that old theatrical convention, the stage entrance, for the *offstage* audience's benefit lies precisely in the difference between *onstage* and *offstage* space, in bridging that difference. It assumes greater theatrical, even ritual emphasis as Collins generally formally announces the characters' names on their first entrance from the tower. The entrances of the two most important characters, St. John Hotchkiss, the groom's best man and a snob, and the coal merchant's promiscuous wife, the Lady Mayoress Mrs. George, mark the divisions of this single act play into three parts.[12] Mrs. George, a Shavian version of a *dea ex machina*, makes the grandest stage entrance of all, emerging from the tower's winding stair preceded by her officially costumed Beadle, who announces her impending arrival, while Collins announces her name as she appears.

The play begins with a seemingly innocuous *onstage* conversation on the subject of wedding days between the Bishop's wife while she placidly *reads The Times* and Collins, the greengrocer doubling as wedding planner, who *counts* napkins. Later we learn that *offstage* at more or less the same time the mail was delivered with tracts for Edith the bride and Cecil the bridegroom warning against the dangers of marrying. Unknown both to each other and to the other characters, they *read* the tracts, thus stalling the wedding preparations and thereby providing the motive for the play's action. While more immediately *offstage*, the Bishop in his study-library is *writing* a treatise on the history of marriage, thus reinforcing the play's reflexivity. This insistence on the reading/writing binary is as important as the on-/offstage and circle/straight oppositions to this "disquisitory play," as it is subtitled, on marriage. A good third of the play, the play's *onstage* discussion, will be a failed attempt to *write* a reasonable marriage contract in response to the bridal couple's *reading* of the tracts.[13]

The play's climactic *onstage* scene of Mrs. George in a clairvoyant trance, delivering an oracular revelation as the mouthpiece for womanhood in general in their relations with men, lays bare something of the essence of the mystery of marriage when comprehended *retrospectively* as having taken place at the same time as the *offstage* wedding.

Shaw may have had in mind a *Hieros Gamos*, a ritual sacred marriage with the god and/or the goddess performed by the nominally celibate hierophant and the priestess of the temple during the Classical mysteries.[14] Here, the Bishop of Chelsea as priest of this particular temple is attended by his resolutely celibate sexton, while the incarnation of the goddess or her priestess, the promiscuous Mrs. George, reveals a marriage contemplated years earlier, a spiritual, epistolary marriage between the otherwise sensual Incognita Apassionata (Mrs. George) and the Bishop, happily married with six daughters. The mystical moment of one soul touching another occurred years earlier, when the Bishop preached a sermon on essential human equality, leaving Mrs. George with a lasting sense of self-worth, unfelt previously. In this play of expanding circles of meaning we can retrospectively note another item delivered by the mailman *offstage* that morning: the latest love letter addressed to the Bishop from Incognita Apassionata.[15]

The dramatic relevance of Mrs. George's *onstage* trance and revelation of this sacred marriage to the *offstage* wedding also becomes easier to understand retrospectively, with Shaw's stage direction for the groom suggesting sexual satiation when the now-married couple return *onstage*: *Sykes, with an unnatural air, half foolish, half rakish, as if he had lost all his self-respect and were determined not to let it prey on his spirits, throws himself into a chair at the end of the table near the hearth, and thrusts his hands into his pockets like Hogarth's Rake, without waiting for Edith to sit down* (*CPP* III:648).

What, though, may be lost in this complex counterpoint of dramatic meanings is how Shaw transforms his drama, already heavily inflected by costume and theatricality, into a type of initiation ritual for St. John Hotchkiss. Listening *offstage* before he enters toward the end of the trance, he and the audience become beneficiaries of the revelation on marriage and human equality presented as a religious initiatory mystery rite.

In the play's penultimate scene, with all the other characters *offstage* preparing for Mrs. George's appearance at the wedding breakfast, St. John and Mrs. George in front of the Sexton settle the terms for their proposed union, more profane, yet as chaste as Incognita's mystical marriage with the Bishop. Illustrating the desideratum of intermarriageability, this marrying of social unequals, a coal merchant's wife and an upper-class snob, provides the second of the weddings that Shaw originally planned.

The play as a model of reflexivity concludes with a *coup de théâtre* when the biggest *onstage* stage exit simultaneously becomes the most important of *offstage* stage entrances. Preceded by her mace-bearing Beadle declaiming "Make way there, gentlemen, please. Way for the worshipful the Mayoress," Mrs. George exits with St. John Hotchkiss to ascend the tower's winding stair. This exit becomes a grand entrance, the arrival of the goddess to consecrate the bridal couple's marriage, for that other *offstage* audience: the reassembled wedding guests at the wedding breakfast in the hall above.[16] This marriage discussion play can then end on a doubly ironic grace note of silence: left alone *onstage* the celibate Sexton "resumes his *writing* tranquilly" (*CPP* III:662).

Misalliance

Although *Misalliance*, which concludes with the pairing-off of two couples, is neither a wedding nor a marriage play per se, it surveys attractions and desires that sometimes lead to sexual consummation, mating, or even marriage, and their consequential intergenerational family conflicts.

Shaw's title, which highlights the type of socially denigrated marriage between people of different class backgrounds, provides the key to his politics of equality as applied to this play: the best prospects for human social development, he argued, lay in maximizing intermarriageability by minimizing economic—and therefore class—differences. Shaw's title is also ironic, for though politically he wants to make the idea of social misalliance redundant, he also wants to encourage every other imaginable type of attraction between opposites, as, for example, when the brainy but physically challenged Bentley Summerhayes pairs off with the superb, physically accomplished acrobat and aviatrix Lina Szczepanowska.

For *Misalliance*, Shaw again discovers a formal metaphoric structuring device useful to his thematic concerns on mating. Rather than the abstract onstage/offstage binary of *Getting Married*, he uses binary oppositions here more generally, even in the name of the location, Hindhead, an actual place that Shaw knew well. Oppositions between high and low, or between air and earth, are pervasive throughout: Bentley's nickname Bunny, for example, suggests the earth (rabbits live underground), while Lina, an acrobat and aviatrix, is of the air.

Inside/outside is another important opposition stressed by the set itself, as peculiar yet as thematically important as that of *Getting Married*: a glass conservatory (Shaw requires an architecturally-challenging "*spacious half hemisphere of glass*") literally built into the side wall of the large country house so that it is neither *inside* nor *outside*, or, rather, is both ("*the glass pavilion springs from a bridgelike arch in the wall of the house*"; *CPP* IV:143). Analogous to Shaw's proscenium stage, the interface dividing the audience from the play's diegesis, the pavilion occupies a liminal in-between space while also being both solid and transparent, making *outside* visible from *inside*. Tarleton's Underwear also occupies a liminal position, both sartorially and metaphorically/metaphysically, if we accept Shaw's analogy of it to a soul.

Shaw again adapts to his own purposes Athenian drama's stage device of the *deus ex machina* to facilitate a spectacular entrance for the goddess, when Lina's plane crash-lands into the nearby greenhouse (another glass structure), but breaking "*some of the glass at the top*" of the pavillion on its way.

The play's main focus on sexual attraction leading to marriage, however, is Hypatia, the lively, modern, independent daughter of the house. Frustrated and stifled in her enclosed, talkative family world, Hypatia has been longing for an adventure to fall from the sky to release her pent-up, Maenad-like energies. Facilitated by the obliging playwright, Lina's fellow aviator, Joey Percival, duly drops down, setting the ball rolling for the later climactic sexual chase between Joey and Hypatia, which reveals sexual attraction as the engine that, in its way, powers the world. She pursues him *outside* the house onto the heather on the hill and into the magical woods visible beyond, where he turns to pursue her. The first part of this encounter *inside* the house is witnessed by the providential stranger, the burglar hiding (*half inside*—his body; *half outside*—his head comically popping in and out) in Tarleton's recently delivered Turkish bath! His name Baker suggests Bacchus (Dionysus), the god finally releasing irrational energies amidst all the rational discussion.[17]

In an ironic twist on Cusins's and Barbara's more elevated discussion with Undershaft toward the end of *Major Barbara*, Hypatia bluntly tells her wealthy father to "buy the brute [Joey]" (*CPP* IV:241) for her. The climax of the play, however, follows with Lina Szczepanowska's great tirade against marriage. Sexual proposals have been made to her all afternoon until at last comes the highest insult, Tarleton's son's offer of marriage and his unwitting promise to make her economically dependent. Refusing to be thus bought, this idealized, economically independent woman will remain unmarried so as to continue risking her life once every day to satisfy her own family code of honor.

Throughout, Shaw has played with the criticism that his plays are all words, and especially has Hypatia complained of getting no respite from the perpetual talk in her father's house: "How I envy the animals! They can't talk" (*CPP* IV:175). The play's volubility finally peters out with the loquacious Tarleton for once stuck for words: "Well, I suppose—er—I suppose theres nothing more to be said," to which his daughter Hypatia "fervently" responds: "Thank goodness!" (*CPP* IV:253).

GRANVILLE BARKER'S *THE MADRAS HOUSE*

Granville Barker in *The Madras House* presents an array of predicaments for the modern woman: stifled daughters of a dominating mother in a prosperous upper-middle-class family, sweated employees or independent workers in clothes manufacturing and retail, fashion objects, a deserted wife or an equal partner in marriage. Act I's six unmarried Huxtable daughters ironically refer to *Getting Married*'s six married (by the end of the play) daughters. Tyrannized by their mother, all are frustrated in different ways by their wealthy family circumstances, unable to extricate themselves either to work or to marry. Act II, however, presents just such an economically independent modern, young working-class woman, Marion Yates, an employee of the Huxtable clothes manufacturing firm. She has become pregnant, though she refuses to tell who the father is. A married fellow employee, who has been flirting with her, is wrongly suspected. That this man cannot live with his wife, or even recognize her as such, because she has to live in for her job at the same firm allows Barker the socialist to raise the always problematic labor conditions in the clothes business.

The father is, in fact, Constantine Madras, co-owner with the Huxtables of not only the manufacturing business but also the Madras House, the fashion house that provides the setting of Acts II and III as well as the title of the play. Its boardroom provides the setting for a fashion show, in which the mannequins are objectified in terms of their being merely dress wearers. In interplay dialogue, the boardroom's glass roof nods to *Misalliance*'s conservatory, while John Tarleton is even referred to at one point in the dialogue. Shaw will return the compliment by setting *Fanny's First Play* in Denmark Hill, where Barker's Huxtable family live, while in the frame play the critics will hold a discussion on *The Madras House* and its author.

For the end of Barker's Act III, Shaw wrote a scene (not taken up by Barker) of the elder Madras encountering the young woman he has made pregnant.[18] Shaw has her refuse both his offer of financial help in rearing the child and his acknowledgment as its father. Madras here is Barker's parallel to *Misalliance*'s promiscuous John Tarleton's past relationship with Lucy Titmus and their son, Julius Baker—the burglar who came to the house with the intention of shooting his heretofore unacknowledged father.[19]

Act IV of *The Madras House* highlights opposite conditions for two married women: Constantine Madras's pitiable and embittered deserted wife, still unreconciled to the breakup of her marriage years earlier; and Jessica, elegantly dressed and highly cultured wife of Constantine's son Philip Madras. At the end, Jessica is prepared to exchange her sterile existence playing the wealthy wife for the hurly-burly of political life, with which Philip now proposes to concern himself once the firm has been sold off to an American chain. Barker plays his own variation here on the characters at the end of Shaw's *Major Barbara*: the returning estranged husband, the abandoned wife, and a young couple determined to use the wealth from the family business to change the world's social conditions for the better.

Fanny's First Play

Given the formal structural and thematic complexities of his previous two plays, along with Barker's *The Madras House*, which all left the critics baffled, Shaw seemingly simplified matters in his next, subtitled "An Easy Play for a Little Theatre."

Fanny's First Play comprises two plays: the young Fanny O'Dowda's three-act play, which provides lighter variations on the themes permeating the other plays, and a frame play showing the offstage scenes immediately before and after the first private production of Fanny's play for a select group of London critics. The *inner* play features two families, as in *The Madras House*, who run a clothes-related business, and a frustrated adult daughter, Margaret Knox, like Hypatia in *Misalliance*, determined to break the cocoon of her family environment. Her mother provides something of a parallel to the elder Mrs. Madras, although not at all as pathetic, being spiritually fortified by an eloquent evangelical Puritanism—in ironic counterpoint to the self-serving Islamic sympathies of the promiscuous patriarchs, Madras in *The Madras House* and Tarleton in *Misalliance*. Mrs. Knox's religious nature makes her sympathetic if not necessarily approving of her daughter's actions that landed her in gaol.

Fanny O'Dowda in the *outer* (frame) play demonstrates independence from her father, for whom the elegant artifice of the eighteenth century represents the height of artistic achievement. She joins the Fabian Society at Cambridge, becomes a Suffragette, spends time in gaol, and writes a twentieth-century play of Ibsenite social realism on lower-middle-class family life. Its apparently sordid naturalism, ironically derived from the *commedia del'arte* he so adores, duly horrifies the aesthetically sensitive Count. Fanny's characters Bobby and Margaret, engaged at the beginning of the inner play, end up, like Hypatia and Bentley in *Misalliance*, dis-engaging. Both land in prison following adventures with a prostitute and that most risqué of theatrical clichés, a married French sailor, respectively. Shaw, along with his audience, has almost cartoonish fun in dismantling those rigid class barriers that give potency to the idea of a social misalliance. In spite of his family's respectability, Bobby decides to walk out together with "Darling" Dora Delaney, while Margaret matches up with the footman, Juggins. In fact this seeming misalliance operates in the opposite direction as, in another well-worn stage cliché, the footman, whose first name is Rudolph, is brother to a duke!

Juggins underwent a religious conversion to social equality similar to Hotchkiss's at the end of *Getting Married*, which

> only Mrs. Knox will understand. I once insulted a servant—rashly; for he was a sincere Christian. He rebuked me for trifling with a girl of his own class. I told him to remember what he was, and to whom he was speaking. He said God would remember. I discharged him on the spot. … It stuck like a poisoned arrow. It rankled for months. Then I gave in. I apprenticed myself to an old butler of ours who kept a hotel. He taught me my present business, and got me a place as footman with Mr. Gilbey. If ever I meet that man again I shall be able to look him in the face. (*CPP* IV:431–432)

When Mr. Gilbey, jealous of the Knox daughter marrying into the nobility, voices horror at his son's proposed misalliance with a prostitute, Dora assures him that Rudolph will teach her good manners. The following year Shaw would write another play on social mobility involving an impoverished street girl, one Eliza Doolittle, who will learn good manners—and a new linguistic idiom—so as to pass herself off and make herself marriageable in respectable society (Fig. 7.1).

Fig. 7.1 Harley Granville Barker sitting on a bench holding a brush. This photograph, probably by Shaw himself, was taken between c.1895–c.1905. Reproduced by the kind permission of the Society of Authors on behalf on the Bernard Shaw Estate, the National Trust and the London School of Economics

CONCLUSION

Shaw's and Barker's "sartorial" tetralogy can be seen as crucial to the development of twentieth-century theatre. Barker and Shaw, having firmly established twentieth-century English-speaking literary (as opposed to commercial) theatre with the 1904–1907 repertory seasons at the Court Theatre, now had to show that this new type of theatre, what might be called the first wave of theatrical modernism coming in the wake of Ibsen, could exist beyond the Court. While it remains true that, with the exception of *Fanny's First Play*, none of the four plays was initially a great success, they all demonstrate their writers' ambitions to go beyond their achievements at the Court. In Shaw's case, this can best be guaged by a critical understanding of his complex formal procedures in *Getting Married* and *Misalliance*, capped by the reflexive metatheatricality of *Fanny's First Play*. In the first two, Shaw goes back to the origins of western drama in Ancient Greece, incorporating elements of the Classical world, its religion and its drama, which was inextricably part of its religious practice, into his plays' formal and poetic structures. Further, more than any other modern playwright, he provides practically a religious experience for the spectators in his theatre, while breaking it down into a structure of abstract elements, all placed into the very contemporary context of the younger generation and the struggle for social equality and women' rights in the years 1908–1911. This embedding of both dramatic history and forms into his own plays' themes and structures may well have been unprecedented, which makes these plays in particular pre-eminent as not only modern, but as modernist theatrical artifacts.

NOTES

1. Having written three of the most ambitious, not to mention lengthiest, plays of modern literary drama with *Man and Superman* (1900–1903), *John Bull's Other Island* (1904), and *Major Barbara* (1905), Shaw briefly scaled back, if only in the sense of *reculer pour mieux sauter*, to write his Molièresque comedy *The Doctor's Dilemma: A Tragedy* (1907). Most of the general studies on Shaw's plays then tend to skip straight over the plays discussed in this chapter to 1912s *Androcles and the Lion* and *Pygmalion*. However, Christopher Innes's essay ""Nothing but Talk, Talk, Talk": Discussion Plays and the Making of Modern Drama," in the *Cambridge Guide to George Bernard Shaw*. Cambridge: Cambridge University Press, 1998), 162–179, offers an excellent introduction to this

group of discussion plays, while Margery Morgan's chapters on *Getting Married* and *Misalliance*, especially Shaw's allusions to Greek drama, in *The Shavian Playground* (London: Methuen, 1972) remain indispensable. Sections on these plays in Martin Meisel's groundbreaking *Shaw and Nineteenth Century Theatre* (New York: Princeton University Press, 1963), showing how Shaw roots his plays in earlier forms, and J. Ellen Gainor's *Shaw's Daughters: Dramatic and Narrative Constructions of Gender* (Ann Arbor: University of Michigan Press, 1991), a not uncritical take on Shaw's feminism, also remain valuable. Peter Gahan looks at Shaw's use of reflexivity in *Getting Married* as well as his complex structuring in the supposedly simple *Fanny's First Play* in *Shaw Shadows: Rereading the Texts of Bernard Shaw* (Florida: University Press of Florida, 2004), 213–227, 166–188 (Innes 1998; Morgan 1972; Meisel 1963; Gainor 1991; Gahan 2004).

2. Contemporary London theatre critics, including Shaw's friends and colleagues like William Archer and Arthur Bingham Walkley, who called *Misalliance* "the debating society of a lunatic asylum" in *The Times* (qtd. in *File on Shaw*, compiled by Margery Morgan (London: Methuen, 1989), 63), were even more unenthusiastic about this group of plays than they had been about the plays presented at the Court Theatre from 1904 to 1907. H. Hamilton Fyfe's review of *Getting Married* and Max Beerbohm's of *Misalliance*, both reprinted in *Shaw: The Critical Heritage*, edited by T.F. Evans (London: Routledge & Kegan Paul, 1976), 190–193, 200–202, can be taken as representative. P.P. Howe offered a singularly perceptive corrective to other contemporary critics in *The Repertory Theatre* (London: Martin Secker, 1910), 92, 101, reprinted in Morgan, *File on Shaw*, 63: "*Misalliance* was as enjoyable as was the discomfort of the critics in face of it... There is nothing high about it except its spirits, and they are splendid.... Shall we call *Misalliance* a symbolist farce." Perhaps no better label describes the Shavian play (Morgan 1989; Evans 1976).

3. Indeed, another element in the plot of *The Archaians*, the taking hostage of a basket of charcoal, may have contributed to the husband of *Getting Married*'s leading character, Mrs. George, being a coal merchant.

4. One of the other uses of tarlatan, relevant for this particular character obsessed with books in this play of excessive words, is for wiping away excess ink in the intaglio printing process, whether engraving or etching.

5. Shaw wrote to Maud Churton Braby on May 18, 1907: "But you may not have noticed that the play, besides being a disquisition on the marriage problem, is also a sermon on equality" (*CL*, 786). He had made the same point to Lillah McCarthy on May 13 (*CL*, 781). Philippa Burt's essay "Granville Barker's Ensemble as a Model of Fabian Theatre," *New*

Theatre Quarterly 28:4 (November 2012): 307–324, offers an interesting perspective on Barker the director as socialist (Burt 2012).

6. Shaw's names are often significant, and that of the character of his upper-class young snob St. John "Sonny" Hotchkiss suggests a link to, rather than a portrait of, St. John Hankin, Shaw's fellow Court Theatre playwright whose plays had satirized snobbery and class consciousness. Indeed, Shaw's names offer multiple resonances: St. John's Christian connotations counterpoint the play's many Classical allusions, while St. John's insistence on the Word ("In the beginning was the Word") is also relevant to this wordy play. The character also has an autobiographical aspect: "Sonny" had been Shaw's own nickname as a teenager, while Hotchkiss's age is 29, the age Shaw tells us he lost his own virginity.

7. A metaphysical concept common to almost all religions, the soul as understood by Shaw is essentially a Christian notion derived from Greek philosophy, especially Platonism and its intellectual derivations, Aristotelianism and neo-Platonism. An invisible, immaterial, yet substantial metaphysical entity, apprehended by reason, and the spiritual counterpart of the physical body known to the senses, it may pertain to human beings only, or to all animals, to all living things, or even the entire physical universe.

8. Harley Granville Barker, *The Madras House* (New York: Mitchell Kennerley, 1914), 133. Barker's 1925 revision of the play is not considered here (Barker 1914).

9. Preface to *Major Barbara*.

10. Margery Morgan, *The Shavian Playground* (London: Methuen, 1972), 180, note 1.

11. Shaw asked that the stage designer visit the Norman-built Tower of London to get an idea of what he wanted: "Tell [J.J.M.] Davis to go and look through the Tower on a sunny morning. There must be NO PANNELLING ... It must be clean Norman stone work, supposed to be lit by big windows in the proscenium opening—big oak doors (not painted, but axe-cut raw oak doors with big latches—clean and splendid ... Nothing like it has ever been done on the stage." Letter of April 19, 1908 to J.E. Verdrenne, in *Bernard Shaw Theatrics. Selected Correspondence of Bernard Shaw*, edited by Dan H. Laurence (Toronto: University of Toronto Press, 1995), 88 (Laurence 1995).

12. See Shaw's letter to Siegfried Trebitsch of January 15, 1909: "In Getting Married the curtain falls immediately before the first entrance of Hotchkiss, at the conclusion of the Bishop's speech.... The second time is immediately after the first entry of Mrs. George. As she appears on the stage, and before she has spoken." *Bernard Shaw's Letters to Siegfried Trebitsch*, edited by Samuel A. Weiss (Stanford: Stanford University Press, 1986) 141–142 (Weiss 1986).

13. Both first and last names of the puritanical Sexton suggest that Shaw had in mind that well-known painting subject of the late Middle Ages, the "Temptations of St. Anthony"—*soma* being Greek for body.

14. Shaw would have known about *hieros gamos* from Frazer's *Golden Bough*, and possibly Jane Harrison's recently published *Prolegomena to the Study of Greek Religion* (Cambridge: The Univeristy Press, 1903). He may also have consulted his friend, and Harrison's colleague, Gilbert Murray, as he had previously for information about the Classical world (Harrison 1903).

15. Part of this play's reflexivity, indicated by the circulation of letters by mail, is that letters generate letters. Indeed, the Bishop as Alfred Bridgenorth, Chelsea, can be literally reduced to the alphabet, ABC. Shaw is also reflexively drawing on the convention of writing dramatic dialogue by denoting male characters in order of importance with the first letters of the alphabet (A, B, C) and the female characters working backwards from the last (Z, Y, X). Consequently Mrs. George's first of many names is Zenobia! Shaw would later incorporate this reflexive convention into *Village Wooing* (1933), where the two characters presented at the beginning as a writer and a reader are only ever known as A and Z. See Peter Gahan, *Shaw Shadows*, 151–156. Shaw had as model for his Bishop Mandell Creighton (1843–1901), Bishop of London, whose residence was Fulham Palace. A historian and founder of the *English Historical Review*, his wife Louise Creighton was also a historian and activist for women's suffrage. See letter of September 3, 1916 on actor Walter Creighton, the Bishop's son, to William Faversham (*CL* III:411–412).

16. Shaw may have had the architecture of the temple at Eleusis in mind, with its Great Hall [Telesterion = Initiation Hall], where the sacred objects were exposed to the crowd; Shaw's sacred objects are the wedding cake and the Beadle's "baubel," as Mrs. George calls the mace, which will be revealed to the assembled guests in the hall of the Bishop's Palace above. In which case, the Anaktoron [palace], the dark chamber in the middle of the Telesterion, corresponds to the Norman kitchen where the drama of *Getting Married* has been staged. Its food associations make it appropriate for invoking this festival celebrating Demeter, goddess of corn. The never-opened chest of Shaw's set might correspond to the Kiste, the chest which held some of the sacred objects in Eleusis. For Shaw's use of the Eleusinian mysteries in *Candida* and *Getting Married* (in some ways a reworking of the themes of the earlier play), see Peter Gahan, *Shaw Shadows*, 209–218.

17. See Peter Gahan, "Bernard Shaw's Dionysian Trilogy: Reworkings of Gilbert Murray's Translation of Euripides's *Bacchae* in *Major Barbara, Misalliance*, and *Heartbreak House*," in *SHAW 37.1: Shaw and the*

Classics, edited by Gustavo Rodríguez Martín. University Park: Pennsylvania State University Press, 2017: 28–74.
18. Shaw's scene for *The Madras House* is published in *CPP7*, 609–612.
19. Perhaps even more than *Major Barbara*, Shaw modeled *Misalliance* after Euripides's *Bacchae*. Julius Baker represents Dionysus/Bacchus, son of Jupiter and Semele. In a stream of word associations (Lucinda, Cindy, Cinderella, cinders), the name Lucy can be seen to be synonymous with Semele, incinerated when struck by a thunderbolt from Jupiter, an association that Shaw himself later made with rather poor taste after attending his sister Lucy's cremation: "Lucy is now Cinderella," he wrote to Mrs. Patrick Campbell, March 31, 1920 (CL, 674). Lucinda was also his mother's first name, appropriate in as much as Julius Baker's life as a clerk seems drawn from Shaw's own experience as a Dublin teenager. Shaw figures the androgynous cross-dressing aspect of Dionysos in Lina Szczepanowska, who, due to sartorial indirection (male aviator's attire), is at first mistaken as a man. The year before writing *Misalliance*, Shaw coached actress Lillah McCarthy for the role of Dionysus in Euripides's *Bacchae*. See Shaw's letter of November 15, 1908 to Granville Barker, *The Shaw-Barker Letters*, edited by C.B. Purdum (London: Phoenix House, 1956), 138–139 (Purdon 1956).

REFERENCES

Barker, Harley Granville. 1914. *The Madras House*. New York: Mitchell Kennerley.
Burt, Philippa. 2012. Granville Barker's Ensemble as a Model of Fabian Theatre. *New Theatre Quarterly* 28 (4): 307–324.
Evans, T.F. (ed.). 1976. *Shaw: The Critical Heritage*. London: Routledge & Kegan Paul.
Gahan, Peter. 2004. *Shaw Shadows: Rereading the Texts of Bernard Shaw*. Gainesville: University Press of Florida.
Gainor, J. Ellen. 1991. *Shaw's Daughters: Dramatic and Narrative Constructions of Gender*. Ann Arbor: University of Michigan Press.
Harrison, Jane. 1903. *Prolegomena to the Study of Greek Religion*. Cambridge: Cambridge University Press.
Innes, Christopher (ed.). 1998. *The Cambridge Companion to George Bernard Shaw*. Cambridge: Cambridge University Press.
Laurence, Dan H. (ed.). 1995. *Bernard Shaw. Theatrics: Selected Correspondence of Bernard Shaw*. Toronto, ON: University of Toronto Press.
Meisel, Martin. 1963. *Shaw and the Nineteenth-Century Theater*. Princeton, NJ: Princeton University Press.

Morgan, Margery. 1972. *The Shavian Playground: An Exploration of the Art of George Bernard Shaw*. London: Methuen.
Morgan, Margery. 1989. *File on Shaw*. London: Methuen.
Purdon, C.B. 1956. *The Shaw-Barker Letters*. London: Phoenix House.
Weiss, Samuel A. (ed.). 1986. *Bernard Shaw's Letters to Siegfried Trebitsch*. Stanford, CA: Stanford University Press.

AUTHOR BIOGRAPHY

Peter Gahan is an independent scholar living in Los Angeles, CA, USA. A graduate in philosophy from Trinity College, Dublin, he has written many essays on Shaw, is author most recently of the book *Bernard Shaw and Beatrice Webb on Poverty and Equality in the Modern World, 1905–1914* (2017), of *Shaw Shadows: Rereading the Texts of Bernard Shaw* (2004), editor of the anthology, *Shaw and The Irish Literary Tradition* (2010), and serves as a member of the editorial board of *SHAW: The Journal of Bernard Shaw Studies*. He currently co-editor of the *Bernard Shaw and His Contemporaries* series for Palgrave Macmillan.

CHAPTER 8

Ruled by Autonomy: Women's Evolving Marital Choices from *the Doctor's Dilemma* (1906) to *Pygmalion* (1914)

Ellen Ecker Dolgin

Spanning genres, the group of plays that this chapter considers—*The Doctor's Dilemma* (1906), *Overruled* (1912), *Androcles and the Lion* (1913), and *Pygmalion* (1914)—delineate Shaw's evolving and diverse attitudes toward marriage. The push–pull between traditional ways of life and the innate need to forge an individual identity reverberates in each of these works. By tracing characters and situations chronologically and contextually, this chapter will show how Shaw steers readers and audiences to reflect upon the pressures of obligatory matches that engender misalliances. More importantly, this grouping of plays highlights some of the key issues and strides of the more radical women's suffrage movement that occurred during those very years. Beginning with *The Doctor's Dilemma* (première 1906 in the Royal Court Seasons), the schism between inner and outer perceptions of domestic emotional ties boldly comes to the fore in these plays. Between 1906 and 1914, women's organized activism not only grew in size and number of participants,

E.E. Dolgin (✉)
Dominican College of Blauvelt, Orangeburg, New York, USA
e-mail: ellen.dolgin@dc.edu

© The Author(s) 2017
R.A. Gaines (ed.), *Bernard Shaw's Marriages and Misalliances,*
Bernard Shaw and His Contemporaries,
DOI 10.1057/978-1-349-95170-3_8

125

but also blended the various reforms that women's activism had formerly divided into distinct efforts: legal rights (suffrage) and advocacy for women's workers—from prostitutes, sweatshop workers, and shop girls to pursuit of women's placement in the professions, including theatre.

The Actresses' Franchise League, formed in 1908, was yet another vital layer of cross-fertilization in the push for full citizenship for women. By 1912, women had begun to picket Parliament and hold mass demonstrations. The Vice-President of the Actresses' Franchise League, Lillah McCarthy (Jennifer Dubedat in *The Doctor's Dilemma (1906)* and Lavinia in 1913s *Androcles and the Lion*), was a key organizer. Lavinia dares to defy convention by becoming a Christian and assuming the role of social activist. This character's confrontation with Roman authority is a direct parallel to Lillah's own multi-pronged public persona as actress/theatre manager/activist. Lavinia likewise represents the stance of activists like Cicely Hamilton (see discussion of her work below) and many other women that they did not need men to have complete lives.

The lighter play from the prior year, *Overruled (1912)*, removes all pretense in its concise and precise illustration that marriages based on rules, without the "sexless" aspect of friendship, can easily become shams. Each of the four characters lacks the intellectual stimulation to sustain conflict; marriages that are complacent can be just as fraught as those that are incompatible. Here, Shaw playfully responds to the Edwardian era's skepticism of the institution of marriage, even as the play veers away from any rationale for divorce or separation within two marriages.

Pygmalion, written in 1912 but not performed in English until 1914, goes beyond any of the other works in this chapter in its evocation of the dangerous liaison that could have existed between a teacher and his pupil, had either of them been truly conventional. In Henry Higgins, Shaw offers us a man too absorbed in his work and his financial privilege to "need" a wife in any way; Eliza does not seek marriage or sexual connection because her girlhood had shown her enough of the downsides. Both of them are realists and neither can be said to represent an individual in search of a soul mate. Henry's social status precludes any demands to find a wife, on the cusp of World War I, Eliza comes to recognize that upper-class young women are, in a sense, more constrained than working-class women. It is likely no accident that the "war" between Eliza and Higgins was written and performed at a time when Parliament repeatedly promised to enact women's suffrage and then reneged.[1]

The plays both incorporate the continuation of the institution of marriage as economic surety to pass down through biological descendants and reflect the emerging "companionable" love matches of the younger generation. These fostered egalitarian alliances that ran counter to the business side of things that Cicely Hamilton's 1909 tract, *Marriage as a Trade*, examines. Hamilton's sociological approach equips readers to see the institution rather than individual relationships. Marriage as a woman's "career," in the context of her economic dependence on her husband, pinpointed the contradiction. Self-development in its usual sense, through hard work (a career), was not part of the bargain for wives. Tellingly, the choices that Shaw gives some women in these plays disrupt the tacit acceptance of marriage as a woman's sole interest.

The marriage conflict was of course at the heart of the obsessive concern with challenges to marriage that had existed internationally since the last decade of the nineteenth century. Shaw's plays began to emerge when the New Woman controversy raged in the 1890s, frequently centered around the generational contest outlined in "The Revolt of Daughters" by B.A. Crackenthorpe in her 1894 essay. This writer came out on the side of the daughters even though she was herself a mother. Crackenthorpe likened the struggle to the labor strikes that were headline news, with daughters having the "vitality, 'go', and the muscle strength to pick themselves up [after an encounter] only a surface bruise or two the worse, while the elder and less supple opponent has possibly received wounds which, bleeding inwardly, poison the joy of life at its purest source." The power of tradition (the mothers) clearly was replaced by the new opportunities for young women in the urban centers, even if the jobs were not at the highest level. Crackenthorpe succinctly warns that mothers cannot resolve this conflict as something to be "lightly laughed away as a passing trouble, to be speedily cured by marriage."[2]

The challenge to the mores of married life had begun decades earlier, when the long-established social class system that kept family life separate from the rapid changes in the industrial world likewise began to fray in the 1880s. Elaine Showalter, in *Sexual Anarchy*, explains that what might have remained separate issues came together in the public imagination because of the legislative gains for at least some women that were achieved by then: the Married Women's Property Act of 1882 and the Guardianship of Infants Act in 1886. Predicting the tactics that women's activism would pursue at the turn of the century, the underclass began to agitate for workers' rights to higher wages and shorter hours. The serious economic depression of 1887 emblematized the conflation of the changing social scene. This was the first time the word "unemployment" was used and the homeless of London began "camping out in Trafalgar Square and St. James' Park, arousing both compassion and fear. Charities, which were run more and more by women, brought food by cartloads and gave out lodging tickets." When business owners fretted over lost business and demanded police action, the result was Bloody Sunday, November 13, 1887.[3]

Shaw was fully engaged in these activities. The Fabian Society had participated in many public demonstrations since 1885, and Shaw spoke regularly, along with the feminist orator Annie Besant. On Bloody Sunday, William Morris had planned a very large demonstration; the police had closed Trafalgar Square days earlier. When people turned to Shaw for guidance, Michael Holroyd notes that Shaw's answer was "firm and unparadoxical." He told them to do "nothing except get to the Square however they could." Shaw managed to take his own advice and noted that the police likely let him through "in consideration of my genteel appearance."[4] He would use his observation of costume-as-character to great advantage as a playwright, prompting audiences to recognize their own appearance-based assumptions.

Fast-forward 20 years: militant suffragettes marched in picture hats and ladylike ensembles. Donned by demonstrators on both sides of the Atlantic, this costume choice was a tactic used to ensure press coverage and to assert that a push for full citizenship and autonomy did not automatically preclude an appreciation of fashion or dignified public appearance. What perplexed those indifferent or opposed to women's rights was the guise of a womanly woman that the activists stretched over the resolve of a warrior. Assembling by hundreds and thousands, these women marched and spoke in Trafalgar Square, and they staunchly refused to remove an iota of their agenda for full citizenship for women across class lines.

In April 1906, a few months prior to *The Doctor's Dilemma* première at the Royal Court Theatre under the direction of Granville Barker, a Resolution for women's suffrage was slated for debate in Parliament. Twelve leaders of the WSPU (Women's Social and Political Union, the Suffragettes) obtained tickets to observe in the ladies' gallery in the balcony. Unsurprisingly, this was the last item of business and the time allowed for discussion was short. Once it became clear to the women that the bill would be "talked out" and would receive no action, they rose in protest and demanded the MPs bring the matter to a vote. This caused a commotion and led to the removal of the women from the chamber. The Resolution was talked out, but the publicity was widespread and international.[5] The following year, Granville Barker directed Elizabeth Robins's play at the Royal Court, *Votes for Women*; Robins, herself a WSPU leader, included a discussion of this specific disruption in Parliament in the first act of the play, which takes place in a country house just before lunch on a Sunday afternoon.

Several of the older, married women bemoan the folly of the Suffragettes' action because they believe the supporters of the Resolution are close to getting somewhere, and they are angry that the most radical WSPU branch of suffrage activists has thrown everything away in five minutes. The protagonist of the play, Vida Levering, suggests the Suffragettes "realize they've waked up interest in the Woman Question. ... Don't you think *they* know there's been more said and written about it in these ten days since the scene, than in the ten years before it?" Levering's implications prompt the key questions: had the MPs deliberately foiled the possibility of converting the Resolution into a Bill, or, conversely, how could the women get anything accomplished without the help of men? She states: "It does rather look to the outsider as if the well-behaved women had worked for forty years and made less impression on the world than those fiery young women made in five minutes."[6]

Robins would expand her connections between women's decorum and their own inner struggles in a 1907 article she wrote for *Collier's Weekly* that describes her own inner journey toward feminism. She describes attending a Trafalgar Square meeting "out of shamefaced curiosity ... head full of masculine criticism about woman's limitations." Before this day, Robins had felt women needed more education and discipline ... "not realizing that the higher discipline can come only through liberty."[7]

A London editor expressed concern that women, like men, would feel the "deteriorating" effect of public life. Robins's reply could not be more telling. Then aged 45, she pointed to her acting career as her proof: "I had spent a good part of my adult existence under conditions where I could see the effect on character of just these fierce tests ... [but] the necessary focus on self that acting demands contrasts with the 'civilizing, ennobling' service to others that suffrage work was."[8]

Shaw often features independent single women in his plays, but how do his younger married women fare in their quest for self-development? Jennifer Dubedat, in *The Doctor's Dilemma* (1906), makes her entrance into the play as an arresting presence, determined to see the doctor just knighted for his cure for consumption so he can save her dying artist husband. She is devoted, to be sure, but in no way behaves as a helpless, handwringing damsel. Rather, Jennifer employs the strategies of a charity fundraiser working for the public good, as Robins describes above. Ridgeon is dismissive at first, saying he cannot take any more patients in his sanatorium. He ruthlessly tells her that taking her husband's case will kill one of the ten patients he has chosen from fifty that were put before him. Worse, the doctor reveals his despicable arrogance, stating that his selections were not primarily based on the specifics of the patient's medical condition and the match to his treatment methods, but on whether Ridgeon thought their lives "worth saving" (*CPP* III:353–355).

Jennifer demonstrates her acute observational skills when she flatters Ridgeon by complimenting his knowledge of good art and shows him her husband's portfolio. Once again, her behavior as well as her dialogue aligns her with the outspoken and assertive suffrage and trade union speakers. As the doctor looks through the portfolio, Jennifer explains she was her husband's model when he first began, to save money. By then Ridgeon is attracted to Jennifer's beauty, vitality, and the high quality of Louis's work. Ridgeon impulsively invites the Dubedats to join him and his colleagues at a dinner celebrating his knighthood so Louis can see several doctors all at once.

At the dinner in Act II, both Jennifer and Louis charm all the doctors there, until the melodramatic plot twist—the hotel worker who recognizes Louis Dubedat and claims to be his wife. It is then that each doctor admits he has loaned money to Dubedat. Tables have turned, but the promise to see Dubedat together is something their gentlemanly code of honor cannot dismiss. Dr. Ridgeon's supposed dilemma about whose life to save has deteriorated as Shaw peels away his professionalism and that of many of the other physicians. The one exception is Dr. Blenkinsop, who has working-class patients who cannot afford treatment and is therefore in financial straits himself. This doctor also has consumption, which he reveals only after the Dubedats leave. When Blenkinsop leaves, Sir Patrick Cullen asks Ridgeon: "Well, Mr Savior of Lives: which is it to be? That honest decent man Blenkinsop, or that rotten blackguard of an artist, eh?" Ridgeon then divulges his true "dilemma": should he sacrifice Dubedat because he wants to marry Jennifer? Then Shaw ends the act with a well-made touch. Ridgeon decides to pass Dubedat to one of their colleagues with a great reputation but who is incompetent, and to save their colleague (*CPP* III:3735–4378).

Jennifer's admirable ability to be at once totally immersed in her emotional tie to Dubedat while transcending stereotypical maudlin or dysfunctional behavior emerges fully in the death scene. As he had in Act III when the doctors visit their home, Louis charms, manipulates, or directly disrupts social norms when he hires a journalist to document his death scene. Desmond MacCarthy, critic for the première production, depicts the absolutely spellbinding but excruciating scene, which got its power from being the polar opposite of a crescendo: "Granville Barker acted the onstage death naturally and realistically. Dubedat dies in a pose ... His last picture is painted on his wife's mind."[9]

While she never faces the truth about Louis's actions or character, Jennifer takes from the marriage what she needs to move forward. She remarries quickly, as Louis asked her to do on his deathbed, and publishes a book about Louis. A more conventional playwright would have put Jennifer and her self-absorbed husband in more dire circumstances, and certainly would not have allowed Jennifer a second husband who supports her self-development as well as her finances. Shaw wisely chooses not to introduce us to this man, showing the character's generosity as selfless (*CPP* III:433–436).

Between 1906 and 1912, the theme of marriage and women as chattel resounded in suffrage campaigns. Parliament continued to appear willing to consider a Bill for suffrage and then change its mind. In June 1908, a remark by the Home Secretary Herbert Gladstone absolutely backfired. Gladstone implied that the women's case for gaining a hearing and potential vote on suffrage was solid, but that they could not convince Parliament to give them this because, unlike the activist labor movement run by men, women could not possibly assemble thousands in a public square to demonstrate. That kind of public support moves governments, he noted.[10] In response, the WSPU organized a demonstration on June 21 and transported women in 30 trains from distant locales to London. Organized into seven processions, the women were led by well-known personalities, including actresses. Well over 250,000 people attended, including Shaw.[11]

Women writers, activists, and even actresses were clearly introducing the idea that a woman's psychological self-sufficiency was just as important as her economic independence. In her tract *Marriage as Trade* (1909), Cicely Hamilton examines why relegating so many women to the "trade" of marriage, with no regard for their potential individual contributions to society, was a loss on many levels: "Even while growing up, a girl was trained to be a pleaser so that any abilities she had were not directed towards self-development." She was "fitted for her trade by the discouragement of individuality."[12] On a more psychological level, Hamilton acknowledges that the economic basis for marriage, from the woman's perspective, is not in a man's best interest either: "Woman does not support life to obtain a husband, but frequently obtains a husband only in order to support life."[13] In this way the trade of Hamilton's title has a double meaning.

On the positive side, Hamilton emphasizes the growing awareness within women and men that they were capable of change. She stresses that her own conception of an individual woman is not tied to sexual status in any way. Unlike stereotypical images that regard a woman not as a "human being … but as a breeding machine and the necessary adjunct to a frying pan," Hamilton considers the growing number of egalitarian marriages of two professionals based on mutual respect; they do not result in the "evaporation of a woman's personality." Working-class couples are interdependent because each contributes financially. It is only the "comfortable classes" that retain the malaise, since these women have "narrow duties and a few petty responsibilities."[14]

During these same years, Shaw wrote a number of playlets that Holroyd considers a unit of sorts. They are "one-act trifles—skits, farces, extravaganzas for the stage—often anesthetizing his fears of sex or death" (*Holroyd* II:268). The two couples in *Overruled* (1912) are under 35 and have gone on separate vacations to revitalize themselves, but the question is whether as couples or as individuals. What is unmistakable is that both the men and women are bored with the fixed roles in their personal lives, as well as those dictated by their privileged social class. The issue Shaw presents is a staple of farce: adultery. Michael Holroyd gives a fuller context for this: "In his own plays he had either replaced adultery with other passions or rephrased it impersonally as the workings of a biological technology" (*Holroyd* II:270).

In *Overruled*, biological technology is mixed with socio-psychological overtones. As is so often the case with Shaw's plays, the "talk" in *Overruled* is the action, except for the play's opening moments between Mrs. Juno and Gregory Lunn, when he has gone beyond restraint and is passionately embracing her. Shaw claimed that he had actually shown the sexual act onstage but no one noticed, which Eric Bentley believes is an amazing statement.[15]

Mrs. Juno implores Lunn not to be "horrid." He replies that he is "happy" because "I only want you. As long as I have a want, I have a reason to go on living. Satisfaction is death" (*CPP* IV:846–847). Lunn is far more interested in good conversation than dalliance, but their conversations have clearly led to their sexual fascination. The mood is broken when they realize each was mistaken about the other's being married. As a gentleman, he should leave at once. He cannot. Neither can she. Their attempt to return to the "normalcy" of convention fails utterly, and they are again locked together in the lounge until a voice in the corridor disrupts their interlude; it is Mr. Juno. With him is Mrs. Lunn, Mrs. Juno and Mr. Lunn slip away from the lounge and out of the room (*CPP* IV:852–856).

The second couple's scene is quite different. They own up to being married and immediately begin a frank and captivating conversation about love, marriage, sexual attraction, and the allure of adultery, which Mr. Juno terms "romance." His distinction is both telling and hilarious, because he has already established the happiness he has found with his wife, despite his longing for a "guilty passion—for the real thing—the wicked thing ... Marriage is all very well; but it isn't romance. Theres nothing wrong in it, you see." Rather than stupefaction, Mrs. Lunn says what is normally a conventionally nurturing thing from woman to man, but in this context wholly unexpected: "Poor man! How you must have suffered!" (*CPP* IV:856–857).

However, when Mr. Juno urges Mrs. Lunn to divorce her husband, he signals the boundary that cannot be broached. The shift comes when she is unimpressed with his idea of being madly in love with her (it has been a regular occurrence since she was 17); she calls it an "unmitigated bore." Further, she is "hopelessly respectable." His reply does not convey pain, but insult: "Mrs Lunn: do you think a man's heart is a potato? Or a turnip? Or a ball of knitting wool? That you can throw it away like this?" Her reply is razor sharp: "I don't throw away balls of knitting wool. A man's heart seems to me much like a sponge, it sops up dirty water as well as clean" (*CPP* IV:860). Moments later, Mrs. Juno and Mr. Lunn return and the resolution emerges: it will be fine for the alternate pairings to meet from time to time to talk and enjoy their feelings for one another, but no one will divorce, no one will become ill, and all will be well.

What makes Shaw's play funny is not its farcical roots, but rather its frank conversation about feelings, urges, and boredom. A potential assumption that there must be at least one misalliance between the married couples proves false. Everyone goes into dinner at the end and, true to custom, each of the women goes in on the arm of someone other than her own husband. When Alfred Turco asked Eric Bentley what he thought of the ending of *Overruled*, he exclaimed: "It's a wonderful comma! There's no formulated conclusion ... It's an invitation to look at something in a way we never have—with sweet reasonableness."[16]

Shaw's *Overruled* was likewise on the pulse of the other central phenomenon of this time, psychoanalysis and the popularization of Sigmund Freud's theories. Into the nascent experimental theatre in the United States came Susan Glaspell's two-scene satire *Suppressed Desires* in 1915. In Linda Ben-Zvi and J. Ellen Gainor's introduction to *Suppressed Desires*, they emphasize the popularization of Freud's materials from the lectures he gave in 1909, but also the play's focus on the implications of a half-baked understanding of psychoanalysis.[17] The play involves a married couple, Henrietta and Stephen, her visiting sister, Mabel, and Dr. Russell, the psychiatrist who never appears but whose authority looms over the play. Henrietta talks of little but psychoanalysis, and is bent on converting her husband and sister to this new science. At Henrietta's urging, they both go to Dr. Russell and he has diagnosed their suppressed desires as their need to leave their spouses. The final "wink" of the play is the introduction of the term "sublimation," so that Mabel can return to her husband and not act upon her suppressed desire for Stephen.[18]

With the popularization of Carl Jung's theories of archetypes, re-examinations of old tales and folklore began to happen. A play that appears light-hearted on the surface and features aspects of Aesop's fable, a Christmas pantomime for children, and Christian melodrama is *Androcles and the Lion*, which premièred in 1913. Aesop's original story was about the sufferings of a slave and of a wounded lion who encounter each other when each creature is vulnerable; the ability of the slave to come to the dangerous animal's aid and relieve its sufferings is in itself a fully satisfying one. The recognition of the man by the hungry lion in the Coliseum, and the mercy shown the man by the beast, could never fail to delight a reader or viewer. Charles Berst posits that the blended form Shaw created yields the true and full import of the play: "The frivolity of pantomime and the charm of fable serve as a context which, ironically, clarifies the spiritual message." Berst sees Shaw's Androcles as a "gentle humanitarian Christian" for whom "doctrine is subordinate to kindliness and good will."[19]

Shaw changes the slaves into Christians, thereby shifting the focus to Christian martyrs and ruthless Roman pagans. Giving Androcles a wife who does not share Christian beliefs and is unloving, demand-ing, and complaining appears more Gilbertian than Shavian, but of course it allows Shaw to highlight the gentle forbearance of Androcles. Androcles's shrewish wife, Megaera, represents the merchant class of her day, and the exasperation that a pagan probably felt if a spouse made the dangerous choice of converting to Christianity in those times. In her angry speech to Androcles in the forest, she complains not only of her physical discomfort, but also of the emotional burden she carries as the one blamed for her husband's downcast state. She says it is not her fault that she is married to him. No, that is my fault, he says. "That's a nice thing to say to me. Arent you happy with me?" she asks. "I dont com-plain, my love," is Androcles's reply. Misalliance—not exhaustion—is the malady here. Megaera demands that Androcles return to his home, friends, and "sacrifice to the gods as all respectable people do" (*CPP* IV:586–587). The coming of the lion interrupts their quarrel and, after some comic scrambling, Androcles goes to help the wounded lion and she chases after him, but that is the only scene with Megaera.

As the Great War loomed, the significance of these choices would of course become almost startling. Judith Evans points out that Shaw's work around the time of the war pointed more and more to the teach-ings of Christ.[20] Lavinia, a role written specifically for Lillah McCarthy, speaks forthrightly on behalf of her fellow Christians. She is a patrician and therefore is used to assessing situations and asserting some authority. She also has resolve and dignity, and refuses to burn incense and sacrifice to the gods to escape her fate. Most impressively, Lavinia is prepared to die even when she realizes that her faith is not absolute.

Shaw's Lavinia is a true New Woman even as she also has qualities reminiscent of activist women saints; she thinks things through on the spot, bolsters the spirits and faith of others, and is a calm presence. Berst calls her a "free thinker with her feet on the ground and her ideals in the heavens, surviving doubt through intuitive optimism."[21] That same kind of optimism has given her the understanding that she belongs to herself. That Lillah McCarthy played the role more than once would also have underscored this combination of qualities for many in the audiences. She an actress, and principal suffrage activist.[22]

In Act II, several Christians are eaten by the lions, and Ferrovius, who has enormous faith, finds himself compelled to use his sword when he goes to face the gladiators. Lavinia will not allow herself to be saved by marrying the handsome Roman captain with whom there is an obvious mutual attraction. In Shaw's envisioning of the story, Ferrovius does not die in the arena: he kills six gladiators, which amazes and captivates the Emperor. Ferrovius is ashamed that he has retained his patrician and pagan values, but because of these, he is made a Roman officer and the other Christians are freed. When her life is spared, Lavinia offers the Captain friendship and will allow him to visit her, thereby retaining her autonomy, both as an independent woman and as an individual on a spiritual quest. There is neither marriage nor misalliance here. The magic of the mixed genres in *Androcles and the Lion* was received quite differently in the New York revival in 1915. The United States was not yet at war, but Europe was. Martin Meisel notes that audiences for this production of Shaw's play reacted very viscerally when the swift shifts among the "fun, satire, the historical study of manners and characters and the deadly deep earnest were all on the stage as the same moment. It was a deeply disturbing psychological moment."[23]

Shaw's *Pygmalion* (1914) runs contrary to both Ovid's original myth about Pygmalion, who made an "idol"/statue because no woman was good enough for him, and W.S. Gilbert's *Pygmalion and Galatea* (1871), which retained the statue-turned-love-interest from Ovid, and added the wife who substituted for the idealized woman and of course was a jealous woman once the statue came to life. Venus granting the statue, Galatea, life in Ovid is a reward for Pygmalion recognizing that he is not perfect. In Gilbert, Pygmalion's wife Cynisca is a former votary of Artemis; the goddess gave the wife as well as the husband power to blind the other in the event of adulterous thoughts or behavior. Jane Stedman explains that Gilbert retold the story to emphasize King Phanor's conclusion that man cannot live with complete truth.[24] Of course, Shaw would have no patience for either of these basic concepts. However, the Pygmalion/Galatea story was a trope in Victorian arts and literature: the grace, silence, and stillness of the "statue as woman" formed an antidote to women's increasing activism. Martin Meisel points to Galatea's importance in Victorian romantic comedy. There were several motifs that theatregoers came to expect: "misalliance between classes"; a "Cinderella–Galatea motif of transformation and testing"; "the opposition of youth and age."[25] Shaw's conflation of the first two Victorian motifs, as well as the unresolved conclusion, could be contributing factors to the propensity of the actors in the original London production, and the last-minute screenplay changes to the 1938 film version (which led directly to the book/screenplay of Alan J. Lerner's *My Fair*

Lady), to return to the familiar territory of romantic attachment between Pygmalion and Galatea.

Aside from any objections we should rightly raise about these actions' disingenuous treatment of Shaw's text, the fact that there is no Galatea per se in Shaw's play should alone make such conclusions egregious. Eliza may owe a great deal to Higgins's teaching and mentoring, but we must never forget that it was she who came to him to learn proper English. Shaw is not ambiguous in the least about Eliza fusing both Galatea and Pygmalion into her transformed self. Moreover, Pygmalion (Higgins) retains his self-absorption and contempt for people around him—men as well as women—throughout Shaw's text. The question becomes whether Shaw's "Pygmalion" figure in the play cares more about his "creation"—ladylike Eliza and the possibility for individuals to rise in social status based upon their speech—or the power that he wields to produce this result. Shaw's characterization of both Higgins and Eliza shows that he was strongly on the side of Eliza and her sense of self. Cicely Hamilton does not label it as such, but a salient point of her tract on marriage cited above concerns the conception of single women in society's collective mind's eye. The growing numbers of women who chose to live a single life in the Edwardian era were still often perceived as "incomplete," which is almost unfathomable to Hamilton in 1909. A woman alone "is not a woman at all—until man has made her so. Until the moment when he takes her in hand she is merely the raw material of womanhood—the undeveloped and unfinished article."[26] Hamilton does not mention the Pygmalion myth here, but the overtones are unmistakable. Shaw's portraits of single women in this play veer in the opposite direction of the problem Hamilton outlines.

Eliza may be poor, but she's supported herself since she was 14, when her father tossed her out, and she has a head for figures and a knack for observing strangers. She knows what she can or cannot do—sell flowers from the street, but not on the curb—and also recognizes an opportunity to improve her life when she overhears Higgins explain to Col. Pickering that it is really this flower girl's "kerbstone English" that will keep her down. Although it is hardly an idealized view of the struggle for gender and class equality in Shaw's play, Eliza has also imbibed some of the "penny weekly" stories that had been appearing in inexpensive periodicals since the 1840s, and is thereby alert to the social coding contained in Higgins's observation to Pickering. Written in an anecdotal style, these articles concentrated on a formula for success for young women: respectability in appearance and, more importantly, as a moral guide, and aspirations for good-paying employment that would expose them to potential husbands and increased self-esteem.[27] Eliza's constant insistence that she is a "good girl" echoes these readings. What Higgins will term her "Lisson Grove prudery" illustrates Eliza's belief in genteel relations, even between the social classes. Eliza wants to work in a flower shop, but knows she must speak better to obtain the position. Eliza knows what lessons should cost based upon the experience of a friend.

Higgins proposes that she live there with him, Col. Pickering, and the housekeeper, Mrs. Pearce, for three months for an intense course of study. More disturbing are the threats of violence leveled at Eliza by Higgins before and after her father comes to him to sell his daughter for five pounds and advises Higgins to give her the strap. Higgins's character combines elitism, misogyny, and iconoclasm. His manners offend everyone, especially his housekeeper and his mother, who shows her displeasure each time he visits her. Mrs. Pearce is snobby and harsh with Eliza at first, but is also stern with her employer. She recognizes what neither Higgins, Pickering, nor even Eliza does: for a single young woman from the working class, living with men outside of marriage is not in her best interest. Mrs. Pearce demands to know what Eliza's status will be in the house and what will happen to Eliza when the teaching is finished. She says: "You must look ahead a little" (*CPP* IV:688–695). Higgins's reference to Eliza as "baggage" and "guttersnipe" recur from Act II onward; on the other hand, his plea that she learn to speak her language reverently because she "has a soul" (*CPP* IV:679) in Act I is about the clearest contradiction in comedy, although even that cannot remove the smart of his callousness.

It is Mrs. Higgins who reproves Henry and Pickering for being a "pair of babies playing with your live doll" (*CPP* IV:734), a reference to Ovid and, more importantly, Ibsen's Nora simultaneously. When Eliza has her "tryout" at Mrs. Higgins's at-home tea, it is clear that the demeanor and pronunciation are polished, but Eliza's inability to match conversation and the company she keeps is a social catastrophe, albeit a scene of infinite enjoyment. These older women watch out for Eliza and help her develop her confidence as a young woman who will join "society" one way or another.

After Eliza wins Higgins's bet for him at the Ambassador's ball (Pickering tells Eliza she had done it ten times over), the three of them return home. She is treated abominably. In true anti-feminist form, the two men congratulate each other and ignore Eliza altogether. Suddenly, she realizes that she has no clear-cut future and asks Higgins what will become of her, a precise echo of Mrs. Pearce's and Mrs. Higgins's questions to him.

Marriage is not on Eliza's mind at all, until she realizes that Higgins's transformation of her bearing as well as her speech has turned her into a lady. Here is Shaw's feminist point, in solidarity with the suffrage campaign at its height outside the theatre doors. Even Higgins rises to the occasion at this one juncture in the scene. He suggests that Eliza might marry. Her reply: "We were above that at the corner of Tottenham Court Road." He does not understand, so she explains: "I sold flowers. I didn't sell myself. Now you've made a lady of me I'm not fit to sell anything else." Higgins responds: "Tosh, Eliza. Don't you insult human relations by dragging all this cant about buying and selling into it. You needn't marry the fellow if you don't like him." He reminds her that she has other options, including the flower shop (*CPP* IV:750–751). Higgins saying she has options is not the same as proscriptive orders. Charles Berst encapsulates Eliza's coming into her own full power here: "Through successive stages of inspiration, purgation, illumination, despair, and final brilliant personal fulfillment, Eliza progresses towards self-awareness as a human being."[28] Without Act V, back in Mrs. Higgins's house, the full import of Berst's statement or Eliza's transformation could not be recognized. It matters not if Eliza ever goes back to that house, because it can never again be on the same terms.

Whether or not Eliza marries Freddie, she certainly is not pining for marriage with Higgins; throughout the text, she separates them not only because of age, but because he represents a higher intellectual as well as social status, sure signs of a misalliance. Although biographical explanations of the "unfinished" ending of *Pygmalion* may be of interest, leaving Eliza with the ability to choose her future based on her own hard work and what she has learned from Higgins and Pickering feels even more modern than Shaw himself might have imagined.

Viewed collectively, the premises as well as the characters in these four plays point to Shaw's finger on the pulse of the social movement from 1906 to 1914. As the social structures that supported traditional marriage began to adapt to wives, mothers, and daughters being capable and self-sufficient, successful playwrights were scripting life offstage as well as on. As this author has argued in *Shaw and the Actresses Franchise League:*

Staging Equality, this era's recognition that roles are chosen as well as mandated changed the way audiences viewed the plays. Shaw placed his characters in situations that often replicated those that the audience members experienced. Ultimately, the plays offer a conclusion that must have appeared wondrous: a woman can belong to herself.

NOTES

1. Julie Holledge, *Innocent Flowers: Women in Edwardian Theatre* (London: Virago, 1981) & See also Ellen Ecker Dolgin, *Shaw and the Actress Franchise League: Staging Equality* (N. Carolina & London: McFarland & Co., 2015)—Ch. 5.

2. B.A. Crackenthorpe, "The Revolt of the Daughters" in *A New Woman Reader: Fiction, Articles and Drama of the 1890s*. Ed. Carolyn Christensen Nelson (Ontario: Broadview Press, 2001), 261–262.

3. Elaine Showalter, *Sexual Anarchy: Gender and Culture at the Fin-de-Siècle* (NY: Viking, 1990), 6–7.

4. Michael Holroyd, *Bernard Shaw:* Volume I-1856–1898 (NY: Vintage, 1990), 183–185.

5. Andrew Rosen, *Rise Up Women!* (London: Routledge and Kegan Paul, 1974), 63–64.

6. Elizabeth Robins, *Votes for Women: A Play in Three Acts* (Create Space Publishing, 2014), 49–52.

7. Elizabeth Robins, in *Way Stations*, 1913. Free Google E Book. Retrieved 1 May 2011.

8. Ibid.

9. Desmond MacCarthy, *The Court Theatre, 1904–1907: A Commentary and Criticism* (London: A.H. Bullen 1907-Nabu Public Domain rpt.), 97–98.

10. Julie Holledge, *Innocent Flowers: Women in Edwardian Theatre* (London: Virago, 1981), 52–53.

11. Ibid., 53. See also Ellen Ecker Dolgin, *Shaw and the Actresses Franchise League: Staging Equality* (N. Carolina & London: McFarland & Co., 2015) Ch. 5 for the discussion of this event and others that led to the establishment of the Actresses' Franchise League and other professional women's segments of the suffrage movement in 1908.

12. Cicely Hamilton, *Marriage As A Trade* (London, Dodo Press rpt. of 1909 text), 24.

13. Ibid., 8.

14. Ibid., 46.

15. Alfred Turco, Jr. "Shaw 40 Years Later—Eric Bentley Speaks His Mind on Eleven Neglected Plays: *Getting Married, Overruled, On the Rocks*, and Others." *SHAW*, Vol. 7 (*SHAW: The Neglected Plays* (1987), 16.

16. Bentley qtd. in Turco, 17.
17. Linda Ben-Zvi and J. Ellen Gainor, Eds., *Susan Glaspell: The Complete Plays* (N. Carolina & London: McFarland & Co., Inc., 2010), 11–12.
18. Susan Glaspell (in collaboration with George Cram), "Suppressed Desires." In Ben-Zvi & Gainor, 13–23.
19. Charles Berst. *Bernard Shaw and the Art of Drama* (Urbana: University of Illinois Press, 1973), 178.
20. Judith Evans, *The Plays and Politics of Bernard Shaw* (N. Carolina & London: McFarland & Co., Inc., 2003), 100.
21. Berst, 181.
22. Lillah McCarthy was an officer in the Actresses' Franchise League and lobbied Asquith directly. See Holledge, cited above, and Dolgin, cited above, for further details.
23. Meisel, 325.
24. Jane Stedman, *W.S. Gilbert: A Classic Victorian and His Theatre* (London: Oxford Univ. Press, 1996), 91.
25. See Meisel on the motifs of nineteenth-century romantic comedy, 161.
26. Hamilton, 2.
27. See Sally Mitchell's article, "the Forgotten Woman of the Period: Penny Weekly Family Magazines of the 1840s and 1850s." In *The Widening Sphere: Changing Roles of Victorian Women*, Ed. Martha Vicinus (Bloomington: Indiana University Press, 1977), 34.
28. Berst, 197.

References

Ben-Zvi, Linda and J. Ellen Gainor (eds.). 2010. *Susan Glaspell: The Complete Plays*. Jefferson, NC: McFarland.
Berst, Charles A. 1973. *Bernard Shaw and the Art of the Drama*. Urbana: University of Illinois Press.
Crackenthrope, B.A. 2001. The Revolt of the Daughters. *A New Woman Reader: Fiction, Articles and Drama of the 1890s*, ed. Carolyn Christensen Nelson, 261–262. Peterborough, ON: Broadview Press.
Dolgin, Ellen Ecker. 2015. *Shaw and the Actresses Franchise League: Staging Equality*. Jefferson, NC: McFarland.
Evans, Judith. 2003. *The Plays and Politics of Bernard Shaw*. Jefferson, NC: McFarland.
Hamilton, Cicely. 1909. *Marriage as a Trade*. London: Dodo Press, n.d.
Holledge, Julie. 1981. *Innocent Flowers: Women in Edwardian Theatre*. London: Virago.
Holroyd, Michael. 1990. *Bernard Shaw:* vol. I-1856–1898. 183–185. New York: Vintage.

MacCarthy, Desmond. 1907. The Court Theatre, 1904–1907. In *A Commentary and Social Criticism*, ed. A.H. Bullen. London: Nabu Public Domain Reprint.

Mitchell, Sally. 1977. The Forgotten Women of the Period: Penny Weekly Family Magazine of the 1840s and 1850s. In *The Widening Sphere: Changing Roles of Victorian Women*, ed. Martha Vicinus, 29–51. Bloomington: Indiana University Press.

Robins, Elizabeth. 1913. *Way Stations*. Free Google eBook. https://archive.org/stream/waystations00robigoog#page/n294/mode/2up. Accessed 1 May 2011.

Robins, Elizabeth. 2014. *Votes for Women: A Play in Three Acts*. Crate Space Publishing.

Rosen, Andrew. 1974. *Rise Up Women!* London: Routledge & Kegan Paul.

Showalter, Elaine. 1990. *Sexual Anarchy: Gender and Culture at the Fin de Siècle*. New York: Viking.

Stedman, Jane. 1996. *W.S. Gilbert: A Classic Victorian and His Theatre*, 91. London: Oxford Univ. Press.

Turco, Alfred, Jr. 1987. Shaw 40 Years Later—Eric Bentley Speaks His Mind on Eleven Neglected Plays: *Getting Married, Overruled, On the Rocks*, and Others. *SHAW*, vol. 7 *SHAW: The Neglected Plays*, 16.

AUTHOR BIOGRAPHY

Ellen Ecker Dolgin is Professor and Chair of English and Co-Chair, Gender Studies, at Dominican College in Orangeburg, NY, USA, where she teaches courses in drama, multicultural American literature, and women's literature. Her books include *Modernizing Joan of Arc: Conceptions, Costumes and Canonization* (2008) and *Shaw and the Actresses Franchise League: Staging Equality* (2015). "History Plays" appears in *Shaw in Context* (2015), edited by Brad Kent. She is Vice-President of the International Shaw Society and Past President of NeMLA, the Northeast Modern Language Association.

CHAPTER 9

From Ellie to Eve: The Quintessence of Marriage in Shaw's *Heartbreak House*, *Annajanska, the Bolshevik Empress*, and *Back to Methuselah*

Audrey McNamara

In his 1905 Preface to *The Irrational Knot* (1880), Bernard Shaw argued "that marriage did not stagger me as it staggered Europe."[1] He continued through a commentary on Ibsen's *A Doll's House* where he maintained that he himself had "made a morally original study of marriage."[2] He explored the notion of ownership and equality within relationships and marriages, and how gender roles in marriages were polarized in the nineteenth century. He stated in *The Quintessence of Ibsenism* (1891):

> it is not surprising that our society, being directly dominated by men, come to regard Woman, not as an end in herself like Man, but solely as a means of ministering to his appetite. … Now to treat a person as a means to an end is to deny that person's right to live.[3]

A. McNamara (✉)
University College Dublin (UCD), Dublin, Ireland
e-mail: bernardshawindublin@gmail.com

© The Author(s) 2017
R.A. Gaines (ed.), *Bernard Shaw's Marriages and Misalliances*,
Bernard Shaw and His Contemporaries,
DOI 10.1057/978-1-349-95170-3_9

143

In this very self-explanatory statement, Shaw's allegiance to gender equality is apparent. There were two very different models in operation within a marriage for both parties, in effect making a mockery of the word itself. Shaw believed that the institution needed reform and stated that "there is no question of abolishing marriage; but there is a very pressing question of improving its conditions" (*CPP* III:456). This chapter will, through an analysis of *Heartbreak House* (1916), *Annajanska, The Bolshevik Empress* (1917), and *Back to Methuselah* (1920), investigate how Shaw demonstrates that marriage underpins the very stability of society, and, by association, the nation, during a period when the "war to end all wars" turned societal expectations on their head.[4] *Heartbreak House*, written against the backdrop of World War 1, depicts a society in a state of flux. The very foundation of society, the family, is interrogated, and in creating that fractured familial scenario raises the question of how society can operate if the very basis of it is dysfunctional. *Annajanska, The Bolshevik Empress* approaches the topic in a completely different way. Writing in the year of the Russian Revolution, Shaw uses societal expectations of woman's role in society to expose the inadequacies of such expectations to an audience, especially in relation to equality. In *Back to Methuselah*, his epic play after *Annajanska* written in the aftermath of the Great War, Shaw continues the debate by returning to the beginning of time and the first marriage, the pledge of Adam and Eve to love one another and take no other partner for the rest of their lives, inventing, as the Serpent says, "the word marriage" (*CPP* V:357). Shaw stretches the debate over five parts that are actually full-length plays in their own right. The time span for the five parts is approximately 36,000 years. Arguably, by bringing the final part full circle, Shaw's purpose was to demonstrate that whatever progress is made in society is tenuous at best, and the decisions that are made regarding marriage and relationships need to be carefully engineered or the mistakes of past generations could resonate far beyond future imagination. On the subject of marriage, Shaw maintains that "if marriage cannot be made to produce something better than we are, marriage will have to go, or else the nation will have to go" (*CPP* III:466). *Heartbreak House, Annajanska,* The Bolshevik Empress, and *Back to Methuselah* deal dramaturgically with the fundamental debate that Shaw raises in this very provocative statement.

Marriage was considered one of the most significant issues in a woman's life in the Victorian period, as it was a necessity for both her moral and her economic survival. H.E. Harvey, writing in the period, observed:

The artificial distinction conferred on society on the married woman as compared with the unmarried, combined with the difficulty of qualifying for other professions, is, of course the great inducement to marriage with the majority of women, as very many women do not care for domestic life and would greatly prefer independence and liberty. But they marry because society expects it of them, and tempts them with its favours.[5]

Shaw's preface to *Getting Married* deals in depth with all the issues surrounding the marriage question, but more importantly he plays with the notional options of the varying social issues surrounding marriage through the female characters in his plays. Blanche Sartorius in *Widower's Houses* (1892) is representative of marriage for social position, as is Nora Reilly in *John Bull's Other Island* (1904), while Vivie Warren in *Mrs Warren's Profession* (1893) represents the New Woman and the single professional life. Patriarchal dominance is questioned in *Candida* (1894), while every possible marital and relationship status is explored in *Getting Married* (1908). Shaw experiments with the "other profession" open to women in *Mrs Warren's Profession* (1893) and *The Shewing-up of Blanco Posnet* (1909), and alludes to it in *Pygmalion* (1912). By the time World War I began, the idea for *Heartbreak House* had been fermenting in his mind, and there is no doubt that the years that followed the completion of it, and the other two plays under discussion, Shaw's outlook on the traditional values in which society had embedded itself had changed utterly.

Arguably, in stating in the preface to *Heartbreak House* that "It is a cultured leisured Europe before the war," Shaw was making a cynical observation. An analysis of the play demonstrates that the "culture" in it is imagined and the "leisure" that he points to actually exposes the idle stagnation of the moneyed classes in wartime Britain. Shaw is quoted by Holroyd as stating to Nugent Monck, "The captain's house and gardens are not only a place but an atmosphere"; Holroyd analyzes this to mean "the house is all inclusive. It contains light and dark, land and sea, sleeping and waking, fantasy and fact" (*Holroyd* III:14). Holroyd's definition of the all-inclusiveness of *Heartbreak House*, and especially his reference to fantasy which permeates all the other descriptions of "waking, sleeping, light, dark, land, sea," culminates in the word "fact," a word which grounds all these other notions in the fantasy element of the play. The very word "fact" questions the perceptions of both the characters and the audience. What is real and what is not? From the outset, as Holroyd observes, sleeping and dreaming set the tone for the unfolding plot. The concept of the house as a ship further conveys a sense of the distorted reality that is to come, a sense that all is "at sea." This distorted reality underpins a vacuous instability that Shaw has identified and explored through a fractured familial scenario and an impending marriage question, that of Ellie Dunn to Boss Mangan. In addition, however, to this ostensible marriage question is the marriage status of all the other characters in the play.

Heartbreak House and its inhabitants depict a society in a state of flux. Chaos and disorder reign from the outset: Ellie arrives at Heartbreak House, at the invitation of Hesione Hushabye, Captain Shotover's eldest daughter, and finds there is no one to welcome her. The arrival of the second daughter of the house, Lady Ariadne Utterword, is no less fraught with confusion, for not only is she not greeted, she is not even recognized by her father, Captain Shotover, or her sister. It is learned that Captain Shotover is an inventor and that Hector Hushabye, Hesione's husband, is an "inventor" of stories. All the members of the house have pet names, which adds to the play's world of make-believe. Ellie encapsulates the nucleus of the house when she finds that Hesione's hair is false by stating that "everything is false" (*CPP* V:126). Lady Utterword's arrival is followed by Mazzini Dunne, Ellie's father, whom Captain Shotover mistakes for a ship's boatswain that he once sailed with and who later turns out to be Nurse Guinness's husband, and finally by Boss Mangan, Ellie's fiancé and her father's boss. Hesione has little time for Ellie's father, Mazzini Dunne, calling him "an old brute" (*CPP* V:73) and, in reaction to Ellie's defense of her father, tells her that she'll "give that born soldier of freedom a piece" of her "mind that will stand him on his selfish old head for a week" (*CPP* V:75). Hesione's reasoning soon becomes clear: she feels that Ellie is being traded as a business commodity in gratitude for Mangan's so-called role as her father's savior. Mrs. Hushabye does not believe in self-sacrifice, telling Ellie "that it is not honourable or grateful to marry a man you don't love" (*CPP* V:77–78). She is determined to put a stop to Ellie's marriage to Mangan and constructs the conversation in such a manner as to glean Ellie's real thoughts.

Nicholas Grene declares that "Hesione ... is a character of enormous charm and real good will in her efforts to extricate Ellie from the clutches of Boss Mangan. She uses her charm selflessly in Ellie's interests ...."[6] Though she is a character of great charm, her motivation for helping Ellie is not as selfless as Grene believes. Hesione Hushabye is a self-serving character who seeks amusement and entertainment through the lives of others. She satisfies the profile of an establishment whose actions display the futility of the lives of the inhabitants of the house. She attempts to cause mischief by drawing from Ellie a confession of her love for one Marcus Darnley, who turns out to be Hector Hushabye, Hesione's husband. Hesione's reaction to the flirtation between Ellie and Hector says a lot about her own marriage and points to a lethargy inherent in an idle society. Hector is a day dreamer who, in choosing the alter ego "Marcus Darnley," illustrates an attitude that is not in touch with reality. Hesione feeds into this inertia by rejecting her father's suggestion that Hector should earn a living, saying he "should do nothing of the sort. I should never see you from breakfast to dinner. I want my husband" (*CPP* V:103). Although Hesione appears to be amused by her husband's flirtatious nature, there is an underlying darkness in her comment: she wants him where she can see him. This undertone points once again to the insecurities that resound in the house.

Lady Ariadne Utterword's marriage to "Sir Hastings Utterword, who has been governor of all the crown colonies in succession" (*CPP* V:66) tells a wider tale of domination and colonization, which is also alluded to when Hector Hushabye talks of Shotover's marriage to a "black witch" and that the two "demon daughters are their mystical progeny" (*CPP* V:156). These unions convey a patriarchal power that points to the inequalities both in marriage and in empire. For Shaw, "the [marriage] service was really only an honest attempt to make the best of a commercial contract of property and slavery" (*CPP* III:477). Ania Loomba states of colonialism that it "can be defined as the conquest and control of other people's lands and goods."[7] She maintains this "process of forming a new community ... meant *unforming* or reforming what existed there already, and involved a wide range of practices including trade, plunder, negotiation, warfare, genocide, enslavement and rebellions."[8] Shaw, in the preface to *Getting Married*, maintains that within marriage in that era, there was no question but that it imposed an economic slavery on the woman in terms of her subservient dependence on her husband.

The theme of colonization is also reinforced through the character of Boss Mangan. David Clare in his article in the *New Hibernia Review* refers to Mangan as a "particularly intriguing Irish diasporic character,"[9] and the position he holds within the play as a member of a syndicate, like Broadbent's syndicate in *John Bull's Other Island*, conveys a sense of empire. However, the development of Ellie's character acts as a bid for change. Her interaction with Mangan reveals an inner strength that had not been heretofore acknowledged. The verbal interaction in Act II reduces Mangan to a nearly insignificant entity as Ellie demonstrates how well she has thought out her marriage to him and how to capitalize on the benefits of the marriage arrangement. Mangan reveals to Ellie that he deliberately ruined her father as an attempt at control, though it is not until Act III that events take a distinct twist and the truth about Mangan is revealed. It is a revelation which compounds the illusory appearances that are integral to *Heartbreak House*. Ellie's reaction to Mangan's confession is indifference, and she uses emotional blackmail to prevent him from backing out of their arrangement. However, she ultimately rejects Mangan when, central to the final act, she commands the attention of the other members of the house. She announces her marriage to Captain Shotover, stating that it is a spiritual union "made in heaven, where all true marriages are made" (*CPP* V:168). The implication of the word "marriage" implies a consensual union. The case of Nora and Broadbent's union in *John Bull's Other Island* was a marriage for the purpose of financial gain on Nora's part, and acceptance of community on the part of Broadbent. Ellie, on the other hand, rejects that notion of materialism with Mangan and opts for a union that looks beyond the immediate merging of wisdom, experience, and enthusiasm. Shaw felt that "if ... domestic laws are kept so inhuman that they at last provoke a furious general insurrection against them ... we shall in a very literal sense empty the baby out with the bath by abolishing an institution which needs nothing more than a little obvious and easy rationalizing to make it not only harmless but comfortable, honorable, and useful" (*CPP* III:541–542). There is a perception that all the characters in the house are strangers to each other, even those related by blood, conveying an air of disconnect, a lack of coherence or community. They are symbolic of a society that is trapped in a notional and outdated way of living, as outdated as the marriage laws that govern them.

In writing *Annajanska*, The Bolshevik Empress after *Heartbreak House* in 1917, Shaw stated that it was a 'bravura piece' (*CPP* V:231). It has to be argued that it is much more than technically skillful, in that Shaw has taken the character of Annajanska and used the trope of marriage once again to present a societal and political situation. Russia in 1917 was on the brink of change. Revolution had been part of the political landscape since 1905. By 1917, the toll of World War I and the autonomy of Tsar Nicholas II, who believed that his reign was a divine right and nothing to do with the will of the people, had created an atmosphere of mutiny, and many small rebellions began to take place. In fact, Nicholas II, then the archaic symbol of patriarchal power, was forced to abdicate in March 1917, making way for provincial government; this, in turn, suggested the possibility of great change to the western world. In recounting an incident that took place in July of that year, Orlando Figes argued of one situation that "Centuries of serfdom and subservience had not prepared him to stand up to his political masters—and in that lay the whole tragedy of the Russian people."[10] Shaw's cleverness lay in his knowledge and interest in the conflict in Russia. A situation of dual power (*dvoevlastie*) was at play; struggles were rife between the provisional government and a rising Bolshevik party.[11] In creating an illusion of duality in the character of Annajanska by creating her role as both male and female, Shaw is highlighting the equality of the sexes while also mirroring the political duality at play. The "metaphorical dagger" (*CPP* V:236) is symbolic of the impending fracture of the nation state, as represented by Annajanska. Strammfest's horror at Annajanska joining the revolution is heightened by the fact that he thinks she also has "eloped with a young officer" (*CPP* V:236). There is a definite inference here to a "marriage" of two opposing sides. Strammfest's reaction to Schneidekind's question "Committed suicide?" (*CPP* V:236) reflects a Shavian view on the viability of marriage between an incompatible couple and the case for dissolving such a union through divorce. His rationale was that divorce would improve the institution of marriage, that "in fact, it is not the destruction of marriage, but the first condition of its maintenance" (*CPP* III:522).

Annajanska's appearance does nothing to rationalize a bizarre scene; in fact, if anything it increases the confusion. The indecision of what to do with her creates a comedic dilemma. True to Shavian form, Annajanska is presented as a strong female character—determined and in control. She manages to make the men around her look like indecisive fools, and she plays with their misconceptions of her status. Convinced she is going to elope, Strammfest cannot countenance the notion of a woman traveling on her own. This reflects the patriarchal thinking of the time: that marriage was the only respectable occupation for a woman. Shaw, in handing the power to "the Grand Duchess," as Strammfest addresses Annajanska in the final stages of this one-act play, creates the surprise twist at the end that speaks to the revolutionary times of the twentieth century's second decade, which turned patriarchal thinking on its head. Strammfest's question "how can I obey six dictators at once?" (*CPP* V:244) signals the societal chaos that was present in international politics. Annajanska's reply echoes Hector Hushabye's treatise on the world that "we are what is wrong with it" (*CPP* V:159) when she states: "We are so decayed, so out of date, so feeble, so wicked in our own despite, that we have come at last to will our own destruction" (*CPP* V:245). The duplicity of Annajanska's disguise holds a mirror to Shaw's contemporary society in order to demonstrate that nothing is what it seems.

Shaw began *Back to Methuselah* seven months before the end of World War I and completed it two years later. It was his way of presenting a future model for consideration from what was a demoralized present. Shaw, as Michael Holroyd argues, "struggled to discover what this discouraged generation needed to have said to it" (*Holroyd* III:35). In the *Postscript after Twenty-Five Years*, Shaw states:

> The history of modern thought now teaches us that when we are forced to give up the creeds by their childishness and their conflicts with science we must either embrace Creative Evolution or fall into the bottomless pit of an utterly discouraging pessimism. (*CPP* V:702)

Back to Methuselah was Shaw's contribution to a hopeful post-war modern world. The five-play cycle embraces a Shavian Life Force through the catechism of Creative Evolution, a concept devised by French philosopher Henri Bergson in 1907[12] and borrowed by Shaw. The first play of the cycle, titled *In the Beginning*, is set in the Garden of Eden, with the characters of Adam and Eve and the Serpent. Cleverly, Shaw uses a discussion on death as the starting point of the first act, an acknowledgment of the somber mood after the war as society attempted to come to terms with the catastrophic loss of the "flower of a generation." However, out of death comes hope, as the ensuing conversation with the Serpent reveals. Although displaying an abhorrence of death, Adam wishes for "an end some day, and yet no end. If only I can be relieved of the horror of having to endure myself for ever!" (*CPP* V:351). Shaw opens the debate on the necessity of death for the future of life, and in essence turns the discourse from the morbidity of death to birth and love. The first act ends with the invention of the word "marriage":

Adam:	I will live a thousand years: and then I will endure no more: I will die and take my rest. And I shall love Eve all that time and no other woman
Eve:	And if Adam keeps his vow I will love no other man until he dies
The Serpent:	You have both invented marriage and what he will be to you and no other woman is husband: and what you will be to him and no other man is wife. (*CPP* V:357)

In ending this, the first act in the first play of the cycle, with the union of Adam and Eve in marriage, Shaw has set up the very basis and foundation of society and, by default, the nation. The message is one of hope for the future: that men and women working together can help build and shape future generations. Holroyd argues that Eve represents hope and "identifies improvement with the species rather than herself and accepts uncertainty, even death, as the inevitable risk in the process of creation" (*Holroyd* III:44). Through the marriage of Adam and Eve the cycle of life is developed, and the second act opens many centuries later with the result of that union. The theme of death as a means of renewal continues when it is learned that Cain has killed his brother Abel. Cain represents modernity by rejecting the lifestyle of his parents. He rejects the land in favor of blood sports, a trait he envied in Abel. He sees killing as meaning he is a man of spirit: "stronger, happier, freer" (*CPP* V:362). Adam tells him to "Be thankful to your parents, who enabled you to hand on your burden to new and better men, and won you eternal rest; for we invented death" (*CPP* V:376). The closing message of the play suggests that the marriage of death and birth leads on to progression when Eve states" "there is something else. We do not know what it is yet but someday we shall find out" (*CPP* V:377).

This search for that "something else" continues in *The Gospel of the Brothers Barnabas*. The action takes place in the first years after World War I and introduces the idea of "will" and the prospect of living for 300 years. It is linked once again to the question of marriage when the brothers Barnabas and Haslam decide that the parlormaid's decision to get married is foolish, as "She has to die before she knows." In response to Conrad's statement, Franklyn clarifies: "She hasn't time to form a well-instructed conscience." He maintains that "A world without conscience, that is the horror of our condition" (*CPP* V:383). The condition he speaks of is, of course, life, and the futility of not reaching the maturation needed for the development of the human spirit. The parlormaid gives Conrad pause for thought in answer to his question on her thoughts on living "a devil of a long time" (*CPP* V:387), when she muses on the idea of the compatibility of long life and marriage: "he must take me for better or worse, til death do us part. Do you think he would be ready to do that, sir, if he thought it might be for several hundred years?" (*CPP* V:387). Shaw has posed a particularly pertinent question in light of the validity of marriage if society were to continue functioning as it was. It goes back to the discussion on the need for people to be married more than once in order for society to thrive and evolve. He argued that "Divorce only reasserts couples … it makes people much more willing to marry, especially prudent people and people with a high sense of self-respect" (*CPP* III:522). Underpinning the basis of the Life Force and longevity is the discussion of the fundamental basis of the formation of society through marriage.

The theme continues in Part III, *The Thing Happens*, when the gospel of the brothers Barnabas becomes a reality for two of the characters, the parlormaid and the Reverend Haslam; a pair whom the brothers did not consider worthy of Creative Evolution. Because of class prejudice, Savvy, Franklyn's daughter, considered longevity improbable if it meant the parlormaid were to be a long-liver. Set in the future year of 2170 AD in the Office of the President of the British Isles, the introductory characters bear resemblance to the characters from the earlier play. Burge-Lubin is a mix between the older Burge and the younger Lubin, and Barnabas resembles Conrad but as a younger version. This speaks to an evolutionary trajectory of the human species. However, the revelation of the parlormaid having metamorphosed into long-liver Mrs. Lutestring, the Domestic Minister, and the Reverend Haslam into the Archbishop of York, propels the dramatic plot forward. The implications and the problems that surround this are discussed, especially in relation to marriage. Consternation ensues when Mrs. Lutestring refers to the other characters as children and speaks to the difficulties in meeting grown-up people. She confessed to getting married on her "hundred and first birthday. But of course I had to marry an elderly man: a man over sixty" (*CPP* V:474). The ensuing discussion on age in relation to marriage exposes a view that marriage needs to be between mature equals in order for it to form a solid base. The Archbishop begs the question: "Can you short lived people not understand that as the confusion and immaturity and primitive animalism in which we live for the first hundred years of our life is worse in this matter of sex than in any other, you are intolerable to us in that relation" (*CPP* V:475). The point that seems to be being made here is one of conscience and governance, with marriage being the template from which all morality stems. It appears to challenge the viability of a society that does not give due consideration to what Shaw termed "the cornerstone of the system that produced us," specifically "the family and the institution of marriage" (*CPP* III:466). The trope of marriage is once again used to protect the system when the discussion on race, color, and creed becomes so broad that Mrs. Lutestring's reaction to the ramblings of Burge-Lubin is to approach the Archbishop, her contemporary, with the line: "If the white race is to be saved, our destiny is apparent" (*CPP* V:480). Although this statement would not be seen as politically correct, it must be remembered that era from which it sprang was all about nations that were trying to regroup and rebuild after a horrendous and annihilating war. The sense of an unknown and uncertain future intrinsic to this play is articulated by the character of Confucius when he states:

> Every mortal man and woman in the community will begin to count on living for three centuries. Things will happen which you could not foresee: terrible things. The family will dissolve: parents and children will no longer be the old and the young: brothers and sisters will meet as strangers after a hundred years separation: the ties of blood will lose their innocence. The imaginations of men, let loose over the possibilities of three centuries of life will drive them mad and wreck human society. (*CPP* V:483–484)

This play could be described as the epicenter of the cycle, the one that has exploded to a conscious surface and prepared the audience for what is to follow. Shaw definitely seems to suggest through *The Thing Happens* that the concept of irreversible Creative Evolution needs to be examined to see how creative it actually is.

Moving to the year 3000 AD, *The Tragedy of an Elderly Gentleman* fast-forwards the audience to a time when "short-livers" are becoming a thing of the past, as a new race of people have come into existence who can live as long as they choose. It quickly becomes obvious that marriage is now an outdated notion. In his introductory conversation with Zoo, the Elderly Gentleman inquires whether she is a "Miss" or a "Mrs" When he speaks to her about marriage, she is baffled and says: "You are getting out of my depth: I don't understand a word that you are saying.

Married and questionable taste convey nothing to me. Stop, though. Is married an old form of the word mothered?" (*CPP* V:505). As the play progresses, so does the sense of chaos. The emphasis appears to be on creating a society in order to lengthen the lifespan of its members (or entities). Suggestive of a sterile society, where marriage and family have no place, Zoo reveals that her function is to "specialize in babies" (*CPP* V:506). The sterility of society is mirrored by the landscape when it is learned that there are "no cities" and "no ruins" (*CPP* V:530). The Elderly Gentleman, in remarking at the end of Act I "Sic transit gloria mundi!" (Thus passes the glory of the world; *CPP* V:530), enforces a vision of an apocalyptic landscape where creativeness has been stymied through a collective singular mindset.

Almost farcically, Act II opens with the appearance of Napoleon, "the man of destiny," and his discussion with the Oracle on war, which becomes a battle of wits between Napoleon and the Oracle. This continues the chaotic tone of the play, and the Shavian technique of no resolution is very much in evidence. A family arrives on the scene, the Envoy, his wife, and his daughter, adding to the confusion as Napoleon departs. This "family" is foreign and alien to the social order being dramatized. There is a sense that they are almost exhibits, rather like animals in a zoo, especially as the Elderly Gentleman and his family are paraded in front of the Oracle inside the temple in Act III. Shaw reveals the foolishness of wasted opportunity, as well as the human desire to know what the future holds. Zoo states: "how often must you be told we cannot see the future? There is no such thing as the future until it is the present" (*CPP* V:559). This belies the whole premise of her society, whose goal is long life. In the final minutes of the act, the Elderly Gentleman, in choosing to die from "discouragement" rather than "disgust and despair" (*CPP* V:562), points to a notion of irresolvable futility that transcends the question of creative evolution.

The final play, *As Far as Thought Can Reach*, presents an evolved human society where not only are there no marriages, but no mammal-type births either. All new humans are formed in an egg, and the concept of time is distorted. The new young are born as adolescents and their journey to maturation as fully informed adults takes place over 4 years, following a process that bears a remarkable similarity to human development as it formerly was, until they reach a stage where they become members of "the ancients," at which point the only way to death is through an accident. Shaw yet again plays with history and creativity when he introduces the character of Pygmalion who, along with the other young artists, has learned how to create human beings. The man and woman they create introduce the notion of marriage into this, the final play. They also introduce the concept of feelings and stimulus, even though they are referred to as "mere automata" (*CPP* V:599) by the ancients, who kill them by discouraging them. The male and female figures are presented as man and wife, and their deaths represented as the death of a traditional way of life, one that had marriage and family as a basis for society. Arguably, this demise of traditional values creates an endless vacuum, devoid of creativity and independent thought. This is telling when one of the youths, Ecrasia, wishes for her "fatal accident" before the day dawns that brings life eternal as prophesied by the He-Ancient. In response, Arjillax states:

> *Ecrasia*: For once, I agree with you. A world in which there were nothing plastic would be an utterly miserable one. No limbs, no contours, no exquisite lines and elegant shapes, no worship of beautiful bodies, no poetic embraces in which cultivated lovers pretend that their caressing hands are wandering over celestial hills and enchanted valleys. (*CPP* V:621)

Yet again, Shaw has painted an apocalyptic picture: a barren wasteland, devoid of human emotion, pleasure, and consciousness. In a form of reflection, the final minutes of this one-act play revert to the beginning as the ghosts of Adam, Eve, Cain, the Serpent, and Lilith appear, and what has been achieved is interrogated. Adam and Eve, as husband and wife, ponder the results of their endeavors. Adam states:

> he can make nothing of it, neither head nor tail. What is it all for? Why? Whither? Whence? We were well enough in the garden. And now the fools have killed all the animals; and they are dissatisfied because they cannot be bothered with their bodies. Foolishness, I call it. (*CPP* V:629)

The cycle has come full circle and the closing lines are given to Lilith. Purdon argues that giving her the last words was "Shaw's attempt to get free from the limitations of the natural world, the world of the senses, and the course of natural life."[13] Arguably, however, Shaw was creating a stark image of life without the accepted traditional structure of marriage and family, and presenting a grim portrayal of an aimless society whose main purpose is to achieve eternal life. Lilith's final words bear testament to this thinking: "And for what may be beyond, the eyesight of Lilith is too short. It is enough that there is a beyond" (*CPP* V:631). There is a resounding note of hope seasoned with common sense in these words, a latent message for mankind to live for the present in order to protect the future.

World War I created a fracture in both societal and family life. Millions of young men went to war and never returned. The course of a generation was changed forever for both men and women. Women who had manned the munitions factories were forced back into the home to make way for the returning workforce. Through all this Shaw realized there was no going back to the older way of life. Old values had to be interrogated and adapted to a changing modern society. It is obvious that he felt that without marriage, society had no hope of healing, but also that marriage, in the form it retained, was equally inoperable. His idea of a Life Force combined with Creative Evolution was to guide people to see beyond the narrowness that governed them and fashion a change that would create a stronger, independent society and nation.

Notes

1. Bernard Shaw (1905) *The Irrational Knot* (London: Heron Books), p. xix.
2. Bernard Shaw (1905) *The Irrational Knot*, p. xix.
3. Bernard Shaw (1926) *The Quintessence of Ibsenism* (London: Constable & Company), p. 36 (Shaw 1926).
4. Due to the sheer size of both *Heartbreak House* and *Back to Methuselah* and the word limitations for the chapter, it will not be possible to give an in-depth analysis of more than the theme under discussion.
5. H.E. Harvey (2001) The Voice of Woman in *A New Woman Reader*, ed. Carolyn Christensen Nelson (Canada: Broadview Press), p. 209 (Harvey 2001).
6. Nicholas Grene (1984) *Bernard Shaw: A Critical View* (New York: St. Martin's Press), p. 125 (Grene 1984).
7. Ania Loomba (1998) *Colonialism/Postcolonialism* (London and New York: Routledge), p. 2 (Loomba 1998).
8. Ania Loomba (1998) *Colonialism/Postcolonialism*, p. 2.
9. David Clare *Bernard Shaw, Henry Higgins and the Irish Diaspora* in *New Hibernia Review* 18:1 (Earrach/Spring 2014) 93–105, p. 103 (Clare 2014).
10. Orlando Figes (1996) *A People's Tragedy: The Russian Revolution 1891–1924* (London: Pimlico), p. 432 (Figes 1996).

11. See Chaps. 10 and 11 in Orlando Figes (1996) *A People's Tragedy: The Russian Revolution 1891–1924*).
12. Bergson's book *Creative Evolution* was translated into English by Arthur Mitchell in 1911.
13. C.B. Purdon (1963) *A Guide to the Plays of Bernard Shaw* (London; Methuen & Co Ltd), p. 270 (Purdon 1963).

REFERENCES

Clare, David. 2014. Bernard Shaw, Henry Higgins and the Irish Diaspora. *New Hibernia Review, Spring*, 18 (1): 93–105.
Figes, Orlando. 1996. *A People's Tragedy: The Russian Revolution 1891–1924*. London: Pimlico.
Grene, Nicholas. 1984. *Bernard Shaw: A Critical View*. New York: St. Martin's Press.
Harvey, H.E. 2001. The Voice of Woman. In *A New Woman's Reader: Fiction, Articles and Drama of the 1890s*, ed. Carolyn Christensen Nelson, 207–210. Peterborough, ON: Broadview Press.
Loomba, Ania. 1998. *Colonialism/Post Colonialism*. London: Routledge.
Purdon, C.B. 1963. *A Guide to the Plays of Bernard Shaw*. London: Methuen.
Shaw, Bernard. 1926. *The Quintessence of Ibsenism*. London: Constable.

AUTHOR BIOGRAPHY

Audrey McNamara a Ph.D. in drama from University College Dublin, Ireland, is currently working on a monograph, *Bernard Shaw: From Womanhood to Nationhood—The Irish Shaw*. She is also co-editing an anthology of essays, *Shaw and the Making of Modern Ireland* due 2017 and volume 36.1 of *SHAW: The Journal of Bernard Shaw Studies: Shaw and Money*, published June 2016. She organized the first ever Irish Shaw international conference in 2012, co-sponsored by UCD Humanities Institute and the International Shaw Society, which was opened by the President of Ireland, Michael D. Higgins.

CHAPTER 10

Beyond *Married Love*: Shaw, Stopes, and Female Desire in the Drama Between the Wars, 1923–1934

D.A. Hadfield

In her 2006 work *The Marriage Paradox: Modernist Novels and the Cultural Imperative to Marry*, Davida Pines argues that the modernist period offered "the likeliest moment" for literature to loosen "the cultural hold of the marriage plot."[1] The period between the world wars offered a unique moment where the interests of both feminist campaigners and literary artists converged in a desire to break from the confining values and traditions of the Victorian and Edwardian eras. Of all the traditions desiring to be broken, few were as stifling as the domesticating cage of marriage. Pines argues, however, that the critique of marriage in many major novels of the modernist period is marked by an ambivalence that "paradoxically reinforce[s] the marital norm." For Pines, this paradox goes a long way toward explaining why the marriage plot continues to dominate contemporary culture as the "only thinkable form of adult social relations" and the "crucial marker of [women's] personal success," even for

D.A. Hadfield (✉)
Department of English Language and Literature,
University of Waterloo, Waterloo, Canada
e-mail: dhadfield@uwaterloo.ca

© The Author(s) 2017
R.A. Gaines (ed.), *Bernard Shaw's Marriages and Misalliances*,
Bernard Shaw and His Contemporaries,
DOI 10.1057/978-1-349-95170-3_10

159

women who are financially and otherwise independent of men.[2] Katherine Holden concurs that, even though single women now have a broader range of acceptable behavior, including sexual activity, "the single are viewed in relation to the supposed permanence and solidity of the married state as in a temporary and generally inferior position," reinforcing marriage as an institution integral to a sense of cultural stability.[3] Holden specifically credits the landmark 1918 publication of Marie Stopes's *Married Love* as a major contributor to this persistent validation of marriage. Both Holden and Karen Chow[4] point out the ambivalent feminism of Stopes's book, which simultaneously affirmed women's sexual autonomy and agency, and insisted that their natural and healthy sex drives could only be expressed and satisfied within traditional marriage relationships.

Even before the advent of literary modernism or the appearance of Stopes's landmark work after World War I, Shaw had been an outspoken critic of marriage as an institution, in print and in person. He also clearly aligned himself with Ibsen and theatrical modernism, often risking dramatic censorship for plays that critiqued social constructions of marriage and gender. Shaw's four interwar plays discussed in this chapter—*Saint Joan, Too True to Be Good, The Millionairess,* and *The Six of Calais*—show him continuing his critiques, specifically considering what role marriage might play among women for whom suffrage victories, wartime employment, *Married Love,* and access to birth control had brought gains in political, physical, economic, and sexual autonomy. For Shaw, too, this was a likely moment to question the marriage plot, and, like his modernist cohort, Shaw ultimately demonstrates some ambivalence. While Shaw's plays compare favorably to *Married Love* and Stopes's play *Our Ostriches* in advocating for women's equality and autonomy outside marriage, he also increasingly accepted marriage as the normative social arrangement, focusing on possible ways in which newly empowered women could help redefine marriage as an institution, but not necessarily escape it.

Marianne DeKoven identifies "a male Modernist fear of women's new power" in the ambivalent treatment of powerful women in modernist works, where a fascination with "the empowered feminine" always contends with "masculinist misogyny."[5] This is the central dialectic of *Saint Joan,* but Shaw's experiments with history and narrative form are fairly unequivocal in their attempt to let the empowered feminine triumph. Shaw's play follows Joan of Arc through her military victories and the crowning of the Dauphin at Rheims, increasingly exposing the misogyny and fear the maid inspires in the political power brokers whose authority she refuses to recognize. In the play's climax, the Catholic Inquisition condones Joan's death when it becomes clear she will not be domesticated into a submissive woman's role, but Shaw refuses to end Joan's story with her defeat by church and state. He added a controversial epilogue after the burning in which Joan reappears and offers to resurrect herself for a contemporary society that claims it no longer fears her power—only to be rejected all over again. Shaw's attempt to imagine an alternative ending for her that is neither marriage nor inevitable death affirms Joan's identity as an empowered, independent woman, and lays the blame for her fate on the misogynistic society—historical and contemporary—that fears the independent woman as much as the saint. Even though the play's central conflict is ostensibly about "the individual, the spirit and genius that were capable of transcending the body,"[6] the action relentlessly plays itself out on the protagonist's undomesticated female body, which presents too much of a threat to patriarchal order to be allowed to survive.

Critics commonly take their cue from lines like "I will never take a husband ... I do not want to be thought of as a woman" (*CPP* VI:120), and Joan's insistence on male military dress to focus on her identity as an unsexed and ungendered warrior. However, Shaw himself readily admitted the connection between the Joan of Arc he staged and the icon of the pre-war suffrage campaign,[7] a movement that was fundamentally imbricated with empowered, specifically female, identity. Moreover, he also insisted in his preface that Joan "was not sexless: in spite of the virginity she had vowed up to a point, and preserved to her death, she never excluded the possibility of marriage for herself," but only "seemed neutral in the conflict of sex because men were too much afraid of her to fall in love with her" (*CPP* VI:21). During the Inquisition scene, Shaw has Joan defend her domesticity by boasting, "I will do a lady's work in the house—spin or weave—against any woman in Rouen" and identifying with a female role, "I could drag about in a skirt; I could let the banners and the trumpets and the knights and soldiers pass me and leave me behind as they leave the other women" (*CPP* VI:172, 183). In highlighting Joan's eligibility and fitness for conventional female domesticity, Shaw normalizes her to an audience for whom "spinsterhood was often aligned with frigidity: if a woman chose to be single her choice was perceived as somehow abnormal; independence from a marital relationship was not seen as being healthy"[8]—an attitude that perfectly aligned Shaw's contemporaries with Joan's.

Unmarried, independent women presented a source of such anxiety after World War I for similar reasons that the New Woman unsettled the *fin de siècle*. First, because there were so many of them: by some estimates, two million women were rendered "surplus" in England by the shortage of marriageable men. It followed that if there were no husbands to support them, the economy had to accommodate the women's need to support themselves. Working women should have caused less anxiety for a society that had relied on women's labor during the war, but post-war jobs were scarce, and unemployed men did not welcome competing with women for them. So despite the first women's suffrage victory in 1918 and other gains like the Sex Disqualification (Removal) Act of 1919,[9] the interwar period actually saw an erosion of feminist gains and increasing pressure on women to relinquish their jobs and independence to the men back from the war. Married women were more vulnerable because, while various marriage reform acts had given them rights to a legal identity and property, they still did not have the right to control their own person. Discrimination against female workers took advantage of the fact that husbands still controlled what kinds of labor their wives' bodies were used for.[10]

As an unmarried woman, then, Joan manifests for Shaw's audience as an uncontrolled and uncontrollable body. Her "commonsense" (*CPP* VI:177) insistence on wearing a soldier's uniform scandalizes her accusers explicitly because men's clothes do not belong on her woman's body; rather than disguising her gender from the authorities, her sartorial misalignment serves to highlight it. But if Joan's refusal to submit to the authority of the patriarchal institutions of church and state seems unnatural, other aspects of her crusade emphasize a normative female identity: she is willing to sacrifice herself for love, just not her love for a husband and children. She is "in love with" war and religion (*CPP* VI:120) and she expresses her love for France in the maternal language of protection and nurture (*CPP* VI:154). Shaw implies that Joan—his Protestant and nationalist saint—is a threat mainly for the patriarchal and misogynistic society that fears women it cannot domesticate. And by trying to revive Joan in the epilogue, only to have her rejected all over again, Shaw explicitly points out that this fear is not just historical artifact, but contemporary reality. In Joan, Shaw creates a woman who is simultaneously historical and contemporary, whose threat as a fifteenth-century heretic is amplified in the context of the twentieth-century unmarried woman.

Shaw's epilogue attempts to overwrite the convenient collusion between history and conventional narrative form to imagine an ending other than marriage or death for independent women, creating a more radical female identity than even an ardent fellow crusader like Marie Stopes could imagine. At the same time as Shaw was writing *Saint Joan*, Stopes was writing *Our Ostriches*, whose upper-class heroine, Evadne Carillon, defies her family, rejects her fiancé, and faces her own hostile tribunal in her fight to bring relief to the poor in the form of birth control. As defiant as Stopes makes Evadne, she ultimately recuperates her heroine in the most conventional way possible, with Evadne anticipating a happily married future.

By 1923 when these plays were written, Marie Stopes was as well known as Bernard Shaw, thanks to the publication of *Married Love* and follow-up works, as well as her opening of England's first birth control clinic in 1921. The two celebrities shared a prolific correspondence, an interest in eugenics, and an enthusiastic support for birth control education. They also shared a frustration with dramatic censorship, having both fallen afoul of the Lord Chamberlain's office. According to Stopes, her play *Vectia* was already in rehearsal when it was unexpectedly denied a license, and she wrote *Our Ostriches* in the space of a day to replace it.[11] *Our Ostriches* opens with a park scene that emphasizes the collusion of interests and control between upper-class society and the church, represented by Brother Peter, a "stout, elderly rubicund priest, ... beneath a surface of kindly joviality, ruthless."[12] Evadne becomes engaged to the desirable Lord Simplex, but almost immediately scandalizes everyone by insisting on "taking [her] fiancé slumming" (*CPP* VI:348) so she can visit her old nurse. Lord Simplex retreats in disgust to wait in the car, while Evadne sees at first hand the suffering of the women and their numerous, sickly children in the brutally impoverished tenements. While visiting, she encounters the "athletic, youthful ... bright, intelligent" (*CPP* VI:345) Dr. Verro Hodges, who has just delivered a woman's third stillborn child upstairs and arrives in time to attend another woman about to deliver what Evadne believes is a seventh child. Brother Peter also appears, clearly a familiar visitor, and "collects [the six children] easily, like a little flock, driving them before him" (*CPP* VI:358) to get them out of their laboring mother's way. When Brother Peter tells Evadne that devout Mrs. Flinker has five more babies "safe in heaven," she turns on him with indignation for the suffering of the women and children, and he questions her religious fealty. Just before Lord Simplex takes Evadne away, Dr. Hodges confirms that "science" could help control the number of stillborn and sickly babies in the slums, but is silenced by Brother Peter. Evadne's condemnation expresses a worldly version of Joan's indictment of church and state:

> You good, religious priests, you humane and learned medicals, you pater-
> nal Government officials all of you—are in the secret for yourselves—but
> what do you care for Mrs. Flinker *really*? Nothing! She's a parishioner,
> a patient, a subject—but a free woman? *Never*! *You* will not give her the
> knowledge you possess so that she may be saved torturing misery … well,
> I'll find out—I will find out for myself. (*CPP* VI:362)

Evadne returns to the slums two days later to find Mrs. Flinker's new-born also dead, and Brother Peter comforting the starving children with Bible stories, but still refusing to let Dr. Hodges explain how to control the birth of sick and unwanted children. Brother Peter directs Evadne to go home in terms evocative of Joan: "You are playing with fire. You don't know what you are speaking of. You must leave the world to wiser, older folk to manage." The stage direction describes Evadne's somewhat melodramatic response: "*She looks towards* BROTHER PETER, *but he is remote from her, separated by a gulf. In the silence cries up from the street. Meanwhile the world suffers.* EVADNE *lifts her arms slowly as though in her helpless isolation, she invokes God's help*," as she echoes Joan's anguish in her final line, "I will find out how to help alone, *alone!*" (*CPP* VI:366).

In the final act, Stopes sets Evadne in her own Inquisition scene when she appears in front of a smug and hostile Commission to argue that the poor should have access to birth control information. The scene opens with the Commission members—including Brother Peter and Dr. Hodges, and representing Government, middle- and upper-class society, church, and the medical profession—sitting at a long table with a witness whose learned opinion satisfactorily affirms their own anti-birth control stance. The next witness is Evadne, who comes in "*very soberly and beautifully dressed … She bows, looks very timid, almost frightened. The CHAIRMAN … speaks to her in a very encouraging, paternal fashion, and the girl quiets her fears and sits waiting, bowing slightly to the Commission*" (*CPP* VI:371–372). Evadne uses both logic and scripture to make her argument, in the process exposing the capitalist interest in maintaining a plentiful but weak working class. As the Commission becomes "stolidly hostile," Evadne defies them one last time: "You have no hearts … out-side real people need help—you could give and won't—I must go—*alone* and try to help them! [*She goes blindly out sobbing uncontrollably*]" (*CPP* VI:378), while the Commission is relieved to be quit of the "hot-headed little thing" (*CPP* VI:381). Unlike Joan, Evadne obviously does not go to the stake; instead, Stopes provides the other ending as common as death for the independent woman, marrying her to a suitable mate. In the final scene, Evadne breaks off her engagement to Lord Simplex when he refuses to discuss family planning with her, but immediately receives another proposal from Dr. Hodges, who had conveniently been falling in love with Evadne even as her passionate crusading was awakening his own reformist zeal. As the curtain goes down, Evadne rejoices that she can continue the crusade together with her new husband. Where Shaw tries to pry open the handcuffs of history to empower the unmarried, independent-minded woman that Joan of Arc represented, Stopes scripts the most traditional marriage plot for her fictional Joan figure, unable to dare a future without the marriage imperative.

Almost a decade later, Shaw continues to advocate for strong women in *Too True to Be Good*, but begins to display more ambivalence toward their empowered independence. As with *Saint Joan*, where marriage and its limitations loom large in their absence, Shaw critiques marriage mainly by contrasting it to the freedom of women who reject its institutional confines. And where Marie Stopes buries her own head in the sand around the possibility of single women's sexuality, Shaw openly acknowledges it. During the severe economic depression of the 1930s, however, Shaw is more equivocal about letting women—particularly working-class women—retain their absolute independence, and he reintroduces marriage, at least provisionally, as an appropriate possible ending for the independent, employable woman who represents the most "sexually and economically disruptive force."[13] Posing as a nurse, Sweetie masterminds a plan to rob her wealthy female client, but when the young invalid falls in love with Sweetie's former lover Aubrey, the three all run away together to enjoy a life of freedom and adventure, until the women get bored and look for fulfillment through more meaningful relationships. Miss Mopply eventually reunites with her mother, who has come looking for her invalid daughter and finds instead a healthy young woman who insists that "there should be only ... strong women able to stand by themselves ... No more lovers for me ... Since I came here I have been wanting to join the army, like Joan of Arc" (*CPP* VI:509, 512). Free to invent his own ending this time, Shaw offers this Joan of Arc freedom and independence, an intriguing alternative to marriage or death. But he is less generous with the sexually active, working-class Sweetie, for whom fulfillment means the possibility of giving up her autonomy and freedom to "settle down" in a marriage relationship with Private Meek.

The prospect of marriage is not promising in *Too True to Be Good*: there are no happy examples. The married characters are marked by disillusion, describing their marriages as disappointing, bitter, and confining. Only Sweetie claims her sister achieved the improbable ideal of a husband whose wedding day ardor never cooled, but only because "he beat her on their wedding day; and he beat her just as hard every day afterwards" (*CPP* VI:474). When Tallboys bashes Mrs. Mopply over the head, the umbrella-induced epiphany paradoxically makes her realize how much wives suffer even without physical beatings. In contrast to earlier plays like *Man and Superman* or *Candida*, Shaw can no longer pretend that women find total fulfillment and empowerment in marriage and motherhood. Instead, Mrs. Mopply comes to recognize that the self-sacrificing "angel in the house" is a dangerous and detestable figure: "I wasn't a bit like what they said I ought to be. I thought I had to pretend. ... I was told to sacrifice myself—to live for others; and I did it if ever a woman did. They told me that everyone would love me for it; and I thought they would; but ... now I find it was not only my daughter that hated me but all my friends ... I hate my daughter and my daughter hates me, because I sacrificed myself to her" (*CPP* VI:519–522). She further recognizes that the maternal care she was told to lavish on her children actually killed them, an idea that Shaw also expressed to Marie Stopes about his own upbringing, crediting his longevity to his mother's "complete neglect of me during my infancy ... because if she had attempted to take care of me her stupendous ladylike ignorance would certainly have killed me. ... motherhood is not every woman's vocation" (*Holroyd* I:18).

When Shaw portrays marriage as stifling and unrewarding rather than woman's natural vocation, he contradicts interwar media efforts to naturalize and "popularize the career of housewife and mother."[14] Stopes herself reinforced this ideal in *Married Love*, which made women's sexual satisfaction a legitimate pursuit, but continued to insist on happy marriage and motherhood as the only appropriate reasons to pursue it. Stopes's adamant commitment to "married love," in fact, undermined her own insistence that desiring sexual fulfillment was wholesome and natural by insisting that this ostensibly "natural" instinct could only be fulfilled within marriage. This contradiction between "the supposedly natural sex instinct and the moral codes surrounding marital status," which many of her unmarried correspondents even recognized, can be understood in terms of Stopes's desire to separate her birth control crusade from any possible fear that she was promoting immorality or promiscuity, which would have classified *Married Love* as obscenity.[15] But, as the title of *Too True to Be Good* implies, Shaw is more concerned with truth than moral codes, and that includes truth about sex and the single population.

In contrast to Stopes's willful ignorance, Shaw acknowledges the reality of non-conjugal sex. When Sweetie tells Miss Mopply she is expecting a gentleman friend, the invalid immediately infers indecent behavior. Sweetie herself, in fact, is the product of an illicit liaison between people who were "united in the sight of Heaven" but "not legally married" (*CPP* VI:451). Instead of offering Sweetie's origin story as a cautionary moral tale about the dangers of pre-marital sex, Shaw uses it to implicitly highlight the greater sexual freedom that Sweetie enjoys—the more consequence-free sexuality that Marie Stopes's birth control crusade had helped broker for Sweetie's generation. Sweetie epitomizes the single, working female, able to pursue economic independence *and* sexual satisfaction (even acknowledging that the two are sometimes linked) without risking pregnancy and giving up her mobility to a conventional domestic arrangement. In Aubrey's sermon on Sweetie, Shaw exposes the link between acknowledging an independent woman's sexual appetites, her "lower centres," and the unsettling collapse of patriarchal marriage: "Since the war the lower centres have become vocal. And the effect is that of an earthquake. For they speak truths that have never been spoken before—truths that the makers of our domestic institutions have tried to ignore. And now that Sweetie goes shouting them all over the place, the institutions are rocking and splitting and sundering" (*CPP* VI:478). The cautionary moral tale that Sweetie does embody is about the possibility that women might enjoy sexual freedom and adventure as much as men have.

But here Shaw exhibits that modernist ambivalence about women's freedom, and while he demolishes Stopes's hypocrisy about sex and singles, he proceeds to set Sweetie and the Sergeant back on the very path Stopes described in *Married Love*: "The great majority of our citizens—both men and women—after a time of waiting, or of exploring, or of oscillating from one attraction to another, 'settle down' and marry."[16] The only hope is that Shaw does not commit to the disappointingly conventional ending he scripts for the energetic Sweetie, at least not entirely. Sweetie and the Sergeant could hardly have a "conventional" marriage: there are no idealistic illusions about each other's innocence or purity, and the Sergeant also recognizes that he needs her as much as she needs him (*CPP* VI:518). More importantly, getting—and staying—married is never a certainty: they admit that constancy is neither's strong point, and the most they agree to is "keeping company for a while ... just to see how [they] get along together." Sweetie has already predicted this might be a fortnight or at most a month; the Sergeant will presumably have to work hard to continue satisfying her need for "variety" (*CPP* VI:518–519) beyond that. This may, after all, be less marriage imperative than marriage provisional, lasting only if it satisfies them both in body and mind and proves a "true" marriage rather than a misalliance.

Saint Joan and *Too True to Be Good* critiqued marriage indirectly by focusing on women's greater potential for autonomy and power available outside it; in *The Millionairess* and *The Six of Calais*, Shaw moves increasingly into line with the modernist ambivalence about the "marriage plot." While he offers some critique of marriage by considering what happens when empowered women decide to "settle down" within it, he nonetheless affirms it as the only option for his female characters. In *The Millionairess*, financially and physically powerful Epifania Ognisanti di Parerga has entered into a misalliance with her husband Alastair, who won her hand by improbably succeeding at a money-making test that her father had set. But Alastair does not satisfy Eppy sexually and Eppy does not satisfy Alastair emotionally, so they both take lovers—Alastair's is an "angel in the house" named Polly, while Eppy settles for the compliance of the aptly named Adrian Blenderbland—and consider divorce. Eppy eventually acknowledges that her money and power are meaningless without love, and her best hope for happiness is the prospect of a more appropriate marriage with the Egyptian doctor who has stood up to her.

Eppy is a natural successor to Sweetie and her energetic enjoyment of physical love without intellectual, spiritual, or maternal aspects. Eppy has a mind as well as a body, but marries Alastair Fitzfassenden, "*a splendid athlete, with most of his brains in his muscles*" (*CPP* VI:893), because of his "sex appeal" (*CPP* VI:892). Like Sweetie, Eppy unashamedly lets her "lower centres" do the talking, but is infuriated to find that Alastair cannot keep up his end of the conversation: "I thought that this irresistible athlete would be an ardent lover. He was nothing of the kind" (*CPP* VI:892). Eppy's expectation that her husband should satisfy her physically is another idea made possible by Stopes's *Married Love*, which not only explained women's sexual responses, but also for the first time asserted married women's rights to sexual desire and fulfillment. Stopes's intent was to make marriages happier and more rewarding for both husband and wife, but the volumes of correspondence she received from men and women anxious about marriages that lacked sexual satisfaction suggest that "the message that sex should now be for individual gratification rather than simply a reproductive duty had as much potential to destabilize as it did to strengthen marriages."[17] Clearly for Eppy, whose only maternal inclination emerges when she bullies the sweatshop owner and his wife into feeling like children (*CPP* VI:941), a marriage that does not deliver her individual gratification is a misalliance.

Yet even with divorce law reforms making it easier for her to divorce the "sexless fish" (*CPP* VI:897), Eppy explicitly prefers to remain married. In dismissing her lawyer's advice, she initially cites the convenience and freedom that being married offers, but her later outburst bespeaks a more emotional cause: "Is it just that I, because I am a millionairess, cannot keep my husband, cannot keep even a lover, cannot keep anything but my money? ... Well, be it so. I shall sit in my lonely house, and be myself, and pile up my millions until I find a man good enough to be to me what Alastair is to Seedystockings" (*CPP* VI:958–959). Legally but unhappily married, Eppy recasts herself as a reviled and ridiculed spinster, lonely and still looking for Mr. Right. Her response confirms that divorce law reforms actually reinforced the marriage imperative by offering people more chances to find the right partner rather than considering possible alternatives to marriage.[18] Similarly, the suitor tests are intended to help Eppy and the doctor marry the right people, but still assume that marriage is inevitable. And when her father's test does not protect Eppy from a misalliance, the focus on her unsatisfactory marriage mirrors the modernist critique that Pines identifies in novels, where "mismatched couples, disappointed expectations, and routine infidelity" are the norm.[19] Shaw brings the Fitzfassendens' infidelities into the open, not to suggest alternatives to marriage, but to show alternative marriage relationships, both of which are clearly inadequate to accommodate the powerful, independently capable woman.

Alastair is clearly not the right candidate to be Eppy's soul mate. Their marriage is characterized by a profound inequality, as Alastair comes to realize (*CPP* VI:914), where Eppy holds all the economic, intellectual, and will power. All Alastair brings to the table is his brute strength, a commodity with little value in a society that sweats manual labor and disapproves of men who beat their wives (even if they are still legally allowed to do it). The only marriage in which Alastair belongs is the profoundly old-fashioned domestic arrangement represented by Polly, the self-proclaimed "angel in the house" (*CPP* VI:899). As a more modern woman, Eppy is not dependent on Alastair's muscle; she has taken her father's advice and cultivated her own physical strength, learning judo and all-in wrestling, and even sitting with the kind of force that breaks chairs.[20] Even so, Eppy only reinforces the caution against the role of physical force in marriage. She can physically dominate Adrian, but he elicits much sympathy (although not legal redress) after she assaults him "as a child smashes a disappointing toy" (*CPP* VI:958). Her previous instance of expressing disappointment by physical attack led to Alastair's instinctive solar plexus punch that left her in fear of her husband's fists (*CPP* VI:893), a reminder that anyone who relies on physical domination in a marriage is always at risk of running into someone stronger.

Eppy is financially, intellectually, and physically self-sufficient, yet her yearning for a partner indicates that something is still missing. The doctor's piety and charity represent the missing element: in pursuing independence and power, Eppy has lost touch with her spiritual side, the domain previously associated with woman as the angel in the house, and the domain from which Joan of Arc derived her mission. Eppy already possesses the traditionally male qualities in a marriage, and the doctor will supply the traditionally female elements. When Eppy finally instructs her lawyer to negotiate her divorce from Alastair so she can marry the doctor, Shaw suggests that marriages still need a proper balance, but in a world where women have increasing access to broader domains of power, any domestic institution will have to let go of rigid gendered expectations around how that balance will be embodied.

In the same week he finished *The Millionairess*, Shaw dashed off *The Six of Calais*, "an acting piece and nothing else" (*CPP* VI:975). For Shaw, this emphasis on acting has significant feminist resonances. He believed that physical fitness comprised a crucial aspect of female emancipation, and the athleticism that his female roles required ensured that the actresses who portrayed them had to practice what he preached.[21] Within a few weeks of requiring a millionairess to perform judo, Shaw scripted the equally extraordinary physical challenge of the visibly pregnant Queen Philippa, who intervenes in her husband Edward III's plan to execute the six Burghers of Calais as punishment for the city's resistance against him. Shaw's return to history and the medieval period here gives him another opportunity to explore the dynamics of power as they play out on women's bodies, as he did with *Saint Joan*. This time, without necessarily supporting any explicit alternatives to marriage, Shaw presents a cautionary reminder to the women of his own time—those being encouraged, and in some cases legislated, to retire from the workforce and focus on their "jobs" as wives and mothers—that they were making themselves vulnerable by returning to a state of dependence on men.

In the way that Epifania is a successor to Sweetie in *Too True to Be Good*, Queen Philippa can be seen as a successor to Polly Seedystockings in *The Millionairess*. Polly is proud of her role as the traditional angel in the house and defends herself against Eppy's insult that she is a doormat by logically countering that "Doormats are useful things if you want the house kept tidy" (*CPP* VI:899). Moreover, Polly turns out to be absolutely right when she tells Sagamore that she can win a battle of wills against Eppy, even though she has "no will at all. But I get what I want, somehow" (*CPP* VI:915). Yet if Polly intimates the viability of the position, Queen Philippa demonstrates its limitations.

Philippa is the angel in the house incarnate: she nurtures the children, frets over her husband, "the biggest baby of them all," and dismisses any protective concern about her own "delicate state of health" (*CPP* VI:977–979). The emphasis on the Queen's pregnancy serves as a reminder of women's connection to the procreative and evolutionary power of the Life Force, and their mysterious, spiritual connection to nature and the universe that modernism both revered and feared. The Queen has power in the marriage *because of* her female biology and maternal self-abnegation. Even the king's men-at-arms recognize her power in acknowledging that "the Queen's arrival washes out all the King's orders" (*CPP* VI:984). She negotiates the prisoners' release by emphasizing her unworthiness to make the request, and successfully exploits her pregnancy to gain her husband's sympathy by arguing: "Their ransom will hardly buy me a new girdle; and oh, dear sir, you know that my old one is becoming too strait for me" (*CPP* VI:986–987). Even the King acknowledges the power of her female submissiveness, recognizing that "you ask nothing because you know you will get everything" (*CPP* VI:987). However, the intrusion of one "dog of lousy Champagne" (*CPP* VI:989) shows the Queen how easily the balance of power she derives from her womanliness can be upset. The King asserts his dominance over her body by making a bawdy joke that celebrates his masculinity at her expense, and when she objects that "you mock my condition before this insolent man and before the world ... Oh for shame! for shame! Have men no decency?" (*CPP* VI:990–991), he "*stops her mouth with a kiss*," asserting his male prerogative to silence her, as the men all laugh at her outrage. Even for a Queen, the inverse power of domestic submission is overridden in the dog-eat-dog world of men.

Shaw's treatment of marriage in these four interwar plays often shows him ahead of his literary and social contemporaries in advocating for women's autonomy and empowerment, and initially even their independence from marriage. The latter was a particularly difficult proposition during a period when women's post-war experiences of financial and physical independence conflicted with an economic need to eliminate them from the workforce, and Shaw increasingly succumbed to the marriage imperative. Even then, however, his plays support an institution that is reformed to accommodate independent women, empowered by their experiences and Marie Stopes's landmark publication to need something more from married love.

Notes

1. Davida Pines, *The Marriage Paradox: Modernist Novels and the Cultural Imperative to Marry* (Gainesville: University Press of Florida, 2006), 2 (Pines 2006).
2. Pines, *Marriage Paradox*, 3.
3. Katherine Holden, "'Nature Takes No Notice of Morality': Singleness and *Married Love* in Interwar Britain," *Women's History Review* 11, No. 3 (2002): 482 (Holden 2002).
4. Karen Chow, "Popular Sexual Knowledges and Women's Agency in 1920s England: Marie Stopes's *Married Love* and E.M. Hull's *The Sheik*," *Feminist Review* 63 (1999): 67–68 (Chow 1999).
5. Marianne DeKoven, "Modernism and Gender," in *The Cambridge Companion to Modernism*, ed. Michael Levenson (Cambridge: Cambridge University Press, 2011), 212 (DeKoven 2011).
6. Karma Waltonen, "Saint Joan: From Renaissance Witch to New Woman," *SHAW* 24 (2004): 187 (Waltonen 2004).
7. See Sheila Stowell, "Dame Joan, Saint Christabel," *Modern Drama* 37, No. 3 (Fall 1994) for a discussion of the suffrage resonances in *Saint Joan* (Stowell 1994).
8. Maggie B. Gale, *West End Women: Women and the London Stage, 1918–1962* (London and New York: Routledge, 1996), 32 (Gale 1996).
9. The Sex Disqualification (Removal) Act (1919) made it illegal to discriminate on the basis of sex or marriage against candidates for senior civil

service posts, juries, and professions. It also required universities to admit women to membership and degrees, and made provisions to accredit women whose education and training would qualify them as solicitors if they were men. See http://www.legislation.gov.uk/ukpga/Geo5/9-10/71/contents/enacted for the original content of the Act. It was in many ways astonishingly progressive, but was rarely enforced, and often actively undermined by "marriage bars" that made it easy to remove married women from employment, especially teaching jobs. See Gale, *West End Women*, Chap. 4, and Ellen M. Holtzman, "The Pursuit of Married Love: Women's Attitudes Toward Sexuality and Marriage in Great Britain, 1918–1939," *Journal of Social History* 16, No. 2 (Winter 1982) (Holtzman 1982).

10. As late as the mid-1980s, legal opinion in England explicitly upheld the precept that a husband could not be charged with raping his wife. The marital rape exemption was finally abolished in England and Wales in 1991.

11. See Marie Stopes, "Preface on the Censorship," in *Banned Play and a Preface on the Censorship* (London: John Bale, Sons & Danielsson, Ltd., 1926), for Stopes's account of the unexpected censorship and rush to write a replacement play (Stopes 1926).

12. Marie Stopes, "Our Ostriches," in *Plays and Performance Texts by Women 1880–1930*, ed. Maggie B. Gale and Gilli Bush-Bailey (Manchester and New York: Manchester University Press, 2012), 343. All subsequent quotes from this play are cited parenthetically by page number in the text (Stopes 2012).

13. Holden, "Nature Takes No Notice of Morality," 487.

14. Qtd. in Holtzman, "Pursuit of Married Love," 42; see also Gale, *West End Women*, 21–37, for a discussion of how women's career aspirations were redefined based on biology and gender to suit economic needs.

15. Holden, "Nature Takes No Notice of Morality," 487.

16. Marie Stopes, *Married Love*, 6th ed. (London: A.C. Fifield, 1919), 2 (Stopes 1919).

17. Holden, "Nature Takes No Notice of Morality," 485.

18. Pines, *Marriage Paradox*, 7.

19. Ibid., 13.

20. See Tracy J.R. Collins, "Shaw's Athletic-Minded Women," in *Shaw and Feminisms: On Stage and Off*, ed. D.A. Hadfield and Jean Reynolds (Gainesville: University Press of Florida, 2013), for a discussion of Shaw's commitment to the importance of physical fitness for emancipated women (Collins 2013).

21. Collins, "Shaw's Athletic-Minded Women," 20.

References

Chow, Karen. 1999. Popular Sexual Knowledges and Women's Agency in 1920s England: Marie Stopes's *Married Love* and E. M. Hull's *The Sheik*. *Feminist Review* 63: 64–87.

Collins, Tracy J.R. 2013. Shaw's Athletic-Minded Women. In *Shaw and Feminisms: On Stage and Off*, ed. D.A. Hadfield and Jean Reynolds, 19–36. Gainesville: University Press of Florida.

DeKoven, Marianne. 2011. Modernism and Gender. In *The Cambridge Companion to Modernism*, ed. Michael Levenson, 212–231. Cambridge: Cambridge University Press.

Gale, Maggie B. 1996. *West End Women: Women and the London Stage, 1918–1962*. London: Routledge.

Holden, Katherine. 2002. 'Nature Takes No Notice of Morality': Singleness and *Married Love* in Interwar Britain. *Women's History Review* 11 (3): 481–503.

Holtzman, Ellen M. 1982. The Pursuit of Married Love: Women's Attitudes Toward Sexuality and Marriage in Great Britain, 1918–1939. *Journal of Social History* 16 (2): 39–51.

Pines, Davida. 2006. *The Marriage Paradox: Modern Novels and the Cultural Imperative to Marry*. Gainesville: University Press of Florida.

Stopes, Marie. 1919. *Married Love*, 6th ed. London: A.C. Fifield.

Stopes, Marie. 1926. Preface on Censorship. *A Banned Play and a Preface on Censorship*, 1–50. London: John Bale, Sons & Danielsson, Ltd.

Stopes, Marie. 2012. Our Ostriches. In *Plays and Performance Texts by Women 1880–1930*. ed. Maggie B. Gale and Gilli Bush-Bailey, 342–387. Manchester: Manchester University Press.

Stowell, Sheila. 1994. Dame Joan, Saint Christabel. *Modern Drama* 37 (3): 421–436.

Waltonen, Karma. 2004. Saint Joan from Renaissance Witch to New Woman. *SHAW: The Annual of Bernard Shaw Studies* 24 (3): 186–203.

Author Biography

D. A. Hadfield is Faculty Lecturer in the Department of English Language and Literature at the University of Waterloo, Ontario, Canada. She has published books and articles on feminist theatre and on Shaw, most recently as co-editor of and contributor to *Bernard Shaw and Feminisms: On Stage and Off* in the University Press of Florida's Bernard Shaw series (2013).

CHAPTER 11

Definitions of Marriage: *Village Wooing, On the Rocks*, and *The Simpleton of the Unexpected Isles: A Vision of Judgment*

Jean Reynolds

Of the three plays Bernard Shaw wrote in 1933 and the early part of 1934, only *On the Rocks* deals with the devastating economic depression in Great Britain. Many critics see similarities between *On the Rocks* and *Heartbreak House*, another Shavian play that uses a troubled family as a metaphor for a country headed toward social and political destruction. The other two plays from this period are far removed not only from Britain's social unrest, but from Shaw's usual playwriting practices. *Village Wooing* is a romantic comedy written not in acts but in three "conversations." There are only two speaking roles, and the usual Shavian preface is missing, perhaps because the quiet village seems untouched by Britain's economic crisis. In *The Simpleton of the Unexpected Isles*, Shaw takes that detachment from contemporary political problems to extremes by creating a futuristic island paradise that features goddesses, pirates, and an angel.

J. Reynolds (✉)
Polk State College, Winter Haven, FL, USA
e-mail: ballroom16@aol.com

© The Author(s) 2017   175
R.A. Gaines (ed.), *Bernard Shaw's Marriages and Misalliances*,
Bernard Shaw and His Contemporaries,
DOI 10.1057/978-1-349-95170-3_11

One common thread in all three plays, however, is their down-to-earth depiction of marriage and its attendant misalliances. Even the group marriage in *The Simpleton of the Unexpected Isles* often seems pragmatic and familiar. In *Village Wooing*, the two unlikely lovers take a practical view of marriage that seems refreshingly real, and the Prime Minister's family in *On the Rocks* is so conventionally dysfunctional that we could be watching a situation comedy.

By contrast, Shaw's own experience with marriage was decidedly unconventional—he postponed marriage until he was 41, and the union was probably never consummated. But because he was an astute student of human behavior, he recognized that marriage is central to human life: "Marriage nevertheless Inevitable" is one of the headings in the preface to *Getting Married* (*CPP* VI:453). The "inevitable" marriages in these three plays give us a window into Shaw's views of both marriage and the human condition.

Village Wooing

Village Wooing (1933) begins on a cruise ship where A, a successful travel writer, meets and instantly dislikes Z, a village shopkeeper who is spending her winnings from a newspaper contest. (The characters are never named.) After the cruise, Z returns to the village shop. When A drops in with a shopping list, he is surprised to see her again—and dismayed to learn that she intends to marry him. Nevertheless, he purchases the shop, keeps her on as his assistant, and finally agrees to marry her.

Audiences soon realize that the title of the play is ironic: A never "woos" Z, and there is none of the romance we might expect from a shipboard meeting. Their relationship is a misalliance right from the beginning, and we are left to guess how successful their marriage will be. Audiences familiar with Shaw might notice that what J. Ellen Gainor calls "an important Shavian archetype"[1] is missing: Z never speaks of wanting a baby. All she wants is to marry A: "there come times when I want to get hold of you in my arms, every bit of you; and when I do I'll give you something better to think about than the starry heavens" (*CPP* VI:566–567).

The play does feature one typically Shavian characteristic: a preoccupation with language. John Bertolini describes *Village Wooing* as "a play of reading and writing,"[2] and Peter Gahan finds in it "the poststructuralist textual implications of the larger works."[3] As Gahan explains, "Marriage, with its implications of generation, is a metaphor for the process of language itself, though Derrida would caution that dissemination often falls on fallow ground."[4] As the author of the *Marco Polo Series of Chatty Guide Books*, A is naturally interested in language, and he is a stickler for grammatical correctness, correcting both Z's lapses and his own:

A: Who does this shop belong to? I mean to whom does this shop belong? (*CPP* VI:561)
A: What, exactly, do you mean by my second marriage? I have only been married once. I mean I have been married only once. (*CPP* VI:564)
Z: If it doesnt matter who anybody marries, then it doesnt matter who I marry and it doesnt matter who you marry.
A: Whom, not who. (*CPP* VI:565)

Other language-related elements in *Village Wooing* include a discussion of why the Red Sea and Black Sea are blue (*CPP* VI:538) and a joke about Z's father:

Z: My father used to say that men and women are always driving one-another mad.
A: That sounds literary. Was your father a man of letters?
Z: Yes: I should think he was. A postman. (*CPP* VI:542)

Village Wooing is equally preoccupied with numbers—another hint that we are watching an unconventional romance. Z spends her days dealing with telephone numbers and counting, measuring, and weighing items for sale; A is committed to writing 2000 words every day; and both A and Z often discuss money:

Z: Cheese threepence: two and a penny; butter sixpence: two and sevenpence; apples we sell by the pound. Hadnt you better have a pound?
A: How many to the pound?
Z: Three. (*CPP* VI:551)

The first softening in A's attitude occurs when Z tells him, "I hate wasting money." "Thats an extremely attractive point in your character," he replies. "My wife used to waste my money. Stick to that and you will get married in no time" (*CPP* VI:545). In the Third Conversation, A starts to submit to Z's will while he is working on a balance sheet: "Crusoe drew up a balance sheet of the advantages and disadvantages of being cast away on a desert island. I am cast away in a village on the Wiltshire Downs. I am drawing up a similar balance sheet" (*CPP* VI:559). Z joins in, unsuccessfully at first, with her own version of a balance sheet—about marriage: "it's really cheaper to keep a wife than to pay an assistant. Let alone that you dont have to live a single life" (*CPP* VI:562). A few minutes later she remarks, "I might be one of the amenities of the estate of holy matrimony, mightn't I?" (*CPP* VI:566). With Shavian irony, love blossoms not on the deck of a ship, but in the businesslike setting of a shop. Marriage, Shaw seems to be saying, is as much about the everyday business of living as about passion and romance.

Margery Morgan has noted "an economy of understatement"[5] in much of Shaw's late work, and that stylistic development is apparent in some brief but telling conversational exchanges in *Village Wooing*. One remark from Z, for example, shows that she has highly developed powers of observation—and that A is not the recluse he claims to be. On the ship, she tells him, "you looked at all the women out of the corner of your eye in spite of your keeping yourself so much to yourself" (*CPP* VI:565). Another conversation contains similar revelations—Z is an attractive woman (and knows it), and A has too much self-respect to make a fool of himself over a woman:

> *Z:* But there was something about you: I dont exactly know what; but it made me feel that I could do with you in the house; and then I could fall in love with anyone I liked without any fear of making a fool of myself. I suppose it was because you are one of the quiet sort and dont run after women.
>
> *A:* How do you know I dont run after women?
>
> *Z:* Well, if you want to know, it's because you didnt run after me. You mightnt believe it; but men do run after me. (*CPP* VI:555)

Shaw uses the same economy to show that A's resistance is softening: "But you have not acquired any of the reserves. You say what you think. You announce all the plans that well-bred women conceal. You play with your cards on the table instead of keeping them where a lady should keep them: up your sleeve" (*CPP* VI:556).

But in the last moments of the play, the "economy of understatement" evaporates, and Z begins to speak as a passionate woman—"Youll find that you have senses to gratify as well as fine things to say" (*CPP* VI:567)—and A agrees to marry her:

A: I shall expect more than you have ever dreamt of giving, in spite of the boundless audacity of women. What great men would ever have been married if the female nobodies who snapped them up had known the enormity of their own presumption? I believe they all thought they were going to refine, to educate, to make real gentlemen of their husbands. What do you intend to make of me, I wonder?

Z: Well, I have made a decent shopkeeper of you already, havnt I? But you neednt be afraid of my not appreciating you. I want a fancy sort of husband, not a common villager that any woman could pick up. I shall be proud of you. (*CPP* VI:569)

In *Village Wooing*, Shaw bypasses the grand social, political, and philosophical ideas that often dominate his plays to show us how a particular man and woman decide to get married. The absence of romantic dialogue challenges us to focus our attention on the larger, impersonal forces that can bring two unlikely people into a loving relationship—and to wonder whether a misalliance will be the ultimate outcome.

On the Rocks

Unlike *Village Wooing*, which focuses entirely on its two unlikely lovers, *On the Rocks* uses marriage as a minor theme to the political ideas that dominate the play. The Chavender family is conventional and comical: Sir Arthur, the British Prime Minister, is bumbling and good-natured; Lady Chavender runs the family but pretends her husband is in charge; and the two almost-grown children endlessly defy their parents, who respond by shaking their heads and wondering how things could have gone so wrong.

At the beginning of the play we learn that Britain is suffering a national economic crisis. Lady Chavender, concerned about her husband's exhaustion, calls in a mysterious female healer who insists that Chavender's real problem is "a want of mental exercise." Sir Arthur is nonplussed, but agrees to treatment at the female healer's Welsh retreat. He returns, transformed, to make a speech proposing drastic changes that include compulsory service and nationalization of industry. When the Cabinet refuses to back his plan, Sir Arthur resigns. As the play ends, a mob is smashing the windows near his office.

The Chavender family seems to have just two purposes in the play: providing comic relief and underlining Sir Arthur's incompetence. One example comes just a few minutes into the play, when Sir Arthur brags to his wife about his success in "governing the country." She quickly shocks him back into reality: "But you dont govern the country, Arthur. The country isnt governed: it just slummocks along anyhow" (*CPP* VI:644).

Closer examination, however, raises two important questions about marriage—what it is intended to accomplish and whether it can ever fulfill that purpose. Lady Chavender soon emerges as the most interesting member of the family. Shaw describes her as "nice," "goodlooking," and "bored" (*CPP* VI:643). Lady Chavender is a potential Shavian New Woman with an unusual ability to recognize the truth and give it a voice. In the end, however, she chooses not to follow her husband's example of breaking away from society's expectations.

As the play ends, Sir Arthur is looking forward to a new and better life: "Do you realize that we two are free at last? Free, dearest: think of that! No more children. ... A cottage near a good golf links seems to be indicated." He clearly wants her to be part of it—"What would you like?" (*CPP* VI:733)—but she does not answer his question. Sir Arthur is excited about the new possibilities ahead: "I am enjoying the enormous freedom of having found myself out and got myself off my mind. That looks like despair; but it is really the beginning of hope, and the end of hypocrisy" (*CPP* VI:733). Lady Chavender, however, does not express hope or propose to renounce hypocrisy—perhaps because she has been speaking the truth all along, and he has not listened to her. The following exchange with her husband hints what an exceptional person she is—or, at the very least, could be:

Lady Chavender:	I am so tired of wellbred people, and party politics, and the London season, and all the rest of it.
Sir Arthur:	I sometimes think you are the only really revolutionary revolutionist I have ever met.
Lady Chavender:	Oh, lots of us are like that. We were born into good society; and we are through with it: we have no illusions about it, even if we are fit for nothing better. (*CPP* VI:731–732)

Clearly she loves her husband, declaring: "You are certainly the best of husbands, Arthur. You are the best of everything" (*CPP* VI:643). But she does not hesitate to tell him how ineffectual he has been. When Sir Arthur boasts about his success and reminds her that he has "climbed to the top of the tree" (*CPP* VI:644), she responds with "Yes, yes, very

very busy doing nothing. And it wears you out far more than if your mind had something sensible to work on!" (*CPP* VI:645). She cannot talk frankly to him because "you live in fairyland and I live in the hard wicked world." A moment later, however, she turns her critical eye away from his inadequacies and back onto herself: "Thats why I cant be a good wife and take an interest in your career" (*CPP* VI:645). Earlier she had said, "I suppose it's something wrong in my constitution. I was not born for wifing and mothering" (*CPP* VI:644). In a conversation with Aloysia Brollikins, the woman who wants to marry the Chavenders' son, Lady Chavender says, "Nobody ought to marry anybody, Aloysia. But they do" (*CPP* VI:730) (Aloysia herself says, "Marriage is a lottery" [*CPP* VI:727]). Lady Chavender calls her husband "dearest love" and "a duck and a darling," and she worries that he is close to "a nervous breakdown" (*CPP* VI:645). But she also confesses, "I treat you abominably" (*CPP* VI:644). She considers herself a failure, telling her husband, "I am a bad wife and a bad mother" (*CPP* VI:643–644).

Yet surely some of her problems can be blamed on her husband, who worships the idea of a Womanly Woman: "I know that you have sacrificed yourself to keeping my house and sewing on my buttons; and I am not ungrateful," he tells her (*CPP* VI:645). Sir Arthur is appalled by the socialist notion of the nationalization of women, and he has strong opinions about women and their proper role. "We are above all a domestic nation," he intones when he rehearses his speech about the family (*CPP* VI:665), and he thinks a working wife might threaten his own political future:

Sir Arthur:	Thank God I have not a political wife. Look at Higginbotham! He was just ripe for the Cabinet when his wife went into Parliament and made money by journalism. That was the end of him.
Lady Chavender:	And I married a man with a hopelessly parliamentary mind; and that was the end of me. (*CPP* VI:645)

When Lady Chavender says "I have a grudge against your career," he completely misses the point: "Of course I know it keeps me too much away from home," he tells her (*CPP* VI:644). He never wonders why, if she is so lonely for him, she is urging him to spend 6 weeks away from her at a retreat in Wales—and why she makes sure he knows that it is run by "a rather interesting and attractive woman" (*CPP* VI:646).

Because *On the Rocks* is preoccupied with politics, Shaw is careful not to allow the Chavenders' marriage to overwhelm the debate about parliamentary government. As the play is ending, the question of what is wrong with the Chavender family is still largely unanswered. Daughter Flavia believes she is the target of endless parental criticism: "I have considered you and given up all the things I wanted for you until I have no individuality left. If I take up a book you want me to read something else. If I want to see anybody you want me to see somebody else" (*CPP* VI:641). Lady Chavender, on the other hand, thinks she and Sir Arthur have neglected their children: "It serves us right, dear, for letting them bring themselves up in the post-war fashion instead of teaching them to be ladies and gentlemen" (*CPP* VI:643). Aloysia—David's intended—has still another viewpoint. When David complains about his upbringing, Aloysia retorts: "your parents are too good for you, you uncivilized lout" (*CPP* VI:731).

Shaw may have been remembering his own unconventional upbringing when he created the Chavender family. His mother, "Bessie" Shaw, endured an oppressive childhood and was, her famous son thought, "too humane to inflict what she had suffered on any child; besides I think she imagined that correct behavior is inborn, and that much of what she had been taught was natural to her. Anyhow, she never taught it to us."[6] Bessie thought marriage would liberate her, but she soon realized that her husband was an alcoholic and her marriage a mistake. Her salvation, GBS explained, "came through music. She had a mezzosoprano voice of extraordinary purity of tone."[7] Bessie found a gifted voice teacher, George John Vandeleur Lee, who—incredibly—moved into the Shaw household. Does Lady Chavender harbor undiscovered gifts and secret dreams? If so, she lacks Bessie Shaw's determination to bring them to fruition.

The Chavender offspring seem destined for their own misalliances. If David marries Aloysia—the woman who had set her sights on him—they may end up with a relationship that copies the elder Chavenders', but with the gender roles reversed. Aloysia, like Sir Arthur, instantly knew what she wanted: "Well, the moment I laid eyes on David I went all over like that" (*CPP* VI:726). She calls the attraction "the evolutionary appetite," and her plan—before she is put off by David's rudeness to his mother—is to "develop the race"; a nod to the theme of human improvement in **Man and Superman** (*CPP* VI:726). But David's happiness (like Lady Chavender's) matters little to her: "he's coming along nicely" is her only comment (*CPP* VI:727). Another complication is Aloysia's gift for leadership: "Wherever I went I rose because I couldn't keep down," she says (*CPP* VI:729). If she indeed plans to focus her energies on "developing the race" through marriage and motherhood, her passion for social change may have to be set aside. Aloysia breaks off the relationship when she hears David rant against his parents, but it seems likely that the "evolutionary appetite" will pull her back to him.

What about Flavia, the Chavenders' daughter? Like David, she seems not to know what she wants. Viscount Barking from the Isle of Cats is determined to marry her, despite his comment that "all I can get out of her is that she is not a gold digger" (*CPP* VI:723). Sir Arthur amiably offers to "order her to marry you if you think that will get you any further" (*CPP* VI:723)—another hint of a future misalliance.

As the play ends, Sir Arthur is headed for the golf links, Lady Chavender has no plans, and their children seem headed for problematic marriages. Only one person seems open to new possibilities—Hilda Hanways, the unmarried and self-effacing secretary who changes her lunch plans at the behest of Lady Chavender, efficiently shepherds visitors in and out of Sir Arthur's office, and worries about his lack of sleep: "Really, Sir Arthur, you should have come home to bed" (*CPP* VI:638). But the demonstrations outside the Cabinet Room awaken something new inside her: "Well, but cant the police let them run away without breaking their heads? Oh look: that policeman has just clubbed a quite old man" (*CPP* VI:735). The stage directions say that Sir Arthur *draws her away, placing himself between her and the window* (*CPP* VI:735).

Nevertheless, moments later, "suddenly hysterical," she shouts "Oh, my God! I will go out and join them" and rushes out. Sir Arthur soothes his worried wife with "Never mind, dear: the police all know her: she'll come to no harm. She'll be back for tea" (*CPP* VI:735)—but the play ends before we can discover whether he is right. What we do know is that Sir Arthur will enjoy his golf games, Lady Chavender will feel bored, Britain will founder—and husbands and wives will continue to have contrary views about the life they have chosen.

THE SIMPLETON OF THE UNEXPECTED ISLES: A VISION OF JUDGMENT

In the two previous plays, Shaw showed us believable people grappling with the realities of marriage. *The Simpleton of the Unexpected Isles* (1934) is different—a fable about "a eugenic experiment in group marriage" (*CPP* VI:763). This "Superfamily" includes two Englishwomen, two Englishmen, an Asiatic couple, and the offspring of the experiment—two daughters and two sons. In his preface Shaw explains that he is not advocating "that method of peopling the world" (*CPP* VI:763); his real purpose is to explore the concept of usefulness. "In a living society," he says, "every day is a day of judgment; and its recognition as such is not the end of all things but the beginning of a real civilization" (*CPP* VI:760). Near the end of the play, an angel descends upon the Unexpected Isles to tell the inhabitants that it is Judgment Day, and "your records are now being looked into with a view to deciding whether you are worth your salt or not." Those judged to be unworthy "will simply disappear: that is all. You will no longer exist" (*CPP* VI: 822). It is not, Shaw insists, a story to be taken seriously: The "four lovely phantasms" (offspring of the group marriage) "never did exist" (*CPP* VI:763). As Rodelle Weintraub explains, "At several points in the play, Shaw reminds us that what we are seeing just might be a dream."[8]

A dreamlike fable about group marriage might seem to have little to say about the marital experiences of ordinary people. But *The Simpleton* is a surprisingly honest assessment of a marriage between two idealists who undertake a noble experiment and fail. When an angel descends on the Unexpected Isles to make his judgments, Pra—an Asiatic priest—decides that he and his wife, Prola, will probably be eliminated: "we two have made a precious mess of our job of producing the coming race by a mixture of east and west. We are failures" (*CPP* VI:838). Prola acknowledges their mistakes, but she disagrees about their fate: "I do not feel like that. I feel like the leader of a cavalry charge whose horse has been shot through the head and dropped dead under him. Well, a dead hobby horse is not the end of the world" (*CPP* VI:839).

After the judgment Prola is proven right: she and Pra are still standing in spite of their failures. What is even more surprising is that they both knew from the beginning how absurd the experiment was. After the angel departs, Pra says, "We are awaiting judgment here quite simply as a union of a madwoman with a fool" (*CPP* VI:838). Earlier Prola had said, "nobody but a fool would be frivolous enough to join me in doing all the mad things I wanted to do" (*CPP* VI:837).

The foundation for this "mad" experiment is laid in the three scenes that form the Prologue to the play. Lawrence Switzky explains that these are "brief vaudeville sketches, sped up so that events of high seriousness (including suicides, suicide attempts, and religious conversions) appear as farce"[9] (*CPP* VI:195). These sketches also include sexual content. Rodelle Weintraub, reading *The Simpleton* as one of Shaw's "Freudian-type dream plays,"[10] catalogues many examples of sexual imagery, including a loaded pistol, a spear, and ships and caves.[11] Most important, the characters are involved in extramarital sexual experiences intended to recruit new members for the Superfamily, including a young woman who is a British tourist and an English couple, Sir Charles Farwaters and his devoutly Christian wife, Lady Farwaters. Only one English member of the Superfamily does not undergo this sexual initiation: a suicidal emigration officer whose spiritual rebirth comes after Pra kicks him over a cliff into the safety nets below.

The emphasis on sexual desire is a departure from the previous two plays. In *Village Wooing*, for example, Z's desire for the state of matrimony is almost as strong as her desire for physical union with A: there is only one speech about her desire to "hold" him, and A dismissively replies that he can find pleasure in other ways. In *On the Rocks*, neither Sir Arthur nor Lady Chavender ever mentions their desire for each other: marriage means domestic life.

The most important sexual encounter in *The Simpleton* occurs in Act I of the play, following the three scenes of the Prologue. When a young Anglican clergyman arrives on the Unexpected Isles, sexual desire lures him into the Superfamily experiment as a prospective husband to the two beautiful daughters: "They must have children," exclaims Sir Charles Farwaters (*CPP* VI:799). This clergyman is the "simpleton" in the play's title—since childhood he has been called "Iddy," for idiot, instead of his real name, Phosphor Hammingtap. When he first sees the two beautiful young women, he mistakes them for statues, and there is a Pygmalion moment when he kisses one of them: "You make me feel as I have never felt before. I must kiss you." According to Shaw's stage directions, *He does so and finds that she is alive. She smiles as her eyes turn bewitchingly towards him* (*CPP* VI:789).

Yet when Iddy learns he must marry both daughters he is appalled: "An English clergyman could not marry two women" (*CPP* VI:799).

But eventually the marriage does take place—and soon turns into a mis-alliance: the two daughters are "wonderful and beautiful, but sterile," and they lack common sense: "we made fools of them," Mrs. Hyering says (*CPP* VI:831). Making matters worse, their husband is an "impo-tent simpleton" (*CPP* VI:807). As the adults try to figure out what went wrong, the mystical language of Act I gives way to blame and regrets. Lawrence Switzky explains, "Marriage is finally envisioned as a series of catastrophes and rebirths and as a continuing attempt to place the threat of tragedy within a comic frame."[12] Margery Morgan says that the failure of the Superfamily experiment instigates "the same psycho-logical crisis as Shaw had earlier designated 'heartbreak', when the shock of reality penetrates and disperses illusion and makes sound judgement possible."[13]

One problem is the split between East and West that has persisted in the Superfamily. Lady Farwaters recalls, "Well, from the time when as tiny tots they could speak, they invented fairy stories. I thought it silly and dangerous, and wanted to stop them; but Prola would not let me" (*CPP* VI:798). Sir Charles adds, "Pra and Prola think they understand it; but Lady Farwaters and I dont; and we dont pretend to. We are too English" (*CPP* VI:799).

That phrase "Lady Farwaters and I" hints at a second problem: the six adults still sort themselves into three couples rather than a unified Superfamily. Often the four British spouses line up against Pra and Prola, sounding like adolescents rebelling against their parents (Flavia in *On the Rocks*, for example). Sir Hugo Hyering (the former emigration officer) complains to Pra, "You kicked me into the sea." Sir Charles feels that he and his wife were manipulated into the group marriage: "You made love to Lady Farwaters" (*CPP* VI:806). Pra aligns with Prola, and his expla-nation borders on insult:

> *Pra*:   I had to use that method with very crude novices; and Lady
>   Farwaters, with her English ladylike bringing-up, was so crude that
>   she really could not understand any purely intellectual appeal. Your
>   own mind … was in an even worse condition; and Prola had to
>   convert you by the same elementary method. (*CPP* VI:806)

Despite their haughty superiority, Pra and Prola have had problems of their own. When they talk about their children, Prola confesses to the same boredom that afflicts Lady Chavender:

Pra:	They grew up to bore me more intensely than I have ever been bored by any other set of human creatures. Come, confess: did they not bore you?
Prola:	Have I denied it? Of course they bored me. They must have bored one another terribly in spite of all their dressing up and pretending that their fairyland was real. …
Pra:	The coming race will not be like them. Meanwhile we are face to face with the fact that we two have made a precious mess of our job of producing the coming race by a mixture of east and west. (*CPP* VI:838)

We get glimpses of past tensions in their marriage (the Priest and the Priestess here are Pra and Prola):

The Priestess:	He inspires a doglike devotion in women. He once did in me; so I know.
The Priest:	Dont be vindictive, Prola. I dont do it on purpose. …
The Priestess:	No: you do it by instinct. That, also, is rather doglike. (*CPP* VI:779)

And:

Prola:	Tell me the truth, Prola. Are you waiting for me to disappear? Do you feel that you can do better without me? Have you always felt that you could do better without me?
Prola:	That is a murderer's thought. Have you ever let yourself think it? How often have you said to yourself "I could do better alone, or with another woman"?
Prola:	Fairly often, my dear, when we were younger. But I did not murder you. Thats the answer. (*CPP* VI:836–837).

As the cracks in the Superfamily appear, the marriages in the play begin to sound more real and believable, and *The Simpleton* starts to deconstruct a common misconception about Shaw: that his characters are only mouthpieces for his social and political views. In *Shaw's Daughters*, for example, Gainor declares, "What does emerge is Shaw's concern with social problems … rather than the issue of the individual trying to assert him- or herself within society, or within the family as a microcosm of that larger social environment."[14] But *The Simpleton* is about both social change and a wife who does assert herself throughout her marriage:

Prola: Ive grown fond enough of you for all practical purposes;—
Pra: Thank you.
Prola: —but Ive never allowed you or any other man to cut me off my
            own stem and make me a parasite on his. That sort of love and
            sacrifice is not the consummation of a capable woman's existence:
            it is the temptation she must resist at all costs.
Pra: That temptation lies in the man's path too. The worst sacrifices I
            have seen have been those of men's highest careers to women's
            vulgarities and follies. (*CPP* VI:837–838)

Pra shares his wife's view, and Iddy—despite his role as the designated "simpleton" in the play—recognizes a similar truth. The women in the Superfamily love him "wonderfully," he says. "But it is my belief that someday we'll have to try something else. If we don't we'll come to hate one another" (*CPP* VI:811).

The Simpleton seems to be questioning the persistent messages about the importance of love that we hear from religion and popular culture. But if life is not about giving and receiving love, what else is there? In the last moments of the play, Prola opens the door to yet-unknown possibilities:

Remember: we are in the Unexpected Isles; and in the Unexpected Isles all plans fail. So much the better: plans are only jigsaw puzzles: one gets tired of them long before one can piece them together. There are still a million lives beyond all the Utopias and the Millenniums and the rest of the jigsaw puzzles: I am a woman and I know it. (*CPP* VI:839)

CONCLUSION

These three plays offer an intimate look at people who have arrived at marriage with different expectations and found varying degrees of satisfaction in their misalliances. Both A in *Village Wooing* and Lady Chavender in *On the Rocks* have had unhappy marriages, and Shaw hints that one problem might be their failure to define what they wanted. A was married for a while to a woman who, he says, "used to waste my money" (*CPP* VI:545). Did he know beforehand that money was so important to him (that phrase "*my* money" is telling), and will Z's frugality and love prove strong enough to sustain their marriage?

Lady Chavender too has experienced disappointment. "I suppose it's something wrong in my constitution," she confesses to her husband. "I was not born for wifing and mothering" (*CPP* VI:644). Her grasp of political realities is stronger than her husband's, and she admits she is bored by family life. Very likely she always knew she had a distaste for domesticity. Did she just drift into marriage?

The contented spouses in these three plays, on the other hand, seem to have known exactly what they wanted. Z, in *Village Wooing*, is attracted to A because he does not chase women—and because she felt physically attracted to him: "there come times when I want to get hold of you in my arms, every bit of you" (*CPP* VI:566). Sir Arthur Chavender wanted (and, blissfully ignorant, thinks he has found) a domestic goddess—"I know that you have sacrificed yourself to keeping my house and sewing on my buttons; and I am not ungrateful," he tells her (*CPP* VI:645).

The couple with the strongest bond is found in *The Simpleton*. Pra and Prola are united not only by their commitment to the Superfamily experiment, but by their deep connection to each other. Nevertheless, their marriage has been a stormy one. As we saw earlier, when Prola asks, "How often have you said to yourself 'I could do better alone, or with another woman'?" Pra answers, "Fairly often, my dear, when we were younger. But I did not murder you" (*CPP* VI:836).

Marriage, it seems, is always problematical—and yet it is still going strong, despite Shaw's warning in 1908 that "if marriage cannot be made to produce something better than we are, marriage will have to go, or else the nation will have to go" (*CPP* III:418). More than a century later, hopeful couples continue to think that *their* version of marriage will "produce something better than we are." The three plays in this chapter hint at reasons why we continue to cling to this hope—and why we so often find disappointment instead.

NOTES

1. J. Ellen Gainor. *Shaw's Daughters: Dramatic and Narrative Constructions of Gender*. (Ann Arbor: Michigan University Press, 1991), 155.
2. John A. Bertolini. *The Playwrighting Self of Bernard Shaw*. (Carbondale: Southern Illinois University Press, 1991), 1: 65.
3. Peter Gahan. *Shaw Shadows: Rereading the Texts of Bernard Shaw*. (Gainesville: University Press of Florida, 2004), 139.
4. Gahan, 155.
5. Margery M. Morgan. *The Shavian Playground: An Exploration of the Art of George Bernard Shaw*. (London: Methuen, 1972), 279.

6. Bernard Shaw. *Immaturity*. (London: Constable, 1950), xiii.
7. Bernard Shaw. *Sixteen Self Sketches*. (London: Constable, 1949), 30.
8. Rodelle Weintraub. "Bernard Shaw's Fantasy Island: *Simpleton of the Unexpected Isles.*" *SHAW: The Annual of Bernard Shaw Studies* 17 (1997), 103.
9. Lawrence Switzky. "'The Last Word On Last Words: Shaw and Catastrophic Drama." *SHAW: The Annual of Bernard Shaw Studies* 27 (2007), 195.
10. Weintraub, 97.
11. Ibid., 102–103.
12. Switzky, 199.
13. Morgan, 28: 6.
14. Gainor, 21.

Author Biography

Jean Reynolds Ph.D., from the University of South Florida, is Professor Emerita at Polk State College, Florida. Author of *Pygmalion's Wordplay: The Postmodern Shaw* (1998) and co-editor with D.A. Hadfield of *Shaw and Feminisms: On Stage and Off* (2013), she wrote the chapter on "Education" in *Shaw in Context* (2015). She has published in *SHAW: The Journal of Bernard Shaw Studies* and in *ELT*, and is a member of the editorial board of the *SHAW Journal*.

CHAPTER 12

Matrimonial Partnerships and Politics in Three Late Plays: "*In Good King Charles's Golden Days*": *A True History That Never Happened, The Apple Cart: A Political Extravaganza*, and *Geneva: Another Political Extravaganza*

Matthew Yde

It is not always remembered that in 1898, the year Shaw married, he was an invalid, and was nursed back to health by Charlotte Payne-Townshend, his future wife. Learning of his condition, Charlotte cut short her trip to Rome and was "appalled" to discover the condition of his room at Fitzroy Square when she returned to London:

> Under its drifting surface of smuts and dust, Shaw's programme of work-and-hygiene had filled the place with such chaos that Charlotte could only squeeze in sideways. Unshoe'd, his mobility had "contracted itself to within hopping distance from my chair". He was unable to do housework;

M. Yde (✉)
University of New Mexico, Albuquerque, USA
e-mail: matthewblairyde@aol.com

© The Author(s) 2017
R.A. Gaines (ed.), *Bernard Shaw's Marriages and Misalliances*,
Bernard Shaw and His Contemporaries,
DOI 10.1057/978-1-349-95170-3_12

191

could no longer look after himself—and no one else there had any interest in him. (*Holroyd* I:458)

The "no one else there" refers to Shaw's distant and emotionally unavailable mother, with whom he had been living since he arrived in London 22 years earlier. Charlotte arrived in London on May 1, immediately set herself up as Shaw's nurse, and the two were married informally at the office of the registrar in London, with Shaw hobbling about on crutches, on June 1. As Michael Holroyd has written, Shaw "did not want to bully Charlotte—he wanted her to bully him. He did not want a replacement for Mrs Salt [his secretary] but for Mrs. Shaw" (*Holroyd* I:458).

I begin this exploration of Shaw and marriage in three late plays with this brief anecdote because much of what we will see of Shaw's representation of marriage will inevitably draw our minds back to this episode, the beginnings of his own relatively happy marriage with Charlotte. Both *The Apple Cart* and *Good King Charles* are very much concerned with the condition of marriage, especially as the institution relates to busy, competent statesmen like King Magnus and King Charles II. The third play analyzed in this essay, *Geneva*, looks at marriage from a different perspective, not as it relates to an efficacious statesman (although the play is equally concerned with politics and politicians), but how marriage fits into the life of a vacuous and meddlesome politician of another sort; that is, someone with no talent for statecraft but whose ability to captivate the electorate gets her into politics, a modern condition at which Shaw shuddered with foreboding. In *Geneva* Miss Begonia Brown enters successfully on a political career, despite her unfitness for such a role, due to the inanities of the public and democracy's penchant for electing persons with no qualifications to govern whatsoever. Her relationship to her betrothed is just as vacuous as her relationship to her constituents, and equally without substance. Electoral politics, and many marriages, Shaw seems to be saying, are based on sex appeal, a recipe for disaster in his view. In *Good King Charles* and *The Apple Cart* we see effective rulers in satisfying marital relationships that are not based on sex but on intellectual companionship, an equitable partnership between two strong persons, which was also the basis of Shaw's marriage to Charlotte.

Good King Charles and *The Apple Cart* share remarkable similarities, both structurally and thematically. In both plays we only see the ruler with his wife in the last, much shorter act, near the end of the play. In *Good King Charles* we see Charles with his mistresses in Act I, but not in Act II; and in *The Apple Cart* we see the king with his mistress only in the interlude between the two acts. In both plays the wife is a rational partner and caregiver, even protector, but the relationships are not discernibly sexual. Neither does either king engage in copulation with his mistresses; they serve other purposes. Charles was famous (or infamous) for his dalliances, but in Shaw's play it is clear that the 50-year-old "merry monarch" has done with the messiness of sex; he continues his relationships with Nell Gwynn and Louise de Kérouaille, but not for the purposes of sexual fulfillment, while Barbara Villiers—although "the handsomest woman in England" (*CPP* VII:278)—is ferocious, violently possessive, hell on two legs: he would clearly prefer to see her no more. As he says, "I am done with all bodies. They are all alike: all cats are grey in the dark. It is the souls and the brains that are different. In the end one learns to leave the body out" (*CPP* VII:289). Likewise, Magnus in *The Apple Cart* visits Orinthia when he wants "to talk freely," or, as Orinthia puts it, unhappily, when "the model household becomes a bore, I am the diversion" (*CPP* VI:346). He is attracted by her beauty and vitality, but knows better than to entangle himself sexually:

> Do not let us fall into the common mistake of expecting to become one flesh and one spirit. Every star has its own orbit; and between it and its nearest neighbor there is not only a powerful attraction but an infinite distance. When the attraction becomes stronger than the distance the two do not embrace: they crash together in ruin: we two also have our orbits, and we must keep an infinite distance between us to avoid a disastrous collision. (*CPP* VI:346–347)

The danger of sexual entanglement was clear in Shaw's early play, *The Philanderer* (1894), an autobiographical work based on the disastrous love affair of Shaw and Jenny Patterson, a mistake of his early manhood that he was careful never to repeat.[1] Shaw learned his lesson and for the most part kept his flirtations free of the mess of sexual contact. His ideal is clear as early as *Caesar and Cleopatra* (1898), where Caesar studiously refuses to get involved with Cleopatra in a sexual way. It was no different with the monarchs in these much later plays.

In fact, the chaos that ensues from sexual entanglement, so hilariously dramatized in *The Philanderer*, is also present in the first act of *Good King Charles*. Nell is charming and kind and not prone to jealousy, and that is all to the good; but Louise de Kérouaille wants to procure a love potion so she can possess Charles, while Barbara Villiers is a ruthless termagant, constantly making scenes. Charles had had a sexual relationship with the tempestuous beauty, but now he just longs to be rid of her. By contrast, the second act—which only features Charles and his wife Catherine—is calm, placid, and homely, full of strong but demonstrably non-tempestuous fellow feeling. In *The Apple Cart* also, the act with Magnus and his wife Jemima immediately follows the interlude with Orinthia, where Magnus is driven to violent "*fury*," calling her a "she-devil" as he "*tackles her in earnest*" (*CPP* VI:349). In contrast, the time spent with his wife is calm, orderly, and occupied by rational discourse between the two partners. It is no mistaken perception either that the chaotic first act of *The Apple Cart*, while not a scene of monarch wrangling with mistresses, is one of monarch wrangling with unruly and selfish politicians.

After the bedlam of the first act in Sir Isaac Newton's home, *Good King Charles* moves in the second act to the home of Charles and his queen, Catherine of Braganza, later that same day, with Charles sleeping on a couch in Catherine's boudoir, no doubt recovering from the day's pandemonium. Charles has left the room in great disorder, but there is a *prie-dieu* to suggest Catherine's piety and a clock to indicate the orderliness of the household:

> Catherine, aged 42, enters. She contemplates her husband and the untidiness he has made. With a Portuguese shake of the head (about six times) she sets to work to put the room in order by taking up the boots and putting them tidily at the foot of the couch. She then takes out the coat and hangs it on the rail of the landing. (CPP VII:287)

Catherine then wakes her husband up and there ensues one of the finest depictions of domestic amity in all of Shaw. When Catherine asks Charles why he is resting in her room, he says, "it is the only place where the women cannot come after me." Catherine replies that "[a] wife is some use then, after all," to which Charles, echoing the Book of Proverbs, concurs, "There is nobody like a wife"—meaning, of course, there is no one like a good wife (*CPP* VII:288).[2]

Catherine for her part is of like mind, for she says that Charles is "the very best husband that ever lived" (*CPP* VII:291). In this scene Charles worries about his "unfaithfulness" to his wife, although in the previous act he confesses: "To her only I can never be unfaithful" (*CPP* VII:232). In other words, his infidelities do not make him unfaithful, because his love is true and the infidelities are meaningless. Catherine agrees, saying in the later act, "What care I about your women? your concubines? your handmaidens? the servants of your common pleasures? They have set me free to be something more to you than they are or can ever be. You have never been really unfaithful to me" (*CPP* VII:291–292). The partnership is based on something that Shaw valued much more than sex and that was brains, ability, and mutual esteem. Charles tells her that "she has more brains and character than all the rest of the court put together," to which Catherine replies, "I am nothing except what you have made me"; adding that with what she has learned from him she will, after his death, "govern Portugal" (*CPP* VII: 292). The act continues with the two amicably discussing politics and the inability of the English to be governed, and concludes with Catherine dressing him for his Council meeting:

Catherine:	No no: you have forgotten your wig. [*She takes his hat off and fetches the wig*]. Fancy your going into the Council Chamber like that! Nobody would take you for King Charles the Second without that wig. Now. [*She puts the wig on him; then the hat. A few final pats and pulls complete his toilet*]. Now you look every inch a king. [*Making him a formal curtsy*]. Your majesty's visit has made me very happy. Long live the King!
Charles:	May the Queen live forever! (*CPP* VII300–301)

With that the play ends. Just as Charlotte helped Shaw when he was an invalid and continued to do so throughout his life, so here Catherine babies and bullies and adores her husband, helping him to be the man he was destined to be.

This is an ideal image of marriage, and of Shaw's own marriage, but there is more to the story, of course; an ideal is never the whole truth. Despite what Catherine says, we know that she must have felt pain at times during the lonely nights when Charles was with, for instance, the beautiful Barbara Villiers, Duchess of Cleveland, Countess of Castlemaine. Charles was, at one time at least, deeply attracted sexually to Barbara, and he still enjoys the company of Nell. If these plays reveal something of the domestic life of Shaw, they also reveal his sexual ambivalence: his sexual desire with its concomitant wariness of that same desire; not willing to renounce it, but usually keeping it at a safe distance. Shaw believed it was essential for marriage partners each to have friends of their own of the opposite sex. In a long speech in *The Apple Cart*, Magnus tells Orinthia:

there is no wife on earth so precious … that it is impossible ever to get tired of them. … we are like all other married couples: that is, there are subjects which can never be discussed between us because they are sore subjects. … My wife doesn't like your sort, doesn't understand it, mistrusts and dreads it. Not without reason; for women like you are dangerous to wives. But I don't dislike your sort: I understand it, being a little in that line myself. … So when I want to talk freely about it I come and talk to you. And I take it she talks to friends of hers about people of whom she never talks to me. She has men friends from whom she can get some things that she cannot get from me. If she didn't do so she would be limited by my limitations, which would end in her hating me. So I always do my best to make her men friends feel at home with us. (*CPP* VI:346)

Shaw knew the importance of outside interests in a marriage, but in his own life when he himself was the "friend" of the woman in another marriage or relationship, it often threatened to become a misalliance as the women sometimes fell in love with him, in which case he usually disappeared from the couple's life. Examples of such triangles are Herbert Bland, Edith Bland, and Shaw; May Morris, Harry Sparling, and Shaw; Ellen Terry, Henry Irving, and Shaw; Janet Achurch, Charles Charrington, and Shaw; and Kate Salt, Henry Salt, and Shaw. Shaw, like everyone else, longed for peaceful domesticity and an enduring, stable partnership, but like everyone else he also desired passion and beauty, even if usually sexually unconsummated.

For Shaw, marriage was principally an institution where two persons agree to remain domestic partners and friends for the duration of their lives, but it was not about sex or procreation. Marriage was not a suitable institution for the procreation of children; in fact, it was disastrous. Suitable partners for the making of desirable human beings were not likely to make congenial living partners. As he writes in the preface to *Good King Charles*, when considering the much more sexually active historical figure (in his sexual proclivities Shaw's Charles resembles Shaw much more than he does the historical king):

As a husband he took his marriage very seriously, and his sex adventures as calls of nature on an entirely different footing. In this he was in the line of evolution, which leads to an increasing separation of the unique and intensely personal and permanent marriage relation from the carnal intercourse described in Shakespeare's sonnet. This, being a response to the biological decree that the world must be peopled, may arise irresistibly between persons who could not live together endurably for a week but can produce excellent children. Historians who confuse Charles's feelings for his wife with his appetite for Barbara Villiers do not know chalk from cheese biologically. (*CPP* VII:208)

The sonnet Shaw alludes to is sonnet 129, Shakespeare's famous sonnet about the disastrously wasteful effects of lust, the first two quatrains of which read:

> The expense of spirit in a waste of shame
> Is lust in action; and till action, lust
> Is perjured, murderous, bloody, full of blame,
> Savage, extreme, rude, cruel, not to trust,
> Enjoy'd no sooner but despised straight,
> Past reason hunted, and no sooner had
> Past reason hated, as a swallow'd bait
> On purpose laid to make the taker mad.

Tanner marries Ann to produce a child only because his society requires him to do so. We remember the opprobrium that Violet endures when it is believed she is pregnant out of wedlock, although Tanner congratulates her for her courage. For Shaw, procreation and sexual fulfillment are much better dealt with outside of marriage, while marriage is suitable for the union of minds, as in Shakespeare's equally famous sonnet 116, which begins, "Let me not to the marriage of true minds/Admit impediments." Shaw married, yet he and Charlotte produced no offspring; it was a marriage of minds and a marriage of affectionate partnership.

Shaw's marriage to Charlotte and his extramarital relationship with Stella Campbell were the impetus behind the Magnus–Jemima–Orinthia triangle in *The Apple Cart*, much to Campbell's chagrin. In fact, *The Apple Cart* is one of Shaw's most autobiographical plays, in the same way that *The Philanderer* is autobiographical. Shaw used the triangle of himself, Jenny Patterson, and Francis Farr to generate comedy in *The Philanderer* and he used a similar triangle in *The Apple Cart*, but only in part to generate comedy. Shaw admitted that the interlude with King Magnus and his mistress Orinthia was "comic relief," but went on to say that the interlude "completes the portrait of the King who in the middle of the crisis is seen, not merely as a statesman but as a human being with a domestic life" (*CPP* VI:383). We only see Orinthia in the middle section of the play, the interlude that divides Act I from Act II, but it is a part that has attracted great actresses, such as Edith Evans and Helen Mirren. And no wonder, Orinthia is one of Shaw's "vital geniuses," as he referred to Ann in *Man and Superman*.

Orinthia is a dynamic and captivating personality, but she is demonic, a cruel and capricious sex goddess. She tells Magnus to "drown" his wife, to "shoot her: tell your chauffeur to drive her into the Serpentine and leave her there. The woman makes you ridiculous" (*CPP* VI:342). She believes that she is the "real queen" (*CPP* VI:342) and that as king he "should wipe [his] boots on the common people" (*CPP* VI:347). It is a very unflattering portrait, and Shaw avoided showing it to Stella for as long as he could. When she finally read it she exhorted him to "Tear it up … and re-write it with every scrap of the mischievous vulgarian omitted" (*Holroyd* III:152).

For all her beauty and vitality, Orinthia is not regarded as a prime progenitor, as Ann is in *Man and Superman*. In her attempt to take the king away from his wedded wife, Jemima, Orinthia says, "I can give you beautiful, wonderful children: have you ever seen a lovelier boy than my Basil?" Magnus replies, "Your children are beautiful; but they are fairy children; and I have several very real ones already. A divorce would not sweep them out of the way of the fairies" (*CPP* VI:344). Shaw originally had Magnus reply, "Basil is a very good-looking young man, but he has the morals of a tramp" (*Holroyd* III:152). Campbell lost her son in the war, and was furious with this line; she accused Shaw of hitting "below the belt when you juggle with gossip picked up about my dead son" (*Holroyd* III:152). Shaw tried to please her where he could, and so he changed the line to the one quoted above.

Shaw was attracted to beauty, charm, and vitality, but it was essential that he keep the would-be lover at a distance; that the flirtation remain, for the most part, a game, lest the two "embrace … [and] crash together in ruin." Magnus describes his relationship with Orinthia as "two children at play" (*CPP* VI:347), and while Jemima is a part of his "real workaday self; you [Orinthia] belong to fairyland" (*CPP* VI:344). However pleasing her company, she is neither material for making children with, nor is she one for marriage, at least as far as Magnus (and Shaw) is concerned; after all, Orinthia despises politics and derides the women in Magnus's Cabinet. Finally the king tells her, "My dear Orinthia, I had rather marry the devil" (*CPP* VI:344).

Yet this fairyland world, removed as it is from the pleasures and rewards of marriage, is clearly a compelling and in some way necessary part of life for both Magnus and Shaw, however essential that it be kept at a safe distance to avoid crashing and ruin; although this is easier said than done, and the incident when Shaw pursued Stella to the coast of Kent was an unusual instance of Shaw pursuing his fantasies beyond a safe distance. Luckily for Shaw, Stella would not have him then, and was furious that he followed her (she was engaged to be married at the time). On the train back Shaw wrote Stella, begging that his fantasy become reality, "About you I am a mass of illusions. It is impossible that I should not tire soon: nothing so wonderful could last ... I will hurry through my dream as fast as I can; only let me have my dream out" (*Holroyd* II:314). This was a rare instance of Shaw pursuing his fantasy and flirtations to the point of fleshly embrace, but nothing came of it. It would be almost ten years before Shaw would have another one of these tempestuous love affairs, this time with Molly Tompkins, and this time apparently consummated.[3]

In her fastidious motherly attentions to her husband, Jemima resembles Queen Catherine, and Charlotte. In fact, the play ends very much like *Good King Charles*, with Jemima peremptorily making certain that the king is dressed properly and fed:

The Queen:	Now Magnus: it's time to dress for dinner.
Magnus [*much disturbed*]:	Oh, not now. I have something very big to think about. I don't want any dinner.
The Queen [*peremptorily*]:	No dinner! Did anyone ever hear of such a thing! You know you will not sleep if you think after seven o'clock.
Magnus [*worried*]:	But really, Jemima—
The Queen [*going to him and taking his arm*]:	Now, now, now! Don't be naughty. I mustn't be late for dinner. Come on, like a good little boy.

The King, with a grimace of hopeless tenderness, allows himself to be led away. (*CPP* VI:374–375)

Some small part of Magnus needs Orinthia for amusement and diversion, but it is to his wife that he is devoted. Orinthia is a pretty flower, lovely and perhaps even aesthetically necessary, but like a rose can also sting; Jemima is aliment itself, essential. When the regal Orinthia says, "Oh, you are blind. You are worse than blind: you have low tastes. Heaven is offering you a rose; and you cling to a cabbage," Magnus sensibly replies, "But what wise man, if you forced him to choose between doing without roses and doing without cabbages, would not secure the cabbages?" (*CPP* VI:338–339). It is the homely, motherly Jemima who complements the model ruler Magnus. Orinthia as wife would destroy him.

While the relationship between king and queen, model ruler and model wife, is an essential part of both *The Apple Cart* and *Good King Charles*, it is *The Apple Cart* and *Geneva* that bear almost the same subtitle: *The Apple Cart*: A Political Extravaganza; *Geneva*: Another Political Extravaganza. Structurally *The Apple Cart* and *Good King Charles* bear superficial resemblance, but thematically the former play perhaps has even more in common with *Geneva*. Both plays concern the potential destruction of society under democratic or mob rule. Orinthia wishes to take Jemima's place as queen because, she believes, her beauty will captivate the mob and complement the dynamic king far better than the prosaic Jemima. As Holroyd puts it, "What she [Orinthia] offers the King is the exploitation of democratic popularity to establish a pop-star dictatorship of the masses by beautiful people" (*Holroyd* III:154). This is very much what we see in *Geneva* with Begonia Brown and her betrothed— "*a cheerful young gentleman, powerfully built*" (*CPP* VII:113)—although she is the politician whom he will complement with his cheerful, powerful presence. This democratic partnership is in stark contrast to the dictators Bombardone and Battler, who were modeled on Mussolini and Hitler. In the play the domestic lives of the dictators are of no concern, while Begonia's married life, as intimated, is a key part of her portrait, so much so that when her partner is introduced in the fourth act his character name is The Betrothed, as if he exists only as a complement to her.

At the start of the play, Begonia is typist in the office of the International Committee for Intellectual Cooperation. This was a real adjunct to the League of Nations, although nobody knew anything about it. At the top of the play Begonia is seen sitting in the dilapidated office in Geneva, but she is not working, instead she "*is smoking and reading an illustrated magazine with her heels on the table.*" This description of the *"self-satisfied ... fairly attractive and well aware of it"* Begonia tells us everything we need to know about this character, whose *"speech and manners are London suburban"* (*CPP* VII:44). Begonia is the typical ignorant modern person who thinks they know all they need to know and who, given the chance, would bring the world to complete destruction with utter insouciance. In fact, when she learns that she has sparked a "series of political convulsions which may end in the destruction of civilization," she is *"flattered"* that she is such "a big success" and "wont pretend [she is] not gratified" (*CPP* VII:71–72). In short, she is the opposite of Magnus and Charles, but it is she and those like her, and not the aforementioned statesmen, whom the voting public are more likely to put in power in the democratic age, if for no other reason than that they resemble the public and so flatter their egos.[4] Because Begonia files the complaints of the disgruntled plaintiffs who visit her office—which before had never received anyone at all—and the complaints are processed by an energetic and idealistic judge in the International Court of Justice in The Hague, Begonia is thrust into the limelight. She is an instant celebrity and is made a Dame by the British Empire.

Early in the play an American journalist, not dissimilar to Begonia, enters the office and the two begin to kiss, but when there is a knock on the door they quickly separate. Despite this dalliance, Begonia is soon engaged to the British Foreign Secretary Sir Orpheus Midlander's nephew, "Benjy" (as his uncle calls him), who we are to understand is as vacuous as Begonia. Sir Orpheus tells us that Benjy—or The Betrothed, as he is denominated in the play—is no more intelligent than "a blue behinded ape" and has not exchanged 20 words with him since he "tipped him when he was going from Eton to Oxford" (*CPP* VII:76). No one believes Begonia could have written the complaints herself, and when the Secretary of the League of Nations suggests to Sir Orpheus that perhaps his nephew wrote them, Sir Orpheus says that if "the work shews political ability and presentable style, you may accept my assurance that Sue's boy has nothing to do with it. Besides, he is at present in Singapore, where the native dancing girls are irresistible" (*CPP* VII:76). The inbred blue bloods molded at Eton and Oxford are no better than middle-class suburbanites like Begonia.[5]

When Sir Orpheus learns from Begonia herself that Lord Middlesex is dead and the Conservative Party has invited her to run in the Camberwell by-election, the Foreign Secretary reminds her that his nephew is running as the government candidate. No, Begonia tells him, he "has withdrawn and proposed to me. He will pay my election expenses" (*CPP* VII:84). It turns out that "Billikins" (as Begonia calls him) never wanted to run anyway, was doing it for his mother, and no amount of coaching could have prepared him for public interrogation in any case, whereas Begonia has a knack for saying just what the public want to hear.[6] Sir Orpheus is appalled, because she has no political experience at all; it does not matter, she says, "I shall pick up all the politics I need when I get into the House; and I shall get into the House because there are lots of people in Camberwell who think as I do. You bet I shall romp in at the head of the poll" (*CPP* VII:85). As a political partnership, Begonia and "Billikins" are as far away from Magnus and Jemima or Charles and Catherine as it is possible to conceive.

Despite learning about The Betrothed's character over the first three acts of the play, we do not actually meet him until the fourth act, when everyone has gathered at The Hague for the trial, initially waiting to see if the dictators will even show up. The plaintiffs and the few others gathered read newspapers while they wait, but *"Begonia and her young man have one excessively illustrated newspaper between them. He has his arm around her waist and is shamelessly enjoying their physical contact"* (*CPP* VII:113). Whereas Magnus and Charles carefully separate their official duties from their grosser pleasures, with Begonia and her betrothed they are merged and contaminated. Whereas the two monarchs choose wives who will help them in their duties, the dangerous synergy of the attractive young couple here will only hasten any disaster likely to ensue from their involvement in politics.

In *Geneva* there is one other character who derives her name from her marital status, and that is The Widow, a fiery Central American woman with very definite opinions of right and wrong and social etiquette, which are the consequence of her origin in the Earthly Paradise, "one of the leading States in the world in culture and purity of race" (*CPP* VII:55). Actually her own opinions are null and void; she is compelled to act according to public opinion, and it is often difficult to tell whether an opinion is her own or simply derived from the public. The Widow is one of the plaintiffs at the Court, and wants the murderer of her husband brought to justice. She tells Begonia that if they do not comply with her request, her "son will be obliged to take up a blood feud and shoot the murderer with his own hands, though they are at the same school and devoted to one another. It is against Nature, against God: if your committee does not stop it I will shoot every member of it, and you too"

(*CPP* VII:58). She has already shot her husband's lover dead, although she was her "dearest friend" (*CPP* VII:57). She did not mind the affair at all, but had to kill her friend because public opinion demanded it of her "as a self-respecting wife and mother" (*CPP* VII:57). One of the motifs of the play is stimulus response violence. Begonia hates anyone from Peckham—"You have only to say Peckham to the representative of the Intellectual Committee of the League of Nations to reveal her as an irreconcilable belligerent" (*CPP* VII:144)—and for all their differences, The Widow is subject to a similar conditioned violence. The compulsion to act according to the dictate of public opinion is equally powerful whether accompanied by hostility or not. Shaw is concerned here with the danger of run-away violence, always a threat to civilization, but now capable of destroying the world. The very moment in history when modern industrial weapons enter the political sphere, democratic electoral politics puts the levers of global destruction into the hands of persons like Begonia and The Widow.

The Widow's late husband was the President of the Earthly Paradise, "the most civilized country in the world. Its constitution is absolutely democratic: every president must swear to observe it in every particular. The Church is abolished: no moral authority is recognized except that of the people's will. The president and parliament are elected by adult suffrage every two years" (*CPP* VI:56). All these reforms were introduced by the Widow's late husband, "the father of his country" (*CPP* VII:57), who had been re-elected three times. Begonia fails to see why someone loved by his people would be murdered, and The Widow explains that her husband "had certain weaknesses. He was an affectionate husband: I may even say an uxorious one; but he was very far from being faithful to me. When he abolished the Church he would have abolished marriage also if public opinion would have stood for it" (*CPP* VII:57). It turns out that his kind nature also extended to his opponent for public office, who finally succeeded in murdering him. What do we make of this strange tale? Like Charles II, the President of the Earthly Paradise was a good husband who had extramarital relations as a matter of necessity. But he lacked real power because in his nation "the people's will" had all real authority, and so the title Earthly Paradise is a misnomer, an ironic designation for a land that is destined to destruction.

After nearly 45 years of marriage, it was Shaw's turn to care for Charlotte at the end, as she suffered terribly from a crippling case of rheumatism and finally died in 1943. Shaw lived on for seven more years, serviceably cared for by his private secretary, Blanche Patch. Charlotte had characteristics of royalty, according to many—Lady Rhondda said she had "a number of the attributes of a Queen"—and so, according to Michael Holroyd, it was no "wonder that Shaw had set the scene of their marriage as the finale to '*In Good King Charles's Golden Days*'" (*Holroyd* III:446–447). The two were not your average couple, Shaw very much the elderly statesman of British literature and senior member of the Fabian Society, Charlotte the regal Irish aristocrat. They were as far removed as possible from the likes of Begonia Brown and her young man, and the intense fear of what Miss Brown represented to the future of humanity stimulated Shaw to a lifetime commitment to political solutions. He had an opinion on everything, of course, including marriage. His views on the institution of marriage and the best means of producing a higher type of human being, not always consistent—as we would expect in over 70 years of writing—can be found in works as disparate as *Cashel Byron's Profession* (1882), *The Quintessence of Ibsenism* (1891), *Man and Superman* (1902), *Getting Married* (1908), *The Simpleton of the Unexpected Isles* (1934), and *Farfetched Fables* (1950). But perhaps the best place to look is to his own childless but relatively happy marriage to Charlotte, and the dramatic representations of that marriage, especially in *The Apple Cart* and *"In Good King Charles's Golden Days."*

NOTES

1. Although, as we will see, he came dangerously close to repeating it with Stella Campbell.
2. "He who finds a wife finds what is good and receives favor from the LORD." Proverbs 18:22 NIV.
3. See Charles Berst, "Passion at Lake Maggiore: Shaw, Molly Tompkins, and Italy, 1921–1950." *The Annual of Bernard Shaw Studies* Vol. 5, SHAW ABROAD (1985) 81–114. Penn State University Press. Stable URL: http://www.jstor.org/stable/40681152 (Berst 1985).
4. In *The Apple Cart* Shaw gives an example of a competent and public-spirited politician tactically considering how he may exploit his celebrity for electoral victory, but for the people's good, an unusual inversion to the status quo of electoral politics.
5. Another British character in the play worth noting is The Newcomer, who, although a duly elected MP in the House of Commons, has been locked out of Parliament by a Hitler-like Prime Minister, which is being enforced by the police and by a "body of young men called the Clean Shirts" (*CPP*

VII:52). At the close of the play, when the end of the world seems imminent, the uxorious Newcomer says, "I must depart now and cheer up the missus" (*CPP* VII:160). As might be guessed, his democratic principles and commitment to electoral politics are almost as mercilessly satirized as Begonia's stupidity.

6. I cannot refrain from saying it: Begonia reminds one of Sarah Palin.

REFERENCE

Berst, Charles A. 1985. Passion at Lake Maggiore: Shaw, Molly Tompkins, and Italy, 1921–1950. *SHAW: The Annual of Bernard Shaw Studies* 5: 81–114. www.jstor.org/stable/40681152.

AUTHOR BIOGRAPHY

Matthew Yde Visiting Assistant Professor in the Department of Theatre and Dance at the University of New Mexico, USA, specializes in modern and contemporary theatre and drama. He is the author of *Bernard Shaw and Totalitarianism: Longing for Utopia* (2013) and of numerous articles in *Modern Drama* and *SHAW: The Journal of Bernard Shaw Studies*. He is currently writing a monograph on contemporary American dramatist Stephen Adly Guirgis.

APPENDIX A
DIVORCE DECREES, DIVORCE RATE PER 1000 MARRIED COUPLES, AND PETITIONS FOR JUDICIAL SEPARATION (ENGLAND AND WALES), 1851–1987

Republished from *Science Today* with the kind permission of Palgrave Macmillan Publishing and reprinted from 1990 edition of *The Road to Divorce: England 1530–1897* by Lawrence Stone pp. 435–436 with the kind permission of Oxford University Press.

Year	Divorce decrees	Divorce rate per 1000 married couples	Petitions for judicial separation
1851	4	0.0001	
1857	4	0.0001	
1861	141	0.04	49
1866			64
1871	161	0.04	86
1876	208	0.05	136
1881	311	0.07	119
1886	325	0.07	133
1891	369	0.07	110
1896	459	0.08	110
1901	477	0.08	89
1906	546	0.09	92
1911	580	0.09	58
1912	587	0.08	
1913	577	0.08	
1914	856	0.12	
1915	680	0.1	
1916	990	0.14	68
1917	700	0.09	

(continued)

© The Editor(s) (if applicable) and The Author(s) 2017
R.A. Gaines (ed.), *Bernard Shaw's Marriages and Misalliances*,
Bernard Shaw and His Contemporaries,
DOI 10.1057/978-1-349-95170-3

Year	Divorce decrees	Divorce rate per 1000 married couples	Petitions for judicial separation
1918	1100	0.15	
1919	1600	0.22	
1920	3100	0.41	120
1921	3500	0.46	
1922	2600	0.34	
1923	2700	0.35	115
1924	2300	0.29	
1925	2600	0.32	
1926	2600	0.32	
1927	3200	0.39	
1928	4000	0.48	
1929	3400	0.4	
1930	3600	0.42	
1931	3800	0.44	
1932	3900	0.45	
1933	4000	0.45	
1934	4300	0.47	
1935	4100	0.45	
1936	5100	0.55	96
1937	4900	0.52	
1938	6200	0.64	99
1939	8200	0.84	
1940	7800	0.79	101
1941	6400	0.63	101
1942	7700	0.75	102
1943	10,000	0.98	103
1944	12,300	1.2	104
1945	15,600	1.4	105
1946	29,800	2.8	106
1947	60,300	5.6	107
1948	43,700	4	108
1949	34,900	3.2	109
1950	31,000	2.8	83
1951	29,000	2.8	
1952	34,000	3	
1953	30,000	2.7	
1954	28,000	2.5	
1955	27,000	2.3	
1956	26,000	2.3	
1957	24,000	2	
1958	23,000	1.9	
1959	24,000	2.1	
1960	24,000	2	
1961	25,000	2.1	128

(continued)

Year	Divorce decrees	Divorce rate per 1000 married couples	Petitions for judicial separation
1962	29,000	2.4	
1963	32,000	2.7	
1964	35,000	2.9	
1965	38,000	3.1	
1966	39,000	3.3	99
1967	43,000	3.5	
1968	46,000	3.7	
1969	51,000	4.1	119
1970	58,000	4.7	90
1971	74,000	6	94
1972	1,19,000	9.4	
1973	1,06,000	8.4	
1974	1,13,000	9	
1975	1,20,000	9.6	
1976	1,27,000	10.1	
1977	1,29,000	10.3	
1978	1,44,000	11.6	
1979	1,39,000	11.2	
1980	1,48,000	12	
1981	1,46,000	11.9	
1982	1,47,000	12.1	
1983	1,47,000	12.2	
1984	1,45,000	12	
1985	1,60,000	13.4	
1986	1,54,000	12.9	
1987	1,51,000	12.6	

Appendix B
Marriage and Divorce: Liturgy and Legislation: Edited by
L.W. Conolly

Although civil marriages had been legally recognized in England since 1836 (Shaw himself was married in a civil ceremony in 1898), the bulk of marriages in late Victorian England still took place in church, predominantly in the Church of England. The liturgy of the Solemnization of Marriage has changed little since the Victorian era, except that the bride is no longer required to promise to "obey" her husband.

1. From the Solemnization of Matrimony, *The Book of Common Prayer.* **Oxford: Oxford University Press, [1901], 303–305.**

At the day and time appointed for solemnization of Matrimony, the persons to be married shall come into the body of the Church with their friends and neighbours: and there standing together, the Man on the right hand, and the woman on the left, the Priest[1] shall say,

Dearly beloved, we are gathered together here in the sight of God, and in the face of this congregation, to join together this Man and this Woman in holy Matrimony; which is an honourable estate, instituted of God in the time of man's innocency, signifying unto us the mystical union that is betwixt Christ and his Church; which holy estate Christ adorned and beautified with his presence, and first miracle that he wrought, in Cana of Galilee; and is commended of Saint Paul to be honourable among all men: and therefore is not by any to be enterprised, nor taken in hand, unadvisedly, lightly, or wantonly, to satisfy men's carnal lusts and appetites, like brute beasts that have no understanding; but

© The Editor(s) (if applicable) and The Author(s) 2017
R.A. Gaines (ed.), *Bernard Shaw's Marriages and Misalliances*,
Bernard Shaw and His Contemporaries,
DOI 10.1057/978-1-349-95170-3

reverently, discreetly, advisedly, soberly, and in the fear of God; duly considering the causes for which Matrimony was ordained.

First, It was ordained for the procreation of children, to be brought up in the fear and nurture of the Lord, and to the praise of his holy Name.

Secondly, It was ordained for a remedy against sin, and to avoid fornication; that such persons as have not the gift of continency might marry, and keep themselves undefiled members of Christ's body.

Thirdly, It was ordained for the mutual society, help, and comfort, that the one ought to have of the other, both in prosperity and adversity. Into which holy estate these two persons present come now to be joined. Therefore if any man can shew any just cause, why they may not lawfully be joined together, let him now speak, or else hereafter for ever hold his peace.

And also, speaking unto the persons that shall be married, he shall say,

I require and charge you both, as ye will answer at the dreadful day of judgement when the secrets of all hearts shall be disclosed, that if either of you know any impediment, why ye may not be lawfully joined together in Matrimony, ye do now confess it. For be ye well assured, that so many as are coupled together otherwise than God's Word doth allow are not joined together by God; neither is their Matrimony lawful. ...

If no impediment be alleged then shall the Curate say unto the Man,

Wilt thou have this Woman to thy wedded wife, to live together after God's ordinance in the holy estate of Matrimony? Wilt thou love her, comfort her, honour, and keep her in sickness and in health; and forsaking all other, keep thee only unto her, so long as ye both shall live?

The Man shall answer,

I will.

Then shall the Priest say unto the Woman,

Wilt thou have this Man to thy wedded husband, to live together after God's ordinance in the holy estate of Matrimony? Wilt thou obey him, and serve him, love, honour, and keep him in sickness and in health; and forsaking all other, keep thee only unto him, so long as ye both shall live?

The Woman will answer,

I will.

Then shall the Minister say,

Who giveth this Woman to be married to this Man?

Then shall they give their troth to each other in this manner. The Minister, receiving the Woman at her father's or friend's hands, shall cause the Man with his right hand to take the Woman by her right hand, and to say after him as followeth.

I take thee [name] to my wedded wife, to have and to hold from this day forward, for better for worse, for richer for poorer, in sickness and in health, to love and to cherish, till death us do part, according to God's holy ordinance; and thereto I plight thee my troth.

Then shall they loose their hands; and the Woman, with her right hand taking the Man by his right hand, shall likewise say after the Minister,

I take thee [name] to my wedded husband, to have and to hold from this day forward, for better for worse, for richer for poorer, in sickness and in health, to love, cherish, and to obey, till death us do part, according to God's holy ordinance; and therefore I give thee my troth.

Then shall they again loose their hands; and the Man shall give unto the Woman a Ring, laying the same upon the book with the accustomed duty to the Priest and Clerk. And the Priest, taking the Ring, shall deliver it unto the Man, to put it upon the fourth finger of the Woman's left hand. And the Man holding the Ring there, and taught by the Priest, shall say,

With this Ring I thee wed, with my body I thee worship, and with all my worldly goods I thee endow: In the Name of the Father, and of the Son, and of the Holy Ghost. Amen.

Then the Man leaving the Ring upon the fourth finger of the Woman's left hand, they shall both kneel down; and the Minister shall say,

Let us pray. Oh eternal God, Creator and Preserver of all mankind, Giver of all spiritual grace, the Author of everlasting life; Send thy blessing upon these thy servants, this man and this woman, whom we bless in thy Name; that, as Isaac and Rebecca lived faithfully together, so these persons may surely perform and keep the vow and covenant betwixt them made (whereof this Ring given and received is a token and pledge) and may ever remain in perfect love and peace together, and live according to thy laws; through Jesus Christ our Lord. Amen.

Then shall the Priest join their right hands together, and say,
Those whom God hath joined together let no man put asunder.
Then shall the Minister speak unto the people.

Forasmuch as [name] and [name] have consented together in holy wedlock, and have witnessed the same before God and this company, and thereto have given and pledged their troth either to other, and have declared the same by giving and receiving of a Ring, and by joining of hands; I pronounce that they be Man and Wife together, in the Name of the Father, and of the Son, and of the Holy Ghost. Amen.

2. From *An Act to Amend the Law Relating to Divorce and Matrimonial Causes in England, 28 August 1857. A Collection of the Public General Statutes Passed in the Twentieth and Twenty-First Years of the Reign of Her Majesty Queen Victoria*. London: Eyre and Spottiswoode, 1857, 847–862

Having made such a solemn commitment to marriage, couples who subsequently wished to end their marriage found the divorce law a formidable obstacle, especially for women. For most of Shaw's life, divorce was governed by the 1857 Divorce and Matrimonial Causes Act, the most relevant clauses of which are given here. There were no significant changes to divorce laws in England until 1937, after which divorce rates rose (by 1939) to 0.84 per 1000 married couples.[2] For other important legislation affecting women's rights (e.g., the Married Women's Property Act of 1892), see Kester.[3]

XVI A Sentence of Judicial Separation ... may be obtained, either by the Husband or the Wife, on the Ground of Adultery, or Cruelty, or Desertion without Cause for Two Years and upwards.

XXVII It shall be lawful for any Husband to present a Petition to the said Court, praying that his Marriage may be dissolved, on the Ground that his Wife has since the Celebration thereof been guilty of Adultery; and it shall be lawful for any Wife to present a Petition to the said Court, praying that her Marriage may be dissolved, on the Ground that since the Celebration thereof her Husband has been guilty of incestuous Adultery, or of Bigamy with Adultery, or of Rape, or of Sodomy or Bestiality, or of Adultery coupled with such Cruelty as without Adultery would have entitled her to a Divorce *à Mensâ et Thoro*,[4] or of Adultery coupled with Desertion, without reasonable excuse, for Two Years or upwards ....

XXX In case the Court, on the Evidence in relation to any such petition, shall not be satisfied that the alleged Adultery has been committed, or shall find that the Petitioner has during the Marriage been accessory to or conniving at the Adultery of the other Party to the Marriage, or has condoned the Adultery complained of, or that the Petition is presented or prosecuted in collusion with either of the Respondents, then and in any of the said Cases the Court shall dismiss the said Petition.

LVII When the Time hereby limited for appealing against any Decree dissolving a Marriage shall have expired, and no Appeal shall have been presented against such a Decree, or when any such appeal shall have been dismissed, or when in the Result of any Appeal any Marriage shall be declared to be dissolved, but not sooner, it shall be lawful for the respective Parties thereto to marry again, as if the prior Marriage had been dissolved by Death: Provided always, that no Clergyman in Holy Orders of the United Church of England and Ireland shall be compelled to solemnize the Marriage of any Person whose former Marriage may have been dissolved on the Ground of his or her Adultery, or shall be liable to any Suit, Penalty, or Censure for solemnizing or refusing to solemnize the Marriage of any such person.

NOTES

1. Used interchangeably in the service with "Curate" and "Minister."
2. Stone, Lawrence. *Road to Divorce. England 1530–1987.* Oxford: Oxford University Press, 1990, 435.
3. Kester, Dolores. "The Legal Climate of Shaw's Problem Plays." In Rodelle Weintraub, *Fabian Feminist*, 68–83.
4. "From table and bed" (Latin), i.e., a legal separation, but not divorce.

BIBLIOGRAPHY

All sources are print unless noted otherwise

Auerbach, Nina. 1997. *Ellen Terry: Player in Her Time*. Philadelphia: University of Pennsylvania Press.

Bergson, Henri. 1998. *Creative Evolution,* trans. Arthur Mitchel. New York, Dover.

Billington, Michael. 2007. *State of the Nation: British Theatre Since 1945*. London: Faber & Faber.

Carpenter, Charles A. 1969. *Bernard Shaw and the Art of Destroying Ideals: The Early Plays*. Madison: University of Wisconsin Press.

Chothia, Jean (ed.). 1998. *The New Woman and Other Emancipated Woman Plays*. London: Oxford World Classics.

Clare, David. 2015. *Bernard Shaw's Irish Outlook*. London: Palgrave Macmillan.

Dietrich, Richard Farr. 1989. *British Drama 1890–1950: A Critical History*. Boston: Twayne.

Dietrich, Richard Farr. 1995. Shaw and Yeats: Two Irishman Divided by a Common Language. *SHAW: The Annual of Bernard Shaw Studies* 15: 65–84.

Dukore, Bernard F. 2000. *Shaw's Theater*. Gainesville: University Press of Florida.

Dunbar, Janet. 1963. *Mrs. G.B.S.* New York: Harper and Row.

Ford, Ronald (ed.). 2007. *The Letters of Bernard Shaw to The Times, 1898–1950*. Dublin: Irish Academic Press.

Grose, Captain (comp.). 1994. *The 1811 Dictionary of Buckish Slang, University Wit and Pickpocket Eloquence*. London: Studio Edition Ltd. Rpt.

Hadfield, D.A., and Jean Reynolds (eds.). 2013. *Shaw and Feminisms: On Stage and Off*. Gainesville: University Press of Florida.

© The Editor(s) (if applicable) and The Author(s) 2017   217
R.A. Gaines (ed.), *Bernard Shaw's Marriages and Misalliances*,
Bernard Shaw and His Contemporaries,
DOI 10.1057/978-1-349-95170-3

Hellman, Jesse M. 2015. Lady Hamilton: *Nelson's Enchantress*, and the Creation of *Pygmalion. SHAW: The Journal of Bernard Shaw Studies* 35 (2): 213–237.

Hiaasen, Carl. Satire. BrainyQuote. www.brainyquote.com.

Holroyd, Michael. 1988. *Bernard Shaw. Vol. I: 1856–1898. The Search for Love*. London: Chatto & Windus.

Holroyd, Michael. 1989. *Bernard Shaw. Vol. II: 1898–1918. The Pursuit of Power*. London: Chatto & Windus.

Holroyd, Michael. 1991. *Bernard Shaw. Vol. III: 1918–1950. The Lure of Fantasy*. London: Chatto & Windus.

Holroyd, Michael. 1992. *Bernard Shaw. Vol. IV: 1950–1991. The Last Laugh*. London: Chatto & Windus.

Ibsen, Henrik. 2001. *Four Major Plays*, vol. 2, trans. Rolf Fjelde. New York: Penguin.

Innes, Christopher (ed.). 2002. *Modern British Drama. The Twentieth Century 1890–1990*. Cambridge: Cambridge University Press.

Kennedy, Dennis. 1985. *Granville Barker and The Dream of Theatre*. Cambridge: Cambridge University Press.

Kent, Brad (ed.). 2015. *George Bernard Shaw in Context*. Cambridge: Cambridge University Press.

Kester, Dolores. The Legal Climate of Shaw's Problem Plays. In *Fabian Feminist*, ed. Rodelle Weintraub, 68–83.

Laurence, Dan H. (ed.). 1965. *Bernard Shaw. Collected Letters, vol. 1: 1874–1897*. New York: Dodd, Mead.

Laurence, Dan H. (ed.). 1985. *Bernard Shaw. Collected Letters, vol. 3: 1911–1925*. New York: Viking.

Laurence, Dan H. (ed.). 1988. *Bernard Shaw. Collected Letters, vol. 4: 1926–1950*. New York: Viking.

Leary, Daniel. 1972. About Nothing in Shaw's *The Simpleton of the Unexpected Isles. Educational Theatre Journal* 24: 139–148.

O'Donovan, John. 1965. *Shaw and the Great Charlatan Genius*. Dublin: Dolmen Press.

Peters, Sally. 1977. Ann and Superman: Type and Archetype. In *Fabian Feminist: Bernard Shaw and Woman*, ed. Rodelle Weintraub, 46–65. University Park: The Pennsylvania State University Press.

Peters, Sally. 1990. From Mystic Betrothal to *Ménage à Trois*: Bernard Shaw and May Morris. *The Independent Shavian* 28 (1–2): 3–16.

Peters, Sally. 1992. A Paper Courtship: Bernard Shaw and Ellen Terry. *Annals of Scholarship* 9 (3): 327–340.

Peters, Sally. 1996. *Bernard Shaw. The Ascent of the Superman*. New Haven and London: Yale University Press.

Peters, Sally. 1998. Shaw's Life: A Feminist in Spite of Himself. In *Biographical introduction to The Cambridge Companion to George Bernard Shaw*, ed. Christopher Innes, 3–24. Cambridge: Cambridge University Press.

Peters, Sally. 2005. The Septuagenarian versus the Siren: Shaw and Molly Tompkins. *The Independent Shavian* 43 (1–2): 20–24.

Powell, Kerry. 2015. Farcical Comedy. In *George Bernard Shaw in Context*, ed. Brad Kent, 85–93. Cambridge: Cambridge University Press.

Purdon, C.B. 1956. *Granville Barker*. Cambridge, MA: Harvard University Press.

Rosset, B.C. 1964. *Shaw of Dublin: The Formative Years*. University Park: The Pennsylvania State University Press.

Saether, Astrid. Interview (27 February 2008) with Saether about her biography of Suzannah Thoresen Ibsen. ibsen.nb.no/id/11163880.0.

Salmon, Eric (ed.). 1986. *Granville Barker and his Correspondents*. Detroit: Wayne State University Press.

Saunders, M. Sean. 2002. From Metropolis to 'Impossible Edges': Shaw's Imperial Abjects. *SHAW: The Annual of Bernard Shaw Studies* 22: 99–115.

Shaw, Bernard. 1926. *The Irrational Knot*. London: Heron Books.

Shaw, Bernard. 1932. *Immaturity*. London: Constable.

Shaw, Bernard. 1934. *Short Stories, Scraps and Shavings*. New York: Dodd, Mead.

Shaw, Bernard. 1971. *The Road to Equality: Ten Unpublished Lectures and Essays 1884–1918*, ed. Louis Crompton. Boston, MA: Beacon Press.

Shaw, Bernard. 1970–1974. *Bernard Shaw: Collected Plays with Their Prefaces*, 7 vols. ed. supervisor Dan H. Laurence. London: Max Reinhardt/The Bodley Head.

Shaw, Bernard. 1975. *Bernard Shaw: Collected Plays with Their Prefaces*. New York: Dodd, Mead.

Shaw, Bernard. 1981a. *Mrs Warren's Profession. A Facsimile of the Holograph Manuscript*, intro. Margot Peters. New York: Garland.

Shaw, Bernard. 1981b. *The Man of Destiny & Caesar and Cleopatra. Facsimiles of the Holograph Manuscripts*, intro. J.L. Wisenthal. New York: Garland.

Shaw, Bernard. 1986. *The Philanderer. A Facsimile of the Holograph Manuscript*, intro. Julius Novick. New York: Garland.

Shaw, Bernard. 2002. *George Bernard Shaw: Eight Interviews by Hayden Church*. Selected by Edward Connery Lathem. Peacham, VT: Perpetua Press.

Shaw, Bernard. 2005. *Mrs Warren's Profession*, ed. L.W. Conolly. Peterborough, ON: Broadview Press.

Shaw, Bernard. 2012. *The Intelligent Woman's Guide to Socialism, Capitalism, Sovietism, and Fascism*. London: Alma Classics.

Smith, J. Percy. 1981. Introduction. In *Candida & How He Lied to Her Husband. Facsimiles of the Holograph Manuscripts*, xiii–xxii. New York: Garland.

Turco, Alfred, Jr. 1986. Shaw 40 Years Later—Eric Bentley Speaks His Mind on Eleven Neglected Plays: *Getting Married, Overruled, On the Rocks*, and Others. *SHAW: The Annual of Bernard Shaw Studies* 7: 7–29.

Tyson, Brian (ed.). 1996 [1991]. *Bernard Shaw's Book Reviews*, 2 vols. University Park: The Pennsylvania State University Press.

Webb, Beatrice. Typescript of diary entry, 12 May 1911. http://digital.library. lse.ac.uk/objects/lse:six767gol.

Weintraub, Rodelle (ed.). 1977. *Fabian Feminist: Bernard Shaw and Woman*. University Park: The Pennsylvania State University Press.

Weintraub, Stanley (ed.). 1970. *Shaw: An Autobiography 1898–1950. The Playwright Years*. New York: Weybright and Talley.

Weintraub, Stanley (ed.). 1986. *Bernard Shaw: The Diaries*, 2 vols. University Park: The Pennsylvania State University Press.

Weintraub, Stanley (ed.). 1989. *Bernard Shaw on the London Art Scene, 1885–1950*. University Park: The Pennsylvania State University Press.

INDEX

© The Editor(s) (if applicable) and The Author(s) 2017
R.A. Gaines (ed.), *Bernard Shaw's Marriages and Misalliances*,
Bernard Shaw and His Contemporaries,
DOI 10.1057/978-1-349-95170-3

221

www.ingramcontent.com/pod-product-compliance
Ingram Content Group UK Ltd.
Pitfield, Milton Keynes, MK11 3LW, UK
UKHW021524140125
4098UKWH00040B/965